CEZANNE IS MISSING

by

Frank McMillan

CAMBRIDGE HOUSE PUBLISHING COMPANY, LLC

Cover art: Celestine Frost

Library of Congress Control Number: 2003114281
ISBN# 0-9711359-4-0

Grateful acknowledgement is made to the following for permission to reprint previously published material:
On the Warsaw Ghetto, quoted on p. 147 of this book: "... the largest Jewish uprising against the Nazis during the Second World War. In the end, it took Nazi troops longer to put down the ghetto revolt than it took them to conquer all of Poland."
On the Ba'al Shem Tov, p. 301 of this book: "Until now I could feel our prayers being blocked as they tried to reach the heavenly court. This young shepherd's whistling was so pure, however, that it broke through the blockage and brought all of our prayers straight up to God."
Both of the above excerpts are quoted from their original source on pp. 369 and 216
From Jewish Literacy by Rabbi Joseph Telushkin
Copyright © 1991 by Rabbi Joseph Telushkin
By permission of HarperCollins Publishers, Inc.

Endnote section at end of this book excerpted from The New York Times:
Copyright © 2001 by The New York Times Co. Reprinted with permission.
"Auschwitz Revisited: the Fullest Picture Yet" by Ralph Blumenthal, January 28, 2001.

Excerpts from "Opening Remarks from the Second Interfaith Concert of Remembrance" written and delivered by Rabbi William H. Lebeau as distinguished guest and featured speaker at the Cathedral of St. John the Divine, November 23, 1991, quoted on pp. 256-257. His full address appears at the end of this book. Reprinted with permission from Rabbi William H. Lebeau.

A portion from the proceeds of this book will be donated to a special fund for educating and disseminating information on the Holocaust, in the name of the Holocaust, and for the prevention of future holocausts.

Printed in the United States of America.

Published by Cambridge House Publishing Company, LLC
331 W. 57th St. #263, New York NY 10019
Printed in 2005

To Sheryl, for being my everything

To Frank and Rob, for their gifts of joy

To my mother, for her abiding love and compassion

To my father, for his wisdom, integrity and moral courage

ACKNOWLEDGEMENTS

This book is a living part of a greater pattern of love and meaning and its publication is the result of much hard work and thoughtfulness by many people to whom I am profoundly grateful. Its story is offered as a testament to the memory of the six million children, women and men who perished in the Shoah, the many hundreds of thousands more whose lives were changed by their annihilation, and their descendents. My hope is that its witness and words move others to seek the paths of Truth and Remembrance, even as I was moved by the words and witness of another so many years ago. Her name was Lisa Pomerantz.

First and foremost, I want to thank my agent, publisher and dear friend, Susan Fisher. Words cannot really encompass all the many things she has done and continues doing for me, but I can truly say that *Cezanne Is Missing* is between book covers today primarily because of her immense talent and dedication. She never gave up. I am blessed to know her.

Tremendous appreciation goes out to Celestine Frost for the grace and beauty of her art work and the brilliant jacket design. The book's spirit soars off the front cover thanks to her.

As a young writer, I was encouraged to persevere by the late Sir Laurens van der Post. My visits with him and his daughter Lucia in London were enlightening and inspiring, and I shall think of them always as my extended family. Special thanks, too, go to Dr. David H. Rosen of Texas A&M University. His ongoing example as a poet and healer of souls means a great deal to me. In the earliest days of the manuscript, vital encouragement was lent by Elliot Fineman whose kind words of enthusiasm were a real gift.

Many special thanks go to Kristopher Mangiafico for his technical expertise and computer wizardry. This project could literally not have been completed without him. A million thanks, too, to Ann Sangis, Esther Gerard, and Sylvia Di Pietro for their invaluable advice and loving support. A kinder, more caring group of individuals could not be imagined. I am a very lucky person indeed to know them. They bring light wherever they go.

I also especially wish to thank the many teenagers from ages 12 to 17 who were given the manuscript to read long before publication in its early drafts, many of whom went out of their way to read it during their school year at the height of other commitments. Their boundless enthusiasm carried me through to the end and their comments are appreciated more than they could ever imagine.

I am honored beyond words by Rabbi William H. Lebeau, vice-chancellor of the Jewish Theological Seminary of America, and his gracious support for this book. A long time ago as distinguished guest and featured speaker, he addressed an audience at the Cathedral of St. John the Divine's second annual concert in honor of all Holocaust victims, "The Interfaith Concert of Remembrance" during Dean James P. Morton's stewardship of the Cathedral. I am grateful to him for permission to cite some of his extraordinary insights on pp. 256-257 in Chapter 21 from his actual sermon that night, heard by many and never forgotten. To me, his luminous words are the spiritual pivot for the turning point of this book, the very place where light emerges from darkness. Nothing I could ever strive to say could capture a fraction of the wisdom he has imparted in these brief lines alone. That I might also include his address in full at the end is a blessing and gift of profound hope to all who read this book.

The New York Public Library presented a very special Exhibit called *What Price Freedom* at its main library on 42nd Street from 1995 to early 1996 to celebrate the 100th anniversary of its founding. While the action of this novel takes place during the early winter of 2002 in New York City, this exhibit is cited in Chapter 21, pp. 262-263, in tribute to the New York Public Library for the profound impact this exhibit had on all those who saw it, as well as its beautiful companion catalogue published in 1995. Very special thanks go to Marie Santora, Public Affairs Director of the New York Public Library, for furnishing this extraordinary material and inspiring this scene in Chapter 21.

The famous story of the young whistler in the temple of the beloved historic teacher and rabbi Ba'al Shem Tov (Chapter 24, p. 301) can be found on pp. 215-16 of Rabbi Joseph Telushkin's superb book, *Jewish Literacy*. The posited wondrous response of the Ba'al Shem Tov, as well as two lines of description of the Warsaw Ghetto uprising (Chapter 12, p.147), are gratefully quoted from p. 369 and p. 216 of his book. I thank Peter London of HarperCollins for granting permission to quote these important lines.

A note of very special thanks to The Very Reverend James Parks

Morton, former Dean of the Cathedral of St. John the Divine and founder of The Interfaith Center of New York. The references here to the Cathedral and to his groundbreaking work, which has inspired life-changes for so many countless souls over the years, come with heart-felt appreciation and thanksgiving. The breadth of Dean Morton's reach, of which he is not even aware, extends even to the final completion of this book. He is not only part of the sacred web, but an architect of it.

Anna Smulowitz is the playwright-director of *Terezin: Children of the Holocaust*, a highly acclaimed NEA-endorsed play that performs at high schools throughout this country and in Europe. Anna, whose mother was a survivor of the Terezin concentration camp, penned a very supportive review of this book that was invaluably important to me at a time when I needed it the most, and I cannot thank her enough.

James Saganiec, history teacher at Garfield High School (and William Paterson University) in New Jersey teaches a course on the Holocaust that has become a badge of honor for his many students over the years. He is one of those rare teachers whom students remember throughout their lives for his gift of imparting knowledge and raising consciousness. His comments have been immensely helpful to me and enormously encouraging; that he wants to add this book to his class curriculum, which I've just been informed of prior to this book going to press, is very gratifying.

There are three people in my life without whom I could do nothing. My mother, Mabel, epitomizes beauty in soul and spirit. An incredibly kind, gentle, and generous person, in her daily thoughts and actions, she embodies Dante's Love that "moves the Sun and the other stars." My late father was the wisest, most honest, and most morally courageous man I ever met. I miss him every day. If I can be half the father to my children that he was to me, I will feel like I have really accomplished something. Ultimately, there is my wife, Sheryl. The smartest, most capable person I know, she is my best friend and my partner in everything, always and always. The day God sent her to me was the luckiest day of my life.

Then there are my two sons, Frank and Rob. Nobody makes me happier. Everything I do, I do for them.

Corpus Christi
Texas

Frank McMillan
November 2003

Special Acknowledgement

For Lisa Pomerantz who, when we were classmates in the third grade, told a story I never forgot about man's inhumanity to man that has haunted me ever since. *Cezanne Is Missing* took shape many years later for me after what she said in class that day that changed my life. She told how young girls and boys, mostly Jewish – as well as others of all ages, creeds and nationalities – were destroyed during World War II in Europe in something called the Holocaust. My nine year old mind could not conceive of such a thing ever happening to anyone, let alone to millions. I have never been the same since and I have never forgotten her words.

Cezanne Is Missing, though it bears no specific resemblance to Lisa's personal story or any person in her family, is nevertheless inspired by the revelation of truth she shared that day and the resolve she instilled in me. While the book shows what despots and their followers are capable of, it is more about the everyday heroes who somehow find strength to stand up to them.

In the face of such destruction, the fact that people are able to draw on their own inner light, and not go against their faith, values, beliefs, and code of morality is finally the essence of who we are. Learning not to compromise our deepest self is perhaps the central issue for each and every one of us as events unfold in the world and in our own personal lives. *Cezanne Is Missing* is written with the hope that it may help keep the memory of the Holocaust alive and in some small way perhaps help readers carry its meaning in our own personal lives.

Since that time I first heard Lisa Pomerantz speak as a child, I have witnessed, simply by being alive in the 20th century, the unthinkable happen again and again to my fellow man, especially to women and children in Armenia, China, Russia, Cambodia, Rwanda, Congo, the Balkans and elsewhere. What does the average person have to do with this? What does a 15 year old, big-city, contemporary American teenager know or care about the reality of genocide in any part of the world? Yet Lauren Robinson, the narrator of *Cezanne Is Missing*, becomes involved when "called upon," as every one of us is undeniably involved by the sheer fact of knowing that such incomprehensible inhumanity can occur at any place and at any time. That is why each of us is a witness because such inescapable events involve our very soul and what it means to be human.

After writing this book, I saw the superb, award-winning BBC series on the History Channel – "The Nazis: A Warning from History" by Lawrence Rees – and was struck by its final words from the persecuted German philosopher Karl Jaspers:

> That which has happened is a warning. To forget it is guilt.
> It was possible for this to happen and it is possible for it to happen again at any minute. Only in knowledge can it be prevented.

Anything that can be done to light up the night, to tell the truth, to raise awareness, and inspire courage to stand up and defy the arrogance of tyrants and their ignorant armies and silent citizenry is of paramount importance for every one of us. For we may each have to stand up and be counted in our own personal lives one day. And to do so will make a difference to those in need and even to our very own soul.

This book comes then with my profoundest gratitude to Lisa Pomerantz who first opened my eyes, and in that sense opened the sacred book to my own adulthood. It is written in honor of the many millions of children, women and men who perished at the hands of prejudice, fanatical adherence to so-called religious dictums, political exploitation, and senseless hatred – and also in honor of the courageous few who in all times and in all places risk their own lives to protect, hide, and deliver the hunted and persecuted from annihilation. *Cezanne Is Missing* is for them.

Frank McMillan

CEZANNE

IS

MISSING

A Novel

by

Frank McMillan

Chapter One

When there was a loud knock on the door, I was standing at the kitchen sink washing clay off my hands and wondering what it would be like to kiss David.

"I'LL GET IT, LAUREN – !" called Mrs. Rosen. "It's probably Gus. Veronica warned me about his always forgetting something."

Gus had left barely 30 seconds ago with the rest of the sculpture class Mrs. Rosen had just taught in place of her friend Veronica. Where was Veronica? At a doctor's appointment with a bad cases of laryngitis. This was Veronica's art studio and they were best friends. Typical of Mrs. Rosen who was always doing nice things for people. Today after school when her friend Veronica telephoned – barely above a whisper, Mrs. Rosen sighed, shaking her head – I was trotted downtown to Soho with her. Veronica's class, all ten of them, were sure shocked to see the great sculptor Dominique Rosen take over for her friend. It was wild watching their expressions when they found her greeting them at the door.

The knock at the door grew louder and more insistent. Mrs. Rosen, who'd been way at the other end of the studio, called out to me again before she got to the door. "LAUREN, WHY DON'T YOU JOIN DAVID AND ME FOR DINNER TONIGHT?"

David! I lathered the nailbrush with dish soap and

1

scrubbed like mad.   Mrs. Rosen, one of the best sculptors in the country and maybe the whole world, I guess, was teaching me how to work in clay. It's messy.

Although she lives just three floors above us, I'd never met Mrs. Rosen until Mom and I bumped into her in the lobby one rainy Saturday. As usual, Mom had towed me along on one of her marathon shopping safaris. They're pretty much a weekend ritual with her. You know, chanting, drums . . . ceremonial credit cards. And I'm not buying her story that I'm an only child. I bet she threw her first kid into a volcano to appease Ralph Lauren. It's not like I exactly mind or anything. I mean, I like to shop as much as the next person. Especially at all those cool places in Soho and the Village. Maybe I'm, you know, codependent or whatever. Or at least, I was. I'm sort of a different person now after . . . after what happened.

Let's see, where was I? Oh, yeah. Anyway, our arms were full, we're sopping wet and we barged into this sweet old lady. It was a classic entrance, believe me. After we chatted a few seconds, Mrs. Rosen politely excused herself. To tell the truth, I was more or less stunned she even spoke to us. Like I said, she's famous. Television famous. Anyway, she said "good-bye" and I trail-drove Mom towards the elevator.

Then came the weird part. On her way out the building, Mrs. Rosen stopped, unrolled her umbrella, and offered to give me art lessons. Just like that. I kid you not.

Well, Mom absolutely detonated. She dropped her Bloomie's bags like they were radioactive and jabbered what a totally huge honor this was and all. To tell the truth, she's kind of a social climber. I immediately wished I was invisible. I can only take Mom up to a certain point and then I don't even want to know her. This was definitely one of those times. For a minute, I was seriously afraid Mom was about to drool all over the poor woman's Ferragamos or something.

Mrs. Rosen handled it real well. She smiled and said it was her pleasure. And that she could tell I was an artist by the look in my eyes. She was serious . . . for some reason. Anyway, she's been giving me lessons for a couple of months now.

David is her only grandchild. A couple of times when I was at her place, he dropped by to run errands for her. He's fifteen, like me. The instant I laid eyes on him I melted. I've had crushes on boys before, but definitely not like this. So when I thought about being invited to dinner at Mrs. Rosen's and seeing David there, my heart raced so fast my shirt buttons jiggled. I was crushing. Big time.

I dried my hands on a dishtowel and took a deep breath. "SURE!" I called back to her, sneaking a peak at my hair in the entry hall mirror. I'd had it highlighted and it was sort of purple. I wasn't sure how I felt about it yet. I was worried it looked a little strange, what with my new tinted contacts and all. It's not like I'm ugly or anything. In fact, I look okay, maybe a little better even, actually . . . but I still wasn't too sure about the flaming magenta-purple hair and green eyes combo.

After I made sure Mrs. Rosen couldn't see me, I stood sideways and checked out my profile. It would definitely help in the boy department if I acquired more of a figure sometime before I die, too. I mean, it's not that I'm obsessive about my looks or anything, but in a sexist society, hey, what can you do?

"*Allo?*" I heard her say when she got to the door, lapsing into her native French. Oh, yeah. She was born in Paris. "Gus, is that you?"

There was no answer. That was strange. We looked at each other as I moved closer to the door. "Gus?" she repeated. "Is that you? Who is – ?"

But instead of Gus's voice, we heard an entirely different voice cut in and boom: "DOMINIQUE ROSEN? I MOST URGENTLY NEED TO SEE YOU! IT IS MOST IMPORTANT!"

The accent was European . . . at least I was pretty sure it was. Mrs. Rosen rubbed her chin, debating about what to do. Nearly every day she gets phone calls and letters from all over the world, usually from struggling artist types desperate for a break. People who want something from her. Sometimes they even show up on her doorstep. Like now maybe. But how did anyone know she was here?

Mrs. Rosen certainly wasn't expecting any visitors and stood there a moment longer deciding what to do. I could almost hear her thoughts. Why let a stranger in just because he knew her name and said it was urgent?

"Whoever you are," she said firmly, "you'll have to call my agent tomorrow. I am not in the habit of opening the door to people I do not know. Especially when it is not even my door. No, you will have to go away." To me she said in a low voice, "Whoever it is must have come in the building when the class was leaving. But why? No one knows I'm here." She wasn't exactly nervous or anything – but, well, more like concerned.

"Unless we were followed here by a fan of yours who waited outside and got through the door when Veronica's class was leaving," I said.

"Ah, yes," she heaved a sigh of relief. "That must be it. There are so many struggling artists, and they're so needy. Art is so important and – " she paused and smiled. "But not more important than safety." She had made up her mind, turned on her heel and started to walk away from the door.

I laughed. "Yes, ma'am, I mean . . . if you say so." She was a gutsy woman, that's for sure, but I'm glad she wasn't so trusting. Though for a moment there she had me worried.

I thought she might actually let the guy in. She really did believe that stuff about art being important. In fact, she was passionate about it. It's her life.

"THIS CONCERNS YOUR FAMILY!" the voice suddenly boomed.

Well, that did it for sure. Like she never even uttered the can't-be-too-careful stuff she just said – she instantly flipped the deadbolt and opened the door.

Three strange men stood in the hall. They were so unusual that it was like opening the door to another century . . . or to some way of life that was ruthless, menacing, and even brutal. Suddenly I thought of September 11th – only four months ago – and everyone in New York was on edge since then. But they didn't look like they were from the Middle East.

Mon Dieu! whispered Mrs. Rosen, fingering the collar of her smock and stepping back in surprise. She knew she had made a mistake right away. So stunned was she by their looks that she couldn't say anything else.

They were big. Real big. Like heavies fronting for some mob boss. All three of them wore expensive-looking leather coats and lots of cheap cologne, which I could smell even though they were still in the hall and I was a few feet behind Mrs. Rosen. They each eyeballed me thoroughly. I thought about bolting past them, but they blocked the doorway.

The man in front bowed stiffly from the waist. His white skin was so thin I could see the veins running through it. His eyes were ice blue and looked like they missed nothing. A rubbery scar ran from one ear to his chin and a blonde buzzcut perched on his head like bad indoor-outdoor carpet. He could have played one of the leads in a vampire movie.

Mrs. Rosen spoke first. "What is the urgent news about my family! What is it? Did something happen? Who are you?" Her voice was filled with alarm and impatience. She'd been duped because they sure didn't act like something was wrong with her family. And she felt exactly as I did that something was very wrong with them. Big time.

"Madame Rosen, I'm Nikolai. It is an honor to meet you," he said, ignoring her questions and bowing slightly. "These are my associates, Vlad and Sergei."

His associates didn't look so hot either. Sergei was particularly scary. Totally bald with whiskers like black sandpaper, he kept glancing down the hall like he was paranoid . . . with a reason. Vlad wasn't as gruesome but definitely not on the up and up. Well, they weren't Muslim terrorists. More like Germans or Russians or East European . . . strong-arm characters from an underground cell on some secret mission, I wondered, my wild imagination having a field day after all the "Nikita" re-runs I watched late at night.

Nikolai, as if hearing my thoughts, suddenly noticed me and took a step forward. "And this is?"

In one quick move, Mrs. Rosen got between us and blocked the door with her body. A shiver went up my spine. "What do you know about my family?" she demanded. "You said it was urgent! Who are you? What do you want?"

Nikolai's accent was thick, but I couldn't place it. He tried to smile . . . sort of. It looked more like he had gas. His stained teeth were small and pointed, and one of them was gold. Then his smile vanished. The novelty of these three characters had long worn off for me – like after the first two seconds – and the bad feeling I had the moment I saw them kept getting worse.

Nikolai, definitely the leader, offered his hand to Mrs. Rosen who just stared at it and made no move at all. Rebuffed, he holstered it in his pocket like a gun. "We have a business transaction of the highest importance to discuss with you, Madame," he said with venom. "It would be very much worth your time to hear what we have to say."

"No." Mrs. Rosen folded her arms across her chest. It was clear she wasn't going to tolerate another second of their strange behavior. "So you lied to me to get in to see me," she said coldly. "It's about business then? Well, this interview is over. Call Lawrence Lascher, my attorney, who handles all my business. He's in the phone book. Now if you'll excuse me, you'll have to leave."

Mrs. Rosen began to close the door in their faces. She was giving them the royal dismissal, the good old heave-ho in style. Even Mrs. Rosen can make mistakes. It was obvious they made up something about her family just to get her to open the door. But she was on to them. Whew, I thought with relief.

But Nikolai, who had positioned his foot a few inches inside the door, didn't budge. He looked as severe suddenly as an executioner. Uh, oh, I thought. This was a guy you didn't say no to. His cheek hardened and it looked like he would strike her. For a split second, his scar even turned red. Then he managed another weak smile, but I could tell he was faking. I could tell that beneath his phony expression, he was someone always used to getting his way.

She tried to shut the door, but his foot prevented her from closing it. "I said you'll have to leave now . . . or I'll call the – "

"Dominique Rosen, listen to me, you do not understand. This is a matter that concerns your brother Joshua!"

Mrs. Rosen gasped.

"YES, JOSHUA. DO YOU NOT KNOW WHAT HAPPENED TO HIM? DO YOU NOT CARE?" he bellowed partly behind the door with supreme authority.

Mrs. Rosen flinched and went stiff. She put her fingers

to her mouth and I saw her hands turn pale under their speckling of coffee-colored age spots. Suddenly her knees buckled and she toppled backwards.

I lunged for her.

Chapter Two

"Nice catch," Nikolai scoffed.

I cradled Mrs. Rosen in my arms. She was moaning and her eyes rolled back in her head . . . white as hard-boiled eggs. For a second, I felt dizzy, too.

"Maybe we ought to stay," Nikolai offered dryly, smirking and snapping his fingers at the others. Get in there and help her," he ordered impatiently. Without hesitation Sergei, the tallest of the three, picked up Mrs. Rosen and carried her over to the living room sofa like she was a sleepy toddler.

With the entranceway now unobstructed, Nikolai strode into the apartment like it was his. Vlad took one last look down the hall and followed him.

"Look," I protested, "I don't think you can just barge in like – "

Nikolai lifted a thick finger to his lips. It was as fat and greasy as a Yankee Stadium frankfurter. "Sssshh," he hissed. Then he grinned and patted me on the cheek. "Don't be nervous, princess. Just do as we say and everything will be fine."

God, he was creepy. His breath reeked of booze and onions. I scrinched my nose. Vlad locked the door and the deadbolt fell with a heavy click. The hair on the back of my neck twitched and I wanted to run. My mind raced as I thought of every exit. But I'd never been to Veronica's studio before. There was only one entrance and exit – the front door. Of that I was sure. Then I'd have to climb out a window. We were on the second floor. The jump wouldn't be so bad if –

Nikolai, stepping forward with a swagger, held out his hand and bowed. "After you."

I was so nervous that for a moment I forgot about Mrs. Rosen. Then I turned back to her . . . really worried about the way she looked, huddled forward on the edge of the sofa with her hands on her knees. I went over to her and touched her shoulder. She shivered in response like she was cold. I leaned down and gently put my arm around her. "Are you all right?" I asked, just as I was starting to shiver, too.

Her voice trembled as she tried to speak. "I . . . I'd . . . I'd like some water, Lauren. I've had a bit of a shock."

Nikolai stopped me and grabbed my arm. Then he turned and gave Vlad an order in a language I didn't understand. When Vlad left the room, I heard his leather overcoat squeaking all the way into the kitchen. "My associate will get it, if you don't mind," Nikolai purred with ultra politeness, his tone belying the fact that he had taken control of Veronica's studio – *and us!* "You might become confused and call your parents . . . or the police, perhaps. I wouldn't want you to make such a silly mistake."

I ignored him and put my hand on Mrs. Rosen's shoulder as she tried to regain her balance. She felt so fragile, like she was made of crystal. Whatever happened, I wanted to protect her. I just wasn't exactly sure how I was going to do that yet. A moment later Vlad returned with a fat wine glass sloshing full of water and gave it to Mrs. Rosen, who took a sip with her eyes closed.

"Joshua . . . Joshua – " she murmured.

"Yes," Nikolai said, "your brother."

She looked at the floor and acted like she was in a daze. Then she lifted her head upward at Nikolai, tears and longing shining in her eyes. "Is he . . . Joshua . . . is he *alive*?"

Nikolai didn't answer. He was too busy sizing up the place, strolling through Veronica's studio and living area in the back like it belonged to him, fingering anything he felt like touching – marble heads, bits of clay, a chisel, and finally a very large sculpture that Mrs. Rosen told me earlier was Veronica's masterpiece, her best work yet, in Mrs. Rosen's opinion. She was going to help her sell it.

"What do you know of him?" Mrs. Rosen asked in a faltering voice, trying to pull herself together. "I haven't seen him in over fifty years. Not since – "

"Yes, of course. Most unfortunate," he said, not meaning it.

She shot a look at him. "What do you know about Joshua? Is he alive?" she cried out, her whole body straining as if she could possibly make it so.

"I'm afraid not," answered Nikolai matter-of-factly. His attention was on a crumpled pack of unfiltered cigarettes he'd taken out of his pocket. He stuck one between his lips and asked, more like an order, "Do you mind?"

Mrs. Rosen meanwhile had slumped back, looking worn-out and defeated. "Does it matter?" she responded with real attitude.

"No, not really," he sniffed, popping open an old-fashioned lighter. The cigarette was long and brown, and he blew two thin streams of smoke from it out his nostrils and tapped its ashes on the Oriental rug beneath his feet. "Your brother was an artist, too, was he not?"

I still didn't understand what was happening. Why wasn't Mrs. Rosen herself? Why didn't she just get up and throw them out? Okay, so she was an older woman and she had just fainted and they were three huge men. But still she was Dominique Rosen! She could do anything, or so I thought.

Yet something else was going on here. They knew each other in some way through her brother. This was between them. Not me. I just wanted outtahere. I was so uncomfortable. Why didn't she call the police? She both hated Nikolai and hung on his every word. Meanwhile, I was trying to decide whether I could somehow sneak past them out a window to run for help or whether I should stay with Mrs. Rosen.

Mrs. Rosen stared at him, her eyes trying to focus. She was coming out of it. "Yes, an artist. One of the best . . . only 20 years old when the war – " she stopped and looked down at the floor, rubbing her forehead as if trying to awaken from a dream. "That was the end of everything."

"Not quite," Nikolai said with emphasis.

"What do you mean?"

"What about the Warsaw Ghetto?" Nikolai was interrogating her like she was a common criminal.

Thunderstruck, as if she just woke up from a trance, Mrs. Rosen struggled to her feet. "What do you know about that? Who are you?" she demanded, her voice filled with outrage. Her balance was a little off, but she was herself again. In another minute, I figured she'd toss them right out of here. So what if this had to do with her brother? These dudes were real bad.

"For now, that's not important," Nikolai answered casually. "But <u>this</u> is," he said reaching inside his coat pocket and pulling out an ancient-looking book. Its brown leather cover was soiled and cracked with age, and it looked like some mildewy old thing you'd find in a trunk in your grandparents' attic. A rubber band kept it from falling apart. "Do you recognize this?"

Mrs. Rosen inspected it. "No," she said. But I could tell she wasn't so sure.

Nikolai narrowed his eyes. "Are you certain?"

"Of course, I'm sure. Why?" She wasn't going to tell him that she wasn't.

"I'll tell you why. Because it's your brother's Diary!"

"What?" She gasped and looked like she was going to topple over again. Her eyes grew wide with astonishment as she moved her right hand to her mouth, stunned beyond words.

"Really, Madame Rosen – pay attention." Nikolai waved the book under her nose. "It belonged to your brother Joshua, as I said. You remember many things about him, surely."

I couldn't understand what was going on. His sarcasm, his snide, cruel way of handling her – her, the great and famous and wonderful Dominique Rosen. It was shocking to see how he treated her. He seemed to know everything about her personal life, and yet he was not someone she ever met. It wasn't like he hated her or anything. Just that Mrs. Rosen as a person didn't matter to him. Nothing mattered to him except what he wanted from her, whatever that was. Her eyes looked glazed, as if she wasn't here in the room with us any more.

"Or perhaps you're getting senile."

I was so shocked that I gasped aloud. That did it! I was positive she'd get up and really let him have it! I wanted to smack him myself. What a low-life. He had no right to talk to her like that. But she didn't move or say anything at all. What was going on? This was so unlike her. How could this stranger have such power over her? I really despised him! For bullying her. For talking down to her.

Mrs. Rosen chewed her lip like a little girl. Tears filled

her eyes and gleamed like liquid fire. I looked at Nikolai whose face was twisted in a grimace of satisfaction. When I turned back to Mrs. Rosen I saw that her tears had turned to rage. She was really furious – I could see that now. Well, finally! I thought to myself.

She stood up to her full height and shouted, stamping her foot. "What do you want? Tell me at once and then get out of here!"

Nikolai was completely unfazed. He only shook his head as if he could care less about what she said or felt. Then he snapped off the rubber band of the Diary and started fanning its pages. "Think what you like. It doesn't really matter." Sighing then, as if bored, he opened the first page and read aloud:

> *To Mother, Papa, Dominique, Sarah, Sonia*
> *and Esther. And, as always, Mrs. Ringlebaum.*
> *I remember.*
>
> *June 1943*

When he finished, Nikolai slapped the book shut and squinted at Mrs. Rosen, watching for a reaction. "Your family, I presume?"

Mrs. Rosen turned to stone again, staring over his shoulder like she was watching a movie on the wall behind him, then took a lace handkerchief from her pocket and daubed the sweat on her upper lip.

"I ASKED YOU A QUESTION!" We both jumped. He wasn't messing around now.

"My parents and sisters," she finally murmured, her voice barely above a whisper. "And . . . and the widow Ringlebaum, God bless her. She took us in when we were deported to the Ghetto." Shaking her head, she stammered, "I

. . . I can't believe it." She sounded so helpless suddenly, like a lost child. "I . . . I've never talked about this to anyone but my husband," she went on in a faraway voice. "No one could know except – "

"Your brother!" Nikolai yelled impatiently. There wasn't an ounce of sympathy in him. Then he shoved the open book in her face. "Recognize anything?"

I couldn't believe his rage. If he could have shaken answers out of her, he would have. Yet I somehow knew this was his medium soft approach. Anyone could see he was capable of anything – but since she seemed to be his means to an end that only he knew, he had to get stuff out of her by jogging her memory in a stream of abuse that I knew was just beginning. He seemed to have mastered the soft sell with the hard sell, and you never knew which was coming at you.

Mrs. Rosen blinked back tears and leaned closer, studying the yellowed pages. It was as though Nikolai controlled her every emotion – and I ached for her, wishing I could do something. "It does look a little like Joshua's handwriting," she whispered, commenting more for herself than him . . . "and maybe it could be one of Poppa's old binders from the university, but it's been so long, I . . . I" – her voice faltered.

"So you are . . . how do you say . . . *satisfied* by the document's authenticity?" Nikolai asked, sounding pleased. His tone changed now.

Mrs. Rosen dropped her head. "Yes." Then, to herself, she added with deep emotion she fought unsuccessfully to hide, "All of them are gone. Lost in the . . . Shoah." Her voice broke suddenly on that word, one I'd never heard before.

SHO-AH. Shoah? This was something new to me. I didn't know what she was talking about.

Nikolai quickly tucked the Diary inside his overcoat

without giving it to her.

Mrs. Rosen stifled a sob and then stuck out her hand. "What are you doing? That Diary is rightfully mine! I am our family's only survivor! It's mine!" she pleaded, her eyes blazing with fury and pain.

But Nikolai only grimaced like he smelled sour milk. "That trifle can be negotiated later. I think the term for now is, how do you say, finders keepers. Let's get down to business. Sit!" he commanded, pointing to the sofa, but his eyes were on me as he reached out suddenly to touch my hair.

Mrs. Rosen clenched her jaw. "First, you must let the girl go! She is only a child. I will not speak to you until you do."

I agreed and nodded my head stupidly. I could still feel the sensation of his hand an inch from my head. And I panicked, big time. All this didn't concern me, I decided. I wanted to bolt. I took her anger as my cue and stood up and said, "Look, I really have to go now. It was nice meeting you and all, but I really – "

"SHUT UP AND SIT DOWN!" Nikolai roared. A wave of contempt flooded his face. "Do you think I'm an idiot? She'll run straight to her mommy. She stays. And she keeps her mouth shut if she knows what's good for her." He looked over at Vlad who found this amusing for some reason.

Mrs. Rosen really looked worried now. She waved me to her, patting the sofa seat next to her, and I sat down beside her in a hurry.

At the snap of Nikolai's fingers, Sergei grabbed one of Veronica's expensive modern chairs, all glistening chrome and black leather, and set it behind his boss. Nikolai ground out his cigarette butt on the rug as he sat down – while Vlad and Sergei stood behind him as if at attention. Picking his front teeth with a thumbnail, Nikolai spat and arched his eyebrows.

"Your brother was a good painter, yes?"

"It is obvious that you know this already," Mrs. Rosen answered stiffly.

"He knew a lot about art history then, too?"

"Of course," she said with impatience, glowering at him. "Where is this leading? Come to the point already!" Her arm tightened around me.

Nikolai held up a finger. "Uh, uh, uh. It's rude to interrupt," he mocked. Then he clapped his hands like a gunshot, and I flinched. "Here's the arrangement," he said finally. "My associates and I have a client, an art collector, a connoisseur, you might say, who came into possession of this little book – "

Mrs. Rosen started to get to her feet. "Just how did he get – "

In a flash, before we ever saw him coming – Sergei leapt across the room and pushed her back onto the sofa. "How dare you lay a hand on me!" she bristled. This was like a bad dream. My legs started to shake.

"Ladies, ladies, please calm down. My associates are simply a little too eager. They don't want you to do something you might regret – that's all," Nikolai chuckled with annoyance, flicking his hand at Sergei who quickly backed off. Then he lit another cigarette and exhaled a cloud of smoke, which made me cough. Noticing this, he made a gesture and blew me a kiss, which made my stomach drop and my eyes bulge out of my head because I was so turned off and scared to death.

He grinned, showing his tiny, pointed weasel teeth again. "Let's start over, shall we? And no more infantile behavior, please." Scowling, he took another deep drag on his cigarette. "As I was saying, my client came into possession of this little book. It's a marvelous thing, really. Your brother was a remarkable fellow, Madame. It seems not only was he a ringleader in the Warsaw Ghetto uprising, he was also an astute businessman. I think *smuggler* is the proper term. Unfortunately, there is also a possibility he cooperated with the Gestapo."

"You're a damned liar!" Mrs. Rosen shouted.

"About some things," said Nikolai, unmoved. "But not this. You see, after the Germans defeated your ill-fated uprising, your brother abandoned you and – "

"Go to hell!" roared Mrs. Rosen. "He was a hero! He fought in the Jewish Resistance! He was a hero of his people, I tell you – like his namesake! I know. I know because I was there!"

"Very interesting. But a hero doesn't leave his family behind, does he?"

"How dare you! We had already been taken! . . . you bas – !" Mrs. Rosen ground out the last word between her teeth and didn't finish.

Then she spoke softly in a far-away voice to no one in particular. "My mother and the rest of us were shipped like cattle to . . . to . . ." – but again she faltered.

Nikolai smirked and gestured with his hand. "Ah, yes – let me refresh your memory." Then he leaned in her face and hissed, "Auschwitz – "

"As if I could ever forget! I don't have to tell you! It's none of your business!" she screamed at him. But then just as suddenly she grew very quiet. Nikolai didn't say anything either. Everything became real still. I could hear the clocks ticking against each other in the hall.

"That hell . . ." whispered Mrs. Rosen, gazing down at the floor, for a moment before lifting her head. When I saw her face, I thought she had completely changed now. I hardly recognized her – so different was the look in her eyes and the tone of her voice. It was as if she'd left the room and was many miles away, seeing something only she could see.

"Your brother ended up there too . . . eventually."

Mrs. Rosen's head snapped back like she'd been slapped.

"Surprised? Yes, he was brought there, too."

"I never knew. What h-happened to – "

"Like all the rest in the end," Nikolai remarked indifferently. "There are the other . . . camps."

"Oh, God – " Mrs. Rosen choked.

"Yes, most unfortunate, but relatively unimportant to matters at hand. You see, my client is extremely interested in this. After your brother escaped from the Ghetto, it seems he smuggled paintings in and out of the occupied zone for a while."

"What? You are insane!" she shouted.

"Mainly Impressionists, according to his Diary," Nikolai droned on ignoring her. "It's a pity because one can't be sure where these, um, rather valuable works are today." Nikolai took another drag, inhaling deeply.

My eyes burned from the smoke he blew my way. Smoke always seems to blow my way, I thought, trying to distance myself from what was going on . . . wishing I could disappear before their eyes.

"Several times in this little book" – he patted his coat pocket – "your brother speaks of hiding canvases. God only knows where he stole them to begin with. Probably from prominent Jewish families who – "

Mrs. Rosen blew up like a volcano. "Never! You are a liar!"

Nikolai calmly filed his nails and looked bored. He stared at his index finger and wiped it on his coat. "Don't act so naive, madam. You know there was a tremendous underground traffic in looted art during the war. Nazi officers themselves skimmed off the top of the plunder pouring back to the *Reichsbank* in Berlin. To this day the odd piece of stolen silver or rare furniture shows up in auction houses. But the point is that rumors of a priceless, mysterious missing art collection have circulated for years. Your brother seems to have handled it. He even mentions the paintings by name. A Renoir here, a Van Gogh there. Pretty expensive merchandise. You get the idea. So does my client. He wants to find the paintings."

"Badly," he added. "Very badly." His eyes narrowed to slits.

"What does all this have to do with me?" Mrs. Rosen asked defiantly.

"Are you serious? You more than anyone would be helpful, let's say, in interpreting some of the Diary entries. Names, places, that sort of thing. After all, you're his sister. You were with him at the time until – " he paused and then coughed. "You can help trace his movements and identify some of the rather vague locations outside the Ghetto he writes about with some sort of inner meaning . . . not exactly a code but . . . well, unfathomable to us. Then there are his non-Jewish contacts he never names outright but refers to in pet nicknames to keep his secrecy intact."

"And this is all for the money, I suppose?"

"It's always for the money, isn't it?" Nikolai chuckled. "Surely, Madame Rosen, you, of all people, can appreciate that. One unknown Van Gogh alone would be worth at least thirty million dollars. Easy. But if one finds three or four, along with a few Renoirs, maybe a Matisse and a spare Cezanne or two . . . well, it's worth an imperial fortune, isn't it?" He smiled grotesquely. "Worth killing for, you might say," he added, while all this was registering with Mrs. Rosen. "Even if only one painting was retrieved."

My mouth felt very dry. If only I didn't have to be here, I thought, listening to all this. What does this have to do with me? I felt guilty at the same time for thinking that because Mrs. Rosen was in trouble. But, still, it was her trouble, not mine. I just wanted to be far, far away from all this.

Mrs. Rosen squared her shoulders. "Give me one good reason why I should cooperate with you," she commanded with disgust in her voice.

"I have a few reasons for you. For starters – "

But she cut him off. "I've met your kind before," Mrs. Rosen spat, her voice dripping contempt. "You don't frighten me – I've seen things you can't imagine. I don't care what you do to me. I'm not afraid to die." She straightened her back proudly. I was amazed at her courage.

Nikolai pretended to be hurt. "Please, Madame, you offend my tender sensibilities." Then he smiled devilishly. "Your bravery is very touching, but you're not the only one involved in this . . . are you? It would be most unfortunate if a crippling accident happened to, say, this pretty young girl here. Think of it as insurance. You know, accident prevention." He swiveled his head like a lizard and winked at me.

I cringed. He hadn't looked at me all this time till now. It was at this point I started to jump out of my skin. She gripped my hand and then embraced me tightly, as if trying to shield me from his very words.

"And while we're on the subject of youth, don't you have a son who lives on West 85th in a brownstone off Columbus Avenue? A celebrated violinist, yes? He and his wife have a son – your only grandson. Yes?"

Mrs. Rosen gasped.

I jumped up and leaped forward a few steps, but Nikolai growled at me. "Don't make a move, princess. It's way too late for that!" The words hit me in the chest like an ice pick. For a second I felt like I couldn't breathe. Then suddenly Vlad, who'd been quiet all this time, entered the conversation, smiling at me crookedly and moving up close to me. "There, there," he whispered with phony reassurance. "Want to come for a ride with us? You will, you know."

While I nearly fainted, Mrs. Rosen gasped and held her arm around me protectively. "Leave her out of this, I say!"

"Vlad!" shouted Nikolai in annoyance. "All in good time. Let me finish please. Madame Rosen wants to help us, I'm sure of it now. I feel it in my bones," he added in a bloodcurdling tone.

"How did you find my brother's Diary? Tell me that at least!" she demanded, removing the attention off me.

"Come, come now. You watch CNN," Nikolai said snidely. "You see, things are rather chaotic in my country. It's a question of who's in control. A question of power. Information is power . . . and power, like anything else, is always for sale. My associates and I simply put buyers and sellers together, that's all. Everyone's happy. Like one big family."

"You're Russian, of course."

Nikolai grinned. "*Touché*, Madame. My accent? Is that what gave me away?"

Mrs. Rosen smiled contemptuously. "I'm not a fool."

Nikolai's smile evaporated. "Nor am I. Make sure you know that about me. For your sake . . . and hers."

A low sound escaped from me. I heard it with surprise myself. I had never felt this terrified. My life had never been threatened before. Nothing felt real. Everything went fuzzy and weird, like I was pumped full of Novocain.

Suddenly Nikolai morphed into Prince Charming and began acting like our host. He was looking at me real hard and then whispered to Sergei, who apparently functioned as his dog or something and obediently trotted away. "I told him to bring you some more nice, cool drinks," he cooed politely to me. I want you to be comfortable. Business should be pleasurable."

It occurred to me that Nikolai might have a split personality like those people you see on talk shows. He obviously enjoyed his soft sell-hard sell approach. Or maybe it was really that he was toying with us for a little while, like a cat does when it bats around a mouse before pouncing. What if she told him what he wanted to know and then we were history? Or maybe he'd just let us go.

Sergei came back with five warm cans of Diet Coke, and I drank about half of mine in one gulp. My tongue felt like a dried-out loofa. I watched Sergei take one for himself and go over to the door after Nikolai snapped his fingers and signaled him with a cock of his head.

Mrs. Rosen refused the drink and slammed her hand down on the coffee table, really impatient now. "You still haven't answered me!"

Nikolai theatrically slapped his forehead. "How rude of me! Yes, well, as I said, much is currently for sale in my country. Times are hard, you know. And with all the new freedoms, well, what can you do? People take advantage. Many things wind up on the black market. Factories, oil rigs, diamonds," he said, his eyes glittering like a rattlesnake. "Then there are the special items. Tanks, missiles, jet fighters, nuclear bomb components, nerve gas . . . you understand, those sorts of things. And sometimes rarities – like the files of the state security agencies."

"I should have known," spat Mrs. Rosen. "It's too apparent."

It was? I was already a few zip codes past clueless.

She sighed and looked far past us. "So, the Nazis took

the Diary from Joshua when they captured him, and Red Army intelligence got their hands on it when they liberated Auschwitz. From there, it vanished into the secret police vaults in Moscow all these years until your so-called client found it, of course. Correct?" She sounded utterly fearless.

Nikolai laughed and applauded. "Bravo, Madame! You should be a detective or a spy like in the movies." He pointed his fingers like pistols. "Arnold Schwarzenegger! Bang, bang!"

Mrs. Rosen wasn't amused. Ignoring his phony sense of play, she questioned him in rapid fire. "How did your 'client' acquire it? Is he with the government? A bureaucrat? Or a spy himself perhaps? What country is he from?"

Nikolai shook his finger at her. "Ah, ah, ah! Naughty, naughty! You know that's a trade secret!" He and Vlad started to laugh.

Suddenly the intercom buzzed. "WHAAAAAAAA!" The sound was so piercing and so unexpected that I almost jumped out of my seat. Nikolai and Vlad spun towards the noise and reached inside their coats. Then Sergei, who'd been standing at the door like a statue, looked out the peephole, gun in hand. "WHAAAAAAAA . . . WHAAAAAAAA!"

Like an air raid siren or fire alarm, the insistent buzzing went on and on, jolting us so completely out of ourselves that it took over everything. I never dreamed there would come a time when the horrible wail of an intercom could sound like heavenly music. I was so relieved that someone was at the door, but my relief was short-lived.

Nikolai frowned. "Are you expecting someone?" His voice was anxious and dead serious. This sure looked like it was ruining his day. He was a different person now as he tried to figure out fast what to do.

Meanwhile Mrs. Rosen had turned white. "This is not

my studio, as you know. It belongs to my friend. It could be anyone."

Nikolai rose to his feet. "Well, whoever it is, get rid of them!" he ordered as the deafening wail again broke through everything. "WHAAAAAAAAA! WHAAAAAAAAA!" Whoever it was, was getting pretty intense now. The ringing was definitely getting on Nikolai's nerves.

Suddenly Nikolai grabbed Mrs. Rosen by the elbow and dragged her to the intercom. "DO WHAT I TELL YOU! GET RID OF THEM!" he yelled.

That's when I saw my chance and bolted. I ran like hell, knocking over chairs and even a sculpture, but Vlad chased me and cornered me when I got to the next room. There was nowhere to go. He dragged me back in and threw me at Nikolai, who grabbed me and covered my mouth.

"YOU SEE THIS?" he barked to Mrs. Rosen. "SHE WON'T GET HURT IF YOU DO WHAT I TELL YOU!" I was panic-stricken and frantically tried to squirm out of his grasp.

"WHAAAAAAAAA!" The intercom wailed on and on. "WHAAAAAAAAA! WHAAAAAAAAAAA!"

Mrs. Rosen lifted the intercom speaker latch and in a shaky voice called out, "Who is it?"

The scariest voice came back, croaking like a monster. But it was only Veronica in her hoarsest voice trying to speak up as loudly as she could without windpipes. "Dominique, it's me, Veronica. I can't find my key!"

Veronica! Well, that threw everyone. She was back way earlier than expected. I was hoping she'd come back soon, but never got behind that thought. When she left earlier she told Mrs. Rosen just to close the door behind us after the class because she wouldn't be returning till after 6:00. If Nikolai and company hadn't showed up, we'd have been long gone way before then. Now what?

Nikolai threw me aside to Vlad and grabbed Mrs. Rosen. "Tell her to come up. Do as I say!" he hissed in her ear, real disturbed.

Won't Veronica be surprised, I thought. Wait till she sees this crew! I felt real sorry for her because nothing could be worse than coming home to this scene.

Mrs. Rosen looked stricken. She was so worried for her friend, worried for me who was still in the clutches of Vlad. We were helpless, all three of us. Nikolai motioned for Sergei to get behind the door as he took Mrs. Rosen further back in the room, away from the vision of the door. And we waited.

When the doorbell rang, Sergei squinted into the peephole again and opened the door, hiding behind the door as he swung it slowly toward him. Though I had been pulled way off to the side by Vlad, I could see Veronica looking around quizzically as she took a few steps inside.

"Dominique?" she strained to say in her wobbly voice.

Instantly Sergei shut the door behind her. Veronica just stood there in shock, gaping at all of us. She started to scream, but no sound came out. She simply had no voice.

"Welcome, dear lady," Nikolai greeted her sarcastically as he let go of Mrs. Rosen. "Now sit over there and answer a few questions please." Casually he lit a cigarette and threw the pack to Sergei who lit one, too.

Veronica stood there as if paralyzed. She looked at Mrs. Rosen and me, both of us strong-armed by Nikolai and Vlad. Her face was panic-stricken. She couldn't believe her eyes. "Who . . . who . . . are you?" she croaked in her fragile, broken voice. "Wh . . . what . . . do you want?"

"Ah, that's just what I will tell you," answered Nikolai as he blew a smoke ring in the air. He was feigning charm again while laughing at her helplessness. "First, tell me please,

26

is anyone else expected here today?"

Veronica bobbed her head up and down. "My brother and . . . and his wife." She was almost choking on her words she was so nervous. "They were . . . to take me to dinner but . . . instead . . . bringing . . . something to eat – " she pointed to her throat, "because . . . not well." Then she added, "No voice!" with her mouth opened wide, almost comically. She was completely flustered.

"Yes, we can see that," Nikolai grunted with a crooked smile. Then in a dead serious voice he asked, "What time are they expected?"

"About six . . . six . . . six o'clock," she stammered.

Nikolai checked his watch. "We have a half hour," he muttered, shaking his head and cursing under his breath. "But I want us to move fast!" he shouted at Vlad and Sergei. "They could come early. And we've got too many people already! So we leave at once!"

"Listen to me carefully," he snapped at Mrs. Rosen. "We're all leaving the building together. All of us – if you do just as I say. If you don't, I will leave your friend here to greet her family – as a corpse! Put on your coats, get your things, and we're out of here in two minutes! You got that? NOW MOVE!" he shouted.

To Veronica who still had on her coat, he said simply, "And you stay right where you are."

Mrs. Rosen and I ran for our things, with Vlad right behind us, and hastily threw on our coats. Veronica sat perfectly still on the couch except for her very visible trembling.

Turning to the door where Sergei was standing, Nikolai jerked his head at him. "Open it and look around you first, just in case." To the rest of us he barked, "If anyone gets any ideas about screaming or running away" – he paused, smirking at Veronica who we all knew was in no condition to scream past a whisper – "you see this?" He showed us a gun in his pocket with a silencer on it. "Be my guest. Try anything and you'll all get it, one, two, three – so no tricks, please. Now let's go!" he commanded.

To Vlad, he added, "Don't let go of that girl!" – at which point, Vlad wrenched me to him like a rag doll and clasped me around the waist with his right arm.

I gasped and I could hear Mrs. Rosen suck in her breath. She and Veronica were together with Nikolai right behind them as Sergei stood in the doorway. We tramped down the stairs, all six of us, sounding like a herd of buffalo. I was praying we'd run into somebody on the stairway or that New Yorkers were less tolerant about noise. But no such luck.

Out on the street, the first thing that hit us was the acrid smell from the horrible pit that used to be the World Trade Center, still spewing smoke after four months. Veronica's place was only around 20 blocks from ground zero, and today had been one of those intense overcast, damp days in early January when you can't breathe anyway. Just thinking about September 11th made me weak at the knees always – and my stubborn hope that we would be released gave way to a sense of panic all over again.

The sickening smell that everyone talked about hit me hard earlier when Mrs. Rosen and I got out of a cab in front of Veronica's place. It was the first time I'd been this far downtown since the day after September 11th when my friends and I almost managed to get past the police cordon around ground zero. We had only wanted to help, but Mom found out later and kept me in the apartment for a week, extracting a vow that I'd stay away. I remember how we stood on line with all the others cheering the exhausted firemen as they returned in shifts from trying to rescue survivors underneath all the debris that once was the twin towers. And how we cheered the other firemen and rescue workers and trained dogs who went in to relieve them.

Remembering them made me feel so cowardly. They were all so brave, so courageous, and I was only thinking of myself today. Why couldn't I be more like the heroes who risked their lives – even sacrificed their lives – to save all those helpless victims of fanatic killers? Why couldn't I have thought of something before to help Mrs. Rosen . . . and now Veronica? I guess that's for other people, special people, not like me.

We were led up the block on Spring Street, the three heavies walking arm in arm with Mrs. Rosen, Veronica and me in pairs. We passed a couple too engrossed in each other to even notice us and then three student types rushing by like they were late for something. Nikolai, holding Mrs. Rosen real tight around the waist, took us around the corner to a street that was completely deserted. It had to be nearly 6:00 by now, but there wasn't a soul in sight. Downtown was like that, especially some of the residential side streets on a cold night at dusk.

Nikolai led Mrs. Rosen to a black car in the middle of the block. He mumbled something to Vlad who looked surprised and started to argue with him. Losing his patience, Nikolai erupted at him: "Don't argue, Vlad! Just do as you're told!"

What was that all about? – I wondered.

Vlad opened the car door and ushered Veronica into the back seat. At first she resisted, but Nikolai whispered something in her ear and she went in without hesitation, as Vlad locked the car with the remote key pad.

"NO!" cried Mrs. Rosen. "Let her go! What are you doing? You can't take her! You can't!"

Nikolai turned to Mrs. Rosen and said, "A long time ago you lost your family. I don't think you want anyone else to disappear. Well, she won't if you listen to me."

Then he jerked his head toward me. Sergei was squeezing me like he could crack my rib cage in the next second. "There's been a change in plan and it works out much better for us. The girl, who I intended to take with us tonight for insurance, would be – let us say – too much trouble. Oh, she's trouble, all right I can tell you that. *N'est pas?*" he slithered in oily French. "But, *voila*, it is simpler now with your friend in her place. She cannot call for help and she cannot run away. What could be better?"

Boy, was I relieved, as I instantly felt guilt in the next second.

Then he lit another cigarette and lowered his voice. It was as if he was leaving a net behind him. "If I were you, I'd think carefully about my offer, which need not take long. Don't do anything foolish, like calling the police. I'd hate for anything to happen to your dear friend Veronica – or your pretty protégé over there, whom we can easily snatch up – or your son and his family. The body of the last bitch who didn't listen to me was found in the East River . . . and over parts of New Jersey."

Nikolai pinched my chin. "You don't want to get hurt, little one," he whispered in mock tenderness, "do you?" – as Mrs. Rosen pushed him aside and held on to me.

I was speechless. I stood frozen in my shoes and cast my eyes down at my feet, then at the long line of parked cars. How could nobody be on the street yet? Not a single soul was around to witness any of this. Only a cold wind came whooshing through, as if to blow the fog away with one powerful thrust after the other.

Nikolai continued, blowing smoke at me, like it was all

a game to him. "In the meantime don't get any ideas. Others are watching your building – other associates of ours, that is – and the brownstone where your son lives with his family. But if you'd rather call the police, go right ahead. Yes, sure, they could protect you for a while, but not all of you, and not forever. On the other hand, *we* are watching everyone closely. And we intend to do so for a very, very long time until we get what we want."

Then he added, "We'd drop the watch for a while till things cool off, if you call the police. But we'd be back. And we'll have your friend the whole time. Besides, they're very busy these days looking for Arab types, not Russians," he said with a smirk.

He looked up and down the street and then leaned closer to Mrs. Rosen. "Think also about this. How easy for us to snatch a young girl or a boy – or your only son. The police mean nothing to us. We have committed so many unsolved crimes that we could keep them busy for ten lifetimes. I advise you to cooperate or we take this girl here or your grandson as collateral, along with your friend in the car who cannot hear a word I'm saying. Disposing of them is so simple to us." His eyes narrowed as he paused for a moment. "I leave that for your imagination for now."

Mrs. Rosen looked like she was staring at a pair of headlights about to run her down, but there was no car coming down the street. "You've thought of everything, haven't you?"

"But of course."

Suddenly she lost it. "Please don't involve them!" she pleaded. "If it's me you want, then let it be between you and me! Take me instead!"

"Madame Rosen, please," Nikolai said, shaking his head. "Tsk tsk tsk . . . what do you take me for? You are so famous that you would be all over the evening news and the front page of newspapers tomorrow! We never intended to take *you*. What's the point? Only that you be willing to do business with us. No, it's much better this way. No one cares about your friends. But *you* on the other hand . . . you would make international headlines. Your picture would be everywhere. Just think of the attention you would attract! The press, as you know, always makes things messy. Other underground operations would grow nosy, others who might find out what we need from you. No competitors, please! We keep it nice and simple."

Nikolai ignored her and started adjusting his coat. Then as if to puff himself up to prove that he never got ruffled unless he permitted it, he turned to Vlad and Sergei and said, "Come on, let's go. We're through here. Let's get something to eat." Sergei grunted and released me as he strode over to the driver's side of the car.

With dripping sarcasm Nikolai said, "Don't bother to memorize the license plate of this car. We'll ditch it so fast before the police could even put out a call on it. They'd never get to your Veronica in time. Have I made myself clear?" He turned on his heel and shouted at Sergei and Vlad: "NOW!"

"Wait!" she cried out as he and Vlad started to get in the car, even grabbing Nikolai by the shoulders. "You never told me how you discovered that Joshua was my brother – and how you found me. This is very important to me – I must know this!"

Was she crazy? Who cares how he found her! I couldn't believe she was delaying their exit. Stalling. How could she ask questions instead of letting them get the hell out of here! I couldn't wait another second for them to leave. Now I was really losing it. Oh, I was worried for Veronica, of course. But where would we be if they took all of us? And what if he changed his mind about me?

Nikolai closed the car door and took a step back on the curb. "The first was easy," he smiled, enjoying himself. "Your *SS* friends kept very efficient records of the families they, um, hosted. And finding you was simple. Our client is an avid collector. In fact, he attended that big show in your honor at the Museum of Modern Art last October. You'll be happy to know he owns one or two of your works."

"Dear God!" she gasped in disbelief.

"And by the way, I appreciate your coming down to Soho this afternoon. We'd been watching your movements for a few days. But when we saw you and 'princess' here leave your building today, we followed and waited outside. How much easier it was for us to have our discussion here and bring back a less troublesome, shall we say, 'guest' back with us . . . in order to get your full attention."

Nikolai lowered his head in a mock bow before Mrs. Rosen who looked desperately confused. Was there no end to how much he would taunt this woman? "Madame Rosen, you look so disappointed that you're not coming with me. It may comfort you to know that that really was our first rudimentary plan. Your name, however, which may protect you briefly, will not protect your loved ones."

"No, please," she pleaded again. "I beg you."

"All in good time. We'll let you know. It really is much less complicated if you simply cooperate of your own free will. The world is a much better place for those who take the path of least resistance. You of all people know this. Today there are more civilized ways of making people do what is needed before resorting to other methods. Less, shall we say, incriminating for us. With your kind, it's so easy." He flicked his cigarette in the street, as the wind caught it in mid-air and carried it off to nowhere.

She ignored his smug preaching and blurted out in one last attempt to get him to change his mind: "I want to go with you! I'll tell my family to keep my absence secret. I will do all this for you. Just please release her! She has nothing to do with this!"

"There, there now. So sorry to disappoint you," he snorted. "You see? We have your full attention. Really, though, it's so much better not to care for anyone else." He laughed like he was the cleverest person in the world and we were the dumbest. "You are all such fools. You make it so easy for us. Ha Ha Ha!"

Nikolai was really wound up now – really full of himself and tickled at pulling off his mission without a hitch. He seemed to love sticking it to her so much that he couldn't tear himself away from her. Gloating the way he did, he made me so furious I forgot my fear. I wanted to smash his face in.

"We'll get together again, I promise you, and maybe I'll even let you have the Diary after you've helped us with it. Remember, I'm keeping an eye on a certain brownstone, too." Then looking over at me, he called out, "And you too, princess."

Mrs. Rosen looked trapped. She was so desperately worried for Veronica. Then there was her son, her grandson and me. The net had been thrown completely over her now. He was leaving, but she was still in his snare. It was all over her face – bewilderment, anger and terror. What could she do? It was as if he owned her now.

Nikolai smiled grimly, took her hand and started to kiss it. "Until we meet again, Madame." But she jerked her hand away from him in disgust as he opened the car door finally. Finally!

His horrible, ugly laughter still rang in our ears after they drove off down the street.

Chapter Three

I felt sick to my stomach and was petrified they'd change their minds and come right back. "Let's get out of here fast!" I croaked, my voice far from normal. "Who were those guys?"

But Mrs. Rosen stood a long time in the middle of the street looking in the direction of the car that was nowhere in sight. She looked so very old and tired. "My poor Veronica," she finally whispered with an agonized sigh.

"What was that all about? What's happening? Who were they? Will they – "

"Gangsters, ex-KGB agents, what does it matter? They have threatened our lives . . . and my family – " her voice quivered when she said that – "what's left of my family. And they took my poor friend with them." Mrs. Rosen looked at me then and feigned putting on a stiff upper lip.

She held out her arms. I went over and hung onto her real tight. "I'm so sorry this happened," she comforted me as we walked back to the curb, tears streaming down her face. "I'm so, so sorry you're involved in this. Dear one, I won't let anything happen to you. Ever. It's me they want. Remember that. Come now, let's get a cab uptown," she said as we walked down the street to Sixth Avenue, my legs feeling like hollow stumps.

"But aren't you going to call the police?" I asked.

"No, not yet. I'm not sure I will. I need to think, to

collect myself and decide what's best to do. It's me they want," she said again. "Not Veronica or any of you. But still . . . I don't know yet. I have to think. Let's go now and find a cab."

"Can I stay with you, please?" I pleaded. "My Mom's not coming home till later and I don't want to be alone now."

"Yes, of course. I asked you to join David and me, I recall, when they – " she grimaced, unable to finish her sentence. "David! I'm so late now!" she exclaimed, looking at her watch. "It's close to 6:00. We must not say anything to him! It's for his protection. I believe they're capable of anything. I cannot jeopardize anyone else now; it's me they really want. Do let us keep silent about this for now till I decide what's best to do – and not tell a soul. For now," she added.

I didn't relish the idea of letting my hysterical Mom in on any of this anyway. She'd ground me for a year, that's for sure. And Dad was away as usual. So who am I gonna tell anyway, I thought, suddenly feeling sorry for myself. My sort of closest friend, Jeannie O'Toole, and I weren't speaking because I wouldn't go out with her cousin. And anyway I wouldn't tell my friends and go against Mrs. Rosen. But, I mean, somebody who really mattered since my best friend moved away? – there was no one.

All I said though to Mrs. Rosen was that I was glad I'd not have to go back to an empty apartment.

"Of course, Lauren, of course. I would rather have you with me, too. You were very courageous, you know. I was filled with admiration for you more than once today," she said as she flagged a taxi to us.

Me? Admiration for me? I couldn't believe my ears! I was filled with shame for myself more than once. How many times had I just been thinking of myself? Just wishing I could escape.

Back in our building on Central Park West, David wasn't there waiting for us. The apartment was eerily quiet. I looked around at the white walls adorned with more paintings than I'd ever seen in any one place, the soft Afghan rugs, her elegant furnishings and her incredibly comfortable, favorite, nearly threadbare chair and sofa. Abstract bronzes dotted pedestals here and there. A crystal vase filled with tulips sat on the fireplace mantel under a small, perfect watercolor of a little boy with a red ball.

It was hard to believe someone as gross as Nikolai could be in Mrs. Rosen's life. But he was. I got a whiff of the sickening scent of his cigarettes in my nostrils as I took my coat off and started to give it to Mrs. Rosen. "No, on second thought, I feel chilly," I said, changing my mind when I noticed I suddenly started trembling.

"Oh, open a window, darling . . . before we asphyxiate," Mrs. Rosen groaned, as if reading my mind. "I can still smell their cigarettes on our coats! I'll be right back."

Where was David? They told us at the front desk he waited a real long time and finally took off. David sure must be jumping out of his skin by now, I thought. Could we pull this off? Would he notice anything different about us? Like the fact that we just barely made it through the last hour with our lives! Could we hide all this from him? Could I hide it from my Mom later? Well, yeah, then again I could hide anything from her, I smirked thinking of my Mom.

I went to the window overlooking the Park and lifted the sash. I felt all shaky, like I was going into shock. Cool air rushed over me, and the curtains puffed like sails. I breathed deeply. Oh, how good it was to be alive!

City noises floated up from below. An ambulance frantically wailed down Central Park West. Taxis honked like a flock of angry seagulls. On the corner, a lone saxophonist blew some jazz. The bare branches of the trees in Central Park stood out above an army of busy joggers circling the reservoir by lamplight. In the distance, the buildings along Fifth Avenue glowed like desert cliffs lit up at night. Outside, life was going on like nothing had happened. Everything was normal again, only it wasn't.

"Lovely, isn't it?" I didn't hear Mrs. Rosen come up behind me. Then her voice changed as she turned away from the window in disgust. "What a hell humans can make of this beautiful world."

My heart nearly blew through my chest. All of a sudden, it hit me like a sledgehammer. "But what are we going to do?"

"I don't know yet, angel. But I feel we must keep silent till he calls . . . and I hear Veronica's voice. Veronica's poor voice." She started to sob, then caught herself. "No, I have to think. Time to cry later," she sighed, holding me to her again.

Just then the doorbell rang. It startled us so much that we both jumped. Mrs. Rosen patted my cheek. "It's David. Dear child, again, don't say anything. You have to give me time to think how to fix this. Please." She stared into the distance. "I don't want to risk any more lives for my sake." Could we pull this off, I wondered? Her voice didn't sound too steady.

David started knocking on the door and calling out impatiently. Finally Mrs. Rosen let him in. "Darling!" She kissed him twice, European-style.

"*Geez!* What took you so long to get back? Where were you all this time? I thought you said you wanted me here at 5:30!" He handed her a rumpled grocery sack. "Is everything all right? You had me worried."

Mrs. Rosen laughed a little too hard. "Of course, darling. We've just had a busy day. We're in the middle of an important project, that's all."

David frowned. "Are you sure you're okay? You sound a little weird. I know your voice. You sound, you know, kind of like something is wrong."

His grandmother quickly changed the subject. "You look famished," she said, taking the groceries from him. "All skin and bones, poor boy."

He wrinkled his nose. "Ugh, who's been smoking?" Unbelievable! I hadn't taken my coat off yet and David could actually smell the stink from Nikolai's cigarettes.

She ignored him. "I'll go put this food in the kitchen and make a pot of tea first."

I tried to give her some cover and awkwardly stepped in front of David, who finally noticed me. "Hi. What's up?"

"Not much," he replied. Ignoring me, he followed his grandmother and left me standing there.

I kicked the sofa. I was starting to feel like myself again. Almost. I took my coat off and threw it on the coat rack in the hallway.

In the kitchen, David and his grandmother unloaded the groceries. He took out the garlic cloves. She put them away. He took out a bag of sun-dried tomatoes. She put them away. They were cute together. Like, you know, a team.

To help keep my mind off the danger Mrs. Rosen and I were in – no, we all were in – I watched David unload the rest of the groceries. He had perfect caramel brown eyes and black wavy hair. Best of all, his hands were tan and looked strong. I liked that. The only thing I was not too excited about was the way he dressed. Not very motivated in that department. Today, he was wearing an oversized army fatigue jacket, dirty blue jeans, and Doc Martens.

I realized I was madly in love with him. It hit me real suddenly. I've heard that people in wartime fell in love a lot. Well, what I'd just been through was pretty close. I could have been killed. Anyway, I now knew that I loved David.

Mrs. Rosen dropped a can of green beans and it rolled under the table. I jumped off the counter where I'd been sitting and grabbed it. Then I gave the can to David who reached over to me for it.

"Thanks, uh – " he stopped. He had forgotten my name!

"Lauren," I mumbled, deflated.

"Thanks, Lauren."

Just then, Mrs. Rosen dropped a potato. It rocked on the floor like a fumbled football. "Oh, how clumsy of me," she said, exasperated, as she wrung her hands.

David retrieved it. "Hey, what's with the two of you? You're so jumpy."

She reached to take the potato, but he didn't let go. "C'mon and tell me what's wrong. Whatever it is, you're not hiding it too well."

Mrs. Rosen went still. She cut her eyes at me, begging me to keep quiet. Then she decided to answer him . . . partly. "I had a visitor today. He knew my brother during the war. It made me . . . sad. That's all."

"Oh, I see," replied David thoughtfully.

She turned her back on him. And then something dreadful happened. In a sort of terrible slow motion, she crumpled to the floor like all of her bones suddenly melted. She pulled her knees tight against her chest and howled like an animal caught in a trap.

"OmiGod!" I blurted. Instantly I wondered if I should tell David about the Russians right then and there, even though Mrs. Rosen had sworn me to secrecy. But she was coming apart before our eyes – and I had to tell him! Then again, I wasn't sure, for I'd be going against her if I did. Yet wouldn't it be better if the truth helped her? I felt really alone now and didn't know what to do.

David looked pained but stayed calm, like he'd seen it all before. "This happens sometimes," he sighed as she cried like a two-year old cradled her in his arms. "*Bubbe*, please, I'm here," he reassured her gently. "I'm here." He stroked her hair. "C'mon, why don't you get some rest?" Turning to me, he motioned with his head to come over. "Could you give me a hand?"

I bent down and took one of Mrs. Rosen's elbows. Her shoulders bounced as she gasped for air, and she repeated over and over, "*Ma famille, ma famille.*" But I couldn't understand her. I looked at David helplessly and choked, "What . . . ?"

"It's French. It means *my family*," David answered with a terrible look of worry on his face.

When we got Mrs. Rosen to her feet, we steered her down the hall to her bedroom. David held her up as I folded back the comforter on her four-poster bed. Then I unlaced her sandals and swung her feet under the covers. David sat on the edge of the bed and whispered something in her ear. A few minutes after I went out into the hall, figuring they needed some privacy, David appeared and quietly closed her bedroom door.

"Is she okay?" I croaked, still freaking out over what I should do.

He rubbed his eyes. "Yeah, she's fine now. The . . . er . . . storm passed. Maybe she'll sleep. This isn't too unusual. Maybe once or twice a year, she'll . . . she'll come apart. The first time I saw it, I was six. We were all sitting at the dining room table during a Passover *seder*, of all things. You sort of get used to it, I guess."

I wrinkled my forehead. What's a *seder*? I wondered.

David watched me closely. "She'll be all right soon," he assured me.

That made me decide to wait a little while before I said anything. David seemed pretty in charge of the situation – concerned but not too surprised. This had happened before. Only I knew what caused it this time. I figured it was best to leave now and check in on her in an hour or so. And if she didn't come out of it, then I'd tell David.

Meanwhile I had to keep cool. I felt funny. Too much was happening at once. First the Russians and Veronica, then Mrs. Rosen and our pact of secrecy, then her going to pieces, and now I was standing alone with David listening to confidential family things. For a few seconds, neither of us said anything. Which was normal, I guess. We were pretty much strangers. Not that it mattered . . . to me, at least. David's face was hard to see.

"So," I finally managed to say, "I guess I better get going. I'm worried about Mrs. Rosen, but if she's resting now . . . well then . . . okay I really should go now because Mom'll wonder," I lied, "what happened to – "

Just then he touched my shoulder. It caught me off guard and I jumped. "Thanks for helping, Lauren."

I smiled. "Sure." It was like my feet were nailed to the floor. I felt awkward. I didn't know whether I should stay or go. "I, uh, guess I need to get my backpack."

We went back to the kitchen. David hit the overhead lights with the bottom of his fist. They flickered on with that depressing buzzing sound fluorescent bulbs always make. "I'll fix her some potato soup," he said. "She'll be fine. In fact, as soon as she hears me rattling pans, she'll burst in here and stop me."

"You're real sweet," I said, smiling at him irresistably.

"I mean, to, you know, to help her so much."

He shrugged his shoulders. "What am I gonna do? She's my grandmother." He opened a small drawer next to the stove and grabbed a potato peeler. Then he rinsed two potatoes under the faucet and peeled them. David really knew his way around the kitchen. On a good day, I can find the microwave.

I checked my watch. It was almost 6:30 pm. I felt awkward. I wanted to get home, but at the same time I didn't want to leave. "You want me to, like, help you?"

David pooched his lower lip. "Well, why not?" He rummaged in the drawer and found a steak knife. "Okay, here – cut." When he handed it to me, our fingers brushed. If he noticed, he didn't show it. I sure noticed.

We stood side by side while he peeled and I sliced. When David was through, he helped me – I went really slow on purpose. The whole time my skin tingled because he was so close. A couple of times our knees and elbows rubbed, and I started getting all warm. I was beginning to feel human again. And in that moment I wanted to tell him everything.

"That's enough," he finally said, just when I opened my mouth to tell him what really happened. He scraped my pile of slices into his. "She doesn't eat too much."

That stopped me cold. I was determined to keep my pact with Mrs. Rosen unless she didn't come out of it. "What was that Mrs. – um, your grandmother – was saying about her family? What was that all about? It sounded so sad."

He scooped the potatoes up in his hands and tossed them into a pot on the stove. "You mean you don't know?"

"No," I answered, not exactly fibbing. Of course, I knew something awful happened to them, but I wasn't going to come right out and say I figured it out during Nikolai's visit.

David wiped his hands on a paper towel. Then he rinsed off the knives in the sink. He cocked his eyebrow. "You see *Schindler's List*?"

"The movie?"

"Yeah. Spielberg."

"No, Mom said it was too, you know, violent." As soon as the words were out of my mouth, I realized I'd said something really stupid.

He shook his head. "Unbelievable. Everyone ought to see that movie."

I felt about a centimeter tall, and I made a lame attempt at damage control. "Well, I really wanted to see it. Maybe I'll rent it."

David put the potatoes in a pot on the stove, turned it on and adjusted the flame. "That'll sit awhile. We can add the other junk later."

My heart pounded. He wanted me to stay. I think.

He scratched his chin. "You got a minute? I mean, before you have to go?"

I tucked my hair behind my ear. "Yeah, I suppose I got a minute or two," I said, trying to act laid back. I was confused. I wanted to be with him, yet knew I should go. I was also still on the edge of telling him what had happened, but kept thinking of my promise to Mrs. Rosen. He was making it pretty difficult for me.

"Excellent. I want to show you something. Follow me."

Anywhere, I thought. Anywhere.

David led me down the hall. We tiptoed by Mrs. Rosen's bedroom and kept going, past the small studio where she worked.

I'd never been this deep into her apartment before. It was a spooky old thing with high ceilings and lots of crown molding. Tons bigger than the cramped box downstairs where Mom and I live now after my parents' divorce. Then David stopped in front of a polished oak door. "Here," he said, twisting the doorknob as the hinges creaked real bad. He turned on the light and we stepped into what looked like the set for an *Indiana Jones* movie. Suddenly I was in another world.

"This is my grandfather's old study."

"Oh, yeah, your grandmother told me about it," I said in awe. Dr. Rosen had been head of the Anthropology Department at Columbia University for years. After he died, Mrs. Rosen hadn't touched a thing in the office. It was sort of like a shrine, I guess. She still talked about how much she loved him.

Dust tickled my nose and I tried not to sneeze. Shelves sagged under the weight of more books I'd seen anywhere in one place except in libraries. Mountains of books spilled over the floor and the window sills, too. While David went to one of the shelves and started digging around, I checked out the rest of the room. Tribal masks scowled down from all over the ceiling, and some wicked-looking spears and painted shields stood piled in a corner. Even a moldy owl and a giant stuffed bat hung from the ceiling. What a place! I could have used some of this stuff for props on my 15th birthday party last month.

"Found it!" David called out, holding a black book about the size of an encyclopedia. "I'm going to loan you this, but you have to promise to return it as soon as you're finished. My grandmother has extra copies, but not that many."

I took the book. Heav-y, I thought, not very interested at all in tackling it. "Thanks," I said, nonetheless. "What's it about?"

"You asked what happened to my grandmother's

45

family.   Well, this tells you.   They were murdered . . . along with ninety percent of the rest of the Jews in Europe."

"They were?   God!   That's unbelievable!" I gasped in horror.

"Have you heard of the Holocaust?"

"Sort of – "

"Hitler?"

"Well, sure."

"How Hitler tried to exterminate us?"

I nodded.   "Yeah.   I think we talked about it in social studies class.   I guess I didn't pay much attention though. History sort of bores me."

His eyes burned a hole in me.   Suddenly I wished I'd paid a lot more attention in history class.   I blushed and looked down at the title on the book's spine.   *Never Again* it read.

"Hey, your grandfather wrote this whole book? Wow!"

David gnawed his thumbnail.   "C'mon, let's get out of here," he said gruffly, flicking off the light.   As I followed him down the hall, I wondered what I'd done wrong.   Somehow the chemistry between us wasn't the same.   In fact, it stunk. All the way back to the kitchen he hardly said two words.

I grabbed my backpack and Discman.   "Well, I guess I better be going.   Mom's a real drama queen when I come home late."

David didn't try to stop me.   "Oh," he replied, uninterested.   Then he went to the stove and stirred the soup. "Don't forget the book."

I picked it up off the table.   "Oh, yeah.   Thanks."   I stuck the book under my arm and took a step towards the door, but stopped.   I bet I stood there for a good fifteen seconds waiting for him to say something.   If he realized I was still around, he sure didn't act like it. "See ya," I finally said.

David looked over his shoulder. "Yeah."

I took a step towards him. "You sure your grandmother's okay and everything?"

He nodded. "She'll be fine. She'll get over it. She always gets over it." He grunted. "She doesn't have much of a choice, does she?"

"Tell her I'll call her tomorrow, okay?"

"I'll let her know."

I stood there for a few more seconds. "I'm gonna let myself out now, okay?"

David kept his back to me. "Be my guest."

At least he didn't have to be so sarcastic, I thought to myself, shrugging my shoulders. I gave up, and then went to the front door and flipped the deadbolt.

"Lauren, wait!" he called out suddenly.

I rested my hand on the doorknob. "Yes?"

"Don't go . . . please."

Things were getting interesting. I counted to five and walked back to the kitchen.

Chapter Four

"I, uh, apologize for being rude."

"You weren't really, just . . . just, I don't know, preoccupied."

"No, I was rude," David repeated emphatically. Then he pulled out a chair at the kitchen table. "Sit down. I owe you an explanation."

I slid my backpack off my shoulder as he took the seat across from me.

"So, you want a soda or what?"

"No, thanks. Actually, I had a Diet Coke not too long ago," I winced, remembering the face of Sergei handing it to me. I shut my eyes wishing I could blot them all out of my mind, tell the truth and just get it over with.

I wanted to shout at the top of my lungs: "David, I was handed a Diet Coke only two hours ago by a Russian thug named Sergei who's part of a gang that kidnapped Veronica because they want something from your grandmother – and we're all in danger including you until she gives them what they want!"

But I didn't. I managed to keep my mouth shut, which sure did surprise me about myself because I never knew I had it in me, especially with someone I wanted to score points with.

David ran his fingers through his hair. Then he stared at the tablecloth and scratched at a crusty spaghetti stain with his thumbnail. The room was quiet except for the sound of the soup bubbling on the stove. It smelled good. I hadn't eaten lunch because I had to keep my figure. That seemed so stupid now. My stomach growled. I put my hand over my belly to muffle the noise. I was still waiting for David to explain himself.

"Okay, here's the deal," he finally said. "Usually, I'm not so . . . ."

I helped him out. "Um, impolite?"

"Right, impolite. But . . . but sometimes certain things, extremely specific things, I don't know, they just bug me."

He looked at me like I knew what he was getting at. I didn't. "Let me put it this way. You're not Jewish, right?"

Duh, I thought. I shook my head no.

"Do you know any Jewish people?"

"A few, I guess. You know, at school. And I'm talking to you, aren't I?"

"I mean, of course I realize you're a gentile, but, see, I just . . . ." His words fizzled like air leaking from a balloon. He stood up and shoved his hands deep in his Levis pockets, giving up. "It's no use. It's not your fault, but it's no use. Why don't you just get out of here!" He scuffed the floor with the toe of his boot.

My face got hot. Things were starting to get out of hand. "I wish you'd at least tell me what I did! You owe me that much!"

He turned around. "You really want to know?"

"Yeah, I do."

"I'm just not sure I can actually tell you. That's the point."

"Well, give it a try," I challenged him with some sarcasm.

"I'm tired of trying. Tired of explaining."

49

"Look, I'm confused here, David. Give me some help. Explaining what?" I cleared my throat.

"Okay, already," he sighed. But a good long minute or two passed before he said anything. Finally, he blurted out, "I'm so thirsty. You sure you don't want a Coke first?"

I blew a lock of hair out of my face. "Now that you mention it, I think I do need one." I watched him as he went to the refrigerator and brought back two cans. Silently he popped them open and handed me one. I kept my eyes on him as I took a sip.

"Do you think I'm a jerk?" he asked out of nowhere.

I took another swallow. "No. I mean, not totally. Should I?"

He nearly smiled. That was a first. "Well, let me tell you a story," he said. "I'm an only child. My mother is a pediatrician and my father plays violin for the New York Philharmonic. Their expectations of me, you know, grades and all that, are pretty high. I can't be good . . . I have to be perfect. Get it?"

I got it. Sort of, anyway. I nodded my head.

"That's just for starters. And you know about my grandmother. Hell, she's even been on the cover of *Time* magazine. The bottom line is that there's a lot expected of me."

"That's pressure," I said. "My Mom is ecstatic if I make my bed."

"Wait," he continued. "You don't know about pressure. To top it all off, I'm also the only grandchild. It's like the entire survival of the family rests on my shoulders." He took a gulp of Coke and wiped his mouth with the back of his hand. "It's a very small family, by the way. And you wanna know why?"

"Why?"

"Read the book I gave you."

I should've seen it coming. I tried not to make a total fool of myself. "They were all killed . . . right?"

"Yes, by the Nazis. My great-grandparents and their relatives, kids and all, except for my grandmother, were all murdered by the Nazis. Starved, burned, gassed, and shot. And all because they were Jews. And you wanna know what else?"

"What?"

"I don't think the world has ever forgiven us for that."

I frowned. "Why? That's a strange thing to say. What do you mean?"

"I think people hate us because we remind them how bad they can be. They hate us because we know. And they hate us because we remember. We're their conscience."

"David, that's nuts. I don't hate you. Nobody – "

He held up his hand to stop me. "Do you know that some idiot at school actually called me a *hymie* today?"

"I'm sorry, but I don't see what one jackass at – "

"And last week, on the cable access channel, I watched two fat rednecks sitting in front of a confederate flag in some stinking studio in Florida squint their little pig-eyes at the camera and say the Holocaust was a hoax." He snorted. "They even called it the 'Hoaxacaust.'"

I shook my head. "But – "

"My point is this, Lauren. People like you, who don't know about the Holocaust, make it possible for schmucks like them to get away with that kind of garbage! That really irritates the hell out of me!"

My face burned up like mad. "God, you're so bitter! And, personally, I think you're being really unfair to me."

"I know it's not your fault, I mean, you have to learn it somewhere. But, jeez, how can you be in high school and not

51

know this stuff? You can't be that dense!"

Embarrassed and hurt, mostly hurt, I leaped to my feet. I could feel my lower lip start to quiver and I tried not to cry. "I'm leaving. I'm sorry I don't know everything like you do. And, as a matter of fact, Mr. Know-It-All, there are a heck of a lot of things you don't know about – "

"WELL, I HOPE I'M NOT INTERRUPTING SOMETHING – "

Mrs. Rosen stood in the doorway. She wore a silk flowered kimono and it looked like she'd put on a little makeup. I don't think she heard what we were saying really because she didn't ask anything. Instead she went right to the stove and lifted the lid on the pan. "Umm. It smells like you two have been busy."

She smiled at me. "Can you still stay for soup, Lauren? My goodness, it's almost 7:30." She gave me a private kind of look and nodded her head as if nothing happened. "Did you speak to your mother yet? I hope you can still stay. It's good to have the two of you around now. But make sure you call her if you haven't already."

I was cinching my backpack straps under my arms and putting on my headphones. "Thanks, but I better be going. She's probably home by now." I was so annoyed with David that I'd almost forgotten about her. And thanks to his moodiness almost forgot about . . . them. I halfway turned to Mrs. Rosen and searched her face closely. "How are you feeling?"

"Rest and time heal," she smiled faintly. She noticed the black book under my arm and raised one eyebrow. "Has my darling grandson assigned you homework?"

David grimaced uncomfortably. "Yes, ma'am, and I think I sort of put my foot in my mouth, too."

She sighed. "Imagine that." She stirred the soup with

a wooden spoon. "The night is young, wonderboy. You still have time to get the other one in there." She tasted the soup and murmured, "Not bad."

"Come on, Lauren, stay for dinner," David pleaded. He flashed me a smile that was irresistible.

This was too much. I just stared at him. Maybe he wasn't as stuck up as he acted. I decided to give him a second chance even though I was pretty mad at him. I pulled off my headphones. "Okay, you twisted my arm."

Mrs. Rosen moved from the stove to the cabinet and reached for some plates. Then, as if sensing I needed support, she said softly to David, "Lauren is not only an exceptional artist, but she also writes well." Turning to me, she coaxed, "You must show David the wonderful short story you wrote last month, Lauren."

I'd rather die first, I thought, picturing David read my first storytelling assignment in English class and passing judgment on it. But seeing Mrs. Rosen back to her old self again made me feel better. Maybe she'd already figured out a plan on how to deal with the Russians.

"Yeah, all right, I'll stay for supper," I repeated, with a dose of drama, "but first I'll call Mom. She should be home by now," I said, reaching for the portable phone. I was about to punch the talk button when the phone tweeted like a bird. Without thinking, I instinctively answered it. "Hello?"

At first, there was silence on the other end of the line. Then an eerily familiar voice drawled out sarcastically, "So, we meet again, *dushenka*."

I broke out into a sweat. It was Nikolai.

Chapter Five

I handed Mrs. Rosen the phone like a hot rock. For an instant, she stared at it like it might bite. She didn't even ask me who was calling – she could tell by the look on my face. The phone's black antenna quivered and shook like a car aerial in the wind when she held it to her ear. Her voice creaked like a rusty gate. "Y-Yes?"

As she listened to Nikolai, her face congealed into a mask, like it was carved from wax. At one point, her wrinkled lids lifted and her eyes got big, flaring white like one of those supernovas you read about. The flare lasted maybe a second. Or less. Then her face went expressionless again, but now it was bluish grey instead of chalky white. It reminded me of the same sick color as skimmed milk.

Finally she nodded and said very quietly, "I understand. Let me speak to her." Then there was a pause. "No, not until I speak to her!" she added firmly. Suddenly Mrs. Rosen's face brightened and her tone changed completely. "Thank God! Oh, Veronica, thank God, you're all right! Please forgive me . . . I have not stopped thinking of – " Another pause as she hung on Veronica's every word.

Then her expression changed. "Yes . . . yes . . . I said I understand." Her voice grew irritated. "Tomorrow!" she spat. Then silence as she listened to what could only be a rebroadcast of Nikolai's threats. "Yes, yes, I remember what you said, but – " She heaved a sigh and didn't say goodbye. Just turned the phone off and rested it on the counter, looking at me without saying anything.

I half-closed my eyes in response, knowing exactly that she'd made her appointment with them and that they let her talk to Veronica for a minute. My heart was heavy and filled with dread for both of them. The call didn't even last two minutes. David caught that look between us, as I noticed from the corner of my eye his head turn from his grandmother to me and then back at her again. How was she going to keep him out of it now, I wondered? He was no longer clueless.

Unable to contain himself, he inserted himself right between us and demanded to know what was going on. He asked her point blank, but got no answer. Then he looked at me and tried to get something out of me.

I didn't dare answer him.

So finally he yelled in exasperation: "WHAT IN THE WORLD IS GOING ON TODAY, YOU TWO?"

Mrs. Rosen scraped a chair across the floor and sank down at the kitchen table. She cradled her head in her hands, her fingers laced together like basket weaving. For the first time, I noticed the arthritic knots twisting her joints. After a moment, she looked up. Some color, not much, but some, was back in her cheeks. She coughed. "David, there are some things you must know . . . ."

Then she told him everything. About Nikolai's visit. About Veronica. About Joshua's Diary. About the mysterious collector and what he wanted from her.

When she was through, David glowered at her. "You mean, all this while since I got here, you both kept this from me? Why didn't you tell me right away? Don't you trust me?"

Mrs. Rosen rubbed her face. "It was for your own

55

good, darling. You didn't need to know."

David pointed at me and blurted, "And SHE does?"

Mrs. Rosen put her arm around my shoulders. "Don't be silly. Lauren was with me when the Russians arrived. And I asked her to keep this secret until I decided what to do tonight. She's a very brave girl, I might add."

David angrily shoved a chair aside and paced around. "What the hell! What did the police say?"

Mrs. Rosen sighed. "What he wants boils down to one thing. Money. And many millions at that. I'm to meet him at noon tomorrow. I don't know where yet. He's to call back in the morning and tell me at which point he will release Veronica. And, no, I haven't called the authorities."

"Why the hell not?" David demanded.

"I don't think it's a wise idea. Not right now, anyway," she answered, not telling him everything.

"What are you talking about, not a wise idea?" David challenged, irritation continuing to rise in his voice.

I couldn't stand it any longer and blurted: "THEY THREATENED TO KILL US, DAVID! Get a clue! Just the other day, they chopped somebody to bits! She doesn't want to risk Veronica's life! They said if we call the police, Veronica will – "

David froze. Then the anger slowly thawed on his face. "You mean – "

Mrs. Rosen nodded. "Yes, that's true. On the phone just now he used a grotesque expression. How did he phrase it exactly? Oh, yes. He said if I didn't cooperate, they'd 'gut' us all like fish."

Omigod, I thought, remembering a point when her eyes got real big when she was on the phone.

Stunned, David slumped in a chair and drummed his fingers on the kitchen table. "How many were there? How many do you think are in this thing?"

"Three.   And there are others, he claims.   I suspect they're all members of the Moscow *mafia*," Mrs. Rosen replied. "That's my best guess, at any rate."

"Geez, those Russian mobsters are hard core killers! They whack guys left and right downtown and in Brighton Beach all the time!   It's been all over the news!"

Ignoring David's excitement, I turned to Mrs. Rosen and asked, "How did Veronica seem to you?   I could tell you were talking to her at one point."

"They only let her speak a moment, but – "

"Because they didn't want to take any chances that you did call the police and they were listening to trace the call, I'm sure," David interrupted.

"Yes, it was very brief and he hung up on me.   Yes, I'm sure you're right.   Well, amazingly it was she who was trying to calm me.   Insisting that she was fine, and that I was not to worry.   Imagine!   Oh, I must get her out of there tomorrow, one way or the other.   I will think of something. It is I, after all, they need.   I'll settle this once and for all with their mysterious ring leader . . . that despicable art collector, whoever he is."

Mrs. Rosen rose to her feet, trying very hard to act like nothing was wrong.   She called David over to reach for some stoneware soup bowls from the cabinet.   "Enough for now. Let me feed the two of you," she announced softly, as if to say *subject closed.*

David snapped his fingers.   "Hey, wait, I think I saw them yesterday!"

Mrs. Rosen nearly lost her balance.   I quickly took the bowls from her and put them on the table.   "What do you mean?" she asked.

"Yeah, big dudes in leather coats.   Right?"

Mrs. Rosen didn't answer him. Instead, she handed me three stainless steel spoons which I set on the table next to the bowls.

"Right," I answered.

"They bumped into me coming out of the elevator when I was still waiting for you to send me up yesterday. I could hear their Russian accent, and I smelled that weird cigarette smoke on the two of you earlier. I watched them pile into a black Mercedes Limo with tinted windows parked out front. Someone was waiting for them in the back seat, too."

"Did you see him? What did he look like?" I asked.

"Let's see, I remember an ancient-looking guy when they opened the door who looked like an old movie actor or something 'cause he wore a fancy pin-striped suit with a red flower in his lapel. Plus, and this is extra weird, he was breathing oxygen out of one of those green tanks like football players use on the sidelines. Oh, and he was wearing black leather gloves. That's all I saw before they slammed the door."

"You saw quite a bit," said Mrs. Rosen, frowning. She was at the table now and lit one of the candles in the sterling silver candlesticks she always used, even when she ate alone. "So he must be the collector behind all this," she said to me. Concern clouded her face. "David, did any of the men get a good look at you?"

"No, I don't think so. They seemed like they were in a big hurry. Why?"

She sighed with relief and blew out the match, but she didn't answer David. Changing the subject, she said, "Come, my darlings, let's eat. I feel relieved a bit after hearing Veronica's voice . . . which is coming back slightly, Lauren," she said, turning to me. "And I think I know what I'm going to do."

We were all ears, dying to know what her plan was, but she didn't say what it was. Instead, she shook her head and whispered, "Thank God, Veronica's all right. She said that they even gave her dinner, though she didn't touch it. She was acting brave for me, certainly. I know her. But then she is an extraordinary friend with such a strong spirit. Her father was very adventurous, and she never tires of telling stories about him. She always said she gets her pluckiness from him. Did I ever tell you about the time she hit a mugger over the head with her umbrella and knocked him unconscious?"

The thought of Veronica stopping a thief cold in the act with an umbrella and beating him senseless struck David and me so comically that we started to roar with laughter in relief from all the tension of the night. Mrs. Rosen chuckled too.

"Veronica has always been a character, a truly passionate soul with strong convictions about standing up for what's right. I could tell you many stories about her. She has been the most wonderful friend in the world. Like a sister to me." Mrs. Rosen bowed her head and repeated *"a sister"*. . . as her voice trailed off.

"Look, let's not talk about this while we have our dinner," she said quietly, her concern for us showing visibly. "Just for a little while. We must eat to keep our strength. So, first, David, please . . . won't you – "

Thunder rumbled outside and a burst of wind blew out one of the candles. "Whoa," David said as he got up and left the room to shut the living room window. Mrs. Rosen shivered and wrapped an intricately woven shawl from the back of the chair tightly around her as David left the room.

Then she leaned towards me and whispered, "You like him, don't you?"

I played dumb. "Who?"

"Oh, who?" Mrs. Rosen cleared her throat. She patted

my hand. "Just be patient with him, Lauren. Sometimes he's too much of a Mr. Smarty-pants for his own good. I know he's quite fond of you, though. I can tell."

My heart fluttered. Just then David came back and I looked down.

"Wow! All of a sudden it's pouring out there!" he exclaimed. Then he caught the looks on our faces. "What's going on? What are you talking about?"

Mrs. Rosen looked impassable, but I thought I saw the slightest smirk on her face. I couldn't be sure though. As for me, if it was possible to turn redder than I already was, I did.

"Okay, okay, I'm not even going to ask," David sighed.

His grandmother gave him a long loving look, and then looked over at me as she took both of our hands. "My darlings who lift my spirit so, come now, let us break bread together and try to eat. Again, we must be strong. David, please, if you would . . . . "

And then David did something I'd never seen before. He took a special candlestick from the cupboard and lit it, too. After that he took some bread and broke it, giving Mrs. Rosen and me a piece each. In the next moment he began saying a prayer in Hebrew. Then Mrs. Rosen said a prayer in Hebrew and I could hear her say the name "Veronica" at the end.

Suddenly I remembered . . . it was their Sabbath. With David's family everything started on Friday night at sundown. It was unusual for me to hear prayers before dinner. I felt somehow proud of David. He looked so serious when he prayed. I bowed my head. To tell the truth, I kind of enjoyed it. My family never goes to church.

The soup, however, wasn't going down so easily. All during dinner, I worried about what David said about how Nikolai and his gang were cold-blooded killers. Mrs. Rosen hardly ate anything either. While we sat at the table, as if everything was normal, they were somewhere out there in the night with Veronica . . . watching and waiting for whatever they wanted of Mrs. Rosen . . . planning to gut us like fish . . . or chop us to bits, or something else too horrible even to imagine. I kept seeing Nikolai's ice blue eyes and how it looked like there wasn't a person behind them, like his eyes were dead.

When Mrs. Rosen served us a dessert of strawberries dipped in powdered sugar, blueberries and custard, which I somehow found room for in my stomach, she decided to tell us about her brother Joshua.

"He was my hero. I idolized Joshua like only a sister can idolize her big brother. Not that he didn't tease me a bit when I was small. He was human, not a saint, thank God. I imagine I was a pest, too. But still, I thought he could do no wrong. And I know he never did. Ever."

"You've never talked about him before. You've never talked about anything from that time before. Could you make an exception for once and tell me about him?" David asked. "Only if it's all right," he added in a tender voice, remembering what happened to her earlier when she collapsed. "It's just that you seem to want to talk about him. And maybe it will be good for you. You know? It's worth a try if it'll help."

While she didn't answer, it seemed to me like she was thinking about it. And it sounded like a good idea. I sure was curious especially that I was involved now since this afternoon. And I agreed that it might help her somehow also. But Mrs. Rosen remained silent, worlds deep in thought.

"Okay, really, I understand. It's all right. I'm sorry I asked," David sighed, backpedaling.

She served David another helping of strawberries, but stopped, as if a shudder ran through her. "I remember the strawberries I loved as a young girl," she said in a far-away voice. "How we all feasted on strawberries when the spring came." Then she put down the strawberry she gazed at so wistfully and sat very still. She looked like she was wrestling a ghost. Or an angel.

Then suddenly her voice changed. "But then the spring came and . . . and – " she hesitated as her voice grew hoarse.

"*Bubbe*," David said affectionately, taking her hand, "it's all right now."

She looked at him with a bitter, worried look in her eyes. "But it isn't all right!" she said, her voice raised in protest. "Don't you see? The world hasn't changed. And I see myself back then in the two of you, for you are so innocent, as I was."

Shaking her head, she said, "I see now that you must be ready for what the world can do to the innocent. It's all around us still. And since the atrocity of September 11th – the terrorist attacks on the World Trade Center and the Pentagon – life has changed for your generation. For all of us. You must be alert to those who destroy innocent lives to serve a fanatic cause. All those innocents . . . all they were doing was going to work that day. Fanatics filled with hate, who will stop at nothing, changed everything forever in this country. I see that nothing is secure any more.

"Europe is erupting in intolerance with the re-emergence of the extreme right these last few years especially. Lies are being manufactured all over again. Especially in illiterate, poverty-stricken countries ruled by an elite whose existence depends on keeping their citizenry ignorant so their media can ceaselessly broadcast outrageous tales that Jews bake babies for bread. Or by those who seek power at the expense of the innocent. All in the name, as always of economic or political survival or a so-called religious crusade. It's become a powder keg again, Europe and the Middle East. Israelis and

Palestinians . . . . Something is happening again in the world and it's clear that this time – this time," she repeated and then stopped abruptly. She caught her breath and looked at us with such tenderness and even sympathy in her eyes, like she felt sorry for us.

"When I was young . . . your age . . . but . . . still . . . I don't know if I should talk about all that . . . I don't know." Her words faltered as we watched her great inner struggle in silence. After a few minutes, though, she nodded her head and gathered herself majestically. It was clear she had made a decision. She cleared her throat.

"Oh, children, now I think . . . I think it's time to tell you some things." Her voice cracked a bit. "It's time you should know. It will not be easy for you to hear and it won't be easy for me to share these things with you. But it is not right that you do not know. I realize that it makes them stronger and you more vulnerable . . . and less prepared for what can happen . . . out of nowhere. Lauren, I'm sorry you are here. But you are part of this now and you must hear this, too. David, some of this I've never even told your father, God bless him."

"Really? Why not?" he asked. His ears perked up. It's not often you get inside information on your parents.

She smiled. "I wanted your father to grow up free of the ghosts that haunt me. So all these years I was silent. In a way, I suppose, I spoke through my art. But now, David, you're old enough to know. As you are, Lauren. What happened here today is proof that some things do not change. You must be witnesses for future generations. My life is almost over – "

David smacked the table. "Don't talk like that!"

"No, please, angel, it's the truth. I'm an old woman. After the war, all I wanted was to forget. Today, what with these men showing up and stirring up the past, remembering Joshua, remembering my lost loved ones, I need to speak and you need to listen. I need to tell you the story after all this time of what happened."

I put my hand on hers. "Are you sure you're all right? You don't have to do this if you don't think you're up to it." I couldn't believe she was going to talk to me about stuff she never told anyone before. And it made me feel older somehow, more important suddenly.

"I know," she said, patting me with affection and looking beyond me . . . deep into the past.

I was concerned for her, but hoped at the same time she'd really tell us. She became silent for a while as my thoughts went racing.

Once after an art lesson, when I noticed there were no photographs of her parents or her childhood in the apartment, I started to ask her about it. But I stopped when I realized she must have lived through World War II. I wondered what it was like growing up in Europe as a young girl then, but she would never speak of it. Now because of what happened this afternoon, she had changed. I'd never seen her like this before. She was always wonderful and warm to me, so poised and distinguished and, well, I don't know, always so unruffled. This was the real side of her she was letting me see. Like there was no need to hide any more. Also, we sure were linked in a new way after today.

I thought about how upset I'd been to see her cry before, and how I hated Nikolai and his gang for doing this to her. I wasn't afraid for myself . . . well, just a little. Maybe more than a little, actually. But most of all I was worried for her and Veronica. I guess that was why it was so hard to tear myself away from her and David; though I have to admit, it's always hard to tear myself away from David. Still, it was something to see her so shaken a few minutes before and yet now be so filled with resolve. Like someone about to dive off the high diving board . . . having doubts but knowing that she had to do it no matter what and that there was no turning back. I loved her all the more for her struggle and her determination to win out over herself.

Again I said gently, "Mrs. Rosen, you don't have to tell us if it will upset you." She looked dazed and far away, not saying anything for a while. Then suddenly –

"I've made up my mind. I know now that I have to. We have all the time in the world until tomorrow, my children. Let us make tonight our time-out from the world. But for now it will help to talk. It will help me for tomorrow. I must remember who I was. What happened today brought back to me a sense of the unnamable darkness that hung over us back then. So I have to. I feel it's my duty to the living – and the dead."

She put her head down. "I am the only one of my whole family who survived. All my relatives, my parents, my sisters, my brother, my aunts, uncles, and cousins . . . all of them were consumed in the conflagration. The nightmare of one man's demented vision and all the soul-less, heartless monsters who helped him."

I suddenly got real thirsty and consumed a glass of water in almost one gulp.

Noticing this, she said, "Here now, dear ones, this will take a while. Bear with me please." She wiped her eyes with the back of her hands and looked at me nurturingly. We need to have some coffee first. Let me – "

"No, I'll get it for you!" I leaped up from my chair, having made coffee here so many times before. Please, let me. You sit. I'll be right back."

David jumped up too. "I'll help you get it."

The coffee was in her great percolator pot that I loved and all I had to do was pour it into cups, but it gave David and me a moment together at the other end of the L-shaped kitchen. "How much of this do you know?" I whispered to him while he got the sugar and milk.

"Well, my parents have mentioned a few things. And I know a lot about the Holocaust – you know, from my grandfather's book and all. But the actual details of her life? No, I don't know so much. Zip, actually."

All of a sudden, hearing him admit he didn't know something, seeing him look vulnerable, I liked him even better. We put everything on a tray and came back to the table. I poured three cups of coffee from the pot and set it on the table.

Mrs. Rosen waved off the milk and sugar and wanted it just black, the first time I ever saw her drink it that way. She sat a moment longer, deep in thought. Then she sighed softly and took a deep breath. When she finally started to tell her story, it was in the most beautiful voice I think I've ever heard.

*

"To this day I cannot bear trains," she began, stirring her spoon in the coffee and then raising the steaming cup to her lips. "I used to love them. My father was a professor of antiquities at the University of Paris. The summer when I was eleven, as a treat, he and I rode the Orient Express to Istanbul, going from one archeological dig to the next in very grand style." She smiled warmly at the memory. "You can't imagine the taste of the croissants, the smell of the fresh-cut roses on the dining tables and the feel of the linen sheets on your skin when you went to sleep in your own cozy berth listening to the train whistle. It was a magical way to travel.

"We rode the train to Warsaw when we moved from Paris, too. Mother, Poppa, Joshua and I had a sleeping car, all to ourselves. It was luxurious. I was six years old – so Joshua was, oh, nine. The whole trip he drove me crazy. He kept pretending he worked for the railroad. The twins and Esther weren't born yet, of course. Poppa had been made a professor in the anthropology department at the University of Warsaw. It was a very prestigious position. We were all so proud.

"He was also offered a post in London. Many times I've wondered what would have happened if he'd taken that one instead. But Warsaw it was. Both Poppa and Mother were born there. All our relatives lived there. I had nearly thirty cousins my own age to play with! It was a little heaven. I missed Paris, where I was born, but Warsaw was like going home. There was such a richness of family and old friends of my parents surrounding us."

She chuckled and her eyes lit up. "You can't imagine what a splendid city Warsaw was! It was like something out of a fairy tale. Castles and magnificent palaces soared above narrow winding streets and tidy houses. In our neighborhood, tree-lined promenades fronted elegant townhouses. Best of all, museums and libraries were everywhere. I was so in love with our life there. At night the city sparkled like a chandelier."

"How romantic," I said.

Mrs. Rosen sighed. "Ah, yes, it was. It was simply beautiful. The largest Jewish community in Europe lived in Warsaw, you know. Intellectually and culturally, it was a very chic place. And the people! Oh, the people! Ballet dancers, painters, actors, violinists, doctors, scholars, writers, rabbis – all on our street! God, it was a world! A wonderful world. Poppa took us to concerts, the opera, plays, sidewalk cafes, picnics in the countryside, ice cream in the park, the zoo, the cinema . . . something nearly every day. In the summer, we sailed on the river and swam. In the winter, we ice-skated. It seemed like the sun always shone."

Lightning flashed over Central Park. As the rumble faded, Mrs. Rosen went on with her story. "In 1939, Joshua was sixteen, I was thirteen, the twins Sarah and Sonia were four years old, and Mother was pregnant with Esther. I was planning to go to the university in a few years to study medicine."

"Medical School! I thought you'd always been an artist!" David interrupted.

She laughed. "Well, I dabbled. A little painting in oil, watercolor, some clay, but, no, at the time I wanted to be a doctor. Joshua was the real artist in the family. He was so much more talented than I."

David looked like he didn't believe her. "Really? I never knew that."

"Oh, yes! Of course, all the children in the family took lessons, from three years old onward. Momma and Poppa were crazy for lessons! *Mon Dieu*! We took ballet, painting, sculpting, piano, violin, Hebrew, English, Latin, Greek, and Russian."

"Wow!" I exclaimed.

Mrs. Rosen chuckled. "Indeed, yes," she said to me, smiling. Then she looked at David. "Oh, how I wish you could have known our family. I never missed Paris after the first year back there. We were our own universe. A universe of love."

A deafening crack of thunder shattered our ears and rattled the kitchen window. The overhead lights flickered. Thunder boomed again, this time like it was in the next room.

Then the lights went out.

Chapter Six

Nobody moved. The candle lit up our faces like the dying embers of a campfire. In one sickening flash, a horrible thought occurred to me. "Do . . . do you think it's *them*? Have they cut the electricity?"

Neither David nor his grandmother spoke. I wasn't alone in my fears. The timing of the power failure was too suspicious. It <u>was</u> Nikolai and his gang taunting us! My mind raced, wondering what fresh torment they had in store for us.

Suddenly David scraped back his chair and went to the kitchen window. "FALSE ALARM!" he called out to us. "It's this whole block!" Then he opened a drawer and took out a flashlight and a few more candles. "The lights are on across the street. Ours oughta be back on soon." He put two candles on the kitchen counter and another on the table. "That ought to help in the meantime."

"Thank you, David," said Mrs. Rosen. "Well, all right, it's only a power failure."

"Whew! What a relief," I gasped, heaving a sigh.

David prodded his grandmother to go on. "So here we are, your captive audience. We have nothing else to do anyway till the lights go back on. Go on, please, and tell us the rest of your story."

Suddenly, like some crazed alarm clock, the telephone rang. All three of us froze and had the same thought at once.

Nikolai!

"Don't answer it!" shouted David.

"I have to!" Mrs. Rosen grimly replied. "You know I do."

David shouted in disgust, "Stay where you are! I'll talk to these bastards!"

"Angel, I've taken enough orders for one day, thank you," Mrs. Rosen said. She stood, picked up the flashlight on the table and disappeared into the shadows with the portable phone. In a few seconds, we heard a door shut. The ringing died.

"I wish I could hear what's going on," David said anxiously.

"How about just picking up the phone on the counter," I suggested, "if she's on the portable? But don't let her hear you lift the receiver."

"Yeah, right," David replied. "Good thinking." He went to the counter and fumbled around in the semi-darkness. "Got it." Then he covered the mouthpiece with his hand and put the phone to his ear.

I couldn't stand the suspense. "Who is it?"

David frowned. "Dial tone."

Then suddenly we both heard – "Actually it was your mother, Lauren. She wants you to stay put until the power's restored."

Mrs. Rosen! David and I spun around. White light blinded me. I threw my arm over my eyes. As I did, I caught a glimpse of Mrs. Rosen holding the biggest flashlight I'd ever seen. For a moment, fat spots swam in front of my eyes like a school of albino guppies.

Mrs. Rosen stood the flashlight on the table. "My husband Victor, God bless him, bought this wonderful device after the big blackout in '65. I always keep it under my bed."

She patted the flashlight like it was an obedient bulldog. "Much better than this little flashlight," she pointed to the other one she'd walked out with.

"As I was saying, Lauren, your Mama is concerned, but I told her not to worry. David will escort you home when the electricity comes back on."

"Thanks," I said. In the panic after Nikolai called, I'd forgotten to call Mom. Not that I cared . . . at least not much. But I figured I had to act like it. "Is Mom okay? Does she need me?"

Mrs. Rosen chuckled quietly. "She's fine, a little anxious, but fine. She said she lit some vanilla-scented candles and is now in the process of trying on some nice new outfits by candlelight that she bought at SAKS after work. She said they look better on her by candlelight and is enjoying herself immensely."

I rolled my eyes. This sounded just like her. Ever since Dad walked out, Mom basically did three things. Work, shop, and sit in bed and watch old black and white movies and cry over a box of Kleenex and a glass of white wine. It got worse every time Dad got a new girlfriend, which was pretty frequent.

"Oh, crap – I thought it was the Russians on the phone!" David groused.

"I could tell," said his grandmother. She narrowed her eyes. "Stay out of this, David. These people are dangerous. I've been around men like them before."

David clenched his jaw and looked away.

"I'm serious," Mrs. Rosen added. "You are all I have left in the world. Promise you won't interfere, darling. I've lost too many people I love. Please promise you'll stay out of this business."

In the dim orange light, I saw David put his hand

behind his back and cross his fingers. A little quake of excitement went through me. Right then and there, I wanted to throw him down and deep kiss him. And then slug him in the arm for being so stupid . . . and so brave.

"Sure, I promise," he groaned. "I . . . I, uh, won't get involved. Promise."

Mrs. Rosen's whole body relaxed. "Good, that's over with." Then she stared into the candle flame.

I scooted my chair closer. She was ready to continue her story.

"All right then, as I was saying, Joshua was the artist in the family. And an athlete, too. In soccer he was a regular dynamo. In January 1939, he went to Paris to study art at the Academy. To tell the truth, I was extremely jealous; yet I cried like a baby on the platform when his train left."

Mrs. Rosen took the candle that was out and lit it on the burning one. Our shadows thickened and spread over the walls.

"Joshua came home unexpectedly one hot afternoon in August. I remember I was playing the piano in our sitting room when he knocked. I thought it was the postman. Joshua came up behind me and put his hands over my eyes. I immediately knew who it was. I squealed and threw my arms around his neck. It was quite a scene." She laughed softly.

"Why did he come home?" David asked.

"To enlist in the Polish Army. He knew war was coming."

"Did you?"

Mrs. Rosen shook her head. "No, not really. There was a lot of talk, of course. The newspapers were full of it, particularly after the Germans occupied Czechoslovakia. But Poppa, a brilliant man who had fought in the Great War for France, didn't think anyone would be stupid enough to start another one. Not even Hitler. He thought he was only bluffing. We did know things were bad for the German Jews. We knew they were stripped of citizenship, that their businesses were confiscated, that they couldn't go to university, that their synagogues were vandalized. But we had no suspicion of the horror that was to come. Joshua did, I think."

David chewed his lip. "What happened? He joined the army?"

Mrs. Rosen stared across the candles at him. "No. There was no time. In an instant, in the blink of an eye, the world ended for our family."

The wind moaned outside the window like a ghost. Mrs. Rosen's voice got all hoarse.

"On the first of September, 1939, the Germans invaded Poland. That afternoon their planes bombed the city. I'd taken the twins for a walk to get away from all the awful news pouring from the radio. Then they appeared like flies. Fat green planes with the ugly, crooked crosses, swastikas, on their tails. They flew so low I saw the pilots' faces. I threw myself across the girls. In a flash, it was all over. Blood ran in the gutters. The first thing I saw when I looked up was a baby carriage on its side. One tire squeaked and spun madly like a pinwheel. A child lay in the street, dead, like a broken china doll. Her mother was beside her, on her knees, white with shock. She opened her mouth and tried to scream. No sound came out."

"Oh, God," David muttered.

"By the end of the month, German soldiers goose-stepped through the streets. My beautiful, magical city was a smoking ruin. We had no running water, no electricity, no heat, and little food. The houses on either side of us were rubble, the neighbors dead. It was like we'd gone to sleep and woke up on the moon. Jews were shot in the streets simply because they were Jews. Rabbis had their beards cut off as groups of grinning Nazis gathered around, slapping and taunting them. Very bad things happened to young Jewish girls. Things that are hard to imagine."

Mrs. Rosen took a sip of cold coffee. Her hand trembled as she lifted the cup.

"It only got worse. The following year, the Germans penned us all in the Ghetto. Ten-foot walls topped by barbed wire were built around the Jewish area, separating it from the rest of the city. That was the Warsaw Ghetto. They kicked us out of our house and gave it to an *SS* officer. It was ghastly.

"Mother sat on the front steps and wept. Poppa had to drag her away screaming and kicking before they arrested us. Finally we got out with only the clothes on our backs. All around us, Jews were being driven into the city from the countryside villages. I can still hear the weeping. Thousands of people milled around in despair, desperate for a place to stay. Lost children wandered everywhere, crying for their mothers. It was chaos. Then it got worse. Soon half a million of us were packed into the most run-down part of the city. For the Gentiles outside the walls, life went on. They went to cafes, motion pictures, to school. We were locked in a nightmare and couldn't wake up."

"What . . . how could . . . what did you do?" asked David.

"We did what we had to. When the Germans kicked us out of our house, they marched us at gunpoint to a filthy Ghetto tenement. Trembling with fear, we climbed the stairs to the first apartment. When Poppa asked if it was all right for us to come in, the people huddling in the shadows shouted there was no room. This was bad news. It was dusk, past curfew. Nazi soldiers roamed the streets, rounding up stragglers. Momma collapsed in the stairwell and started wailing.

"Then the door across the hall opened. An elderly lady, the oldest person I'd ever seen, stuck out her head. When she saw our plight, she sweetly smiled and said, 'Come in children.' That was it, we went to live with the poor widow Ringlebaum – and the six other families she gave shelter. In the middle of savagery and selfishness, she was still human. I imagined that she was an angel. Today, I know she was." Mrs. Rosen slowly nodded and then said again, this time in a whisper, "I know she was."

Mrs. Rosen stood up and walked over to the sink. She ran some cold water on a towel she took out of the drawer, wrung it out and dabbed her face with it. David and I looked at each other, not saying a word, not moving a muscle in our bodies. When she returned to the table, she sat down and asked, "Where was I?"

"You were going to tell us more about the Ghetto and Uncle Joshua," David reminded her. "I mean, if you want to. I really need to know." He looked at me. "So does she."

"Yes, the Ghetto . . . and Joshua." She put her hands together in front of her lips like she was about to pray.

"Children, this story is hard to believe. In truth, it's beyond comprehension, for it concerns forces more diabolical and far older than any words. People who say they understand the Holocaust are profoundly mistaken, I think. In our human weakness, I don't think we can ever truly understand malevolence. Nevertheless, it's our moral responsibility to recognize it and act to stop it as best we can, whenever and wherever we find it.

"How can I say this?" she asked herself aloud. She looked at the ceiling.

"The Shoah . . . "

There was that word again that Nikolai spoke of

earlier.

"The Shoah is the Mount Everest of evil, soaring above the rest of history, there for all to see. Its living taproot is anti-Semitism and its deadly flower, the Holocaust, is a sin that will haunt humanity to the end of time. Paradoxically, it was mostly carried out by rather ordinary men who said they were simply doing their duty. Untold others, in Germany and many other places including America, sad to say, helped them by doing nothing. They simply turned their faces away. Self-imposed ignorance and hypocrisy are killers, too, my children. Always, always be alert for this."

She took a deep breath and glared at us. By candlelight the look in her eyes at that moment was so piercing that I had to turn away for a moment. I was still trying to process what she'd just said.

"I'm sorry, I'm so sorry, my darlings. This is so hard for me – "

David swallowed hard. "Please. Go on. Keep talking. You have to. You know, like you said . . . . "

Rain pattered on the kitchen window. Tears ran down Mrs. Rosen's face, mirroring the wax dripping from the candle stubs. "Well, this I know," she said. "If incomprehensible evil exists, so does equally unimaginable good. Yes, the Nazis existed. But Mrs. Ringlebaum and Joshua existed, too. Later, when I am long gone, and you tell your own children what you are about to hear, never forget the evil, but always remember the good. Promise me."

"I promise," said David in a parched voice.

I glanced at him. "Me, too," I added.

"And remember another thing. The most important things in life cannot be spoken. They can only be lived."

The window creaked. The rain had stopped but the wind was coming up. With the candles flickering in her face,

Mrs. Rosen looked like an old village wise-woman telling ghost stories in front of the fireplace. But her story was scarier than any ghost story I'd ever heard . . . and it was true. And before it was over, I somehow knew my life was never going to be the same again.

"The main thing I remember about the Ghetto are the babies crying," Mrs. Rosen went on. "They were always hungry, you see. We all were. Of course, that was one of the Nazis' goals, to starve us to death."

I thought about all the soup left in my bowl.

"Everyday life was hunger, disease, and fear. The fear was the worst part. We never knew what would happen next. Some residents began to call the ghetto the 'death box.' In the end, it wasn't a place for living at all . . . only for dying.

"Mrs. Ringlebaum did the best she could, of course. Twenty-three men, women, and children were crammed into her little flat, if you can believe it. It was struggle enough just to eat and stay warm. She kept a pristine house, but the whole ghetto swarmed with rats and lice, so epidemics raged all around us. Beggars were everywhere, many of them children . . . ." She held up a finger.

"Pathetic stick figures who died on the street where they fell. You stepped over their raggedy bodies as soon as you walked out the door in the morning." Mrs. Rosen started to breathe fast. "It was awful. The cruelty . . . the sadism. Gangs of soldiers roamed the streets, murdering for sheer pleasure.

"We tried to make a life in the midst of this . . . this terror. Poppa taught the twins their reading and arithmetic lessons. Momma led a kindergarten class for homeless children. A village rabbi lived on our floor and he held services in our kitchen. All these things were against the law. When we could, we attended neighborhood concerts, plays, poetry readings and what not. Some of the greatest artists in the world lived and died in the Ghetto."

Mrs. Rosen sighed. "What a waste of talent and life it all was. Without the food smugglers, though, we all would have perished. At least, sooner than we did. In the end, I think the smugglers were the real heroes of Warsaw."

"Who were they?" asked David.

His grandmother smiled weakly. "Children and teenagers. Like both of you. Only the bravest could crawl under the barbed wire and squeeze through gaps in the Ghetto wall. Joshua kept our family alive. Nearly every day he risked his life to climb over the wall and bring back food. Potatoes, turnips, stale bread . . . anything, anything we could live on. Sometimes I went with him."

"You did?"

"What was I going to do? I was by then sixteen. I thought I was bulletproof. Anyway, I loved my family. I had to help them. Personally, I had no choice."

"If you could get outside the wall, didn't you ever try to escape? I mean, you know, why not?" I asked. That's what I would've done. Or that's what I thought.

Mrs. Rosen shook her head. "Escape? No. Never. I had my family to think of. And . . . and never before had I felt myself so strongly a Jew. I couldn't abandon my people. I vowed to do everything in my power to help them. Sometimes . . . sometimes it wasn't enough. One day Joshua and I went to get milk for our baby sister Esther. She was a year old. A beautiful child. She should have been walking, but couldn't. She was too weak from the starving. It was a rainy day before daylight when we slipped over the wall. That afternoon, when we got back with the milk, we found out they'd come for Poppa."

"Who?" asked David.

"The Gestapo. The Nazi secret police. Poppa was an

intellectual so he was marked to die. They said they wanted him for questioning. He refused to go. They took him downstairs and shot him in the back of the head . . . right in front of Momma."

"Jesus H!" David gasped.

"Joshua never forgave himself for not being there. But it would have been useless. He would've died, too, if he tried to defend Poppa . . . which is exactly what he would've done."

Mrs. Rosen rubbed her forehead. She looked up at the ceiling. "These animals wearing snap-brim fedoras and black leather trench coats drove off in their smart little BMW coupe and left Poppa soaking in his own blood where he fell. Joshua and I carried him upstairs and laid him on the kitchen table. It was no use. I shut his eyelids with my fingers and kissed him on the lips. Joshua chanted Kaddish, the prayer for the dead. When the sun went down, Joshua and I found a wheelbarrow and took Poppa to the Jewish cemetery so he could be with his own people."

She looked at us. "Life is precious, children. And love. And truth. Nothing else really matters. Don't waste the short time you have on this earth on meaningless things."

I thought about what she said. Then I pictured Mom upstairs trying on dresses she'd only wear once.

"In the summer after Poppa died, the deportations began. The Germans decided the Warsaw Jews weren't dying fast enough. Starvation and disease were too slow for them already. In July of 1942, notices appeared on the neighborhood lampposts announcing that Ghetto residents were to be resettled in the East."

David frowned. "Resettled? Like to another town or something?"

Mrs. Rosen gave a tight smile. "That was what they wanted us to think. They wanted us to go quietly. They said they were moving all the Jews to farms in the occupied territories. It was a big lie."

"Where were they really being taken?" I asked.

"To their deaths," Mrs. Rosen replied.

"Oh!" I gasped.

"They told us they'd feed us, that there would be an extra ration of bread and jam if we reported to the part of town where the trains waited. Starving people will do anything. They reported to the trains. They were shoved into the cattle cars and taken straight to a place in the countryside called Treblinka where they were gassed to death upon arrival. We didn't know where they were taken at the time. We were soon to find out though from Joshua's new friend Chaim."

Mrs. Rosen looked at us. "All we knew was that every day in the summer of 1942 trains full of Jews left the ghetto for Treblinka and came back empty. Every single day. Three hundred thousand souls perished this way. And we had no idea."

"But your family didn't go," said David. "Why?"

"Because of Joshua," his grandmother answered. "After Poppa's death he guarded us like a lion. When the first deportations began, he called a family meeting in Mrs. Ringlebaum's living room. Look, he said, all the Germans do is torture and kill people. 'Resettlement in the East'? Why should we believe them? We are not reporting to the trains, he informed us. Never. Why should we trust them?

"We went underground. The deportations increased. When people weren't willing to go, the Germans dragged them out of their houses. One day a squad of soldiers stopped in front of our building. Soon we heard their boots on the stairs."

I leaned forward. "Omigod. How did you get away?"

"We escaped down the back stairwell. I led the way.

Momma carried Esther and Mrs. Ringlebaum had a twin by each hand. Joshua was the lookout. When we reached the alley, we heard the Germans crashing around upstairs, breaking glass and ransacking the apartment, searching for hiding places. We'd escaped, but we were homeless. We'd lost everything but our lives.

"Then Joshua told us about the cellar. It was the bottom floor of an abandoned beer bottling plant. In the cellar, we found blankets, food, water and a lantern. There were even some tins of condensed milk for Esther. It was a miracle."

"Who put them there?" David asked. "Joshua?"

"Yes. He'd planned our escape for days. He'd wanted to collect more but the Germans interrupted. Then he showed us the gun. It was wrapped up in a dirty handkerchief. A Nazi policeman's revolver. And it was loaded. Momma started crying when she saw it. I didn't. I felt proud. To me, my brother was like King David ready to do battle with the Philistines. Or just like his name which he wore so well, the fierce Joshua who Moses trusted more than anyone."

"Do you know how he got it?" David asked.

"He never said and I didn't ask. After everyone calmed down, he told us his plan. We were to live in the basement and leave only when absolutely necessary. Then he asked Mrs. Ringlebaum to take to twins to the far corner of the room because he didn't want them to hear the news he brought us. And that's when we learned about the incomprehensible, shattering purpose of those trains and where they actually were taking their precious human cargo.

"He told us about his new friend Chaim. From a countryside *shtetl*. Someone a few years younger than he. Chaim was only fourteen years old but looked much older. Built like a young Samson, he said, a champion of the people, for his strength was truly astounding. Joshua told us that Chaim jumped from one of the trains just before it arrived at Treblinka, a concentration camp, and that he managed to hide in the bushes while he watched helplessly what was done to his family and all the others brought there. Chaim was never the same after that, of course. Traveling on foot and only by night, he made it back to Warsaw to warn people where the trains were going. That's when they first met and teamed up with one another.

"I can't imagine what he'd have grown up to be, had he lived. He was said to have killed German soldiers at night with his bare hands, even a few at a time. I don't know what happened to him. I can only assume – " Mrs. Rosen sighed with a far-off look in her eyes. When she spoke again, her voice made me shiver.

"Anyway, Chaim was the one that told Joshua that getting on the trains meant certain death! Well, as you can imagine, when Momma heard Joshua tell us this, she started to weep even louder. But then Joshua put his fingers in his mouth and whistled. The cellar stairs creaked under someone's weight and Joshua's friend Chaim appeared.

"He was so powerfully built for one so young that one would never guess his age. He was not as tall as Joshua. But he did indeed look like a biblical hero, a deliverer like Samson, just like Joshua said. In his hands, he held a submachine gun.

"Joshua told us they'd both joined the resistance, the Jewish Fighting Organization. I'd never heard of it, but I was excited. Then Joshua put his hand on my shoulder and looked me in the eye. 'The Germans have marked us for death,' he said. 'There's no hope of rescue. We are going to fight back. We are going to resist! Not a single Jew should go to the railroad cars. People who are unable to fight better go into hiding. But you, Dominique – I want you to join us,' he told me. 'Most of us are only sixteen to twenty years old or so. You're sixteen now. Old enough. Chaim here is even younger.'

"I looked over at Chaim. He looked so formidable, despite not being as tall as Joshua. His eyes burned like black fire under his beret. How could Joshua compare me with him, even if Chaim was two years younger? – I wondered.

"'Help us fight the Nazis! Stand with us and die like a free human being!' Joshua argued passionately. At this point, Momma wailed on and on. The twins ran over to find out what all the commotion was."

David was beside himself. "Awesome!" He couldn't believe his grandmother took on the Nazis when she was young – who could believe that about one's grandmother? "Did you say yes? Did you fight?" he asked, hardly able to contain himself.

Mrs. Rosen leaned back in her chair, sniffed, and lifted her head defiantly. "I most certainly did."

My jaw dropped.

Chapter Seven

David looked like he'd seen a ghost and stammered, "You actually f-fought in the Resistance?"

"Of course I did. I couldn't wait. At first, I helped mix Molotov cocktails, pouring gasoline into the old bottles we found lying around. All winter we collected rifles, knives, bricks, anything. The rebels met in our cellar. The commanders were Joshua, his new friend Chaim, and another fellow nicknamed Angel. My main job was to keep track of the German patrols on our street, for which Joshua gave me a whistle. I used that whistle a lot.

"But first I must tell you something about Chaim. One day when Joshua and I were out on our rounds, some Nazi soldiers randomly searched the area and broke into our hiding place. They had overheard Momma talking to the twins. Momma, Mrs. Ringlebaum, baby Esther and the twins were alone at the time. Before we left, we told them to be as quiet as they could be, but with children that is not always possible.

"Momma said that five soldiers sprang in front of them with their rifles, yelling and shouting and running after the twins who scrambled away. They ordered Momma and Mrs. Ringlebaum to step outside in front of them as they grabbed the children. Momma was holding baby Esther. When she protested, one of the soldiers lifted his rifle butt to her face and was about to knock her down when something happened.

"Suddenly Chaim appeared like a messenger from God, she said. He called out to them, distracting their attention, and they started to fire at him. Two of them chased him and didn't come back. The other three grew a little nervous and started to lead Momma, Mrs. Ringlebaum and the children outside with them when Chaim jumped them with such ferocity and lightning speed that it was as if something superhuman was taking vengeance before her eyes, she said. One of the soldiers knocked Chaim's gun out of his hands, but he lunged back at him so fast that the others could not fire for fear of killing their own. To their amazement, he picked up that soldier like a basket, she said, and threw him at the others, knocking their weapons out of their hands. Then he fought them, kicked them, knocked them down, wrestled them, took their rifles and flung them to Momma and Mrs. Ringlebaum, and managed to even get them out of vision of the children when they heard four shots in rapid succession. Worried that the Nazis had killed Chaim, Momma said that she was stunned to see that it was Chaim who emerged from the shadows instead, assuring them they had nothing to worry about any more. Then Momma said he removed all the soldiers' bodies and they never saw them again. *That* was Chaim Wasserman!

"Well, after that, life took on a strange kind of subterranean normalcy for some time. All winter we hid in the cellars and stockpiled weapons. At night, Joshua and Chaim sneaked out and painted slogans on neighborhood walls. 'Resist! Don't go to the trains!' We also stayed busy turning abandoned building into makeshift fortresses. We tore down attic walls and created a network of secret tunnels. We turned basements into bunkers. When everything was ready, we attacked. The bunkers allowed our fighters to hit the Germans, then vanish, only to pop up in another place. I used Joshua's pistol more than once. We gave them fits!" She chuckled to herself. Then the smile dried like dust on her lips.

"The end came in the spring. The 20th of April was Hitler's birthday. Stroop, the Nazi commander, decided the annihilation of every last Jew in the Ghetto would be his master's birthday present. Ironically, it was also the first day of Passover, the holiday celebrating our ancestors' freedom from tyranny. The attack came early in the morning. No one expected it. Momma and Mrs. Ringlebaum were peeling potatoes for our Seder, the evening's sacred meal. I was feeding Esther some homemade yogurt.

"All of a sudden, Chaim bolted down the stairs. 'THEY'RE COMING!' he yelled. 'GET OUT! QUICK!'

"I cursed and rushed for my stockpile of fire bombs. Momma and Mrs. Ringlebaum grabbed the children and hid them in the cramped bunker beneath the cellar. Then my heart caught in my throat. Joshua was outside the wall. He'd gone to a secret meeting with the Polish Home Army, a group of gentiles who'd also vowed to fight the Nazis. I didn't have time to worry about him, however."

David squirmed in his chair like he was playing Twister. "What did you do?"

"My duty. After Momma and the children were safe, I took my position on the factory roof with my supply of homemade bombs. I didn't have long to wait. A truck full of black uniformed *SS* men turned the corner at the far end of the block. I heard gunshots and screams coming from other parts of the Ghetto. Explosions thudded in the distance. It sounded like the end of the world. As the truck approached, grinding its gears, I struck a match and lit the rag stuffed in the mouth of a beer bottle filled with gasoline."

Now it was my turn to freak. It was like I'd just found out this sweet, little old lady sitting across the table from me was actually Batman or something. God, she was cool.

"The truck stopped directly under me. I tossed my firebomb. It exploded like a deadly scarlet flower smack in the middle of the truck. Burning Germans, flapping their arms like pigeons, ran screaming in all directions."

"No way," I said before I could stop myself.

Mrs. Rosen's eyes boiled with anger. "Yes, it was a terrible thing. But those men were the same ones who every day, every day, mind you, killed innocent children. To me, it was a fate those murdering cowards deserved."

I couldn't believe my ears. Forget Spiderman, Batman, Mad Max, and all those superheroes on the screen. Mrs. Rosen was the real thing – a cross between Picasso and Attila the Hun!

"What happened then?" David asked excitedly.

"They shot back, of course. I ducked and threw my arms over my head. Bullets buzzed all around me, stinging the masonry like hornets. Then I heard someone calling my name. I lifted my head and saw Joshua. Like an avenging angel, he flew towards me, leaping from rooftop to rooftop. When he reached me, he propped his foot on the ledge and emptied his machinegun into the street below. The sound was deafening. Shell casings reverberated around my ears like brass raindrops. Finally it was over and he helped me up. The Germans were dead, their bodies sprawled over the cobblestones like broken china dolls. I hoped they were in hell."

Right then and there, I experienced a total body buzz. Mrs. Rosen was one fierce woman. I wished she were my grandmother, too. All my Granny Martin does back in Minneapolis is play lotto and watch "Who Wants To Be a Millionaire" reruns. But my dad's mother Robinson would have loved Mrs. Rosen if she were still alive.

"Joshua and I hurtled down the stairs," she went on. "There wasn't much time. We both knew reinforcements would soon come to dynamite us out or roast us alive. We pulled Momma and the kids from the bunker and ran. A girl named Judith, one of Poppa's old university students, was captain of a commando team on the next block. She made room for us in her hideout. Once again, we'd left everything behind but the clothes on our backs. Back in our cellar, the table was still set for Passover."

She took a sip of water. The ice cubes in her glass clinked like wind chimes. She squinted like she was trying to see print too small to read.

"For a month, the fighting raged. Block to block. Building to building. Our team went on missions every day. Ambushes, mainly. Firebombing a tank here, shooting up a patrol there. When the revolt began, the Germans cut off our water supply. So sometimes, after dark, I'd sneak out and lap the rainwater in the gutters like a dog, but" – she held up a finger – "but only after I used a bucket or a tin mug to save enough for the little ones hidden underground."

"Wow! Unbelievable! What happened then?" David asked.

Mrs. Rosen waved a hand before her face like someone clearing cobwebs from an abandoned doorway. "It was ghastly. The Nazis no longer talked about deportations. Instead, they exterminated us on the spot. They pumped tear gas into our cellars and blasted whole blocks to dust with artillery. Then they went house to house, using police dogs to hunt us. When Jews, blinded by tear gas and choking on smoke, staggered from their hiding places, soldiers gunned them down in cold blood.

"Of course, we fought back as best we could. More than

once, I watched Nazis die from my bullets. I came to know what hate feels like." She paused. "It felt good. At least, at first. Then it slowly began to kill me, too. Hate, I've found, is a cancer."

She coughed and then shrugged. "The end was never in doubt. The Germans were too strong. What little food, water, and weapons we had were soon gone anyway. Some Jewish fighters used cobblestones, and even their teeth and nails when their ammunition was exhausted. But courage only goes so far. When they realized things were hopeless, Joshua and Chaim made a pact to fight to the bitter end. So did I. I wasn't about to be left out."

"B-but . . . you're here. You survived! How?" I asked in disbelief.

"Sometimes, I wonder the same thing, Lauren. Why did I survive? Why not the rest of my family? Why not – why not Joshua? After all, he saved my life. Every day I live with the guilt. I'll carry it to my grave."

This bugged David. "You shouldn't – it's not right –"

"No, it's true. How can I not feel that way?" She lowered her head and waved us off, as if to say "don't go there." Moments later she said, "Joshua saved my life."

David wrinkled his forehead. "He did? How?"

"Well, it was the afternoon our friend Judith died. Against Joshua's advice, she'd set up a barricade in the middle of our street . . . right out in the open, for God's sake. A German flame-thrower team burned her and her 12 year old brother Moshe alive.

"Then later, the *SS* burnt the whole block. When the smoke got too bad, people jumped from the upper stories of buildings. People of all ages. Some were on fire as they fell. I remember so many of them holding children in their arms. One by one, these human torches descended from the sky before my eyes like a meteor shower. They were God's tears, a sacrifice of falling stars. I could hear the thuds when they hit the pavement."

I shut my eyes.

"It was all over. I knew it and so did Joshua. Earlier he'd discovered a sewer tunnel leading to the gentile side of Warsaw and said it was our only hope of escape. He told me to lead Momma and the children to safety. At first, I refused. I reminded him of our pact. 'It's useless! We're all going to die anyway!' I shouted at him. 'So I want to do it facing the enemy! Like out ancestors, the great Hebrew warriors at Masada! Not running away!'

"I was hysterical. I was in such shock from the horrors I'd witnessed, from the terrible dehumanization we had experienced, from my helplessness to save my family that I found myself lunging for Chaim's gun. I don't know what I wanted. Maybe to run into the street, shooting. I don't know. But Joshua grabbed me and pointed to the girls. 'YOU HAVE TO AT LEAST TRY . . . FOR THEM!'

"He was right, of course. As smoke rolled into our cellar, Momma and I dressed the twins as fast as we could. After I buttoned their coats, I fed them the last bits of bread crust we had and told them we were going on an adventure. The poor darlings clapped their hands." Mrs. Rosen sighed.

David put his hand on the middle of her back. "Please," he said with great affection and concern, "please, this is too much for you now . . . . You don't have to say any more. Really."

She pushed him away. Not too hard. But away. "NO!" she shouted with passion. "I want you to know! I want you to be strong because the evil that caused this to happen is still in the world today! I want you to be strong, not naïve, not insulated from the truth! Sheltering you from what happened only weakens you and gives more power to those who hate other races and religions, those who will stop at nothing because of their burning hatred of anything that is simply different from them.

"Never mistake them for what they are. They can be dressed in the finest clothes and look as scrubbed and wholesome as could be. But inside, their souls are twisted in hatred. And fear, I suppose. I'll never understand such darkness. Nor will you. But don't look away. You must know what has happened. All over Europe, Jews went to their deaths like this. Jews and others who they considered unworthy to live. And I tell you, as surely as I'm sitting here, we bury them all over again if we don't tell their story and remember how they died. And we will help bury the next generation, and the next, if this truth is hidden from the light of day!"

David picked up her empty glass. "Get her some more water, Lauren. Please!"

Glad to have a mission, I flew over to the sink and fumbled for the tap in the candle-lit darkness, then brought Mrs. Rosen her drink, who chugged it down like a construction worker in August. Telling us her story, telling us what she said we needed to know, was hard work. Exhausting, draining, physical work. Like pulling something impossibly heavy out of the earth and then lifting the whole of it on her shoulders.

After taking another sip, she motioned to us. "Sit back down, both of you. And, please, no questions till after. Listen. I'm afraid if I stop I won't have the courage to go on. Despite what I just said."

"All right, all right!" David and I echoed one another.

Outside, down on the street, a car alarm whooped. Mrs. Rosen started to resume her story – "Joshua . . . Josh – " But her voice broke and she moaned like an old dog does when it tries to get up.

David and I looked at one another feeling so bad for her. I wished we could do something to help take away her great sorrow. One of the candles winked out, drowned in its own wax, which she noticed and we watched her pour the hot wax onto her plate. Then she took out a paper matchbook and re-lit the candle. The smell of sulfur hit my nose and burned slightly.

"So," she whispered, after gathering herself together. "This is how it all ended."

Chapter Eight

You know, I've watched my share of scary movies over the years and seen some pretty bad stuff on the evening news. Once Mom and I even saw a dead guy with blood and vomit all over him in the gutter on Lexington Avenue. A heroin overdose, someone said. But nothing I've ever heard or seen bothered me as much as what Mrs. Rosen told us next. The whole time, she talked real low, like those audience members you see who go up on stage and get hypnotized by a magician.

"Joshua led us upstairs to the street. The whole world was on fire. I choked on smoke. Ashes and red-hot embers swirled in the air like molten snowflakes. It was like a scene from the Devil's workshop. Esther screamed. We all started to run. Mrs. Ringlebaum tripped and Joshua went back for her. 'KEEP RUNNING! TO THE CORNER!' he shouted, leading Mrs. Ringlebaum out, as Chaim carried Esther and I held the twins' hands. Somehow we made it.

" '*Here, here*!' Joshua cried out, pointing downward. Where? I didn't understand. We were right in the middle of the street. Joshua bent down and lifted a manhole cover. 'Here! Go!'

"I couldn't see a thing. It was like looking into an abyss. 'Hurry, I'll hand down the children,' I heard Joshua say like someone in a dream. I spotted the ladder and climbed down. My foot hit water. I got scared and stopped. 'Keep going!' he yelled. I took another step down. Then another. Finally, my foot hit bottom. Water and – " Mrs. Rosen's lips trembled.

" – and sewage swirled around my thighs. The smell made me gag. Esther nearly landed on my head. 'Take her, quick!' Joshua cried out. I gathered her to me as Joshua hugged Mother. She wouldn't let go. He pushed her gently and down she came. The twins peeked over the edge, crying. They refused to budge. Chaim leapt into the sewer with a splash. Water hit my face. I gagged again."

"'THROW THEM!' Chaim shouted. Joshua scooped up Sonia and dropped her to Chaim. Then Sarah. Mother took her and I took Sonia. Mrs. Ringlebaum came next. Then she took Esther from me. Chaim started up the ladder. Halfway up, he turned to us and said 'God bless you' in Yiddish. I tell you, I absolutely thought I was going mad. Chaim was leaving us there.

"Joshua took one last look into the pit. Just then the oily black smoke above his head parted and he was framed in a halo of blue sky and sunlight. He glowed like a prophet in a stained glass window. 'Stay to the right. You'll come out of the Ghetto on the gentile side of the city. Find a safe place to hide there. And hurry, Dominique! Hurry!' He lifted the heavy sewer-hole cover and began to put it back.

"'WAIT!' I called to Joshua frantically. He was leaving us, too. Leaving the family in my charge. 'YOU CAN'T LEAVE US. I WON'T KNOW WHAT TO DO!'

"'I must go. Do as I say and you'll be out of the Ghetto. Chaim and I will catch up with you there,' he said. But I didn't believe him.

"'WILL I SEE YOU AGAIN?' I called to him.

"He smiled. 'NEXT YEAR IN JERUSALEM.'

"I grabbed the ladder and screamed. 'JOSHUA!' But the lid clanked down and the world went black. His shadow passed over the little hole in the cover and disappeared. It was the last time I ever saw him.

"With Sarah perched on my hip, I leaned against the slimy bricks with my right hand, feeling my way into the darkness. The children's cries echoed off the walls, making me crazy. I gritted my teeth and kept going. Every once and a while, the sewer shook from the explosions above. We sloshed our way through for I don't know how long. Finally, Esther went to sleep and the twins calmed down, thank God, as the explosions became muffled. Soon the only sound was the water sloshing around our legs. We came to a fork in the tunnel. I kept to the right, like Joshua said. Momma clung to my shawl like a child hanging on to her mother's apron. For the first time in my life, I felt like I was a real adult . . . .

"Then I saw it. A shaft of light. 'We're almost there,' I whispered to my mother. That's when I felt them. I looked down . . . . Corpses floated on the water like a school of dead fish. They were from the Ghetto. On the forehead of a young girl there was a nasty black hole edged by purple bruise. She'd been shot right between the eyes. They were still open.

"Momma nearly climbed up my back like a cat when she saw the bodies. 'Dear God,' she kept saying, as I kept making my way toward the light. It became brighter and brighter until it rained down like a waterfall. Then I noticed the sewerhole cover was missing. Well, that disturbed me. Something wasn't right. I stopped, cocked my head and listened. I could hear the dull booms of the Ghetto fighting. I heard men shouting and then laughing strangely in Polish. I gave Sarah to Momma. 'Shhhhh,' I said, 'Stay here. I'm going to have a look.'

"I put my hands on the rusty ladder rungs. The light hurt my eyes after being submerged in the dark so long. I went up and the first thing I saw was a German soldier wearing one of those ugly helmets that looks like a coal bucket. He was looking straight into my eyes and grinned at me. I was trapped.

"Suddenly, everything went white. I actually saw stars like in one of those old cartoons. As I fell backwards towards, time slowed down and I thought, 'So this is what it's like to be dead.' It was a curious feeling."

"You got shot?" David asked, unable to contain himself.

"No. As soon as I hit the water, I bounced to my feet because I absolutely refused to drown in that mess. As I stood there dripping, the Nazi's rifle barrel poked into the sewer, waving like the feeler of a cockroach. Then he shouted, *'JUDEN RAUS! SCHNELL!'*

"It means *'Jews out! Hurry!'* They were simply waiting for us.

"I wiggled a loose tooth with my tongue. The salty taste of blood filled my I mouth. The *SS* man leaned over the hole. I can still see his red hair and freckles. He wasn't much older than I was. *'Get out of there!'* he snarled. As we started to climb out, Mrs. Ringlebaum was too slow for him so he jerked her out by her coat collar. There all of us stood, blinking and shaking in the middle of the street like moles dug up by an enraged gardener.

"A big truck idled noisily at the curb. In the back sat about twenty men, women, and children. I recognized some of them from our street. Their clothes were wet. They'd escaped through the sewer, too. They sat with their hands in their laps like they were going on a bus ride, but their faces were white with terror. The Nazi poked me in the back with his rifle. *Jump in, you bitch,'* he snarled. *'Now!'*

"I scrambled up on the bed of the truck. 'The girls, Momma!' I shouted. 'Hand me the girls!' I was terrified we'd be separated. Then the *SS* man came over and pushed Mrs. Ringlebaum. *'Hurry up, you old cow,'* he spat at her. She fell to her knees on the cobblestones. He jacked the bolt of his rifle. Momma spun around, so mad she was radiant. Backlit by the sun, her auburn hair gleamed like fire. 'Don't touch her, you swine!' she spat in perfect German. The *SS* man was so surprised he stood there gaping. I pulled Momma quickly onto the truck before he recovered and decided to shoot us all on the spot.

"Instead he yelled at the Polish truck driver, *'There's another load of trash for you. Off you go!'* The truck jerked to life and made a U-turn in the middle of the street. We swayed and fought to keep our balance. Up ahead, the sky was black. We were heading back to the burning Ghetto. My heart dropped into my stomach. The closer we got, the more ghastly it became. The smoke was so thick the sun was blotted out like an eclipse. On every street corner, I saw summary executions. Men hanging from lampposts. Women on their knees begging for the lives of their children. People were lined up against walls and shot in the back of the head. Red blood pumped from them in fountains. The man next to me began to chant the Kaddish, the prayer for the dead.

"Then I felt the heat. Some streets were already burnt out and smoking, but others roared like bonfires. Charred corpses smoldered on the pavement. Trucks full of German troops roared past. My eyes burned. It was like we'd driven inside an oven. Over the crackling flames, I heard the pop-pop-pop of machine gun fire. The battle wasn't over. That meant some of our Resistance fighters were still alive. I prayed Joshua was one of them.

"Our destination soon became apparent. The big plaza next to the railroad tracks. They were going to put us on the trains. A woman on the truck began to tear at her hair and scream hysterically.

"We stopped. Down came the tailgate. *SS* men yelled at us from every side. *'JUDEN RAUS! JUDEN RAUS!'* People stampeded past me in panic. Shots rang out, picking off the stragglers: the elderly, the smallest children on foot who couldn't keep up, and those unlucky enough to catch a heel on a paving stone and trip. Blood pooled on the ground like puddles after a hard rain.

"Then, for one terrible moment, I lost sight of the twins. Scared to death, I spun around like a top. I spotted Sonia's beret. When I made a grab for her hand, I found I'd made a mistake. It was another little girl. She screamed, her eyes wide with terror. All of a sudden, Mother appeared from nowhere with the twins. Mrs. Ringlebaum was carrying Esther piggyback. I vowed never to let them get out of my sight again. Hugging each other, we made for the line of waiting boxcars.

"All around us, people wailed and called out to their loved ones. You can't believe the misery in the voices. It was like the sorrow of lost souls. Pretty soon, the cattle cars were bursting. I saw *SS* men literally throwing toddlers inside, picking them up by their hair and flinging them. I hurried everyone ahead, trying to find a car that was empty.

"Suddenly a wild-eyed soldier blocked our path. *'IN, JEWS! SCHNELL!'* He poked a bayonet under my nose. I quickly scrambled into the nearest car, dragging everyone behind me. More people got on. And still more. I worried the girls were going to be smothered to death in the crush. Just when I thought we couldn't take anymore, soldiers slammed the door shut, plunging us into darkness. Then they sealed the door tight from the outside. Gradually, my eyes adjusted to the dim light filtering through the cracks in the wall.

"All around me, I saw the Ghetto. Wrinkled grandmothers in babushkas. White-bearded rabbis silently praying. Grim-faced fathers in the now threadbare overcoats they'd once worn proudly to the office. One fellow had on his painter's cap. Every once and while he tenderly fingered the brim, making sure it was still there. Mothers rocked babies to keep them quiet. And then there were the children. So, so many of them. A sea of brown and blue and green eyes, shining with terror, grown large in faces thin with hunger. They were only children, yet they looked a hundred years old."

She shook her head and looked down. Neither David or I made a sound. Mrs. Rosen wiped under her eye with a dinner napkin.

"All of a sudden, our cattle car jerked. Everyone staggered like when the subway pulls out of the station. Somewhere in the crowd a woman began to sob. A man cursed. A little boy begged his mother for some water. The whistle sounded. Everyone held their breath. The train picked up speed and began to roll. We were leaving the *Umschagplatz*. Another man muttered 'May God help us!' Out of the darkness, another man answered him. '*Shma Yisroel Hashem Elohenu Hashem Ehad*.' Hear, O Israel, The Lord our God, The Lord Is One.

"For three days and nights we were locked on the train, so crammed together we could barely move. We couldn't sit. We couldn't stretch. Our muscles ached so much it felt like they were on fire. Many people shook so badly that they couldn't stop – that's how scared they were. I had no idea where we were going. I only knew it was probably hopeless. We had no food or water. No toilet . . . .

"You can't – I can't . . . ." Mrs. Rosen stood up. For a

few seconds, she just stared straight ahead. I think maybe for a moment she was back in the cattle car. Then she sat down again.

"I only remember parts of the trip. Most of it is – is gone. Erased. I do remember the smell of acrid body odor from so many terrified people jammed together for so long. The smell of garlic and sweat. The sharp ammonia smell of urine. After a while, the stink of vomit and feces was overpowering. It was like getting hit in the face by a stone wall."

Suddenly she half stood up and squeezed David's hand. "You must understand it was a different time, a different age. Back then we had . . . manners. To soil yourself, I mean, it was unthinkable for an adult to relieve herself in public . . . on the floor . . . the guilt people felt. Of course, they had no choice, they had to, but nevertheless, it was so humiliating for them, so very awful."

Mrs. Rosen fell back in her chair, still clutching David's hand. "You see, mentally we lived in the Victorian age. I think some of the people, particularly the older ladies and gentlemen, nearly died from shame. Famous professors sat soaked in urine. Grandmothers stood in their own excrement. The conditions were completely incomprehensible. Who would impose such things on people? An elderly woman stood by me, still wearing her pearls. She was a very fine lady in her time, I'm sure, and over and over she kept saying, 'I'm sorry, I'm so sorry.' It was shock. The shock that people with dignity feel when they're treated like animals. On the train, that's when I knew. If the Nazis would do this to us, they would do anything.

"I recall sounds, too. The rattle of the cattle car as it rocked along is burned into my brain. For years after the war, I couldn't go near a train. Railway stations made me cry.

Finally, I said to hell with it and went to a psychiatrist. He told me I had a phobic reaction to situations that recall specific memories. Now they call it post-traumatic stress disorder. He wasn't too concerned. But then he wasn't there, was he? I've never ridden the subway."

I glanced at David. He nodded. It was true.

"I can still hear one old man groaning. He'd broken his arm leaping from a burning building. Next to him, a young mother sobbed into her scarf so her husband and small daughter wouldn't see her cry. People chanted prayers. To this day, when I hear the Psalms at synagogue I hear them in the voices on that train. And then there were the babies. Most cried until they exhausted themselves and could only squeak like sparrows. Many didn't survive the trip. Most of all, I remember Mrs. Ringlebaum's voice, so soft, so sweet, telling the twins stories to keep them calm.

"On the first night, as she jostled against me, Momma whispered, 'Where do you think they are taking us, Dominique?' 'I don't know,' I answered, 'but, wherever it is, we'll be together.' As long as we are together, I kept saying to myself. It was the only thing I could cling to. Up ahead, the train's whistle hooted like a lost soul. Momma turned her face away from me.

"Finally, most of all, I remember how tired and thirsty I was. By the last morning of the transport, my tongue was so dry it stuck to the roof of my mouth. I don't think you can understand what three days with no water is like if you haven't lived through it. Some people went mad. Nursing mothers suffered the most. They lost so much liquid, you see. Before it was all over, they cried in agony.

"But there was one brave woman, a stranger, who showed me that even in the midst of the most barbaric conditions people can be honorable. They can remain human.

It seems her baby died the first day of the transport. But how could her body know this? Understand?"

David frowned. I got it.

"She still had milk in her, you know, breasts," I whispered to him.

David was embarassed. "Oh."

"Yes," Mrs. Rosen replied. "She had milk. Without Momma asking her to, she nursed little Esther to keep her alive. Even when it made her own thirst a torture. It's a fact. People can act like Nazis, but they can also be like that woman. Angels. We have free will. The choice is ours. She died before I found out her name.

"As the sun rose on the fourth day of the transport, I passed out. Then I had a dream. Maybe a hallucination. Joshua and I were in a walled garden. It was a warm, sunny day with blue skies. I could smell flowers. Roses. Honeysuckle. We sat beside a splashing fountain. I trailed my bare toes in the cool water. Maybe I dreamed about the fountain because I was so thirsty, I don't know. But there we were, talking, sitting in the shade of a big pomegranate tree. Joshua gave me one of the pomegranates. I took a bite. The sweet nectar trickled down my chin.

"'Where are we? I asked. He laughed. His teeth flashed white in his tan face. He looked good. Strong. He wore the same cap he always wore in the Ghetto. I smiled, too. 'No, seriously, where are we?' 'Jerusalem,' he answered. Well, in the dream, this made perfect sense. The last time I saw him he did say he'd meet me there. Then he added something. 'But wherever you are, I'll always be with you. Right here.' He touched his heart.

"I awoke with a jerk. My heart was pounding. I remembered where I was. On the train. But something was different.

"We'd stopped moving. Dogs barked outside. At first everyone was quiet, too scared to even speak. Then someone asked, 'Where do you think we are?' Before anyone could answer, the cattle car doors slid open with a terrible screech. I blinked, blinded by the sudden burst of sunlight. The barking grew louder, crazier . . . on top of us. A little girl started to cry.

"Dressed all in black, an *SS* officer appeared in the open door. His pale grey eyes surveyed the people cowering before him. Behind him, an *SS* enlisted man restrained a huge German shepherd that lunged on a choke chain, snapping its teeth, spraying flecks of foam. The officer cracked a smile. He paused a second and then shouted at the top of his lungs. *'JUDEN, RAUS, RAUS, RAUS! SCHNELL, SCHNELL! JEWS, OUT, OUT, OUT! QUICK, QUICK, QUICK!'* The dog bared its fangs and barked ferociously, straining on its leash. It wanted to attack us.

"Well, it was like an electric charge went through the cattle car. People panicked and spilled out the door like a human waterfall, crashing every which way onto the station platform below. 'Dear God!' cried Momma. I grabbed baby Esther and yelled, 'Together! Everyone stay together!' Mrs. Ringlebaum put her arms around the twins like a mother hen and clutched them to her chest. Fear boiled in the pit of my stomach. I tried to keep my head. 'Wait, wait for the others to get off!' I shouted. 'The children will be crushed.'

"When the car emptied a bit, I jumped to the platform. Then I helped everyone else down. 'STAY TOGETHER! STAY TOGETHER!' I shouted over and over. All I could think about was Joshua telling me to protect the family. In an instant, we were swept up in the mass of people being driven along the platform by the angry black-shirted men with dogs. Here and there a whip cracked and someone screamed. For the first time, I looked around.

"That's when I saw the strange people in the purple-striped pajama . . . everywhere, stooped over, shuffling like zombies. Barely more than skeletons, they didn't seem human. Then I realized they must be prisoners. On the orders of the SS men, these ghostly-looking figures mixed in the crowd, mumbling directions, shoving people along. They scared me.

"Like in a twirling kaleidoscope, I remember other images. Tall watchtowers and razor wire fences surrounding a sea of wooden barracks. Railroad tracks and the long row of cattle cars spilling their flood of desperate people. Men. Women. Children. Young. Old. Healthy. Sick. Thousands of them, wearing expressions of confused terror as they reached for their families. A few people rushed around wailing and tearing their hair, demented with fear. Others stumbled straight ahead in a daze. Above it all rose the incessant noise of barking dogs and screams of *'SCHNELL! JUDEN RAUS! LOS! ALLES RAUS!'* Later, I found out the Nazis called this 'the *Begrussung*' – the welcome. It was pandemonium. A madhouse. There was something else in the air, too."

Mrs. Rosen stopped. The muscles around her mouth twitched. "Something else. A sweet and sour smell, like overripe fruit. I hated it. The hair on the back of my neck stood and I crinkled my nose. I looked at the sky. The sun was bright, but a grey haze hung low on the horizon. Almost like fog. Something was burning.

"Then I saw it. A fat chimney rising from a red brick building in the distance spewed rolling, black smoke. An orange flame licked its tongue on the lip of the stack. For the first time, I noticed cinders and ashes floating on the wind like grimy snowflakes. Maybe the Germans have taken us to a factory, I thought. Maybe they need us to work. Of course, it had to be a factory, I thought. What else? For the first time in months, a shiver of hope went through me. I grabbed one of the striped pajama-men by his sleeve. His arm felt as brittle as a chicken bone.

"'Where are we?' I shouted at him in German.

"He turned his head in slow motion, like in a dream. His hooded eyes were dull and yellow, almost lifeless. His skin was sallow like the belly of a fish. His head was shaven. A flicker of disbelief passed over his face. 'You don't know?' he asked in Yiddish. I shook my head. *Nein.'* No.

"Then he gave me a look I can only call pity. 'My dear child,' he said, 'you are at Auschwitz.'"

Chapter Nine

"Auschwitz. The name meant nothing to me. Nothing."

David shivered and put his head down. He knew what it meant. I was learning.

Mrs. Rosen looked into my eyes. "In the end, really, I was right. Auschwitz was a factory. An assembly-line. Using science and technology, it processed living, breathing human beings and turned them into smoke and ashes." She sniffed.

David handed her his napkin, and she delicately blew her nose.

"Over the years, I've come to a conclusion," she said. "Auschwitz is the ultimate expression of earthly power, which is the power to control and use people. If this power, sometimes political, sometimes religious, is left unchecked, my children, it ends in blood. Whether in Germany, Russia, Cambodia, China, Croatia, Bosnia, Kosovo, Indonesia, Algeria, Sri Lanka or . . . or Africa." She looked at David. "Where?"

"Rwanda," he whispered. "And Congo, too."

"Yes, thank you. Power gone wrong always ends in killing, whether they call it a 'crusade,' a 'holy war,' 'ethnic cleansing' or a 'final solution.' Nevertheless, to me, the Shoah will remain eternally different and apart. The Holocaust stands alone on the edge of the abyss. And I don't think it's only because I was there. I and my family."

David coughed.

"Why?" I asked in a small voice.

"Because I am convinced that what happened to my family was diabolically unique. The Holocaust is the pre-eminent example of hate, prejudice, and lack of human respect at its most efficient. The absolute nadir, the black hole, of human history. Consciously, rationally, and ever so scientifically, an entire group of people – all its men, women, and children – were efficiently marked for murder. Such a thing had never been attempted before. God forbid it happens again. And it nearly succeeded. But it didn't take place overnight. Two thousand years of anti-Semitism laid the groundwork."

Anti-Semitism. Prejudice against Jewish people. David mentioned that earlier. All of a sudden, he didn't seem so bitter or defensive, just . . . just on target, I guess.

"This ancient hatred particularly prospered in Germany. Led by Hitler, the German people, the cultured people of Goethe, Beethoven and Schiller in their cult-worship of Hitler willingly descended into barbarism and declared the Jews to be to blame for everything. My God, in school they even taught their children to hate us. Their kids even played a colorful board game called 'Get the Jews Out' or read picture books like 'The Poison Mushroom' which depicted Jews as child-molesters. Finally, they began to systematically kill us. In those days, all roads led to a remote railroad siding in Poland. The place where I saw my family for the last time. The place the sad-eyed little man called Auschwitz.

"So, there I was. In a place I'd never heard of before. I didn't have time to think. I let go of the man's arm and he melted into the crowd. Terrified people pressed around me. The barking and screaming grew louder. Then someone pushed me and snarled, *'Get in line, you whore!'*

"An *SS* man. He raised his whip and brought it down on the face of the elderly woman next to me, knocking her to the ground. The string of pearls she wore broke and the white beads bounced crazily around my feet. It was the sweet lady from the train. She stayed down and the Nazi kept beating her. I grabbed for Momma. 'Come on! Come on! Stay together!' Momma held Esther. 'Let me have her,' I told her, 'I'm stronger!' I took my baby sister. Mrs. Ringlebaum ran with the twins, squeezing their hands tightly. Pale with shock, they trotted to keep up. Our little group surged along with the mob, like pieces of driftwood being washed out to sea. Then just as suddenly, we stopped. Something was happening up ahead.

"The *SS* formed a human wall to block us. *'IN LINE! IN LINE!'* they screamed. *'Men over here! Women and small children over there!'* People began to howl when they realized what was happening. The Germans were separating us. The tenderness I witnessed still haunts me. Husbands and wives, boyfriends and girlfriends, parents and grandparents, mothers and sons, fathers and daughters all clutched at one another. Everywhere there were heartbreaking scenes of people kissing and hugging, clinging, refusing to let go. The Germans went into a frenzy with their whips, clubs, and dogs and parted the crowd. Across the divide, weeping men and women called out their good-byes. Amidst all the wailing, I had a selfish thought. 'Thank God, I'm still with my family.'

"The men began to march off. A teenage boy darted from the column and sprinted towards the women. *'Bubbe,* Grandmother! I'll never leave you . . .' was all he said before a German Shepherd caught him and knocked him to the ground. The dog growled and tore at him, shaking his head like a feeding shark. Mrs. Ringlebaum told Sonia and Sarah not to look. There was nothing we could do.

"The column of marching men crossed the railroad tracks and moved further and further away, raising a cloud of dust on the trail beside an ugly, barbed wire fence which stretched to infinity. Then they halted. I squinted, trying to see what was going on. The Germans divided them into two groups. A chill went through me. In one brief sickening flash, I knew the same fate was in store for the women and children. We, too, would be separated."

Mrs. Rosen froze for several seconds, like she was in a trance. She was reliving those terrible events all over again. For a moment, she put her face in her hands. Then she reached for her glass. Her hand shook as she took a sip of water.

"The line lurched forward. Under the gaze of the *SS* guards, the shuffling, zombie-like pajama men pushed us along. 'What's happening? What's happening to us?' asked Momma. I stood on my tip-toes. Over the heads of the women a few feet in front of me bobbed the black caps of *SS* officers. I lied. 'I don't know, Momma. I don't know.'

"Only a few people were between me and the head of the line now. Directly in front of me, a little boy clutching a stuffed clown talked to his mother. 'Mommy, where are they taking Granny?' His young mother stroked his curly hair. 'Some place nice, darling. We're going there, too.' She wrapped him in a tight embrace. A river of tears poured down her face.

"A distinguished-looking Nazi officer watched the touching scene. Everything about him, from his ebony eyes to the tips of his polished boots, shone like a black sun. Then, with a flick of the riding crop in his white-gloved hand, he quietly said, 'To the left, please.' Lost in her love, the woman ignored him. He lashed her across the face, drawing blood. 'Now, please.' His tone of voice never changed. The woman and her child staggered to the left.

"I was nearly to the front of the line when Mrs. Ringlebaum tugged my sleeve. She had a strange look on her face. Tears shone in her eyes, but she was smiling. 'Let me have the baby, darling, you must be tired of carrying her.' The sad-eyed little pajama man stood next to her. Again, he spoke to me in Yiddish. 'Yes, children to the old.' Once more, he melted away. Mrs. Ringlebaum said, 'That's right, angel. Let me have her. It's a good idea.' She smiled, piercing me with the faraway look in her dear, blue eyes. In a daze, I handed Esther to her. Mrs. Ringlebaum cooed at Esther and kissed her nose. When I turned around, there I was in front of the handsome Nazi officer.

"*'How old are you?'* he asked. I realized I was trembling. 'S-sixteen,' I replied. He studied my face. *'To the right,'* he said. Numb, I didn't move. His cheek twitched. All of a sudden, he noticed Momma and the twins. His eyes lit up. Then he grinned like the devil in hell.

"He snapped his fingers. One of the junior *SS* men ran over and smartly saluted. *'Heil Hitler!'* *'Take them aside, Corporal,'* the handsome Nazi ordered. *'I can use them!'* My head reeled. I couldn't believe what I was hearing. My precious mother and sisters? Use them? What on earth did he mean?

"Then the unthinkable happened. It happened quickly, too quickly to react. In an instant, I lost my mother and sisters. We were now part of what they called 'The Selection.'

"The *SS* man wrenched Sonia and Sarah from Momma's hands. She threw herself at him, clawing and kicking. As the twins screamed, two pajama-clad prisoners pulled her off him. I grabbed the Nazi officer. 'IN GOD'S NAME, LET THEM GO WITH ME!' I begged. *'I'll take care of them.'* He squeezed my wrist and slowly removed my hand from his lapel. 'They'll be well taken care of, I promise. Now, go to the right before I shoot you right in front of them.' I hesitated. He unbuttoned his holster and glared at me, his pupils like black bullets. *'Los! Move! To the Right!'*

"Like a sleepwalker, I joined the women on the right side of the platform. Most of them were young like me. 'Come, come, hurry,' said a husky, blonde peasant girl. 'Join us.' But . . . but something was wrong. There were no older women – and no children. None at all. I spun around. 'Momma!' An *SS* man and his huge German Shepherd stepped in front of me. The dog suddenly lunged and snapped wildly, tearing the hem of my dress. I . . . I who for weeks had fought Germans in the Ghetto, could do nothing to save my family. I could only watch what happened next. I still see it in my dreams.

"*'You go that way! Los!'* the officer yelled at Momma. She didn't respond. Meanwhile, the twins, crying and calling 'MOMMY!' were dragged away by the Nazi soldier and tossed into the back of a waiting truck. The truck roared away. Sonia's beret lay in the dust. Weeping madly, my mother sank to her knees and beat her chest. The sad-eyed little man went to help. He put his arm around her and lifted her to her feet. He whispered in her ear. She looked back over her shoulder at me and slowly went to the left. There, waiting for her, huddled together for safety, were the older women and mothers with children. Without a word, the Nazi officer flicked his riding crop and Mrs. Ringlebaum and Esther joined them.

"Now I was alone. For the first time in my life, I was all alone. 'Momma! Momma!' I screamed. The peasant girl tried to comfort me. 'Please, go quietly, it's better this way,' she said. I was in agony. 'Get away from me !' I shouted. 'Momma!' I cried. I reached out my hands, as if I could somehow pull her into my arms across the thirty feet of platform that separated us. Thirty feet that would turn into forever."

Mrs. Rosen reached out with one hand. I wasn't sure she even realized David and I were still in the room. She wasn't there. She was on the ramp at the Auschwitz siding. Nobody said anything as she stared off into space, forgetting about us.

"By now I was sobbing. 'MOMMA! MOMMA!' I cried over and over. One of the guards blew a whistle. Men with dogs surrounded the huddled women and children. The handsome Nazi made a wave with the back of his hand. *'Marchieren! MARCH! IN COLUMN!'* yelled a sergeant. The dogs tugged on their leashes, choking as they tried to get at the women. The hoarse barks and snarling grew more frenzied. The guards indiscriminately whipped their terrified prisoners, forcing them apart, making them fall in line. I prayed Momma, Mrs. Ringlebaum and Esther were spared. The dogs barked louder and louder. Babies cried. Women screamed when the whips fell. The ragged column began to slowly move forward.

"I'd lost sight of Momma. Then I caught a glimpse of her red hair in the crowd. She turned and looked back for me. I waved and made a noise. I was no longer capable of words. She held out her hands and mouthed my name. In that instant, a part of me died, a part that remains forever buried at Auschwitz somewhere deep beneath its blood-stained earth.

"Like a tiny cloud, Mrs. Ringlebaum's puff of snow-white hair floated beside Momma's shoulder. When Momma turned, Mrs. Ringlebaum looked, too. The same strange, otherworldly expression she wore before still graced her face. Somehow she was at peace even amongst the savagery of the guards and their dogs. More than fifty years later, I realize what the expression was. Holiness. She'd used her scarf to swaddle Esther warmly and she held my beautiful baby sister close to her breast. She smiled at me. Then the three of them disappeared, swallowed in the moving throng like grains of sand in the sea.

"I couldn't take any more. I screamed like a wild beast and started to run after them. I wanted to go with them. Anything was better than being alone. It wasn't to be. The big peasant girl squeezed me in her arms like a vise and wouldn't let go. She saved my life. A life I didn't want anymore.

"I watched the line of women and children recede into the morning haze. The guards and their lunging dogs still hovered around them like flies, tormenting their every step. In my desperation, a thought occurred to me. Maybe I could escape and go find Momma. But first, I had to know where they were taking her. Through a film of tears, I saw. At the far end of the railroad tracks was a two-story red brick building. It looked like the barn of a prosperous farmer. From it, rose a chimney, the one I'd noticed earlier. Its fat, flame-tipped stack still spouted a demonic shower of sparks. The forlorn little army of women and children marched on until smoke and ashes swirled over them and blanketed them like the night. Then they were gone."

"In less than an hour, they were dead. Every single person who entered the red brick building at Auschwitz left through the chimney as smoke and a handful of ashes. This is what the Holocaust was. The burning of children. The burning of my baby sister. The burning of my beloved mother and my family."

Like someone waking up from a coma, Mrs. Rosen blinked at David and me. Neither of us said a word. David looked drained of color. Mrs. Rosen brushed some crumbs off the tablecloth into her palm and poured them into her empty coffee cup.

"Of course, the red brick building was the crematorium

where the corpses were fed to the flames. Underground, deep beneath the ovens, was a rat's maze of dimly-lit rooms, all leading to the gas chamber. Did Momma know? I've always wondered. I pray to God she didn't. I think Mrs. Ringlebaum knew, though. She did one little thing. One simple thing, and once again my life was saved.

"You see, that's one reason I'm here today, because people kept saving my life. First Joshua, then the peasant girl, then Mrs. Ringlebaum. I'm only alive today because of the love of others. But that's somehow all beside the point, isn't it? For how can I describe the unspeakable? How much horror is enough? No, my story is simply this. My father was murdered in cold blood; Momma, baby Esther, and Mrs. Ringlebaum perished in the gas chamber; and Sonia and Sarah disappeared, never to be found. And now, only this afternoon, I learn my brother was executed at Auschwitz while I was still a prisoner there. We were just one Jewish family, like hundreds of thousands of other Jewish families, who vanished in the Shoah.

"The love, the laughter, the picnics, the *bat mitzvahs*, the new babies, the funny stories, the painful little secrets – every collection of ordinary, beloved, holy facts that make each family its own unique universe . . . all these things are gone. For me, only memories remain. Memories surrounded by an empty hole that will never be filled. I don't have any knickknacks, letters, photographs . . . nothing . . . nothing except – "

Mrs. Rosen slowly rolled up her sleeve and held out her arm. "This is the only tangible thing I have left to remember my family by. One last present from the *SS*."

In the flickering yellow candlelight, I saw the ugly green numbers tattooed on her skin.

Chapter Ten

David coughed. *"Bubbe?"*

She didn't seem to hear him.

"Bubbe?"

She turned like a robot. "Yes?"

"How did Mrs. Ringlebaum save your life?" asked David, his eyes still on the tattoo.

His grandmother stared into the candle flame. "It was on the ramp . . . when she took Esther from me. The sad-eyed little man said something. Do you remember?"

David shook his head.

I bit my lip. Oh, yeah. "I remember," I whispered. "He said, *'Children to the old.'*"

Mrs. Rosen rolled down her sleeve. "Exactly. After the selection, the Nazis always gassed all the children and the elderly, those they considered unfit for hard labor. And one more group. They also killed anyone holding a child, too.

"You see, you must always remember, they were crafty. They knew that separating mothers and children on the ramp would create too much of a scene, so they automatically sent them to the left . . . down the dusty road to the red brick crematoria.

"After all, the whole system was designed to get people into the gas chamber with a minimum of fuss. The *SS* especially prided themselves on the fact that the machinery of murder moved so smoothly. And, really, the plain truth is that it's easier to kill someone with a child than break them apart. Isn't it? All that unseemly screaming, you know. Mrs. Ringlebaum figured this out. When she took Esther from me she saved my life. She knew. That beautiful woman knew. I'm certain."

"Did you ever find out what happened to the twins?" I asked.

Mrs. Rosen's face dropped. "Honestly, no. And I've never wanted to."

This didn't make sense to me, and I started to ask why when David interrupted, even more agitated than I was. "But why not?"

"There are some things you don't understand. Let me explain," she said patiently. "Of course, I searched for them after the war. I wanted to find them more than anything. And Joshua. For ten years, I checked refugee camps and displaced persons lists all over Europe, the United States, and Israel. The people at the US Immigration and Naturalization Board got heartily sick of my phone calls, I assure you. Even now, I look for their names on rosters of Holocaust survivors. But, no . . . I really don't want to know the particular details of Sonia and Sarah's fate."

"But – "

"Dr. Mengele, David."

The name didn't mean anything to me but it stopped David like a bullet. "You mean – " He sucked in his breath.

Mrs. Rosen nodded. "The handsome officer running the selection on the ramp was Josef Mengele. *Malach-ha-Mawis.*"

I needed help. I looked at David.

"*Malach-ha-Mawis.* It's Yiddish for Angel of Death.

It's what they called Mengele. He conducted medical experiments," he said flatly.

Experiments? I still wasn't sure why this was so bad. "If this guy was a doctor, maybe the twins are still alive. You know, maybe he took care of them or something."

Mrs. Rosen looked at me for a moment as David shook his head. "Oh, Lauren. This is hard." She looked at the ceiling and whispered with great patience, "How can I explain?" Her hands trembled. She took one of my hands and held it.

"You see, Lauren, Dr. Mengele conducted . . . hideous medical experiments on living Jewish prisoners. He was especially fascinated with twins, so they were the only children not immediately gassed at Auschwitz. In his mind, they belonged to him. A fate worse than any death was reserved for them. Do you understand?"

I felt helpless. And so stupid. I hadn't known. How could I?

She was crying again. "I just don't want to find out what happened to my little sisters. Never. I pray to God they didn't suffer long. But please don't ask me about them any more."

I finally understood. David, too. "We won't ask, don't worry," David said in a heavy voice. We know now."

A funny thought crossed my mind. I wanted him to hold me. To just hold me – and make all the bad things go away.

"What happened after the twins disappeared?" asked David. He wanted to hear every last part of the story that led up to her freedom. And so did I.

"After mother disappeared, I went into shock. I don't remember so much. Apparently, the Germans ordered us to march. I fell in line beside the peasant girl. I do remember she squeezed my hand and told me everything would be okay. We went through a metal gate. *'ARBEIT MACHT FREI'* it said, which means 'work makes you free.' Life expectancy for workers at Auschwitz was four months at the most. Beyond the gate, sat an orchestra of horribly malnourished women. In their crisp white shirts and starched navy skirts, moving like puppets, they played something lovely by Bach. They didn't look at us. It was absolutely surreal. Dogs tearing at people to the accompaniment of beautiful music. I thought I was going crazy.

"When we crossed that boundary under the gate, we entered another world. A kingdom where all usual standards were turned on their head, where Wrong was Right, and Life was Death. The kingdom of Auschwitz. Guards impassively peered down at us from watchtowers, following our progress with the noses of their machine-guns. On the other side of the wire squatted rows and rows of long wooden barracks. Primitive hovels you'd be ashamed to keep farm animals in. They were home to thousands of people. The pathetic pajama people. Skeletal, shaven-headed men and women blankly stared, drooling and open-mouthed, as we passed by. A few of the ragged, human scarecrows staggered through the mud like they were in a trance and went to the fence to watch us. Sooner than I knew, I would be one of them.

"*'HALT!'* screamed an officer.

"We stopped outside a long, wooden building. It looked like the dining hall of some a deranged summer camp. The guards and their dogs stepped back a few paces. Out the front door of the wooden building swaggered creatures I'd never seen before. Creatures I couldn't believe existed. Women *SS* guards. Their corpulent, greasy faces leered at us. Faces that hadn't experienced hunger and torture – only inflicted them. The leader, a buxom, ruddy-cheeked blonde, filled her uniform like a sausage casing. She gave a wicked smile. She had no front teeth. She popped a bullwhip above her head.

"*'Strip, girls. NOW!'*

"It was incomprehensible to me. All the women did the same as I. Nothing. So the fat Nazi cracked her whip and yelled, *'SCHNELL, JUDEN! EVERYONE NOT UNDRESSED IN TWO MINUTES WILL BE SHOT!'*

"That did it. The peasant girl whipped off her blouse. She wore nothing underneath. I touched the clasp of my skirt. I paused. Undress in front of other people? Men, included? Other than Momma and our family doctor, no one had ever seen me naked. Like I told you earlier, this was a different era. We were modest people. All around me, young women shucked off their clothes. The *SS* men leered at them. Some of them pointed at the girls they liked. Naked before men? Strangers? I'd had boyfriends, mind you, but . . . I'd never been with a man . . . if you know what I mean. I felt all dizzy.

"The *SS* woman noticed I wasn't moving. She pushed her way through the crowd of half-dressed women. She put her hands on her wide hips and stood in front of me. *"Having a little stage fright, Princess?'*

"What could I do? I nodded yes, blushing with shame. The woman guffawed and turned away, like she was going back to the front of the crowd. In a flash, she whirled around and caught me full in the face with her bullwhip. I fell to my hands and knees.

"*'Strip, you Jewish dog! NOW! Otherwise you can take a nice trip up the chimney with your mommy!'* she screamed.

"Something happened when I was there on my hands and knees. It's funny, but all of a sudden I knew I wanted to live. I had to live. To live and one day tell the truth about the Ghetto, the nightmarish transport, about what happened to my family. I got on one knee, tottered to my feet and obediently got undressed.

"The whip cracked. *'SCHNELL, JUDENHUNDE! HURRY, JEWISH DOGS! INSIDE!'*

"In terror, we ran inside the building where yet more women guards awaited us. In groups of five, we were grabbed and hustled over to a group of prisoners holding scissors and electric razors. As we stood there shivering, they shaved every inch of our bodies. Our head, our armpits, our pubic area. In minutes, we were bald, standing in a circle of our own hair. Before I recovered from this humiliation, they yanked me to a stool. A vacant-faced male prisoner grabbed my left arm. With no deadening and with the same dirty needle he used on everyone else, he tattooed me with my camp number. I was no longer Dominique Levy. For the rest of my time at Auschwitz I was #789456. I still shout out the number sometimes in my sleep."

At the memory, Mrs. Rosen massaged her arm. "I didn't feel the sting of the needle for long, though. I didn't have time for such a luxury. *'MOVE, WHORES! ON THE DOUBLE!'* yelled the guards. Shouting, shouting all the time. In panic, we scurried to the exit, desperate to get out of range of the whips. As we ran through the door, women prisoners handed us each a gray *schmatte*, a rag, to wear.

"Cold, bald and shaking with fear, I was back outside in the prison yard. I threw the sack-like rag over my head. On my naked skin – they gave us no underwear – it itched terribly. It reeked of chemical disinfectant. I wondered who'd worn it last. I wondered what they were like . . . where they were from. No matter, I thought to myself, whoever it was, was probably dead and free of this terrible place.

"We were called to attention. We stood there in rows

in our rags. The heavy-set peasant girl stood two people down from me. She caught my eye and smiled. Then she rubbed her bald head and winked. We were fellow slaves – slaves in the depraved kingdom of Auschwitz.

"We were fed two times a day. If one can call it being fed. Once again German order ruled. Prisoners were put on a diet that, unless somehow supplemented by stealing or bartering, would lead to starvation in three months. Each meal was a small piece of black bread with worms in it and a few ounces of stinking soup. Sometimes the greenish, watery goo was full of nettles or had motor oil in it. Sometimes it stank of sewage or had rat hairs in it. No matter. We were starving. We slurped it down. Gladly.

"Everyday life was a nightmare of sadism and death, pain and starvation. I adapted to the cold and the heat . . . I bartered for rotten pieces of potato, moldy bread, anything, so I wouldn't turn into one of the walking skeletons, the people who had lost the will to live, the poor, listless zombies the prisoners called 'Musselmen.' I vowed to remember all the cruelty I saw around me so that one day, however far off, I could bear witness . . . . I survived.

"Morning was the worst. The 'Appell,' the roll call, was an ordeal straight from hell. For hours, freezing in the winter darkness and melting under the summer sun, we stood there and were endlessly counted. They had a mania, a sickness, about order. Counting. Counting. Counting. The bodies of the women who died in the night – and people died every night – had to be dragged out and counted, too.

"Every week there was a selection. Like on the ramp, people were chosen to live or die. The kapos, the prisoner bosses, would scream 'SELEKTION!' and we'd leap from our planks to run and get in line in the prison yard. Whoever was too tired or too sick to rise would be dragged into the prison yard and shot – or they were hauled to the dreaded Block 13, the waiting room for the gas chamber, where they would rot for a few days without food or water until they went to the gas chamber. Once we got in the yard, the *SS* guards ordered us to strip. Mengele would arrive in his white gloves and saunter over and proceed to inspect the assembled prisoners. Inspect us like we were pieces of meat.

"We all knew this meant life or death. We prayed our bruises or open sores had healed. That our teeth looked good and our ribs didn't stick out too much from the starving. We slapped ourselves and pinched our cheeks to make them look red, to get color in our faces so we'd look healthy. Those who didn't – those who coughed at the wrong time or were feverish or too weak to stand – signed their own death warrant.

"The older women had the worst time. *'How old are you, Mother?'* he would ask in his soft voice. The answer didn't matter. 'You look tired. I'm going to allow you to *rest*,' he'd say to the trembling woman who was someone's beloved mother or favorite aunt. Later that day her ashes would drift up the crematoria chimney into the gray Polish sky.

"One morning, as we waited for Mengele, standing in an inch of ice, our toes going numb with frostbite, the peasant girl, my savior on the ramp, keeled over like a falling tree. I tried to go to her.

"*'Stay where you are or you'll burn, too!'* barked a guard. The girl waved me away. I took another step towards her. I had to do something. She'd saved my life that day on the ramp and now she was my best friend at Auschwitz. Her name was Leni. At night in the barracks, she told me stories about how she grew up on a farm in Czechoslovakia. About the chores and the baby animals. In the first horrible days of captivity, her humor kept me human and her compassionate joy for life gave me strength. Now things were reversed. It was she who needed me.

"'No, Dominique, save yourself!' she pleaded. I looked in her sunken eyes. She shook her head and whispered, 'It's no use. Let me go.'

"She was starving to death. Later, I found out she'd been sharing her bread ration with a new arrival, a sick Hungarian girl. As the girl recovered, Leni withered. Once strong and tan, she was reduced to a loose bag of skin over bones. Mengele spotted her at once. As a guard led her away, she looked over her shoulder at me.

"There in the snow, for the first and only time at Auschwitz after the morning they took my mother away, I cried. I loved that big country girl like she was my sister. I cried and cried and the snow came down. I prayed it would bury me. Like all prayers at Auschwitz, it went unanswered. I still survived.

"After each roll call, we marched to work. By a quirk of fate, I was assigned to the best part of the camp. It was a high-security area known as 'Canada.' Surrounded by razor wire, watchtowers and searchlights, Canada was an enormous mass of barracks, each one stuffed to the roof with the belongings of the Jews who arrived in the daily transports. In the crematoria, they processed our hair, our teeth, and our bones, and they used our ashes as fertilizer in Germany's gardens. In Canada, they looted our clothes, shoes, and valuables while our bodies still burned in the ovens.

"For twelve hours a day, I opened suitcases and sorted their contents into piles. Every morning, after the transports arrived and the chimneys began to smoke, convoys of *SS* trucks chugged into the compound and dumped their load. A mountain of suitcases, packages, carpetbags, backpacks, and valises grew in the yard. A mountain ascending to heaven. My job was to climb up and throw the suitcases down to my coworkers. Then came the hard part.

"Inside the suitcases we found Jewish Europe. From Warsaw, Vienna, and Berlin, from countless villages and *shtetls*, we found photographs. Mothers and children. Stern grocers posing behind the counters of their shops. Grandmothers and grandkids in the park. Beaming parents at a college graduation. A smiling boy on his *bar mitzvah*. Baby's first steps. Sweethearts riding a bicycle built for two. Pictures and more pictures . . . black and white pictures. Pictures of a vanished people, the lost images of a generation of ghosts.

"We sorted through tens of thousands of mementos. Like tiny, golden lockets saving pieces of an infant's curls or a lover's portrait. We found so many special things. Letters sealed with lipstick kisses. School report cards. Jars of homemade baby food. Rubber balls and model airplanes. Wooden steam engines and elegant china dolls that would never feel the caress of their owners loving hands again. Special things.

"Of course, we found many ordinary things, too. Toothbrushes and toothpaste, underwear. Knives, forks and spoons. Pots and pans. Blankets. All the accouterments of everyday life.

"And books and more books. My God, what books. Romances and textbooks. Classics and thrillers. History books and atlases. Novels and religious commentaries. As many books as grains of sand on the beach were in those suitcases – the suitcases of the people of The Book. And then beneath the books there were the *tefillin* and phylacteries. Prayer shawls and Talmuds. Wrapped in tissue paper, hidden . . . cherished.

"We collected mound after mound of clothes. Fancy silk dresses, sensible wool jumpers, cool cotton smocks, and somber pinstriped suits. Mink stoles and Chesterfield coats.

Starched pinafores and knickers. Pink petticoats and small white shirts with Peter Pan collars. Tiny crocheted sweaters and booties with matching hats. Jumbled together, we routinely sorted them into their respective heaps.

"Radiating out from the mountain of suitcases were other mountains. Two I remember very well. There was a hill of baby carriages and a hill of shoes. I can still see the sun reflecting off the spokes of the tangled mass of prams and strollers. None of the girls who worked in the warehouse talked about it. We couldn't. Behind this was a enormous mound of shoes. Boots, sandals, pumps, oxfords, loafers, any kind of shoe you've ever seen . . . some were very humble, others were obviously expensive. Thousands of shoes. Shoes that had walked across Europe, from ghetto to ghetto until they took one last walk down the dusty road to the crematoria. And then I spotted the baby shoes. Dear, dear God.

"But baby shoes or not, the Germans wanted it all. Every last bit we sorted through was inspected and picked over by the black-shirted *SS* vultures. Still, some things they wanted even more. Diamonds. Gold wedding rings. Expensive watches. Sapphire necklaces. Ruby earrings. Emerald brooches. Crystal vases. Oriental carpets. Antique clocks. China. Sterling silver platters. 'Jewelry and valuables . . . jewelry and valuables' – that was a constant refrain from the guards. But good luck to any slave who tried to pocket something and got caught. Before sundown, she twisted on a piano wire strung from the warehouse rafters.

"Our boss was the greediest Nazi of them all, and that's saying something. An *SS Obersturmfuhrer,* he was an even better dresser than Mengele. But he shunned the good doctor's white gloves. No, I would imagine someone of his immaculate taste thought they were a touch vulgar. He much preferred black leather. And he always wore little round sunglasses, day or night, as if he was a mole. In another somewhat freakish touch, his hair was prematurely white. White like snow.

"Just the sight of him made me queasy. I never knew his name. The girls I worked with nicknamed him 'The Curator' for his macabre habit of appraising the valuables taken from his Jewish victims before they were fed to gas chambers. He even kept a little jeweler's glass in his pocket for just that purpose. As we sorted the more expensive items he would invariably stroll over to watch. We kept our heads down and worked even faster as he approached.

"When an item caught his fancy, he'd take out the little jeweler's glass and screw it into his eye and proceed to scrutinize the object, lingering over it like a lover. He was obsessed with silver and gold menorahs and hand-illustrated *Haggadahs*, the ancient book that tells the story of Passover. In fact, he issued a standing order that he was to be notified whenever we found any Judaica or Jewish religious objects. He was particularly interested in our prayer cloths, which we call *tallis*, and *tefillin*, the leather boxes containing scriptural passages we use during prayer.

"One day it was my bad luck to unpack a beautiful set of sterling silver Shabbat cups. I informed an *SS* woman and she summoned the *Curator*. He slowly walked over. It was the first time I'd ever seen him up close. I held my breath. When he took off his sunglasses, his eyes were gray as dirty dishwater. In went the jeweler's glass. For at least five minutes, he carefully examined the cups. I was absolutely petrified. I heard him breathe faster and faster with excitement as he discovered how rare the cups were. His expensive cologne nearly choked me. I kept my head down. His glossy leather boots creaked inches away from my dirty, bare feet. Then, for the first and only time, he spoke to me directly. My heart beat like a rabbit.

"*The world will never believe what we did to you here.*

Pity.' That's all he said. Then he sighed, took the cups and left. His words stayed with me.

"Later that afternoon I was ordered to go rinse blood off some suitcases. I went out into the yard to the place with the hose. There was a lot of mud around the dripping spigot. *'The world will never believe what we did to you here.'* I kept hearing the words, over and over. I looked at the suitcase in my hands. Blood had dried all brown and crusty over it. Beneath the blood were peeling tourist stickers, the kind you proudly stick on to show off where you've been. Venice. Rome. London. Paris. The suitcase's dead owner had been to all those wonderful places, only to die in the back of beyond in Poland.

"In Poland, in the back of beyond, where I was . . . where I was probably going to stay. I fell down on my hands and knees into the mud and wept. I wept for my family. I wept for my people. I wept for Leni. I wept for myself. My life was over. I had just turned eighteen.

"As my tears fell into the mud, something came over me. I began to laugh ecstatically. I must've sounded like a maniac. Out of the corner of my eye, I saw the other prisoners avoiding me, God bless them. I'm sure they expected a guard to run over any second and kick me to a bloody pulp. It didn't matter. I was beyond caring.

"Suddenly I scooped up a handful of mud and tears and began to mold it. More than anything, I wanted to create. In this kingdom of ugliness, lies, and death, I wanted to make something beautiful. Something beautiful – for Life itself. Something beautiful – for Truth. Maybe I was delirious. Maybe the starvation had finally damaged my brain, I don't know.

"I grabbed up more and more mud and kneaded it, pushing it between my fingers. It felt cool and good. Then, like the sun emerging from behind a cloud, a perfect vision burned itself into my mind. The rest of my life, however short it might be, didn't really belong to me, anyway. It belonged to other people. It belonged to Memory. To Imagination. To Truth.

"I've been a sculptor ever since. I create life with my hands. I mold and shape clay and breathe new life into it. I make stone come to life by giving it a heart, a presence, a spirit. I create.

"So . . . there it is. For a year and a half I worked as a slave in Auschwitz's warehouses serving time as an inmate in the house of the dead. A witness to my people's martyrdom.

"Until, one cold morning, when our barracks awoke to thunder in the East. Those who could shuffled to the windows. The faraway boom of guns shook the frost-covered glass. We stared at each other dumbly. We didn't know it, but Hitler's thousand year Reich was crumbling. The Red Army was driving across Poland, the treads of its tanks red with the blood of retreating Germans. Russian scouts were only miles from the camp's gate.

"Nazi high command ordered Auschwitz evacuated. But first, all the evidence of what happened there had to be destroyed. Erased like it never happened, wished into an untold tale, reduced to nothingness and the nonexistence of blackest night. The day the SS dynamited the crematoria the ground shuddered and the red brick chimneys crumbled and fell on their sides like dying dinosaurs. Soon the sky smudged with smoke and ashes floated on the breeze. But this time it was different. This time they burnt paper, not people. They were murdering Truth.

"Heaps of the endless lists and rosters they dearly loved went up in blazes. Names. Dates. Transport schedules. Endless tallies of the families and whole communities who vanished into the gas chambers. The *SS* tossed whole filing cabinet loads of white paper and manila folders into the yard, doused them with petrol and set them on fire. One might suppose this made my fellow prisoners and me happy. It didn't. Just the opposite. It filled us with dread. We knew too much. And we knew our keepers too well. They would never let us live to tell the story. Somehow, someway, they'd find a way to kill us all.

"The burning continued for days. The whole time we were confined to our barracks. Not a good sign. Then one morning before dawn, the *kapos* beat us awake with rubber hoses. *'MARCHIEN! MARCH! SCHNELL! SCHNELL! QUICK!'* I imagined it was our appointment to be shot. At least I don't have to worry anymore, I thought. A strange sense of peace came over me. I was only curious. I wondered what the slap of the bullet against my skull would feel like, how much it would hurt.

"We marched a long time in the dark. In the early morning chill, our breath blew steam like cart horses. A knife-edge wedge of orange showed on the horizon. There in the East, the Russian guns were louder, pounding like angry tom-toms. The camp was in a certified panic. *SS* motorcycles rushed past. Big trucks rumbled by, stinging us with gravel. For the first time, I saw something on the guards' faces I'd never seen before. Fear.

"We stopped beside a row of cattle cars waiting on the ramp. *'ENTRAIN!'* barked our keepers. My comrades and I swarmed towards the cars like a mob of walking dead. There was to be one final test. The people who couldn't climb in the train on their own were made to kneel off to one side. Biting and clawing, pulling up floorboard splinters under my fingernails, I dragged myself into a stinking car, found a corner and curled up like a sick dog.

"Shots popped outside as the girls who couldn't climb were eliminated. A train whistle sounded and the coaches clanked to life. As we rolled through Auschwitz's main gate, the bonfires of burning paper flickered across the plain like the lights of fallen stars. Or maybe candles. Yes . . . candles for my family who died there. I prayed the *Kaddish* as the train sped West . . . towards Germany."

Chapter Eleven

"There was no food or water on the train. One by one, women began to die. I lay in my corner and watched, waiting for my turn. Sometimes when the train stopped, they let us out. A few of the girls tried to eat the straggly grass growing on the railway embankment. Others drank their own urine. At every stop, pistol shots cracked as the sick and dying were murdered.

"One day the train stopped for good. We were deep inside Germany.

"*MARCHIEN! SCHNELL!*' came the orders. The survivors crawled from the train and began a death march. Little did we know it at the time, but all over Europe prisoners like ourselves – whether POWs slave laborers or death camp inmates – were driven into the middle of Germany like water swirling down a bathtub drain. The Nazis pulled us from factories, underground mines, and concentration camps and, through a series of desperate death marches, collected us in the center of the Reich. There was a reason for this. The Allies weren't supposed to find us alive. To paraphrase an old saying, dead men and women tell no tales.

"We were in Bavaria. I saw the Alps in the distance, white like banks of clouds in the sun. The smell of pine trees filled the air. Barely able to put one foot in front of the other, I marched, my eyes locked on the humped back of the walking skeleton in front of me. Every so often, I passed the rag-covered body of yet another person who couldn't take another step.

"I recall a village. It looked like something out of 'The Sound of Music,' a perfect setting where nothing could ever go wrong. Quaint little gingerbread houses with shutters, window boxes and lace curtains lined the cobble-stoned main street. The snow on their roofs looked like spun-sugar frosting. We marched through the middle of the fairytale town like a parade of the damned.

"Today you read where Germans say they didn't know about the concentration camps or what was happening to the Jews. Well, they couldn't help but see us, smeared with our own blood and waste, as we staggered down the deserted main street. The shots of the guards as they killed stragglers echoed off those little cuckoo clock houses like firecrackers exploding in a canyon. And the people were there. I saw them. All those good Germans who supposedly didn't know a thing watched us being herded through their lovely towns and villages. Every once in a while I caught a glimpse of a face before the lace curtains pulled shut like a curtain on a stage. They knew, all right. They knew. They simply chose not to see.

"When we reached our destination, it was a giant pen deep in the forest. Inside the barbed wire fence were a few wretched barracks with neither doors nor glass in the windows. No food or water. Nor blankets. They locked us up and left us to die.

"Days later, a truck pulled up. They'd finally decided to feed us. Standing in the bed of the truck, an elderly *SS* man shoveled some rotten potatoes and moldy turnip tops onto the ground. We fought over them like they were gold. And actually those stinking, black potatoes were more valuable. You can't eat gold.

"Although I had no way of knowing, nearly three months passed. I lost all track of time. I do remember being sick. A raging fever made me delirious. I had the most horrific hallucinations. I kept seeing smoking chimneys and crematoria ovens, their open doors chewing like mouths. I suppose I had typhus. Everyone else in the camp did. Most of them died. I didn't and felt cursed. God had completely abandoned me. He didn't even have the mercy to kill me.

"Out of the thousands of women in the camp when I arrived, only a hundred or so were alive. Barely alive. Most of us couldn't walk. We were too weak. To get to the rotten potatoes now, we crawled on our bellies like snakes.

"Spring came. I knew because one day I saw a flower. I'd dragged myself outside the dark barracks to be in the sun. That's when I noticed it. A tiny, perfect white flower sprouted in the filthy mud of the pen about ten feet away from where I lay. It stood out like a miracle – it was the first thing of beauty I'd seen in three years.

"I used my last bit of strength to get to the flower. I knew I was dying. My body was shutting down and my eyesight was blurry. I wanted to be close to it . . . to have my last sight on earth be something beautiful. I may have felt abandoned by God – but I still believed – despite everything. That little flower in all its modest glory was a testament to something pure and holy and true. Something the Nazis and their hatred could never be part of nor ever destroy. Not its source nor its meaning.

"Using my last bit of strength, I crawled to it until I was about twelve inches away and couldn't go any further. I fought to stay conscious and tried to clasp the flower in my hand. I stretched out to reach it, as far as I could, and stroked its petals with the tip of my fingers. For the briefest moment, I felt its soft, living, magisterial touch. Only then could I finally put my head down – it was so, so heavy. I wanted to sleep – to sleep and never get up.

"Just as I closed my eyes, I had a vision. I saw my family standing beside me. They smiled. Beamed, in fact, with luminosity. Poppa was there. And Momma. And baby Esther and the twins, all dressed in their shining Sabbath best hats and bows. They all looked handsome and healthy. Poppa had on his prayer shawl and the gray in his beard was gone. I think he might have been crying he was so happy, too. Then I saw Joshua. He waved and called me by my childhood nickname. 'DOMI, WE'RE HERE!' he called. 'COME WITH US!' Joshua smiled and offered his hand. I let go of the flower and reached for him. Then everything went black."

"Thank God, you didn't die, *Bubbe*," murmured David, breaking his silence after all this time, as he reached out for Mrs. Rosen's hand.

She smiled at him and shook her head. "No, I didn't die. Not all the way, at least. When I woke up and opened my eyes, all I could see was blue. Deep blue, like the sea. It's an exquisite, warm shade of blue I still try to paint. I don't think I've ever captured it, really. But this blue I saw – well, my first thought was 'So this is what it's like when you're dead. Blue and quiet.' To tell the truth, it didn't seem to be a bad way to spend eternity. I wondered where Joshua was though.

"Then I heard a man's voice. Deep and gentle. He was talking to me. But it wasn't Joshua.

"Other sounds began to fill my ears. Footsteps. Idling trucks. And more men's voices, a great many of them. But something was different. I listened with all my might. And suddenly it hit me. My God! I thought, they're speaking English! Like someone coming out of a fog, I suddenly realized I wasn't dead. I was on my back, looking straight up into the sky.

"Then a large shape hovered over me. It came closer and closer. I squinted my eyes to focus and there he was . . . the most beautiful man I've ever seen. A big, burly African-American sergeant and he had a fat cigar clenched between his teeth. As long as I live, I'll never forget what he said: 'Come on now, honey, it's all over. They can't hurt you any more.' And then he gently picked me up and carried me in his arms like a baby to a waiting ambulance. Later I learned I weighed only fifty-nine pounds when he found me."

Mrs. Rosen stared into the candles. About all that was left of them were wicks floating in pools of wax like lily pads on a pond.

"One year later I came to New York and I've been here ever since. I consider myself fifty-five years old. I was reborn that wonderful day my foot touched the pier on the Lower East Side."

*

We were still sitting by candlelight even though the power failure ended a short while ago, I'd noticed, when the refrigerator jerked and fussed suddenly. The kitchen light hadn't turned on because David flicked off the switch earlier when the lights went out. None of us seemed able to leave our seats, however, even though the blackout was over. Until we heard a voice calling out to someone in the hall.

The spell was broken. I think we all felt a sense of relief. Especially Mrs. Rosen. And hers was a sense of relief a long time in coming. Over half a century, in fact. Tonight she'd finally told her story.

135

Then David coughed and asked, "Did you like America right from the start?"

Mrs. Rosen smiled. "Well, it was definitely different from Europe. I loved the freedom it allows to be oneself, to be who one truly is – which is everyone's real job in life, to my way of thinking. I also loved how America is free of the past, too. One can start over here. And that's what I wanted to do. Start over. I was so young then but my old life was completely gone. Not forgotten, but gone. So, yes, I'm very glad I came here."

For the first time in hours, she laughed a little. "Thank God, I did, or I wouldn't have you," she beamed. She leaned over and mussed David's hair.

Then she stood up with a sigh. "So, there it is. My story. One among six million different stories. All I ask is that you remember. Yes, remember what really happened in the past and act on that memory in the present. And tell your children. Silence isn't an option." She bowed her head. "Never again . . . for me or anybody." Then she looked at her watch. "It is very late, of course, now. I have kept you both a long time."

David stood up and hugged her a long time. He had tears in his eyes.

I had tears in mine too. "Really, Mrs. Rosen, I wouldn't have it any other way," I blurted. "Thank you. I mean that. Thank you for what you told me."

She patted my head and then wrapped her tunic tighter, her signal it was time to go. "Well, Lauren, you better get a move on; your mother will be wondering why you aren't back to the apartment by now."

Doubtful, I thought to myself.

"Not so fast," David said. "What about tomorrow?"

Mrs. Rosen didn't miss a beat. "Tomorrow? Well,

tomorrow, I'm going to meet with the Russians. I must for Veronica. I have made my decision. I've been through the worst already. That's all in the past. I can at least take care of my family now. And my friends. They'll never stop me from doing that again . . . as long as I live."

David tried to take control of the situation. "But it's dangerous! Let me go with you!"

She shook her head. "No! Absolutely not! I forbid it! And promise me here and now that you won't go to the police and you won't tell your father. Promise me!"

David nodded against his will.

"And you too, Lauren! Promise me. I never expected anything like this would happen. Not today. Not ever. And you were with me." Then she looked from me over to David and back at me again. "Dear ones, I trust you both. This is very important to me. Will you do as I ask? Do I have your word?"

We both squirmed a bit, but finally she drew it out of us. "Okay, okay!" we both said, none too convincingly.

"Good!" she exclaimed. "Now don't worry about me, I can take care of myself. My life doesn't belong to me anyway. It belongs to Joshua and Momma and Poppa, my sisters . . . and Leni and Mrs. Ringlebaum. They'll all go with me. With them along, I won't be afraid." Then with great determination she declared, "I *will* get Veronica back. If it's the last thing I do. She will not suffer on my account . . . nor on Joshua's account . . . whatever this is all about. Joshua was not in the black market business with paintings! It's just absurd!"

David tried to say something else, but she shushed him with, "Go on now and walk Lauren downstairs to her apartment . . . and take good care of her. She's my favorite student, you know, exceptionally talented and a natural born artist. And then" – she went over to a kitchen drawer and grabbed her change purse, pulling out a wrinkled twenty – "be sure and take a cab home. It's too late to walk. Keep the change and buy something nice for your computer."

I laughed. Despite everything, she was still a typical grandmother.

David didn't budge. "No, I'm going to stay here with you tonight."

Mrs. Rosen held up her hand. "No. Thank you, but no. I need to be alone. I need to think and plan. This was good for me to tell you all this tonight. It has freed me in a way I hadn't realized I needed. I never spoke of what happened before. Not in all these years. So many decades have passed. Generations! I thank you both for listening. It helped me remember who I am . . . who I was . . . . And now, somehow I feel stronger than when Lauren and I returned home earlier. I know that may be hard for you to believe. But I do."

I was very affected by this because I really saw a kind of transformation in her. This was the hero of the Warsaw resistance talking, and she meant what she said. Almost like she was afraid of nothing because she'd seen it all.

"Go on then, dear ones. David, I'll call you tomorrow, I promise. And give my love to your father and mother. But breathe not a word. Can I count on you?"

"Yes, of course," David groaned, his voice very low.

Then she patted me on the back. "Lauren, try to get sleep. Don't worry. I will not let anything happen to you. This I promise. We'll talk then tomorrow, all of us. And I'm looking forward to having our lesson the same time next week. That's how sure I am that this will be past us by then."

I didn't trust her for a minute. She was really laying it on thick now. How could she be thinking of our lesson next week? It was a decoy to distract me, to make me think everything would be fine. No, she was planning something.

And it was obviously going to be done without David and me.

"You're not going to do something without us, are you?" I blurted. "You'll wait for us in the morning, won't you? Promise?"

She saw the expression on my face change from – How can you think of my lesson when all this is going on? – to – Yeah, right, you're just trying to change the subject to get my mind off everything.

So she took my hand and said very firmly, "You will be here next week and so will I. And so will David. Next week . . . and all the weeks after. I intend to be here for a long time. And I intend for Veronica to be here with me. I have asked her in the past to assist me with students. Today, taking her place with <u>her</u> students, convinced me of that. And now, God Bless her, she has taken my place tonight. Oh, I have so much to make up to her for what I've put her through."

She said this with such peace and conviction that it was hard not to believe that everything would be all right. Something really was different about her after telling us her survival story as a young girl. Then she looked at me and sighed. "As I've put you through, too, today, dear Lauren. Thank you, dear one. You were so very brave."

I suddenly realized I was crying again and gave her a big hug. She wiped the tears under my eyes with her thumb and whispered, "Don't cry now. Just be strong for me . . . and for you. What I shared with you tonight was not to weaken you, but to toughen you. To know who you are and what is right. And to know who <u>they</u> are. They'll always be here. And you may have to stand up to them one day." She patted my cheek and smiled. "Dear Lauren, you already are. Just remember my story and never forget."

She was starting to tear up again herself. But not

Mom's kind of teariness, which was all about desperation and an unnamed fear. Mrs. Rosen really was stronger now than before. I could see it all over her.

"Now if you'll excuse me, I'm going to bed. I need my beauty sleep." She paused in the kitchen door and took a long look at David and me. "You are very special to me. And I'm proud of you both." Then she disappeared through the swinging door.

Chapter Twelve

David and I stood there and looked at each other like we'd just met. I grabbed my backpack. "You don't have to."

"I insist," he said. "You think I'm telling her *NO*?"

We took the stairs. Once we sort of rubbed shoulders in the stairwell, but neither of us said a word until we got to my front door. I dug around in my backpack for my keys. "Thanks."

"No problem." He studied my face like he was trying to figure something out.

I grabbed his arm. "I'm sorry. I never knew, David. Not really. I mean . . . about the Holocaust and all. It's so terrible. I . . . I didn't . . . ." I ran out of words.

"It's all right. I understand. Really," he said. "And, uh, thanks for listening to her. It means a lot to me."

He started to go . . . then stopped and chewed his thumbnail. "So, uh, you coming tomorrow?"

My heart started to beat fast. "What? What do you mean? Where?"

"TO GET THE DIARY BACK! WE'RE GOING TO FOLLOW HER, OF COURSE!" He winked at me.

That sealed it. We were real friends now. My face heated up with a nuclear blush brighter than a thousand suns.

"Look, meet me at 10:00 tomorrow morning outside Computer Warehouse. You know where it is? Oh, and let's put on different jackets or something. You know, to make it a little harder to recognize us." Then he moved closer to me and whispered: "We have to have an alibi why we're meeting."

My head was reeling. I tried not to lose control . . . so I pushed my hair behind my ear real casual-like. "Yeah, sure. And, oh, I know where it is – over by the Banzai Pizza place, right?"

Then as he started to walk backwards he called out as if he wanted everyone behind the closed apartment doors nearby to hear. "Right! I wanna look at a new Sony laptop first! You into computers?"

Even though I knew he only half-meant what he said, I knew he really did love computers. Be careful here, Lauren, I thought. Computers are okay. I mean, I'm pretty good with them and all. But it's not like I'm a hacker or anything, so I told a teensy bit of a lie. A teensy bit? Actually it far overwhelmed the promise I'd just made, and then broken, to Mrs. Rosen.

"Into computers? Totally! You know, hack the planet, surf the net."

He nodded. "Cool! See you at 10:00 a.m. then."

"Definitely!" I called back. My hands were kind of shaking but I managed to get my key in the deadbolt on the second try. David was half-way down the hall by now. Watching him walk away, I got what my Mom calls one of my 'wild hairs.'

"David?"

He turned around. "Yeah?"

After I made sure the door was unlocked, I went over and stood really close to him. "Thanks for everything," I said. Then I put my arms around his neck and kissed him full on the lips.

He was still rubbing his face when I ran inside. I flipped

the deadbolt and rested my head against the door, panting out of breath. I couldn't believe I'd just done that! But I sure was glad I did – it sure made me feel good. Real good!

There wasn't a light on in the whole apartment, but the flashes on the hall ceiling told me Mom was watching television in the living room. I stuck my head around the door. There she was – in the middle of Chinese takeout boxes all over the coffee table and the couch. An empty wine bottle was on the floor behind her.

"I'm home!" I called out.

Mom raised herself up from the couch like Dracula coming out of his coffin. The way she looked scared the hell out of me. Her hair – real moussed – was standing up on end and looked all crazy. I'd woken her out of a deep sleep . . . or from passing out. I could smell the wine across the room. She was drunk again.

She yawned. "Hi ya, baby. Oh, good, the electricity's back on. Must have dozed off. What time is it anyway?" she asked, squinting her eyes. Then she saw the living room clock. It was 10:45. "Wow, I've been out a while."

I went over to her. "Are you okay?"

"Top of the world," she yawned, not too steady getting up. "Did you have a nice time at Mrs. Rosen's? My daughter, the sculptor. Are you learning a lot?"

More than you'll ever know, I said to myself, and more than I'll ever tell you. Well, I just let that sail over my head – I wasn't going to touch it. Then I noticed the wad of Kleenex in her hand. It had been another rough night for her.

"What did Dad do this time?" I asked with a sigh, changing the subject.

"He says he won't pay support this month. He's probably on his way to Cancun with his surgically-enhanced Malibu Barbie lookalike of the week."

I chewed my lip and didn't say anything. I was pretty sick of Mom and Dad acting like a couple of three year olds. All they did was complain about each other. To me! What was I supposed to do? In a way, I really felt sorry for Mom, but it's not like I was the divorce judge or anything. She was really going downhill before my eyes, and I kept waiting for her to wake up and get a hold of herself. I couldn't understand why people threw in the towel like this. Especially my own Mother.

"Can I get you something?" I asked finally.

Mom rubbed her forehead. "I could use a glass of ice water and couple of aspirin now that you mention it."

I went to the kitchen and turned on the faucet. It was hard to find space to get a glass under it because of the pile of dirty dishes in the sink that looked like they had fur on them. Well, if they didn't bother her, they didn't bother me. Then I got her aspirin from the bathroom – another ghastly sight – and took them to her. "You want anything else?" I couldn't wait to say goodnight and escape to my room.

After she gulped the tablets with about half the glass of water, she lay back down and looked at the TV screen. Suddenly she felt like talking. "What did you do in that awful dark for so long? I just got home when the lights went out. I hated it. I missed you. I was kind of nervous . . . imagining the worst as always. I was glad the power failure hadn't happened on your way back from Mrs. Rosen's apartment. I imagined you stumbling down the stairs in the dark, baby. Well, at least you were safe with her. What did you do all that time?"

I fed her the usual "Oh, nothing." On second thought, I figured I ought to say something about what we did in the dark for so long. "Mrs. Rosen told us how her whole family died in the Holocaust."

But Mom's attention was already back on the program

she was watching. "That's nice," she said, a million miles away. It was so rare that she listened to me anyway, why should this night be any different? She stared at the TV screen like it was her sole mission in life. I'd lost her. "Oh, look, the royal family is on *20/20*!" she said all excited, punching up the volume on the remote. "Come and watch."

"Not for me, Mom," I groaned and kissed her on the cheek. "I'm beat. Good night!" I got out of there fast and went to my room.

As I passed Mom's bedroom, I saw all the open dress boxes on her bed. Diane von Furstenberg, Vittadini and Donna Karan outfits with tags still on them were scattered over the floor like confetti, which made me even more depressed. Mom sure didn't need money. I mean, hell, she was a stockbroker at one of the biggest firms in Manhattan and burned cash like gasoline. What she did need was attention, and not from me. Most of the time I was just in the way. I thought of my father and wanted to kill him for doing this to me.

As soon as I hit my room, I checked my answering machine. There was a call from Jeannie O'Toole asking if I wanted to meet her and her boyfriend and her goofy cousin from Long Island for a movie Saturday night. Guess she's giving me a second chance, I thought, chuckling to myself. No dice on that one; that guy's ego was too big for me to ever be interested in maintaining. Three other calls were hang-ups with a lot of background noise like cars and stuff. It sounded like a corner pay phone, which gave me a major dose of the creeps. I wondered how Veronica was.

Just in case, while Mom was thoroughly engrossed in the royal family to notice me, I went to double-check the front door lock. Satisfied after flicking the deadbolt three times, I took a hot bath and then crawled into bed with my Discman. Music didn't help. Barely halfway through the first song, I tossed my headphones on the floor and turned off the light. I was mentally and physically exhausted from everything. Nikolai and his gang – Veronica's kidnapping – and then Mrs. Rosen's shocking story squeezed every ounce of energy I had out of me. I felt all tired and sore like I'd been beaten up in a back alley somewhere.

I rolled over on my side and tried to sleep. But some stupid commercial suddenly blared on the TV down the hall, too loud and too long. Mom must've thought it was pretty funny because she started to laugh and then launched into a major coughing fit. A real hacker, my Mom. The thought of her and my family, such as it was, started to get to me.

I thought about Mrs. Rosen and then Mom. The past and the present. What an amazing life Mrs. Rosen has had. What would I do in the same situation? What if I had been born Jewish in one of the countries the Nazis took over? I mean, she was just about my age when the Nazis came after her and her family. Would I be as brave and stay with Mom in the Ghetto and try to protect her? Or would I try to go over the wall and make a run for it to save my own neck? Would I be a hero or a coward? It kept eating at me.

What would it be like – locked in that hideous train car with no water? To have my Mom ripped away from me on a chaotic railroad platform, screaming and calling for me . . . to be marched away and have all my hair shaved off . . . to be whipped on my bare skin . . . to have everything and everyone I'd ever known, all my friends and relatives, taken from me and not able to do a single thing about it? What would it be like to be stripped naked and ordered to walk through a big wooden door into a dark underground room? – like Mrs. Rosen described. Into a gas chamber!

I sat straight up in bed, my heart beating like a strobe light. Get a grip on yourself, Lauren, I thought, gulping a breath and turning on the bedside lamp. I looked around my room at its familiar, jumbled mess . . . my jeans on the floor, posters half-hanging from the wall, stuffed animals in the window. Everything was okay. Everything was normal. That's when I noticed my backpack on the floor and fished out the book David gave me. I was too awake to sleep anyway.

Propping myself up on a couple of pillows, I flipped open the book to a section of old photographs. More than anything, it was the bodies that got to me. Emaciated human sticks stacked together like firewood. And the children! So many starving children with hollow eyes who stared back at me from behind barbed wire or who lay in dirty street gutters like broken dolls. There were also several pictures taken in the Warsaw Ghetto, right where Mrs. Rosen was. I flipped through the pages and had trouble reading some of the names: *Sobibor, Chelmno, Einsatzgruppen, Sonderaktion.* Then I spotted some of the strange words Mrs. Rosen mentioned, like Special Treatment and Final Solution.

I looked for the Warsaw Ghetto and read that it was "the largest Jewish uprising against the Nazis during the Second World War. In the end, it took Nazi troops longer to put down the ghetto revolt than it took them to conquer all of Poland."* And Mrs. Rosen and Joshua were part of that historic uprising that fought the Nazis so heroically.

I looked for Auschwitz. I didn't know how to spell it but knew it began with an "A." I found it in the index and turned to the chapter on it. There were pictures of barbed wire fences and watchtowers and trains with hundreds of terrified people spilling out. I saw the "pajama men" Mrs. Rosen described and the chimneys. It was beyond imagining. Yet she had actually been there! It really happened, just like she said. Mrs. Rosen's story made it part of me somehow.

Finally I had to close the book when I came across one

picture that nearly did me in. It showed a group of naked women lined up on the edge of a ditch waiting to be shot – some of them holding babies. One little girl about eight years old held her mother's hand and stared into the camera lens. The background was fuzzy but I could make out tangled bodies already in the ditch and the soldiers shooting.

But the children! I thought about hate crimes and stuff on the news that I never like to think about especially when it affects children – the Oklahoma City bombing where so many children died – and the rash of school massacres the last few years with so many psychologists and politicians and preachers spouting their theories. People from all over sending flowers, notes and stuffed teddy bears, and then having to try and explain it to their own kids. Well, what do the experts say? That it's because they're insane – hate crime killers, school murderers, bombers? That they're bored and lost and just looking for excuses to strike out at any cost? Experts say "cold-blooded killers," yet they're not if they feel hate and rage. Is it revenge at any cost? And how can they not see the lives before them that they're blotting out forever? Is there any difference between what makes them tick and what was behind the Holocaust? Does anyone know the answer?

Was there any difference between the terrorists who killed all those people on September 11th – at the World Trade Center and in Washington and everyone on the four planes that day – and those who caused the Holocaust? Is it hatred so extreme that it gets twisted up into some kind of fanaticism that makes no sense?

As I looked at that picture of the women and babies on the edge of the shooting pit, I thought to myself that the answer lay here, right here in what made men kill these innocent, harmless, good people and their little ones. Figure that out and know what happened here, what really happened, and make sure everybody knows it, and then experts will understand why and how to stop it from ever happening again.

Over a million kids were murdered in the Holocaust, the book said. I can't even imagine a million anything. All planned, like Mrs. Rosen told us, with schedules and timetables and all that. Like a business. That really bothered me. About someone who's crazy, you can say, "Oh, he was a psycho, that's why." But what about all the others planning and carrying this stuff out for one cause or another?

My mind was racing. It was like the world was a bigger place to me tonight. I had so many questions. The Nazis shot those women and children because they were Jewish. That's insane, yes. But there has to be more to it than that. Mrs. Rosen talked about hatred tonight. And that's all you heard on the news since September 11th. Not everybody can be crazy, but everybody can hate. At the core there's got to be such extreme hatred to the point that every child, woman and man must be done away with before their fanatic ideas. Yet how could anyone hate mothers holding babies? How could anyone hate the ones in the picture standing on the edge of a ditch so much they wanted them dead?

How could anyone hate to the point that . . . that they're not human any more? That's what it is – they're not human any more. To hate like that means you lose your own self. And for all their talk of racism, they're no longer part of the human race. And isn't that more important than any race or nationality? Why can't people see that?

And how could other people just not care enough to stop them? That's evil too – looking the other way and ignoring it. Ignorance and even a stubborn refusal to see the truth, like Mrs. Rosen said, wherever innocent lives were the targets. And fear too. With a leader like Hitler – were many people just so swept away with his ideas while others were too terrified to stand up and stop it when he gained control? Afraid to be different from the rest?

I didn't know much about the Holocaust before tonight, but David said something about people who say it never even happened. That didn't make sense either. How could something that happened *not happen*?

Six million people . . . six million stories erased one by one. And not only Jews, the book said. Gypsies, gays, Jehovah's Witnesses, political prisoners, and other nationalities looked down upon. So we can't feel any safer about this never happening again if we're not Jewish because plenty of people were exterminated who weren't. And there've been plenty of large-scale massacres, like Mrs. Rosen said, in the last ten years alone. It made me realize that we really have to be on our guard. We have to remember six million special people who taught us about what we must do. But what can be done to stop such evil? What could be done to stop someone like Nikolai? I was confused and miserable and scared. I had to get a hold of myself.

Sometime after 1:00 I finally got sleepy and turned off the light. I started having those dream flashes you get when you're still half-awake. I dreamed that the people in the photographs had the faces of those I knew or cared about . . . Mrs. Rosen, David, Veronica, my friend Jeannie O'Toole, Dad and Mom. What I saw were <u>their</u> faces superimposed on the pictures in the book.

I think my dream was trying to tell me that every life is precious. That every last person killed in the Holocaust was someone special. Every person who died had relatives and friends who knew and loved them. Every one of those six million had their own lives and loved ones – and their own talents and dreams. Some could play the piano, some were great at sports, and others were just ordinary and nice. But each one was unique. There never had been a person just like them before and never will be again. They weren't a bunch of statistics. They had names and faces and families. They were people. Like David and Mrs. Rosen and Veronica. And Mom and me.

I sat up and turned on the light again. I needed to see where I was once more: my pile of clothes in the corner, my CD's, earrings and shoes strewn about the floor. It made me feel better. Like I was more anchored and back in my own life. Then I thought about tomorrow . . . and David. I wondered if I'd be scared. Well, if I was, I figured at least we'd be together. And whatever happened, I knew my life was going to change. Forever! It already had.

I turned off the light again, pulled up the comforter, fluffed my pillow and rolled over on my side. Suddenly I wasn't scared anymore. I don't know why. I mean, after all, Nikolai did threaten our lives and he did take Veronica. No, I was mad now. Mrs. Rosen's story had given me courage. And thinking of my friends and family too in the same situation. There in the dark I was all fired up about tomorrow and protecting Mrs. Rosen somehow. And helping her get poor Veronica back in a daring rescue. And her brother's Diary. A tall order. The stuff of dreams in the middle of the night.

And stories. Six million stories. Now it was up to David and me to speak for them. Somehow. Some way. When I finally went to sleep, I dreamed about the children. And Veronica trying to call out to us with no voice.

Chapter Thirteen

It was one of those blustery mornings in New York when everything happens at once. A day when people move faster in the crosswalks and the taxis honk louder. The sky was electric blue, but deep down in the shadowy canyons between tall buildings, the wind whistled and steam poured from the sewers like dragons' breath. I felt so alive! Like everything looked brand new. Everything had a meaning now. How good it was to be outside and free and doing something important! To feel like I had a purpose for once! A real purpose.

I saw David before he saw me. He stood in a wedge of sunlight on the corner of Amsterdam and Broadway. I yelled at him from across the street. "Yo, David!"

He frowned and squinted in my direction.

I waved and ran across the street against the light. A UPS truck braked and screeched its tires. "WATCH IT! YOU STUPID MORON!" yelled the driver at me. And everybody thinks those brown uniforms are so cute! I crossed my eyes back at him. Yeah, I was definitely manic this morning, overjoyed to be alive and in my own body! Then a bike messenger whizzed past, missing me by inches. Typical. I absolutely didn't care though. I bounced up to David. The river of Saturday shoppers rolling down the sidewalk swirled around us like we were boulders blocking the rapids.

"How's it going?" I gave him a playful punch in the

arm.

He looked at me like my hair was on fire. I shrugged my shoulders and lifted my hands. "What? What?"

"'*YO, DAVID*'? Waving and throwing your arms up in the air? That's undercover? That's what you do when you tail someone?"

My face got hot. "I . . . I . . . I didn't –"

He cracked a smile and chuckled, sort of. "Lauren, I was joking." Then he punched me in the arm. Actually it was good to see you. And we're not there yet anyway."

I rolled my eyes. David with an actual sense of humor was something I was still getting used to. But I approved. He was so cute when he smiled and those sweet little crow's feet crinkled by his eyes I could hardly stand it.

I decided to see if he could take it as well as he dished it out. "Glad to see you got dressed in a different look." Of course, he had on his usual uniform, the fatigue jacket, jeans and army boots combo. But a different fatigue jacket – a Desert Storm one I'd never seen on him before – and a Yankee baseball cap. Some disguise.

He didn't miss a beat. "Don't be so self-conscious. You look fine," he replied.

Fine, I thought. Great. I had only been awake since 7:30 washing my stupid hair and deciding what I was going to wear. I'd settled on jeans, a new pair of blue Converse low tops, and this funky, hooded Guatemalan sweater jacket whatever thingy that Dad brought home from one of his little vacations. I think it was three girlfriends past Mom . . . about a month ago. But I never wore it before and I was sure no one would ever recognize me in it.

David gestured to the Computer Warehouse display window behind us. Not sure what I was supposed to be looking at, I peered in the window.

David cued me. "Cool laptops, huh?"

Like an alien invasion fleet bent on destruction, row after row of sleek black notebook computers lined the bottom shelf. I wasn't impressed. "Those? If you don't care about having enough RAM and don't need a 2.4 Gigahertz Pentium 4 processor. They're obsolete. They're practically growing little grey beards as we speak."

David pushed me. "Get out!"

"Oh, I'm serious. You know, for multimedia graphic applications, those go nowhere without some major add-ons."

"You really do know your stuff, Lauren!"

I might have imagined it, but it seemed like all of a sudden he was standing a lot closer to me.

"So, do you go online a lot?" he asked.

I cocked my head. "I live and breathe to go online. Flame me and you die."

"Man, you really are a webhead. What's your server? We have to get each other's email addresses later."

"Servers are for wussies. I rigged my own web browser application."

David gave me a look like a Chihuahua on an espresso binge. "Wow! That's pretty amazing for a . . . a . . ."

I put my hands on my hips. "Say it. A *girl*?"

"For anybody," he answered. He looked down his nose at me. "So . . . you ready for a stakeout?"

I tossed my hair back and stepped a little closer. "I was born ready, pardner."

I think that made him a little nervous, for he took half a step back. "Uh, good," he said a little tongue-twisted and then looked at his watch. "We better get going. You know how punctual my grandmother is. I called her this morning to check on her. She stonewalled me, said she was fine, that she had heard from them again and that they promised to return Veronica as soon as she could help them decipher the Diary. That they promised she could do this in a public place, and that Veronica would be produced immediately afterward. That it would all be over today."

"A public place? You believe her?" I asked.

"No," he answered.

"Do you think she believed them?"

"No," he frowned.

"Or that Nikolai even said any of that to her? Or *meant* any of it if he did?"

"No, I think she was just pushing me off. Last night, she said that she'd be meeting them at noon. Today she said she had to go out for a while, dodged my questions about the meeting, but that we'd talk later."

I looked at my watch. David and I had both been early, so it was only 10:00 now. I had almost gone up to Mrs. Rosen's apartment before I left, but thought better about it and decided to go straight to David.

"She didn't say anything about the meeting then?"

He shook his head. "Her? Are you kidding? She made me double swear I wouldn't even ask again."

I put my hand on his arm. "Is this going to be dangerous? You can tell me."

He didn't look at me. "Not if we do it right."

"What if we don't, you know, do it right?"

"Oh, we'll do it right, don't worry," he smiled. He was putting up a good front, but I could tell he was nervous, too.

"Well, if . . . I mean, when we get the Diary back, what happens then?"

"I'll think of something."

I smiled. "I bet you will." Then I took a big risk. I reached down and took hold of his hand. "You ready?"

His face went all serious. "Uh, yeah." But he didn't

pull his hand away. In fact, he gave mine a little squeeze. "Let's go."

We went down 72nd Street. I think the few minutes it took to walk to Central Park West were the happiest of my life. Up to that moment. He took my hand as we crossed the street and forgot to let go when we reached the curb. We didn't talk, we just walked hand in hand. I wanted those two blocks to last forever. Like all good things, they didn't, of course. But while they did . . . well, it was pretty fine.

We stopped on the corner of 72nd and Central Park West, right in front of the Dakota, the old creepy-looking apartment building where John Lennon was shot. Sometimes people still left fresh flowers on the sidewalk at the spot where he fell. But no one had today.

David dropped my hand when he checked his watch. A definite bummer. "We need to hurry," he said. Then he just sort of left without me.

Not exactly Captain Romance behavior, I admit, but I figured he was still trainable. And this wasn't the time, that's for sure. There were more important things on his mind. And mine. I put my hand on my cheek. It felt all warm. I kept it there for a second. Then I took off after him.

It took me nearly half a block to catch up with him because he was moving so darned fast. "What's the plan?" I called out, narrowly missing a collision with a very well-preserved, super-rich lady walking three dachshunds wearing matching plaid sweaters. Her purple coat made me remember my hair and how much I'd stand out on the street to Nikolai and company. So I fished in my pocket for my black knit cap and completely covered my hair.

David took a breath. "Cool disguise," he said. "Good thinking. Well, the plan is to follow her wherever she goes. She walks, we walk. She takes a taxi, we take a taxi. We just have to be sure she doesn't shake us!" Then he sped up.

Now we were nearly jogging. My brand new sneakers squeaked on the asphalt like the Knicks on a fast break. Along the way, we earned several one-finger salutes and some very creative cussing from passing taxi drivers as we crossed streets against the light here and there.

As we got closer to our apartment building, David stopped and stared straight ahead, ignoring me, obviously concentrating on our next move. "Here!" he shouted, grabbing me by the arm and yanking me into a nearby doorway. I nearly flew out of my sneakers. Geez! I thought – if this is our next move, it's not very sophisticated.

We stood under the street awning of a building on the next block from ours, half inside the front entrance. Same type of big, old art deco pile with an ornate lobby that looks like something straight from one of those 1930's gangster movies. Black and white tile, chandeliers, and lots of polished marble. You know, good bad taste. Enormous potted ficus trees stood on either side of its revolving door.

David jerked his thumb at them. "You take that one, I'll take this one. We can spy on her from here when she leaves."

"I don't think so, Bucko!" snapped a deep voice with real attitude. I whipped around and saw that it was only the doorman. Out of nowhere – like all great doormen. His red and gold hat and jacket with epaulets combo made him look like a bad cross between Captain Kirk and a George Washington impersonator.

Meanwhile David had already inserted himself behind one of the trees. I have to admit he looked a little odd himself . . . hiding behind a potted plant in broad daylight and right beside a doorman yet.

"YOU KIDS BETTER SCRAM OUTTA HERE!

157

DIS AIN'T A PUBLIC PLAYGROUND!" the doorman growled, taking another step towards us.

"Quick, Lauren! Hide! There she is!" David yelled, ignoring him.

In a flash, I jumped behind my tree. What was going on? It wasn't even 10:30 yet and she was already leaving for her noon appointment. Why had she set off an hour and a half ahead? Was she going that far? Or was she just trying to give David the slip?

The doorman slapped his forehead. "I ain't believin' dis here!"

There was Mrs. Rosen on the sidewalk talking to Mr. Antonelli, our building's doorman, a sweet, old guy with a white mustache like a walrus. Tweeting on the little whistle he wears around his neck on a chain, he summoned a taxi that instantly pulled to the curb for Mrs. Rosen. David's ficus bush rustled and spoke.

"Pssssst! Hey, buddy, be a pal and get us a cab," David whispered to the bemused doorman, as if the tree were talking. "Fast, man, it's an emergency!"

The surly doorman's jaw dropped. "What? Are you kidding me?"

We watched Mr. Antonelli hold the taxi's rear door open for Mrs. Rosen. She was about to get in, but suddenly she stopped short, noticing the sky. It really was a beautiful day for January. The sun was so bright it made her white hair shine silver. She looked great in her favorite cashmere overcoat and a pair of expensive loafers. A pretty scarf was wrapped around her throat and she had a big leather Vuitton bag slung over her shoulder. In one hand was a tightly wrapped umbrella.

She certainly didn't look like she was going to meet up with gangsters. She looked pretty darn sharp. And calm and in control. After looking at her watch, she said something to Mr. Antonelli and handed him the umbrella. Nodding his head in agreement with whatever she said, he slammed the cab's door shut and waved it off without her. What luck for us.

"Whew! She's going to walk," said David with relief.

Mrs. Rosen still tipped Mr. Antonelli and started walking . . . straight for us.

"Freeze!" whispered David.

I froze. So did the doorman.

Then he cut his eyes at me. "Hey, is this one of those Reality TV shows with a hidden camera somewhere?" he asked, frowning.

"How did you guess?" I reassured him boldly. "Let's go inside and discuss this," I grinned, while David and I bolted into the entrance vestibule, moving back deep inside. "Producer's orders."

"Yeah, right. And I'm Tom Hanks and this is suddenly a movie set here – " he went on like a motor mouth, mocking us in a dramatic voice.

I closed my eyes and held my breath. Mrs. Rosen passed right in front of us. Our doorman conspirator, who was half in and half out the door, tipped his cap and bowed. "Mornin', ma'am."

"Good morning," she smiled, bowing her head at him ever so slightly. She walked right on by without seeing us inside the entranceway.

When the sound of her shoes clicked away down the sidewalk, David, now back behind the ficus, emerged from the foliage like Indiana Jones. "Let's go!"

I reached in my pocket and handed the doorman a dollar. "Don't spend it all in one place," I teased. He inspected the bill and raised his eyebrows. "Hey, you were perfect!" I called out to him . . . and added, "Tom!"

"You kids be careful now, you hear? Don't get into trouble!"

"We won't! Only a little!" I called back.

He opened his mouth to say something else that sounded like "wise-ass kids," but we were already gone.

Mrs. Rosen headed north on Central Park West, the direction David and I had just come from. At first we lagged way behind, practically hugging the buildings in case she turned around and we had to duck. We had to duck. Twice. But always like we were in the middle of a major shoelace-tying problem that required both our attention. Then we crossed the street and followed her from the Park side.

The first time was when Mrs. Rosen stopped and chatted with a homeless woman pushing a rusty shopping cart full of old newspapers and aluminum cans. They laughed and talked like they were old friends. The homeless woman was a sweetheart. She was about four feet tall and didn't have any front teeth, but she had the widest, prettiest eyes I've ever seen. Mrs. Rosen gave her some cash before she left. She was always doing stuff like that. One time she told me every human being is a member of the same family.

Mrs. Rosen hadn't gone a block before she stopped again. David and I crouched down on the curb behind a pile of smelly garbage bags while she stopped to admire a pair of chubby twins strapped in a two-seater stroller. Wrapped up in blankets and knit caps, they looked like a couple of regular mummies. Their red-faced English nanny cooed at them and got them to smile for her. Mrs. Rosen blew them a kiss and resumed her hike.

She didn't slow down until she was right in front of the American Museum of Natural History. Then she paused for a moment and gazed up at the enormous castle-like building.

A tidal wave of parents and balloon-toting kids surged towards the entrance. I spotted lots of single dads. Then I remembered it was the weekend. Custody city . . . except at my house. How did I get stuck with these parents I have? – I couldn't help thinking at that moment.

"Do you think she's going in?" I whispered.

"It makes sense," said David. "One of the major public places to meet in the City – and lots of exits." Then he looked at me, puzzled, with his head cocked to the side like a spaniel. "Why are you whispering?"

Mrs. Rosen checked her watch, then walked briskly to the corner and got lost in the crowd waiting for the light to change. "That's strange . . . she's crossing the street," I said, narrating her progress.

"The Park!" David exclaimed.

He was right. She was heading for Central Park.

The "WALK" sign flashed and the knot of people pushed off the curb and hurried across the street. Two kids on skateboards broke from the gate like racehorses. It looked like they couldn't wait to get to the Park and begin thrashing. Mrs. Rosen was the last person to cross. As soon as her foot hit the far sidewalk, the waiting cars and trucks roared to life and took over the street again. After all, it was their turf.

"Come on!" yelled David, yanking my hand. Cool. He pulled me over the wall. Not cool. With a thump we crashed to the ground behind the wall and discovered some really dense azalea bushes to hide behind so Mrs. Rosen couldn't see us.

About fifty yards ahead of us moving along a sidewalk, going deeper into the Park, Mrs. Rosen was smart to walk. It really was an absolutely gorgeous, unusually mild winter day. Last night's powerful thunderstorm had blown through, and now everything looked scrubbed clean. After the misty, humid, overcast spell over New York the last few days, this was a welcome relief for everyone. The park really shone today at its very best in winter. Some of the trees even looked like they were about to bud all green and shiny, and the dirt was spongy under my feet and had that good, loamy wet smell. It sounded like some songbirds had migrated early this year and were trying to outdo each other singing the loudest. Best of all, the sun was back and at its brightest, beaming glorious golden-streaked rays all through the Park.

And it sure was packed! As always on the weekends, especially when the weather was great, tons of cyclists whirred by and kids were running and playing all over the place making a real racket. I love that sound. You know . . . when a bunch of little kids are scrambling around outdoors and don't care how much noise they make. Like a continuous celebration in the air.

Skateboarders and bladers were giving the kids a run for their money though. The boarders were hogging all the hills and stairs, laughing, joshing, and falling down a lot. The bladers terrorized the walks – some because they were speeding too fast and others because they kept bumping into people. Their custom-picked outfits always made me laugh – you know, sort of like school uniforms. Everything on the boarders, for example, was baggy and grungy and screamed Bad Attitude, while the high-tech bladers were all lycra and neon-y with purple helmets and lime green kneepads.

"Hey, David, you ever go rollerblading?" I asked suddenly, growing more manic by the minute. I've always functioned best in tight spots by kidding around.

He shot me a wicked look. "Surely you jest."

"Chicken, huh?" I elbowed him.

He laughed in spite of himself. His sense of humor was coming along nicely, I thought, feeling pretty gratified about that.

By now Mrs. Rosen was crossing the Great Meadow. This meant trouble for us. Tracking her across this wide open section of the park without being seen called for some quick thinking – and fast. "Use the castle for cover!" I said. "We can run around the other side and head her off!"

"What?" David asked, utterly surprised.

"Follow me!" I called.   Now it was his turn to eat dust. I took off running. I figured while Mrs. Rosen walked across the Great Lawn, being careful not to step on the crazy winter sunbathers or get hit in the head with a softball of course, David and I would sprint around the grey stone walls of Belvedere Castle on the edge of the lawn and meet up with her on the other side.

My plan worked! It was just that it nearly killed us. Taking Belvedere Lake and the Delacorte Theater into consideration, which I didn't, it was pretty far to run. We caught our breath on the far side of the Great Lawn behind the obelisk, the big Egyptian-looking needle made of rock.

"Do you see her?" David gasped.

I peeked around the corner. "Not yet." My heart was pounding. And not because David was leaning against me panting like a Labrador Retriever. I was wasted. Now I was convinced I needed to get serious with Mom's treadmill.

Then just when I thought we'd lost her, Mrs. Rosen appeared about forty feet away. I elbowed David. "Pssssst! Here she comes – !" Suddenly my heart dropped through the bottom of my stomach. She wasn't alone!   "Oh, hell!"

"What's wrong?" asked David with alarm.

"It's Nikolai! He's right behind her!"

Chapter Fourteen

"Does she see him?"

"No. Not yet. He's about ten yards back."

"Do you think he saw us?"

"I don't know."

"Where are the others? They can't be far away."

I got chills up my spine. Were they about to spring on us from behind somewhere? I craned my neck, checking the sidewalks and bushes, searching everywhere for where Sergei and Vlad might be hiding to ambush us.

"There!" David freaked, spotting them.

Nikolai's henchmen were about 20 yards away trotting over to him . . . still in their black leather trench coats and gloves. The glove part bothered me. It wasn't very cold, so I figured they had to be worried about leaving fingerprints. Not good. The three Russians put their heads together in a huddle. Sergei, the stocky, bald-headed muscleman, was waving back behind him, shaking his head. I could see Nikolai nodding and turning his head around to see where Mrs. Rosen was.

Still unaware she was being followed, David's grandmother was just now passing to our right. David and I pressed our backs against the obelisk, sucked our stomachs against our spines and held our breath. If she saw us and called out our names with the Russians right there, it would all be over.

Luckily, she didn't notice us and strode right on by.

For no reason I could tell, a faint smile played on her lips. Something about the smile hit me like a lightflash going off in my head. I suddenly realized she was a real hero. I mean, she was 70-something and she was going to a meeting with Russian gangsters . . . and she was smiling. She was so cool.

"I wonder what the bald guy is saying," David whispered.

"His name's Sergei. He's like the complete slave of the arrogant albino creep with the blonde crewcut – Nikolai – who thinks he's the top gang banger or something. I bet Vlad's reporting to him that there are no undercover cops tailing your grandmother. That's probably why they split up and why they were creeping behind her to make sure it's not a set-up or a trick where the cops would surprise them. We're sure lucky they didn't see us."

David whistled in agreement. "They must've spotted her coming toward the Museum. Maybe waiting for her in the trees somewhere. Yeah, but on the other hand, I bet they instructed her to make like she was getting in a cab but then walk through the park where they could see her and follow her for a long distance. Maybe they watched her right from the building. And us too!" he added.

"Not necessarily. We were pretty far behind her, and we always ducked down or were on the opposite side of the street way back. And here in the park, we went around them with my, um, brilliant shortcut trick," I couldn't help saying. "We took a different direction by the castle, remember? And we're sort of in disguise too."

"So now we're tailing them, too, then?"

"I suppose so. This is getting interesting."

Suddenly David and I went real still as the Russians hurried by. I'd forgotten how big they were. Up close, they had about the same dimensions as refrigerators.

"They're gone! Let's go!" I shouted, like all of a sudden I was in charge. Not that I minded. I just wasn't sure what to do next. I figured I'd make up a plan as I went along. I was pretty gutsy this morning. Not like last night. And besides, I wasn't in their clutches. I was tailing them. With David and with a cell phone to call 911 if necessary.

The Russians trailed about twenty yards behind Mrs. Rosen and we kept about twice that distance behind them. It was getting to be a regular parade. Suddenly Vlad stopped short and started to turn around.

I stepped in front of David. "Quick! Hug me!"

"Wha-what?"

I threw my arms around him and buried my face in his neck. "Is he still looking?" I whispered.

"N-no," stammered David. "What was that for?"

"Camouflage," I remarked casually, like a real pro. "Remember, they've seen me before. You, well, we think they don't know." I added, "Except maybe up close."

"Oh, yeah," he said, a little impressed. "It's a good thing you have that cap on your head too, Lauren." Then he really looked into my eyes real direct, longer than any boy had ever done. Like he was about to say something until he glanced over my shoulder. "Come on, one of them just caught up with her."

So he had – it was Nikolai. And he loomed over Mrs. Rosen, gesturing wildly, bullying her. I could see she was listening, but she didn't look at him. Not once. She was a spunky, classy lady and not afraid of anybody this morning. Not for herself, at least. She appeared to be absolutely impenetrable and had such dignity. I was so proud of her. She looked straight ahead, ignoring Nikolai along with Sergei and Vlad lurking behind them like a couple of mangy pit bulls hoping for table scraps.

David got mad. "If it looks like they're going to try to force her into a car or something, I'm going to butt in. There's no way I'm going to let that happen."

"Me neither," I agreed. "And don't forget my cell phone," which I pulled out at that moment.

"Good!" he said. "Glad you have one."

They crossed Park Drive and began to stroll briskly around the Metropolitan Museum of Art. They couldn't possibly be taking her in there, I thought. For a minute, it looked like they were going to cross Fifth Avenue. But when they got to the sidewalk, they turned left as Nikolai led her straight up the steps into the museum.

"They're going inside!" David gaped in amazement. "What on earth for?"

"You got me, but there's the public place he assured her they'd meet at. She wasn't lying to you after all. She just wouldn't tell you where. You ready?"

David grinned and squeezed my hand. "I was born ready . . . pardner."

Hearing that, I took a deep breath and flashed a huge smile back at him. I felt ready for anything, as we watched Mrs. Rosen with the three Russians cross the plaza and climb the broad cliff of steps leading to the museum's door. It was public after all; how much more public could you get? And there were so many police posted at public buildings these days in the city that I felt there was small chance of risk for her.

The magnificent, imposing old building that housed the Metropolitan Museum of Art was my very favorite place in all of New York, and I'd been coming here ever since I was, like, four or something. Some days I felt like I could go in and never come out, staying happily lost forever in the hundreds of galleries, each painting and statue more magical than the one before. I've always loved art ever since I was a kid – and always loved to draw and paint and make things. Somehow Mrs. Rosen recognized that in me the day she first saw me. How did she know?

The soaring columns along its face always reminded me of those old Greek temples you see in tourist brochures. Hung high above the doors, huge yellow and blue banners announcing a new exhibit from Imperial China gently flapped in the breeze. Cool show, I thought to myself, but no time for that now.

Why ever were they taking her in here? I wondered. Maybe to get an idea of the lost works of the Impressionist Masters they were so hot to find or to jog her memory about something. Either way, there sure were plenty of police around, which I'm sure Nikolai noticed. New York was really on guard these days. The sight of them sure made me feel better. We could easily call them for help if something went wrong with Mrs. Rosen's plan. All in all, I felt pretty good about what we were doing.

We waited for Mrs. Rosen and the Russians to disappear inside. Then David and I charged, bounding up the steps two at a time.

Like always, the Great Hall smelled of fresh flowers and hummed with wandering hordes of visitors, most of them with that give-away look, that gawky, big-eyed "it's my first trip to New York" look. You gotta love tourists, though. All New Yorkers do. From the balcony above us came the sounds of a string quartet playing Bach or Mozart or something. I wasn't up on music the way I was about art. Too bad we didn't have time to enjoy it. It was kind of romantic.

David gave me a little metal tag with the big "M" on it that the ticket collector handed him after he paid for our entry tickets. I clipped it on my collar as he scanned the huge hall.

"There they are!" He pointed to Nikolai steering Mrs.

Rosen by her elbow towards the Medieval art galleries.

She looked so vulnerable next to Nikolai. How I hated him. And if I had anything to do with it, he was going to get his. Good and hard. No matter how long it took. *After*, of course, he let Veronica go and Mrs. Rosen alone; after *we* somehow could pull something off, David and I. Was that dreaming on my part? If so, there was always plan B – the police and FBI.

We blended in well – I mean, as well as we could – with a bunch of Japanese exchange students. I'd never seen so many expensive raincoats and cameras in all my life. Really nice kids though. We followed them into the big high-ceilinged room where they always put the great Christmas tree with the famous Neapolitan *creches*.

In an eerie effect, Gregorian chants filtered through the PA system, and sunlight spilled through the room's stained glass windows and splashed on the floor like rainbow confetti. We collided into the Japanese bunch when they stopped short and clustered around a really old statue of Mary and baby Jesus. A really nice man turned around and smiled at us and bowed his head to say he was sorry. We did too.

But we had to rush away because the Russians and Mrs. Rosen were off again. They hurried through the exhibit with the horseback knights in silver armor, the Equestrian Court, and it was bursting with noisy kids. Good cover for us.

"Where are they going? What do you think they're up to?" asked David, frowning, his eyebrows knotted real tight.

I couldn't figure it out either. But as soon as they got to the American wing, Nikolai and his gang stopped in front of the elevators, and I realized what was going on. "Looks like they're taking her to the upper level. We can't exactly get in the elevator with them. *That* would be some scene. We'll have to take the stairs."

The instant the elevators doors closed, we zipped into the stairwell and beat them to the second floor by maybe ten seconds. Just enough time to hide behind a corner wall. The elevator bell "dinged," and David craned his neck around the corner. "Damn," he muttered.

I couldn't see at all. I shoved him and whispered loudly, "What? What?"

"Hey, just the Nikolai dude and my grandmother got off. The other two schmucks must still be lurking around downstairs someplace. I don't like that."

"Yeah, you're right, just what we need. Vlad and Sergei sneaking up behind us. They're sure casing everything around and double-checking their tracks. We gotta look sharp and keep our eyes behind our heads. Like you peel them one way and I'll look the other. They're sure not the type of guys that would take in an exhibit."

"Steal one is more like it," he snorted. "Come on, they're getting away."

Nikolai and Mrs. Rosen crossed a room full of Rembrandts and Vermeers. Whenever we came here, Mrs. Rosen always raved about the Flemish and Dutch painters. She said nobody could depict light like Vermeer did.

But Nikolai wasn't interested in light. His head swiveled on his thick neck like a well-oiled office chair. He was obviously looking for something in particular. Then he yanked Mrs. Rosen past whole universes of medieval Crucifixions and Last Judgments and rows of psychedelic Heavens crammed with smiling, spaced-out angels with bright wings like tropical birds. Mrs. Rosen pointed at a far doorway, and Nikolai jerked her in that direction.

When David saw the big Russian nearly drag his grandmother out of her shoes, he growled, "I'm gonna go postal on his sorry ass!" Two anemic-looking art students behind us sitting cross-legged on the floor sketching a Rubens nearly dropped their charcoal pencils.

I held a finger to my lips and winked at them. "Sssssshh! Sudden moves make him go crazy." At which point one of the girls glared back at me, so I gave her a thumb's up. "Love that black mascara and matching cat suit look. It's so . . . so . . . yesterday." I was getting out of control again. But it kept me loose to let off steam.

"Leave them alone, Lauren, and hurry up!" David hissed, grabbing my hand. Cool! But was this the only way a guy I really liked would take my hand – only on dangerous missions?

Winding through rooms full of Old Masters, we trailed Nikolai and Mrs. Rosen as closely as we dared, stopping often to check behind us for Vlad and Sergei, who must have been still checking out for a undercover cops tailing her. I doubted they were on the lookout for two fired-up kids shadowing Mrs. Rosen, especially since I was such a wimp yesterday. Well, wherever they were, they hadn't spotted us yet.

Once we accidentally drew too close to Mrs. Rosen and Nikolai and had to pretend we were engrossed in a picture, making sure only the back of our heads was visible. Then we loitered in front of a wild dream of El Greco for a minute and watched them out of the sides of our eyes. When they turned a corner, David and I both let out a sigh of relief. I realized how tense I was . . . which was down and out, warp speed, way too much caffeine type tense. My heart was aerobicizing.

We caught up with them again in the Impressionist gallery. Nikolai was talking real loud and jabbing his fingers at some pictures. He positioned Mrs. Rosen in front of Van Gogh's *Cypresses* and stabbed at it like he wanted to push his greasy fist through the canvas. Actually touching it – or the frame – with his hand.

This really got the attention of a very short uniformed attendant. The poor little guy looked like this was the last thing he wanted to do today – confront a big ferocious-looking guy with a Russian accent. But he rose to the occasion and took his radio caller off his belt, ready to call for back-up. This was going to be interesting.

"Sir?" we heard him say as he approached Nikolai. "Pardon me." But Nikolai was too busy griping at David's grandmother to hear him. So the attendant tapped Nikolai on the shoulder. You couldn't fault the attendant for not trying. "Sir, please step back. The museum doesn't allow visitors to get that close to the paintings."

Nikolai suddenly noticed the little guy and turned on him like a rabid Doberman. "Get away from me, you miserable worm, or you'll be eating through a straw the rest of your life!"

The attendant's face went fish-belly white and he backed away fast – lifting his radio phone in his hand. When Nikolai saw the radio caller, he backed off himself, apologizing in the most phony voice, saying he was upset about something else and was sorry he was startled by him. I'm pretty sure it was one of the major shocks of the attendant's life. You don't usually meet people as gross as Nikolai in museums. You're more likely to find them in alleyways like rats. But Nikolai fawned over him, playing Mr. Nice Guy to the hilt. The attendant seemed satisfied and never made his call.

After a brief stop by some Monet lily pads, Nikolai directed Mrs. Rosen over to Cezanne's *Card Players*. Right there in front of the earthy peasants hunched over their cards, Nikolai had a certified tantrum. I noticed he looked all around him to make sure no security guards or attendants were around before he went off. But Mrs. Rosen, cool as the ice at Wollman rink, only stared at him with a raised eyebrow like she would at a screaming toddler. That's when I saw the little attendant guy again, keeping his distance as he watched Nikolai freaking out. Why didn't he call Security? I wondered. Maybe he just thought Nikolai was a bit over-excited. Or maybe he had and we couldn't tell. Then the attendant was called away.

"This is definitely the art tour from hell!" I said under my breath.

Nikolai finally shut up and smoldered for a minute while Mrs. Rosen, ignoring him, studied the painting. She tilted her head in the beautiful way I knew so well. Cezanne was her favorite painter.

I watched David bite his lips and clench his fists while I held him back and managed at the same time to look over my shoulder for Vlad and Sergei.

Sometimes when you're really nervous, you just have to laugh. At least that's how I've always been. And we were both really nervous. I started to laugh a little, as David shot a look at me. I have to admit, looking back, that in a way things actually were kind of funny. For one thing, David and I had to keep ducking around people, which looked really stupid to say the least. Then during Nikolai's little fit, we hid behind a bewildered family of southern tourists and pretended to study one of Gauguin's naked Tahitian girls, her skin all brown like sandalwood. The worried mom wasn't sure their ten-year old son should be staring so hard at the girl's . . . er, chest area, I think she called it.

For his part, little ten year old "Bobby Ray" seemed definitely okay with the whole chest area situation, calling out his satisfaction with "This is really good art."

Then things changed pretty fast.

Chapter Fifteen

Nikolai grunted and grabbed Mrs. Rosen by the arm again. He was losing his patience. "I asked you a question, you withered old bitch!" he suddenly snarled, loud enough for everyone in the whole room to hear. No attendant or security guard was in sight.

"Oh my stars!" the southern mom exclaimed in shock.

"I'll kill him!" spat David, starting to spring.

I grabbed his jacket and held him back. "Wait, David! Don't blow our cover! He's not going to do anything to her here. Let's see where they're going!" I was sure Nikolai wouldn't hurt Mrs. Rosen . . . not here anyway with cameras and guards all over the place.

Nikolai escorted, more like strong-armed, Mrs. Rosen out of the room. And now David and I weren't tailing them any more – we were flat out chasing them. Neither of us wanted to think about what might happen if we lost them.

He whisked her into the wing with all the modern art. Paintings filled with abstract splotches, fluorescent drips and bold brush strokes of green, red, yellow, covered the walls. *My* favorite part of the museum. But this time he didn't look at any paintings. Puffing like an out of shape contestant in the NYC Marathon, he pulled Mrs. Rosen up a flight of stairs at the far end of the room.

"Where in the hell is he taking her now?" David

looked sick to his stomach.

"The Cantor roof garden. That's the only place those stairs lead to."

"Where?"

"The Sculpture Garden. Sometimes your grandmother and I eat lunch there and talk about stuff. That's the only place they could be going."

By now we were running. Vlad and Sergei were still nowhere to be seen. We flew up the stairs and threw open the outside doors. Cool air and sunlight hit us in the face, and I blinked. All across the terrace, a forest of bronze and marble statues were scattered like a chain of volcanic islands rising from the sea. Below us Central Park spread out like a leafy quilt, and in the distance beyond a hedge of trees stood the westside skyline, its steel and glass slabs fanned out like gigantic tombstones. There was also the sound of a siren wailing nearby.

David started to panic. "Where are they? I don't see — "

"Sssssshh!" I pulled him behind a statue. "Over there. Look!" Nikolai and Mrs. Rosen stood by the railing at the far end of the patio. And there suddenly were Sergei and Vlad on either side of them.

"They must've gone on ahead," I almost choked. "They . . . they took the stairs, I guess."

"Yeah," David replied. He nervously scratched the back of his head. "We're damn lucky they didn't catch us on the way."

I swallowed hard and agreed. As the three Russians circled their captive "guest" like wolves, Nikolai reached inside his coat. David sucked in his breath and was halfway in the air, but I grabbed his sleeve and held him back again. I saw that Nikolai had only pulled out a small notebook.

David's forehead wrinkled. "What the hel – ?" Then it dawned on him. "Hey, is that it?"

"Yeah, Joshua's Diary!" I whispered.

Nikolai hit the little book's cover with the back of his hand. Mrs. Rosen turned away and held her head high. Nikolai grabbed her chin and waved the Diary under her nose like it was a knife.

"She's not cooperating," said David, observing every detail as intensely as I was. "I knew she wouldn't. She's too stubborn . . . and too gutsy for her own good," he added.

Nikolai started yelling and waving his arms again. Then he yanked his tie up over his head like a noose and stuck his tongue out the side of his mouth. The expressive type, to be sure.

Without a word, Mrs. Rosen reared back and slapped him. The smack detonated like a shot. A yuppie-looking couple quickly hurried for the exit. "Awesome!" I said to myself, half aloud, with my hand clapped over my mouth.

David lurched forward, but I stopped him once again.

Nikolai was so furious I could see him actually shaking with rage. Sergei and Vlad moved behind Mrs. Rosen, trying to pin her arms, but she swatted at them. What a gal! She looked indestructible. I was really proud of her spunk and fighting spirit. I still knew they wouldn't harm her here, especially with all the heavy security around, and that there was more to come. Of course no security witnessed what we had just now or they'd have been all over them.

"Let's sneak closer," I said. I didn't have to ask twice. David was already gone.

In short bursts David crept from statue to statue, crouching next to their granite pedestals for cover. I caught up with him behind a pair of Rodin's entwined lovers, their bodies melting into each other like hot butter. To our right was a big chunk of black rock shaped like a donut on steroids. Even under pressure, I recognized it as a Henry Moore. Mrs. Rosen had taught me well.

We were on our hands and knees now. Crawling closer until we were only about ten yards away, we hid behind a Brancusi bird, all gleaming like chrome. Then we ducked down behind the last spot of cover between them and us. When I looked up, a bronze ballerina smiled down at me in mid pirouette. My throat tightened at the sight, for the sculpture was one of Mrs. Rosen's.

David elbowed me and nodded his head at them.

Attracted by all the commotion, a security guard was hurrying over to investigate. Finally! But Vlad spotted him and quickly said something to Nikolai, who immediately tucked the Diary inside his coat. Then he lightly placed his hands on her shoulders and turned her around, so they were both facing the guard.

For his part, the young guard looked like the kind of guy who ate lunch every Sunday with his Mom in Brooklyn. He was prematurely bald with a major beer belly on him. It looked like he'd been trying to grow a mustache without much luck, too. Completely clueless about what he was getting into, he walked right up to Mrs. Rosen and her disgusting escorts with the kind of reckless self-confidence determined people sometimes have.

We could hear everything now. Even his popping the wad of gum he was chewing as he confronted them. "WHAT'S THE MATTER HERE? DO YOU NEED ASSISTANCE OR SOMETHING?" he asked irritably and boldly, looking straight at Nikolai. "Like maybe assistance outta here?" The accent was straight from Flatbush Avenue.

After waiting for an explanation with some impatience, he asked Mrs. Rosen if she was all right.

Just at that point, Nikolai whispered in Mrs. Rosen's ear and then eased his hand inside his coat. Damn if he didn't pull out a gun! My heart dropped through my stomach seeing it. But the guard couldn't. Only I could from where I was hiding.

"Jesus Christ!"

"What's going on? You gotta tell me, Lauren," David demanded, unable to see from where he was hiding.

I motioned at him to be quiet and held my breath. Nikolai stuck the pistol's silencer-tipped barrel in the small of Mrs. Rosen's back. She went stiff and the color drained out of her face. Nikolai grinned at the guard like a chimp, but he didn't notice a thing. I thanked God David didn't see the gun because he'd have burst upon the Russians like a rocket and could have ruined everything. I was convinced that our cover was everything.

Mrs. Rosen cleared her throat and said something, but I couldn't hear. She repeated it again, as if to reassure him.

The guard looked skeptical. "Are you sure, lady?" I could hear him clearly. "You're positive you're okay?"

She nodded and waved her hand slightly, royalty style.

"Well, whatever," he sighed. "I was just checking." Turning toward Sergei and Vlad, the guard brayed loudly, "WELCOME TO OUR COUNTRY!" in just the way some Americans talk to foreigners. "You and your aunt have a nice day. Just keep your voices down, why don't you."

Sergei gave a fake smile while Vlad's looked more like a scowl.

The guard then spoke into his radio caller. "This is Sam. Everything's okay here. False alarm. Over." Then he hitched up his belt and strode off.

Nikolai waited until the security guard disappeared and shook his finger in Mrs. Rosen's face. I caught just one word of what he had said. *Veronica.* Then he jerked his head at Sergei and Vlad, who immediately headed for the stairs. David and I had to duck as the two thugs passed within a yard of us. But I still got a big whiff of some hair-curling body odor and stale alcohol.

Nikolai patted Mrs. Rosen's cheek but she turned her face away with revulsion. He just laughed and swaggered off to say something to his buddies.

For a moment Mrs. Rosen swayed on her feet like a boxer about to go down for the count. Nikolai had really gotten to her. She looked a hundred years old. A gust of wind blew a loose strand of hair across her eyes, which seemed to revive her. Carefully tucking the refugee hair back into her bun, she steadied herself on the terrace railing and worked her way to a nearby bench and sat down. That's when she put her face in her hands and wept. She looked so alone.

I rubbed David's shoulder. "I wish we could go over to her. I wonder what Nikolai's up to now."

As if on cue, Nikolai turned and went back to Mrs. Rosen. "Come now," he said in a more civilized voice, as he took her arm and helped her to her feet.

Vlad and Sergei fell in step behind them. As they passed right by us, we dropped to the floor tying our shoelaces behind the sculpture. They could see us, all right, but not our faces. And they weren't looking for kids shadowing them whose heads were ostriches in the floor.

"Uh, oh," I whispered after they passed. "This doesn't look good. I think now's the time for us to do something. David, try to find a security guard fast while I call 911! There's got to be one close by; they're usually all over the place lately."

"I was just about to say the same thing. Damn right! Now's the time."

I fished in my purse for my cell phone neatly zipped in a side pocket. "The police are out in front – lots of them – and can be radioed in an instant. And there were certainly a couple of downstairs. At least we'll all have to pass them leaving the museum anyway." I was so nervous I was half-talking to myself.

Meanwhile Nikolai was whisking Mrs. Rosen so fast ahead of us that he was almost carrying her. "Hurry, we'll lose them!" David half-screamed.

Just then, Vlad turned around and looked straight at us. Or so we thought. We had to make a sharp move to the right and turn our faces toward another sculpture, as though we were admiring it.

When we looked back, they were gone. David was frantic. "Oh, God! We lost them! Hurry, Lauren!" I had just pulled the cell phone out of my purse when David yanked me with him.

We thundered down the stairs and burst into the medieval art wing where we were in for a real surprise. The Museum's Great Hall was a real mob scene now. The noise was deafening with so many voices bouncing off the stone walls like ocean waves crashing on the shore. A hundred buses must have unloaded at the same time, which also meant that almost everyone knew each other and were all talking at once! Also it was the weekend and about lunchtime, too. Wall to wall people not only blocked our path but our vision as well.

"Do you see them, David? Oh, no, where's my cell phone? Oh, David, I must have dropped it when we ran down the stairs! Maybe when you grabbed me. Oh, God, I can't find it!"

"Forget it, we'll find Security – they're all over here." Security Guards were there all right but scattered so far away, they were impossible to reach or call to with such a mob. "But where's my grandmother and those bastards?" David was desperate. We were hemmed in with nowhere to turn. He hopped up and down on his toes, trying to catch a glimpse of them but they were nowhere in sight.

Oh, great, I thought. We lost Mrs. Rosen and Nikolai, *and* my cell phone, *and* we couldn't reach any Security Guards. What a team.

"You look that way, I'll cover this side!" he gasped almost hysterically. "We'll work our way to the front entrance." But it looked hopeless. Jumping up and down to see, while zigzagging a path through the impossibly dense crowd, we tried to push our way to the front of the museum. I'd never seen so many people in my life – it looked like they were giving away free lotto tickets or something.

"THERE THEY ARE!" David shouted. "Over there making their way up the middle!"

"Are there any guards near them? There are some over by the – "

"Too far away. We'll never get to them in time."

"We've got to do something, David!"

I just caught a glimpse of the back of Nikolai's bullet-shaped head before it disappeared into the human flood swirling in the Great Hall. At about the same time the Japanese tour group we'd joined earlier, their guide waving a little flag to keep them in line, struggled against the tide of people streaming in. In fact, one of the guys recognized us and smiled, just as David and I unfortunately charged right through, scattering them like bowling pins. I felt really bad about that.

The Russians and Mrs. Rosen were now only about thirty feet away from the front door. Sergei and Vlad strong-armed her on either side, while Nikolai struggled slightly behind an army of first and second graders who suddenly burst through the entrance and starting shoving through. Their teachers were beside themselves trying to contain them.

"What now?" I asked, after fighting our way close enough so that Mrs. Rosen and her Russian escorts were now only about twelve feet in front of us. With like 500 moving bodies stacked up between them and us.

Meanwhile the parade of exuberant children kept pouring through the door, holding hands and jabbering, their eyes craning all around, their high-pitched voices enthusiastically joining the din in the Great Hall. Nikolai was surrounded by hundreds of tiny little people. I mean, he absolutely could not move in the sea of seven year olds – who aren't exactly the politest people in the world – mowing him down at every turn. It was a regular Oshkosh stampede. I even heard one of their teachers pleading with them to let the "nice man" through, which they ignored, of course.

Now it was Nikolai's turn to look dumb and bewildered. The children were in tight formation, all right. This was finally something he couldn't deal with by being obnoxious and throwing his weight around. He looked with frustration at Sergei and Vlad waiting for him by the door where they were standing arm in arm with Mrs. Rosen in the middle. Vlad, smirking at Nikolai's predicament, let go of Mrs. Rosen and actually lit a cigarette inside the building. A real barbarian.

But right behind him suddenly were two Security Guards. David and I exchanged looks when we saw them. Our last chance. "GUARD! GUARD!" David and I called wildly. But, unable to hear us above the thundering noise all around us, all they did was tell Vlad to put out his cigarette.

"What'll we do if we can't get to them in time?" I yelled as we pressed our way forward through the wall to wall bodies.

My ears ached from all the noise. We were only about ten feet away from Nikolai, still knee deep in all the children, and slightly ahead of him on his left. I hid my face from him and the others.

The second Security Guard moved away, which left the other one standing near the front in our direction. What a tall order. Getting his attention was not only impossible but he didn't exactly look like he could handle three burly fighting machines with weapons who cared nothing about human life or human stampedes at the sound of a gun going off. The Guard looked like a weakling compared to them. And then getting through this colossal crowd on the front steps to the police cars out front wasn't going to be simple either when Nikolai and the others could so easily get lost in the crowd outside. Plus Nikolai's crew were all armed! And Mrs. Rosen would be right in the line of fire! No, none of it was looking good at all. There were other guards but they were way too far away.

"Wait! I have an idea. Watch me!" David blurted out suddenly.

"What?" I didn't like the sound of that. "What's going on?"

"I'm going to get the Diary – "

"You're crazy! How can you possibly – ?"

"I think I can get it out of his coat pocket in this jammed up mess of people. He'll never suspect it. His coat is open now – maybe he doesn't realize it – from making his way through this crowd. I just saw the Diary, the top of it, when he turned to throw a kid out of the way. Also, he's never seen me before. Up close, anyway. I think I can sneak up and bump into him."

"You're crazy!" I groaned, shaking my head.

"Have you any better ideas?

183

He had me there. "Oh, God, David, be careful!"

He turned around and gave me the "Duh" look. Then I heard him say, "Watch me . . . and get ready to haul ass!" as he moved away.

Mrs. Rosen and the others were still at the door waiting for Nikolai to catch up. There were now four Security Guards at the entrance, with at least three cops nearby but Mrs. Rosen hadn't done anything like scream for "Help" or made any other attempt to get their attention. Either they had guns at her back hidden in their coat pockets, and she didn't want to risk anyone's life in this sea of moving flesh, or she had decided that it was best to go with them because of Veronica. No question about it. That was who she was.

David meanwhile had made good progress through a whole other roaring river of kids aimed right in Nikolai's direction. I glanced back at Sergei who moved slightly away from the Security Guards. He joined Vlad and Mrs. Rosen who were standing back further now, though I could barely see them. So none of them were looking at Nikolai now since he was so close to the door finally.

David somehow wedged himself in between the stack of human bodies entering and leaving at the same time and got real close to his mark. Nikolai was only now about ten feet from the main entrance when David saw his chance. He bumped straight into Nikolai. I mean, he really rammed him.

Then, damn, if he didn't do it! Expertly he lifted the Diary out of Nikolai's coat pocket. If I blinked, I would have missed it. It was unbelievable! David didn't even break tempo. He just snatched the Diary, tucked it under his arm and resumed his fussing. He actually adjusted Nikolai's collar! And the whole time he kept up a really exaggerated "I'm-such-a-klutz!" routine, making like a bumbling tourist full of apologies. Even adding a nice touch by actually patting Nikolai and rearranging his coat by the shoulders. What a sight that was!

Nikolai pushed him away in disgust. Between David and the little kids, he was really going nuts.

David winked at me and moved on. I'd gotten real close by this time and fell in right behind him. When we were almost out the door, Vlad darkened the entrance. Oh God, I thought in a panic and froze.

"Keep going, for Chrissakes!" David hissed, pulling his cap down. "He doesn't know me – just look the other way and pull your hat down more so your hair is covered. That way he'll only see the back of your head."

I felt all hot and faint as I started to pass by Vlad with my head down so all he could see was the top of my tight knit hat. We were doomed.

No, we weren't! Vlad had completely missed me because he was too busy ogling back at Nikolai. We walked right past him and got outside where Sergei was standing slightly behind Mrs. Rosen with one hand in his pocket pressed up against her back. There was the gun, all right, though I really couldn't see it except for the slight bulge in his pocket. Mrs. Rosen was looking the other way and didn't see us either!

As we passed through the door with the crush of people behind us, the police were no longer near the entrance. There was some big commotion going on and they were questioning someone who didn't look very happy about it. If only it had been Nikolai or one of the others. It wasn't though. I couldn't figure out what was happening.

Then I noticed three security guards escorting another man over to the police. Either way, they were far beyond our reach or our voices even if we tried to call out to them. They were moving down the stairs fast with the two men in tow. A fire truck's siren was blaring full blast as it passed right in front of the museum on its way down Fifth.

We were half-way down the steps when suddenly from inside the building someone screamed like a wild animal. It was Nikolai. I recognized his voice even over the helicopter that was beating overhead. Vlad jumped like he'd been shot out of a cannon and rushed to the door. Nikolai nearly climbed over him crashing through the doorway.

Murderously red in the face, he kept clawing at his coat and shouting in Russian. That's when he spotted me. "YOOOUU!!!!" he screamed.

"RUN!" yelled David.

He didn't have to tell me twice. The chase was on.

Chapter Sixteen

We bolted down the main steps, three and four at a time, moving so fast we were almost out of control.   All the way down, in a picture of true grace I'm sure, I windmilled my arms like the bald-headed stooge of the Three Stooges.   More than once, I nearly ate concrete.   I could hear the Russians almost on our heels right behind us.   They were in no mood for this.   Their shoes slapped on the pavement like gunshots as we sprinted across the museum's main plaza.   People scattered like pigeons.   And the real pigeons scattered too!

"Where to?" I shouted.

"DOWN FIFTH!" David hollered.

To tell the truth, when I heard that, I didn't think he meant it literally.   I kind of thought we'd, you know, use the sidewalk, not actually run down the middle of the street.   I'll give him one thing – David is full of surprises.

The Fifth Avenue traffic was grid-locked bumper to bumper in front of the Museum.   The fire truck was practically on the sidewalk trying to get past the gridlock, its siren still wailing.   As we shimmied through the cars, David shouted over his shoulder at me.   "Stick tight!"

I screamed just in time.   "David! Look out!"   David teetered on the edge of the curb like a guy about to fall off a tightrope.   A speeding bike messenger whizzed by within a foot of his nose.

"Thanks!" yelled David. Then in one jump, he leapt off the sidewalk like an acrobat right onto a blue Firebird with Jersey plates in the street, sliding across the car's hood.

Just then three Bridge and Tunnelers with major perms screamed and squealed inside the Firebird. As the big-haired driver slapped at the automatic locks, I got a close look at the longest fake nails I'd ever seen in my life. Here goes nothing, I thought and I went up and over the car. The girls inside the car just gawked at me like I was a crook on the run and started screaming all over again.

Vlad slammed into and rolled across the top of the girls' car like a split second after me, holding out his hands to catch me. But he came up empty and crashed. Over my shoulder, I caught a glimpse of him spinning on the asphalt like an amateur breakdancer.

Sergei helped him up but I was long gone by now. Nikolai shrieked bloody murder at them for slowing down.

"Guess what!" I shouted. "They left your grandmother behind! All three of them are after us."

"That's great!"

We began to weave in and out of idling taxis and delivery vans like they were poles on a slalom course. You could track our progress just by the noise alone. Brakes screeched. Horns honked. Taxi drivers cussed. A regular Manhattan chorus.

The Russians weren't built for this kind of work, that's for sure. Breaking arms was one thing; dodging Fed Ex trucks was another. They stayed pretty close to us for a couple of blocks, but then they started to fall back. All that smoking, I guess.

Somewhere pretty far behind us, I heard Nikolai screaming at a cabby. It seemed like the cabby was holding his own – and then some.

We hit the sidewalk on the east side of Fifth Avenue just as a florist's delivery van was unloading on the curb. When a beefy guy suddenly emerged from around the corner of the van with an armload of tulips, we were almost on top of him.

"EXCUSE US!" David shouted.

The delivery guy looked up in mild surprise. But when he saw us coming at him, his eyes got real big and he screamed like a chicken, throwing the flowers up in the air, just like in a sitcom or something. For a second, it rained tulips.

"Sorry!" I shouted as we sprinted past. I'm not sure he accepted my apology. Not after hearing what he told me to do to myself anyway.

We jay-ran through two more intersections getting some stares, double-takes, "Watch it's!" and "Hey you's!" But to tell the truth, most people didn't pay too much attention to us. You see a lot of funny things in New York. Two kids running down the street, ducking down side streets and hiding behind cars, is pretty par for the course. Three men built like refrigerators running – now that's another story. But I couldn't see them behind us any more. We were sprinters, while they were, well, not in the greatest condition from all their booze and cigarettes, I thought to myself, feeling pretty smug at the thought.

Finally we stopped to catch our breath. We were on 76th, rounding the corner near Madison. "David, can you see them?"

He turned and jogged backwards for a few steps scanning the faces of all the many weekend pedestrians behind us. "Guess what! I think maybe we lost them."

I let out a big sigh and slowed to a walk. We lost the Russians. Definitely. "Excellent. That was fun!"

David laughed. "You're weird." He was panting big time as we both started to get back our wind. Then he took the Diary out of his jacket and inspected it. "So this is it, huh?"

"Yeah, that's it!" I, too, examined the small leather book David held in his hands. Its cover was grimy and cracked. It didn't look like anything special, but I knew it was. I really felt it in my heart. And after hearing Mrs. Rosen's story, I felt like I knew Joshua, too. I watched David thumb through its yellowed pages. Maybe in a way I really did know Joshua. At least, I saw his courage reflected in David. And that made me feel good.

"What next?" I asked. "Where's your grandmother?

"Okay now, we gotta get to her! I bet she went straight back home. You know, like . . . so she can wait for Nikolai's next call about Veronica."

"Or better yet, that she went straight to the police!"

"Fat chance of that. She's too careful to call them and risk Veronica's life."

"Yeah, you're right."

"Will she ever be amazed to see this!" he exclaimed, patting Joshua's Diary in his pocket. "This changes everything now! If she's home by the time we get there, we'll get a cab and take her to my house – to my parents – she'll be safe there. But it'll be close. We've got to keep one step ahead of the Russians. Maybe they let her go today because they held all the chips. Or maybe we screwed it all up for them so that she managed to get away when they started chasing us. Now that we have the Diary, well – " Suddenly he looked real worried. "Let's find a phone first and I'll tell her to go straight to my parents and we'll meet her there."

"There's no telling what they might do now," David added. He looked a little queasy as he started to realize that he actually may have put her in jeopardy.

"You think? Maybe we should just call the police."

"Wait. We can't yet. Now that she's okay and not with the Russians, I think it's best to put the ball back in her court. Remember their threat about Veronica. It's got to be my grandmother's decision. And I don't think they'll harm either one of them now that we have the Diary."

But to myself I thought of things like fingers or ears of kidnapped victims cut off and sent to family members to make them act faster handing over ransoms. I shivered and shook the image out of my mind. I couldn't think about that now.

"And the Diary?"

He chewed his lip. "On second thought, you're right. We're in pretty deep now. The police have to be called. But from my parents. We'll tell them everything and I know they'll call the police immediately."

Like David said, let the police take over from here. Despite our promise to Mrs. Rosen. Well, he and his father would just have to convince her that they had to be contacted now.

When we found a pay phone that didn't have a line of two or three people waiting, David got no answer. "She's not there yet. Better get moving fast." He turned to hail a cab, but we couldn't find one. "We better cut through the Park again. There's too much traffic anyway."

A light breeze ruffled the awnings along Madison Avenue. It was a still a beautiful day. Not a cloud in the sky. I felt that kind of good tired you get after you exercise, though we were moving pretty fast up the street. Maybe, just maybe, I thought, everything was going to turn out okay after all. Just maybe.

We passed some fancy shops on our way. Sonia Rykiel. Donna Karan. Chanel. Armani. Cartier. Expensive stationers and parfumiers. Jewelry stores. Typical Mom territory. I noticed a pair of humongous sapphire and diamond earrings in one window that Mom would've loved when a fast-moving blur reflected in the plate glass window caught my eye. I had a bad feeling and whirled around just as a black Mercedes Limo screeched to the curb.

"Oh, hell!" I shouted.

The car hadn't even come to a stop when the back door flew open and Nikolai leaped out, his silencer-equipped pistol drawn. His eyes were demonically focused on David and me, and his face went ballistic with rage. "HEY, YOU!" he shouted, calling out to me with pure venom. "STOP!"

Then Nikolai fired. You couldn't hear the gun shots with the silencer on. Only THUP, THUP, THUP, THUP, THUP. Bullets shattered all the expensive crystal vases in the window next to me as the plate glass broke and fell down in sheets, crashing to bits on the sidewalk.

I shielded my arm over my eyes to keep from getting cut by flying glass. People on the street panicked, screaming and rushing everywhere. A man threw himself on top of his little girl, protecting her with his body. One woman, beyond hysteria, who dropped her shopping bags and ran smack into Nikolai, saved my life. Knocked off balance just as he was aiming for my head, he fired his sixth shot straight up in the air. Hey, this was Giuliani's City! How could he do that in broad daylight! I thought, utterly stupefied and in shock. New York was too protected for this to happen.

David nearly pulled my arm out of its socket. "GO! GO! GO!"

We left the sidewalk and ran into the street without looking. Two taxis rear-ended each other right in front of us. A station wagon tried to brake, went into a fishtail spin, and smashed into them. All down the block, sheet metal crumpled and car alarms shrieked. Madison Avenue was in chaos. Another shot ricocheted near my feet with a splat and

a high-pitched whee sound.   Silent bullets and flying glass!
– this was really serious now.   There I was, slipping on shards,
running for my life.   I was in way over my head.   I had to call
911, I thought, reaching in my pocket, and then remembered
I'd lost my cell phone.

"WE GOTTA GET TO THE PARK!" David shouted.
"We'll lose them in the Ramble."

The Ramble. I loved the Ramble. David was right! It
was a woody, hilly area crisscrossed by footpaths and streams.
Bird-watchers went nuts for this part of the park.   It's like a
jungle, and it's a real great place to hide.   We managed to race
west on 77th, sprint across Fifth, reach the other side of the
street without getting run over, and scramble over the park
wall.   Just as David was swinging his leg over, a bullet smacked
into the wall, showering us in dust and granite chips.

My cheek stung.   What was unnerving was that you
couldn't hear the shots because of the silencers, only hear the
ricochets or *feel* them!   The police down by the Met couldn't
hear any of this.   Especially above the sound of the sirens that
were now blaring by the museum.   And that helicopter was
back too.   What was going on now back there?   They were
needed here!   It was a busy day in New York – that's for sure.

I pulled David down on top of me, and we crouched
down low as another bullet hit the wall.   Then another.   And
another.   It sounded like someone was popping bricks with a
wet towel.   All we could do was keep our heads down.

Suddenly the shots stopped and David peeked over
the wall. "His clip's empty, but he's reloading.   It looks like
the Limo's taking the 79th Street Transverse. "Of course!"
he said, smacking his head.   "They're gonna try to cut us off!
We've got to get to the woods!   If they catch us in the open,
we've had it!"   He looked me in the eyes and took a deep
breath. "One, two, three . . . GO!"

We shot out of there like racehorses at the starting gate. We had to get there before they did! By the time we crossed Park Drive, I had a cramp in my side, but there was no way I was stopping until we got to the trees. We hit the tree line and thrashed through the bushes. Then David pointed to an enormous boulder draped with tangled undergrowth. "There! Over there! We'll hide."

Collapsing behind the rocks, we sat there panting for air while our lungs burned. Police sirens finally wailed in the distance. But were they for us? Children squealed and boom boxes blared. And right next to us, a flock of tiny sparrows landed and flitted through the leaves, chirping and bickering.

Suddenly they scattered with a loud flutter. David held his finger to his lips. But it was only an anorexic blonde in a neon pink crop top and matching shorts roller-blading down the hilly path to where we were. She stopped and took a sip from her Evian bottle. I recognized her from Mom's copies of "W" – one of those supermodels, but I wasn't sure which one – I get them all confused.

After she was gone, David cocked his head and listened some more. When he was satisfied that Nikolai wasn't anywhere around, he leaned towards me. "We're too close to the footpath. We need to move deeper into the bushes." Then he frowned and gently touched my face. "You're bleeding."

I felt my cheek. My fingers were spotted with blood. "I think it's just a scratch," I said, shrugging my shoulders. "Like from – what do they call it on the news? – oh, you know, a bullet fragment." I was really tough.

David dug in his pocket and handed me a blue bandana. "Here, it's clean, I promise. Does it hurt?"

I wrinkled my nose. "Nah." This was a slight lie.

"You see any cops yet?"

"No. Nowhere. Something's going on at the Met.

Or on Fifth. I still hear the sirens," I said.

We were about to move to another spot when we heard voices. Instantly we dropped down and lay flat on our bellies. But it was just four or five guys on mountain bikes whirring down the path talking about the Yankees.

"Okay!" called David. We snuck deeper into the Park, stopping every once and a while to listen. Once we almost stepped right on a couple rolling around and making out in the middle of some ferns. I nearly had a coronary, but they didn't seem to notice us. Finally we found a really thick patch of shrubbery and David said, "This is the place. We can see out and they can't see in. We'll wait them out here."

On our hands and knees we crawled into the bushes – and not an instant too soon, it turned out. Our hiding place was a good one, dark and cool and all with soft ivy to sit in, but we didn't have time to enjoy it. David had just rearranged the bushes to camouflage where we got in when we heard a woman's terrified voice.

"GOOD LORD, VICTOR, HE'S GOT A GUN!"

An older man and woman with a picnic basket hurried past, waddling as fast as they could. A few seconds later, the pair of young lovers we almost stomped on emerged like frightened rabbits. There were bits of leaves and ferns still in their hair and clinging to their backs – the girl had her sweater on backwards – and they ran in the same direction.

"This isn't good," I whispered.

David nodded. "They're still onto us."

"Now that we know they're over there, shouldn't we, um . . ." I pointed, " . . . go that way?"

David looked up and down the trail first to make sure it was safe, and then he motioned to me. "The coast is clear."

Just then we noticed an old man in a hat sitting on a bench reading a Yiddish newspaper and smiling up at us. The old guy seemed really friendly and David called out to him in Yiddish. They exchanged some animated words, after which David thanked him. *"A dank."* The old man smiled and said – *"Nito far vos. Zol zayn mit mazl!"* – and went back to his newspaper.

"What did he say?"

David grinned at me. "That he hadn't seen any *meshuge,* um, crazy *goyim* running around, but if he did he'd say he hadn't seen us. He told us 'Good luck.'"

"What a nice man." I looked back at him and he waved.

We weren't on the path for more than a minute or two when David stopped in his tracks. "I don't like this. It's starting to curve uphill again and we can't see around the bend. We better go cross-country." So we trudged up the slope, balancing on the mossy rocks like a couple of mountain goats. The park was so immense that it was easy to get lost in it. Once I remember my father and I flying over the park when our flight was re-routed pretty low over the City. Looking down, Central Park looked like it was one-fourth of all of Manhattan. That's huge.

I got to the top of the hill first. When I did, I was in for a shock. Nikolai and Sergei were searching the underbrush in the distance, about fifty feet ahead of me, gliding through the shadows with their guns drawn. The predators were out hunting, all right. Hunting for us. But they hadn't seen us yet.

I pushed the palm of my hand towards David, warning him to stay back, and he froze. Slowly I started to back down the hill. Unfortunately, I still had my eye on Nikolai and wasn't watching what I was doing. I stepped on a loose rock and my foot slipped out from under me. A noisy mini-avalanche of rocks and pebbles showered down the hill after me. That's when I heard Nikolai shout – but it wasn't at me!

David helped me up. "Are you all right?"

"Yeah." I took a step. "No!" My ankle felt like it was on fire. I'd twisted it in the fall.

"Put your arm around my shoulder," said David with concern.

"My hero." I hung on to him and, half running, half-hopping, we made it down the hill.

"Did they see you?"

"I don't think so," I answered. "But I don't think we should stick around and ask."

"Neither do I." He looked around. "This is getting old." He adjusted my arm on his shoulder. "This way."

We scrambled back into a thicket, panting and gasping for air. Straight into Vlad!

Chapter Seventeen

Vlad absolutely couldn't believe his luck and just blinked at us. Then he smiled in a big gloating grin, but it didn't improve his features any.

I only thought it worked in movies, but in a flash David picked up a handful of dirt and threw it right into his beady eyes. Vlad cursed in Russian and rubbed his eyes frantically as he took a couple of wild swings at the air.

This was the break we were looking for. My ankle got better . . . real fast! We ran like greyhounds. THUP, THUP, THUP, THUP! Bullets were flying everywhere again. Soundlessly. Leaves fell from the trees. A bee buzzed by my ear. Then I realized it wasn't a bee. It was a bullet. My ankle felt good as new. Better even.

We half-ran, half-tumbled down an incline, splashed across a stream, tore through another batch of dense woods, getting all scratched up from thorns and low tree limbs, and came out on a path full of cyclists and joggers enjoying the afternoon sun. On the benches beside the path, people were playing chess, eating ice cream, laughing with their kids. A street performer juggled for spare change. I even spotted a mime. It was surreal. Everything was so . . . so normal. For them.

David ran over to a neat-looking couple on a two-seater bicycle and trotted alongside them, stripping off his Seiko watch. "Here, I'll give you this if you let us borrow your bike! It's an emergency!" He couldn't have been more sincere or more emphatic.

The woman screamed bloody murder. "GERALD, GIVE HIM YOUR WALLET! HURRY!"

"Wait, lady, you don't get it!" David held up his hand.

"PLEASE DON'T SHOOT!" pleaded Gerald, who looked like he was about to be sick all over his pink Polo shirt while his bike wobbled dangerously.

David rushed back and grabbed my hand. "We don't have time for this! Come on!"

"Look, just call the cops, would you please!" I called back to them. "You have a cell phone? Call them! We need help fast!" But Gerald and the woman on the two-seater cycle couldn't get away from us fast enough. I don't think they got the message.

We found Nikolai and company further down the footpath, wet from the knees down and looking real grim. Sergei pulled out a Mac-10 submachine gun with a silencer as long as a pipe. We dived behind an azalea bush. They hadn't seen us . . . yet. But a lot of people saw them.

Their savage effect on the crowd was something to watch. First, the sidewalk cleared. Then the screaming began. With people rushing back and forth all around them, snatching up kids, hitting the deck or running for their lives – the gangsters slowly paced our way, three abreast. They were so big they took up almost the entire width of the walk. Like terminator robots, they panned their heads side to side, trying to find us. Sergei jacked the bolt on his machinegun. It was only a matter of time before they caught us.

There was nowhere else to run. We were done. Where were New York's finest? Surely they were getting 911 calls now. One of these people had to have a cell phone!

Nikolai cupped a hand to his mouth and called, "COME OUT, COME OUT, WHEREVER YOU ARE, CHILDREN! PLAY TIME'S OVER NOW!"

The hair on the back of my neck stood up. "Pssssst, David."

He turned towards me. "Yeah?"

I gazed deep in his eyes. The Russians got closer and closer.

"What?"

I had to do it. I touched his face. "I love – "

A car honked . . . and kept honking. Three or four blasts followed by a really long one. Then the whole sequence was repeated. And it kept getting louder, like it was getting closer. The Russians stopped in their tracks and listened. So did we.

Nikolai shouted something to Vlad and Sergei in Russian. Instantly after unscrewing the silencer, Sergei put the machine gun inside his coat, as Nikolai and Vlad holstered their pistols.

"Look at the way they're acting," he whispered. "It's a code. Gotta be."

Whatever it was, it saved our hides. The Russians, who would have found us in about another ten steps, mercifully turned off the path and quickly bolted towards the 79th Street cut as the honking got even louder. Then I saw why. There was the black Mercedes Limo honking for Nikolai as he leaped out to flag it down.

"I don't believe it!"

"Holy Moly!" David shouted.

The Limo was actually being pursued by a mounted policewoman about a hundred yards back and gaining. The big old bay horse she rode was lathered in sweat and really moving. And she had her pistol out. Then, damn, if she didn't shoot at one of the Limo's tires. She barely missed. I saw the turf divot somersault where the bullet hit. Reinforcements were right behind her. I heard loud sirens in the distance and coming close fast. At last! Help was on the way! My heart felt like it would jump right out of my chest, I was so relieved and ecstatic.

When the Limo driver spotted Nikolai and his gang, he hit the brakes hard and put it in a nearly terminal slide. Mud splattered everywhere. The car skidded to a halt, and the Russians scrambled toward it.

Then another strange thing happened. The back door of the Limo swung open and I saw a really immaculately dressed older man inside. In his fancy British-cut suit, he looked straight out of a Ralph Lauren ad. His hair was the color of new snow. And then the strangest thing of all happened. He screamed at the thugs in what sounded like German. It all happened so fast, but to me somehow that moment seemed like it was in slow motion.

The Russians sprinted to the car and piled in like clowns at the circus. Its doors barely closed when the Limo spun out, shooting up a roostertail fountain of mud. The mounted policewoman kept right on after it. About ten seconds later, the sound of sirens and whining engines grew unbearable. In a real old-fashioned cavalry charge, four blue NYPD cruisers flew over the crest of a hill at the same time, smashed down on their shocks and roared away after the bad guys.

Like I say, you get used to a lot of things in this city, but even natives had to be impressed by this action. We stood up from behind our bush like meerkats popping out of their burrow. All around us, people slowly got up off the ground as others starting appearing from behind trees. For a few seconds, nobody said a word. I think everyone was just glad to be alive. Especially David and me.

I looked at all the people hugging their kids, the husbands and wives kissing who probably hadn't done that in a while, the people sharing their relief with strangers they ordinarily wouldn't dream of talking to. It was kind of nice. Pretty soon, I figured, everyone would forget and go back to worrying about the same old stuff and acting the same old selfish way.

But . . . but, I don't know, it was weird, I kind of tried to memorize the feeling, sort of imprint it in my brain, I guess, so I could take it out and remember it later. Because it was the sort of thing I <u>had</u> to remember. Mrs. Rosen said so when she told us about the Holocaust. Life is precious, she said; don't waste it on trivial stuff, trivial stuff like being selfish and greedy and mean. That's all fake. Worse than fake. Standing there in the sun, happy to be alive and thrilled to be with David – well, that was precious. That was love. And that was real. The most real thing of all.

"What are you thinking about?"

David startled me. "Oh, uh . . . nothing. Just glad to be alive, I guess."

"You got that right," he smiled, kicking at a dirt clod. "Lauren?"

"Yeah?"

"What, uh, what was that you were going to tell me a minute ago? You know, when the Russians were about to find us."

I blushed. "I just . . . uh, I just wanted you to know, uh . . ."

He looked out over the park. "That's okay. I think I know." He picked an azalea leaf out of my hair. "By the way, how's your ankle?"

"Completely healed."

"Good! If only we had your cell phone! We need

to call my grandmother and warn her to get the hell to my parents and call the police. It's a whole new ballgame now! And she doesn't know it."

If only I hadn't lost it. "Oh, David, I'm sorry."

"It's not your fault. It's theirs. Quick, let's find a pay phone!"

We began to jog towards the West Side. There was one on the corner of 77th and Central Park West, right outside the American Museum of Natural History, which I had used a hundred times before since this was my neighborhood. But we had to wait a minute for some loser in a hooded sweatshirt to quit yelling at his girlfriend and get off the phone.

Finally David dropped his quarter and dialed. "HELLO, *BUBBE*? Thank God, you're there! Yeah, of course I'm fine. It's you I'm worried about! Please listen to me! Get out of there now! . . . What? . . . NO! Listen to me! Don't wait for them to contact you. Something's happened. No time to explain. You have to leave immediately and get to Mom and Dad's now! Lauren and I will meet you there . . . What? . . . Yes, Lauren's with me. We'll meet you there and explain when we – "

I could hear her voice grow louder on the other end of the line.

"Listen. We're already involved, okay? It's too late to change that!" David held up his hand.

Her voice got extra loud. Not mad loud. Just worried grandmother loud.

"We're fine, we're fine." David overrode over her protests. "Look we're wasting time. Just go! . . . Yeah, good idea. Now hurry! . . . Love you, too."

She never knew how we shadowed her every move at the Met and passed right by her on the way out when Nikolai screamed bloody murder and swore at us. If the police hadn't been tied up with something else at that moment, they'd have nabbed him then and there.

As David hung up the phone, he let out a big breath. "I'm glad that's done. She'll be okay at our place. Mom and Dad are home. Wait! I should call them just in case!" He turned back to the phone but two men had already slipped in and were dialing the phone. David said, "Look, this is an emergency! I need to –"

"Get lost, buddy. You already had your chance. We have an emergency too," they said, rolling their eyes.

"Let's go, David. Forget it. What else did she say to you?"

"She knows something's up." He rolled his eyes as he said, "She'll pass out when she finds out what."

"You better believe it."

"Well, it'll be better to tell her in person. But the important thing is she's safe. Drawing their attention away from her worked for now, but they could be there any second. Where else would they go? She said she had already buzzed the doorman to be on the alert and not let them in – and that she'd meet us at my home – and that she'd tell Dad everything so it will all be out in the open and in the hands of the police where it belongs. That she decided herself to go right over to my house and tell my father and call the police together. And that she'd leave this instant."

"Wow! Finally! Well, great minds think alike." I tried to make a lame joke to lighten his load.

Suddenly David looked at the Museum of Natural History and looked like a light bulb flashed over his head. "Wait, I've got an idea! Come on!"

What now? I wondered as he hustled me along with him at top speed through the West 77th Street entrance and up the staircase. David was already ten paces ahead of me when we got through the door into the main hall. And what a sight! It was like everybody who'd been to the Metropolitan Museum was over here now. That's what it looked like anyway! – and like they'd called in all their friends, too. What was this, national museum day or something? Zillions of kids were everywhere.

Then I figured out why – the new Dinosaur Exhibit upstairs that had been advertised all over the City for weeks. It was supposed to even have animatronic things that move and growl and all, which people simply cannot control themselves around. Dinosaurs! I bet if someone founded some kind of Dinosaur Church they'd make tons of money.

For a second, I kind of wished we could take a look at the great whale this museum is famous for. I could never come here without going first to the great room where a life-sized model of a blue whale – something like 100 feet across! – hangs suspended from the ceiling like it's swimming in air. It always amazed me how it didn't come crashing down from the sheer weight of it, especially when I've stood with giddiness directly under it. And then I'd imagine how wonderful it must be to see real live magnificent creatures like this in the ocean. Though I recall someone saying there were only a few blue whales left because most of them have been hunted to extinction.

What a world! Let them all gush over the extinct dinosaurs. But why not save the magnificent whales before they're extinct, too? I shook my head in disgust and went back to thinking about my blue whale here hanging from the ceiling. It was one of my very first memories of my whole life because Dad showed it to me when I was only two years old. So going to see it was kind of like going to visit an old friend, and I always felt better afterwards. If only our path would have taken us through that room. Seeing it would surely make us <u>both</u> feel better – it's that awesome.

But there wasn't time. I tapped David on the shoulder through the crushing trail of kids and grown-ups. "Not that I mind, but what are we here for?"

"To check the Diary for safekeeping at the desk. I . . . I think it's better that way. That way it won't be on me if –" his voice trailed off.

"Brilliant, David! Cool idea. "You mean if we run into our biggest fans again."

"Yeah," he chuckled.

When we checked the Diary, the girl behind the counter acted like it was the most perfectly natural thing in the world. Little did she know how valuable this old shabby book was, and not for what the Russians had in mind. How many lives were in jeopardy – Veronica's, now Mrs. Rosen's, David's and mine, and maybe even his parents – because of this small ordinary-looking, leather bound volume.

And how deeply it was at the very center of so many lives lost when it was written. Lives hunted down for extinction. Another time, another place. And this was now, over fifty years later, and the book still held the power of life and death. It just couldn't have been about smuggled paintings, I thought to myself. There had to be more to Mrs. Rosen's brother Joshua, the hero of the Warsaw Ghetto uprising.

I shrugged and moved away from the check-in desk with David after memorizing the number of the stub he gave me to keep, just in case. The Diary of Joshua, written in the year 1943, would be safe with her in this special place that had my favorite blue whale and the animatronic dinosaurs in the midst of a thousand kids.

Making our way again through the hordes of children all around us, we left the museum through the main Park side entrance and were pretty much on scan mode the whole time we hustled up the street. David lived even closer to the museum than I did so it wasn't far at all to his place. As we approached David's house, a brownstone midway between Columbus Avenue and Central Park West about eight blocks south of our building, we broke into a run. We couldn't wait to finally see his grandmother and call the cops with his Dad.

But she wasn't there! David barely introduced me to his mother when he yanked me back down the steps, calling out to her that we'd forgotten something.

Yeah, his grandmother.

We broke into a frantic run at top speed. My heart was pounding. There was no reason she'd not have arrived at David's place ahead of us. None . . . since she promised to leave the moment she got off the phone with David. She could have been there in five minutes by cab. It took us a good 20 minutes between that phone call and the time it took to check the Diary, run interference through the museum crowds, and run home to his place only blocks away.

My mind was racing as fast as my feet. That could only mean they got to her before she left. But the doorman was alerted. She should have just called the police from the beginning! – right when they kidnapped Veronica. If only I had talked her into it. If only I had tried. If only I had told Mom right off the bat. If only I had called Dad from my cell phone or called the police myself. If only!

Instead Mrs. Rosen bravely faced them all today, and we stole the show from there. But Mrs. Rosen didn't care about her life – she had seen it all – and she certainly wasn't afraid of them. God knows she'd been at the mercy of much worse. So what if the Russians threatened our lives? That was it, of course. It was all because of her concern about Veronica and David's family . . . and me. She sacrificed herself for us.

David and I reached for the front door of my building

207

at the same time.

"HOLD IT! HOLD IT! WHERE'S THE FIRE?" yelled a doorman I'd never met before who blocked our path. Great, I thought, a new guy. Just what we needed now. Red tape and the old getting-to-know-you ID routine. This one looked like he was about sixteen years old. His hat was too big and his ears were mashed down flat. And he was copping an attitude on us.

"Where's Mr. Antonelli?" David demanded to know.

"It's his time off," the new guy answered sarcastically.

"Great!" shouted David with exasperation, trying to push past him.

The doorman grabbed his jacket. "Look, just hold the bus there, hotshot! You're not going anywhere until I say so."

I planted myself between the doorman and David. "Let go of him!" I yelled. "I live here and he's with me and besides you don't understand! His grandmother lives here and she's in trouble! Let us in! Hurry!"

This seemed to throw the doorman. "You have your own apartment?"

I slapped my forehead. "Yes! I live with my mother! Geeez!"

"Let me see your key." He wasn't going to let me pass until I played it by the book. Disgusted, I dug in my pocket and showed him my key.

"Okey, dokey. Go ahead. Just doing my job," he said cheerfully. Which he was, I guess. And I hoped Nikolai and his heavy guns met up with him doing as good a job. But how could he possibly be a match for them?

David looked all wild-eyed and blurted: "Did you see an older woman leave here in the last half hour? Maybe with some men? Big guys – in leather overcoats? Her name is Dominique Rosen," he shouted at the end.

The doorman rubbed his chin. "Sheesh, buddy, this is my first week here. I've seen a few old ladies come in and out, but it's not like I know their names or anything."

"Think!" yelled David.

But the doorman shook his head and kind of looked like he had his feelings hurt. "No, can't say I did . . . not on this shift."

David rushed to the elevator. But both cars were stopped at the top, so we ran for the stairwell and, side by side, attacked the stairs. Our lungs about to pop, we burst out on Mrs. Rosen's landing. Sneaky we weren't any more.

Then David held his arm in front of me. "Tip-toe. Easy. I'll go first."

My initial reaction – "Why, because you're the boy?" – was on the tip of my tongue, but I didn't say it. After all, it was <u>his</u> grandmother in all this trouble. We crept down the hall like thieves. Sure enough, Mrs. Rosen's front door was slightly ajar, and I felt sick to my stomach at the sight. No one leaves their door open.

David mouthed without making a sound: "Stay here!"

"No way!" I mouthed back.

He rolled his eyes and motioned for me to follow him. Expertly, like a federal agent, he ran his fingers along the doorfacing in search of splinters or any other sign of forced entry. Then he gave the door a gentle push; it squeaked on its hinges and made us both cringe and dive down. A few seconds went by as we waited for a reaction from inside. When none came, David slipped through the door and waited for me. My heart pounding, I took a deep breath, and in I went.

Everything looked normal. There was no sign of a struggle – no pulled out drawers, no overturned chairs, no broken lamps. Nothing. The living room was neat and the kitchen looked about like we left it the night before. Mrs.

Rosen's breakfast dishes were still on the table. *The New York Times* was neatly folded back to the international news section at the place where she usually sat.

David pointed to the back of the apartment and we headed down the hall. My heart now was going about 90 miles an hour. The silence was unnerving. This was no fun any more like it was in the Park out in the open and at the Met when David got the best of Nikolai and took Joshua's Diary from him. The exciting part was over.

We stuck our heads in the guest bedroom. Elaborate lace curtains over the window fanned in the breeze. Other than that, everything was still and neat as a pin. The hall bathroom was okay. We checked Dr. Rosen's office – okay just like the afternoon before. The studio was untouched, too. My glob of clay sat atop its newspaper throne, looking all lonely and . . . in desperate need of a lot of work.

The only place left to check was Mrs. Rosen's bedroom. That's when we heard the bumping.

We crouched down and got real still. Down the hall to the front door was a straight enough shot that I figured I could make in about three seconds. But David, looking pretty tense, began to creep towards the bedroom door.

The noise got louder. Bump, bump. Bump! Bump! We stopped just short of the door. I could just imagine Mrs. Rosen gagged and tied to a chair, hopping around the room. That's what the noise sounded like anyway.

David peeked inside. "That's strange."

Whatever it was, it wasn't bad, for I could see his whole body relax as he went in the room. It turned out to be just the screen door leading to the small balcony off Mrs. Rosen's bedroom blowing open in the wind. Sighing in relief, David started to go over and shut it.

"Oh, my God! David, look!" I pointed outside on

the terrace to a potted hibiscus tree knocked over on its side and a man's footprint in the spilled dirt. David rushed to the balustrade and leaned over the side of the building. "They used the fire escape!" But they had long gotten away.

I put my hands on my knees and studied the huge footprint. It could have been Sergei's. He was the tallest. The sight of it really made me sick.

"All right, that's it!" I shouted in disgust, throwing in the towel. "Enough! We're in way over our heads now. They took her! They came straight here after they left us in the park. Or probably notified their other gang members to pick her up when the police were chasing them. And I'm sure the Limo got away too. They had a big head start. Oh, what a fool I was not to beg her to call the police last night! Not to call them myself! We have to call the FBI! She's been kidnapped!"

David sat down in a daze with his head down. "Oh, what have I done! Why did I listen to her and make that promise about not calling the cops? Why did I think I – I mean, *we* could do anything in the meantime? Oh, God, let's call now. Come on!"

We raced back down the hall. "I'll never forgive myself," David was mumbling.

I couldn't let that one slide. "David, it's not your fault! She's so brave! You heard her – she freely chose to meet with them. And, anyway, they're probably not going to hurt her as long as we have the Diary. They <u>need</u> her to interpret. Why would they do anything to her? Think! The Diary is like, you know, a bargaining chip. We can trade for her and Veronica. Hell, you probably saved their lives! Who knows? If you hadn't stolen the Diary, maybe they'd have killed them both!"

David didn't answer me, but I could tell he was listening

intently. I hoped I was getting through to him. I also hoped I was guessing right. On the other hand, I thought grimly, I was a witness who could identify them. And David, too, after today. But I'll worry about that later, I thought. First things first – Mrs. Rosen was all that mattered now.

I spotted the note just as we reached the phone. Something made me turn to the right and notice the living room coffee table with a sheet of paper on it we'd missed earlier. Detouring away from David, I darted in and picked it up. "David, come here! I found something! I think it's a ransom note!" I shouted, ripping open the envelope.

"Wait! Don't touch it!" he yelled, running back.

"Fingerprints, right? Too late now."

The creamy stationery was stiff and thick and obviously expensive, like an invitation to a society wedding. The handwriting, in black fountain pen, was old-fashioned and weirdly precise. It had a simple message, direct and to the point:

GRAND CENTRAL STATION. MIDNIGHT. BY THE CLOCK. BRING THE DIARY OR THE JEWESS DIES. CALL THE POLICE – AND HER FRIEND AND YOUR FAMILIES ARE NEXT.

David looked very pale. "Oh God, we made it worse!"

I swallowed hard. "I know," I choked, filled with a terrible dread. "I know."

Chapter Eighteen

That note changed everything. We didn't dare call the authorities now – the gangsters would kill Mrs. Rosen . . . or maybe even Mom!

We were back on our own. How could I, a 15 year old smart-ass kid, sort of halfway content with my life till yesterday afternoon, have gotten mixed up in this nightmare? I glanced over at David, who looked like he didn't know what to do either. We were going nowhere, but I guess we had to go through the motions.

In a sort of daze, we locked up the apartment, left the building without saying a word, and walked the eight blocks down Central Park West to the Museum of Natural History to retrieve Joshua's Diary from the check-in attendant in the lobby. Two museums in one day – and now back for a third visit to checkout our prize package – I was dizzy from it all!

It's funny how events change the feel of places. Now the museum seemed cavernous and overwhelming, like it could swallow us up whole. That's how small I felt. David looked drained of emotion. We were so sure of ourselves before. Now we had tripped up and lost our way.

When we left the museum, its shadow crawling out towards the Park like a cloud of ink, it was 5:00 p.m. The sun was low and the air was getting much colder. When I looked out over Manhattan, I felt a chill. Night hovered on the horizon like an unwelcome guest. I didn't want it to come, not for a long time, because when it did, it would bring Nikolai with it.

We walked to a copying store over on Columbus Avenue for a counter cartridge so we could use one of the machines. We had to wait for a peroxide-haired attendant who was less than service-oriented, to say the least. And his wispy goatee and pierced eyebrow really depressed me. He was trying so hard to look hip and show biz that it verged on pathetic. I was so low that nothing could possibly look hip to me.

My mind wandered as we waited for what seemed an eternity. When someone else walked in the store, looking just like he'd just come from a TV show, I thought life's gotten too much like television. Not the other way around. TV was supposed to reflect life, I thought. Not any more. Everybody tried to be like their cool favorite character of choice of the week. It was so depressing. And everyone was so obvious about it. You know, a bunch of random, weird stuff surrounded by hype and commercials. That's what people were beginning to look like more and more. I bet you see Nike navel rings any day now. Let's face it, how hip is that?

David finally corralled a vacant copier and yanked me out of my coma. The machine was one of those big ones about the size of a 1948 Buick with a million tiny controls you can't read, much less understand. I mean . . . does anyone really want to shrink something to 17% of its original size? There I was again with my mood going straight downhill.

"Cool tattoos on the Copy dude!" I croaked, not convincingly, in a weak attempt to lighten the mood. I was particularly entranced by the silver stud shaped like a skull sticking out of his tongue. "That guy must be a real date magnet."

I was in rare form now. It was easier to be flip and

sarcastic . . . and in a deep, dark depression . . . than to feel as terrified as I'd been finding the note. This felt much more comfortable, a dark state I knew so well. Yeah, but before – I never knew what from. Now I knew exactly what from . . . now was different. And I felt useless, completely helpless to fix it. I had made bad decisions, bad judgment calls, lost my cell phone when we needed it most, and only helped make things worse.

Watching David make copies, I was losing all sense of belief in anything we were doing. We were like two losers, going through the motions of something that had maybe a two percent chance of working. What could *we* do – two 15 year olds – against guys with guns and a criminal network watching our homes, our families? And how could we stop them from hurting Mrs. Rosen and Veronica? How stupid we were to start trailing Mrs. Rosen this morning.

Apparently David was too preoccupied with the task at hand to notice my descent into major depression. But finally he said in response: "I'm not sure how cutting-edge tattoos are when even the nerd at the corner copy shop has some."

All right! Great minds do think alike! He yanked me out of my mood and I laughed in spite of myself. "Such cynicism, Mr. Rosen. I'm ashamed," I teased.

He took Joshua's Diary out of his jacket pocket.

"Be careful," I cautioned. "That thing has been through a lot." Seeing it now, so fragile and old, the tattered little book captured all my attention. Something was in there, something that was going to change our lives. Well, of course it had already. But *more* than the last 24 hours which had certainly changed my life, big time. I don't know how I knew, but I just did. It began to obsess me.

David gently laid the Diary face down on the machine's glass top and pushed the "Print" button. When the copy slid out, he flipped carefully to the next page and repeated the process over and over in silence. Finally, when he was on the last page, he said something as I began to neatly stack the copied pages: "I wish I'd known him."

"Your Uncle Joshua? Yeah, me too. But don't you feel like you kinda do after hearing your grandmother's story and all?"

He puckered his lower lip. "In a way, I guess. But it's . . . it's like there's this huge hole there. I mean, okay, I have stories about him. I'll grant you that. But I don't have him . . . or any of my other relatives. I've never had any relatives, to speak of, my whole life. They were all destroyed in the Holocaust. No story can change that. And now I'm about to lose the only one I do have, if I'm not careful."

"Oh, David." I couldn't help but hug him. I could tell he was trying not to cry in front of me, for he wouldn't look at me. I shook him then. "Look at me, David!"

He looked up at me and his eyes shone.

I smiled and got in his face. "Nothing is going to happen to her, David. I promise." I meant it. I felt nothing like I did just minutes ago. I was filled with resolve now. It's like when I lost it, he had it and when he lost it, I made up for it.

He turned away again. "How can you be so sure?"

"I'm not sure I can explain it myself, really. It's . . . it's more of a feeling."

"I don't follow you."

"I . . . I mean, it's hard to say. But, okay, here's what I feel. I trust Joshua. I trust his spirit. I mean, look at your grandmother. If he was anything like her . . . my God! . . . then he was a true hero. And I don't believe for a moment he smuggled paintings like <u>they</u> do! It doesn't make sense. He wasn't a crook. He was a hero! There must be some explanation."

David made his cute "listening" face. The one where he makes a face like a puppy that hears a funny noise. That's when I knew I was getting through to him.

"Crooks maybe always think everyone else thinks like them at bottom. But I'm convinced, as sure as I'm standing here, that something deep inside that Diary, something we can't even imagine, is going to help us save your grandmother, David. And, before everything's over – whatever this wonderful thing is – I bet it's going to save us all. Life's going to start over for the better for all of us . . . you, me, and your grandmother. You'll see. In some ways, I think it already has." I caressed his face. "I know it has for me."

He looked at me like I'd just told him I could fly.

"You don't have to understand it, David. Just believe it. This little book is the key. Let's look for the real Joshua. He's in here, I know it. They want him. But we need him more. And he'll come through for us. I feel it in my bones."

I picked up the copied pages. "Come on, let's go pay for this. Then we need to get something to eat. We'll feel better when we have something in our stomachs. We'll think clearer. We didn't even eat lunch! Look, we'll talk over dinner about how we're going to handle Nikolai. This time he's messed with the wrong people."

David smiled at me then, as if I really had a plan that lifted his spirits. All I know is that I felt better with the little book in my hands. It gave me strength somehow. Like some kind of magic was beginning to work over me. Like it was a sacred book. And we were its guardians.

Over a smoked vegetarian pizza, a liter of Pepsi, and frozen vanilla yogurt with crushed Oreos on top, we worked out a plan. The place rocked to the beeps and screeches of video games and the yodels of four year olds full of way too much caffeine and sugar, so we could talk as loud as we wanted. I felt like we were pretty safe. Banzai Pizza didn't seem like old Nikolai's kind of joint anyway – whatever his kind of joint was. I had a hard time getting my mind around the concept of what a person like him did for entertainment. The man was seriously bent in my estimation.

"So, we're set. I'll meet you outside Lincoln Center at 11:00 p.m. Right?"

"Sounds like a plan to me," I agreed. "But are you sure you can get away from your parents so easy?"

"Yeah, I don't think it will be a big deal. They're pretty cool about letting me make my own schedule. Dad's concert should be over around 10:30 or so. I'll just tell them I don't want to go to the party after. I'll say I'm going out front to catch a cab home. It shouldn't be a problem."

"What about your grandmother? Won't they be expecting her at the concert? It's like a really big deal, isn't it? I saw on the news that a bunch of movie stars and Princess somebody or other are supposed to be there."

"No, she can't stand all that celebrity kind of junk. She declined the invitation ages ago. She's heard Dad play at plenty of concerts. One time she told me celebrity worship is the new American religion. On that one, she said, she's an atheist."

I laughed. Was there no end to how much I could love this woman? We definitely had to save her life. No question.

"What about your Mom?"

I made a face. My Mom. "Let's see, I know she doesn't have a date. Otherwise, she'd have been all crazed for days and shopped even more than usual. It'll probably be a chocolate Haagen-Dazs and Harrison Ford video kind of Saturday night. She'll bunker in her bedroom. I won't have a problem slipping out, believe me. She won't even miss me."

"Aren't you kind of hard on her?"

"Well, maybe. But since when has she given a rat's ass about me?"

David pursed his lips. "Whoah! That sounds really angry."

"You think that's angry! That's nothing! The woman is a complete and total narci . . . narciss . . . whatever it is. You know, extremely self-centered. The whole Dad thing was such a rejection for her, all she thinks about is herself."

"Isn't that understandable?"

"What are you, her shrink?"

David chuckled. "No, I just think maybe you're being a little unfair."

"Unfair, my ass. I didn't ask her to have a daughter. But she has. Me. She has some responsibilities, doesn't she?"

"Point taken."

I think David was ready to end this part of the conversation. I didn't blame him. I did overreact, I guess. I tried to compensate. "I love her and all. If I didn't, it wouldn't bother me as much. It's just . . . it's just like I'm her mother most of the time instead of the other way around."

David took a sip of Pepsi and crunched some ice between his teeth. "That's a problem nowadays for a lot of people."

This line of discussion was morphing into a major downer. We'd been down enough. I changed the subject. "So, we're set. I'll go home and get that stuff you suggested and meet you later at 11:00," I repeated. "By the fountain, right?"

"By the fountain." He raised his glass. "Here's to my grandmother Dominique and her friend Veronica."

I clinked glasses with him. "To Dominique and Veronica! And Joshua. And to a successful mission tonight!" We clinked again.

David scooted his chair back like he was ready to leave.

"And I've got one more," I said.

David hoisted his glass. "To?"

"To you."

David looked uncomfortable. "Me? For what?"

"For being so patient with me."

"Me? Patient?" He gave a little laugh. "What do you mean?"

"Last night I looked at your grandfather's book that you gave me."

He grimaced and heaved a sigh. "Good. I just . . . I just wanted to be helpful."

"You were more than that. By telling me the real story about the Holocaust, you and your grandmother taught me a lot. You guys made me a different person. Really."

He started to say something, but I held up my hand. "Please . . . let me finish. You made me a better person, too. Like people say on *Oprah* – I've grown. I have. It sounds corny, but you might say I'm living in a different world today than I was yesterday. For one thing, I really want to learn more about being Jewish. Before, I never really thought very much about how anti . . . anti –"

"Anti-Semitism?" David offered.

"Yeah, thanks. Anti-Semitism. You taught me how anti-Semitism is still so – so widespread and out in the open or brushed under the carpet, but still there. I guess I wasn't paying attention. The most important thing is that you and Mrs. Rosen showed me that hatred and prejudice aren't just crude and bad and uncool and all that, but that they also cause

220

people to get killed. That last part is what I didn't get before. The people who hate aren't the only ones responsible. The people who sit around and ignore it and let them get away with it are guilty, too. That's just as important to learn. Right?"

David nodded his head. "That's how it happened to my family."

"For the first time in my life, I feel . . . I don't know, I don't know how to describe it exactly. Awake, I guess. I feel like I can see. Like I can see the truth. And, I swear to you, David, as long as I live, I'm never going to take my eyes off it."

David looked sort of amazed. He hadn't been expecting this. "Thanks for telling me that, Lauren. It means a lot. I'm . . . I'm kind of . . ." his voice trailed off.

"And one more thing," I added, feeling really self-confident now. I stood up and brushed a lock of hair off his forehead. Then I leaned over and gave him the sweetest, gentlest kiss I could, right above his eyes. "A toast to you for being you."

For the first time ever, I saw him blush.

I slapped him on the back. "Now come on, cowboy, we've got a date with destiny!" I surprised myself. Was this really me? I liked the way I felt now. I liked this brave new me.

Chapter Nineteen

Two and a half hours later, I slipped out the front door of our apartment. Mom never noticed a thing. As I closed the door, I could hear Harrison Ford yelling in the background. Just as I expected. Good old Harrison, Mom's virtual-reality date for the evening. Her favorite guy. Shaking my head, I thought of my father. I could positively have killed him for doing this to me.

As I hurried down the hall, I adjusted the straps of my backpack. Like David suggested, I brought my trusty Patagonia pack along to carry the photocopy of the Diary and this really huge Nikon that Dad gave me for my last birthday. For evidence gathering and stuff. Because Dad hadn't seen me for almost three months, he really came across with the goods that time – really expensive goods. Sickening, I thought.

As an afterthought, I threw in my good luck charm, my trusty Tweetie Bird Pez dispenser, fully loaded, of course. I figured I was gonna need all the luck I could get. And if I ran out of luck and got into trouble . . . well, at least I would be with David. Plus, I thought about Mrs. Rosen fighting the Nazis in the Warsaw Ghetto when she was a teenager. This would be a piece of cake compared to that. Tonight was for her.

I checked my outfit in the mirror by the elevator. I had kind of a Generation Y theme going on. Baggy low rise jeans and a pair of scuffed Vans down below and a generic navy blue Gap sweatshirt and an Urban Outfitters baseball cap on top. Then I popped a Donnas CD in my Discman and went downstairs for a cab. The new guy was still working the door, but I don't think he recognized me. Super, my disguise was operative.

Lincoln Center. David was right where he said he'd be – standing by the big fountain in the Plaza square in the middle of the Lincoln Center for the Performing Arts. The whole fantastic, glass kingdom of concert halls and theaters was lit up for the evening, and the rushing fountain waters sparkled like a rainbow of diamonds and framed David in halo of silver light. I wasn't prepared for what I saw. He was wearing a tie.

"A tie?"

"I had to get dressed up for the concert," he grinned sheepishly.

He did look kind of nice. Besides the tie, a snazzy red thing with abstract shapes, he wore a white, button-down Oxford shirt, a nice wool sweater and navy slacks. In fact, he looked like he was all ready for a school picture. But in an act of David-like rebellion, he still wore his Doc Martens.

I unzipped my pack. "You got the Diary?"

He lifted his sweater and produced the photocopied pages.

"What about the original?"

"They're not getting it that easy," he answered. "It's under my bed at home."

I reached over and loosened his tie. "There, that's better."

He coughed. "It's not like I like this."

"You look nice. Exceptionally cute," I chuckled.

"*Cute*, great. You talk like I'm a panda or something."

"Oh, but you're tons cuter!"

He shook his head. "God! You're hopeless. Let's get a cab and get this over with."

When we walked over to Avery Fisher Hall, the concert had just finished. Men in tuxedos and women in formal long gowns poured out of the building into the plaza – most of them trying to catch a cab. So we ran a block up Columbus Avenue and up-streamed them. And made it to Grand Central Station in no time at that hour. But I was starting to get really nervous. I wasn't exactly looking forward to seeing Nikolai again.

The driver dropped us off by the Park Avenue ramp. After the taxi's tail-lights disappeared, David and I just stood there for a minute. We were early . . . and had plenty of time for reality to hit us. If the way I felt as I stood there on the curb was any indication, this was going to be real hard. My knees started to shake like somebody just pressed the fast-forward button. David didn't look much better. I noticed he kept swallowing like he was fighting to keep his dinner down.

I pulled my backpack straps tight. "You ready?"

He gave a nervous, half-way smile. "I was born ready, pardner."

I reached to open the door when he tapped me on the shoulder. "Lauren, you know, whatever . . . whatever you were about to say when we were hiding from the Russians . . . when they almost found us?"

My heart skipped a beat – several, actually. "Yeah?"

"Well, I feel the same way about you."

Suddenly I felt ten feet tall. Flashing the biggest smile of my life, I held his words close to my heart and couldn't say anything. As he opened the door for me, I just about floated into Grand Central Terminal.

The main concourse was spilling over with people. Not the briefcase-toting, commuting crowd during the weekdays. No, this was the late Saturday night crowd – rowdy, loud, and raucous. Under the concourse's soaring vaulted ceiling and three great, arched windows, New York's nighttime personality paraded itself with no excuses.

Packs of mall rats dissed and joshed each other on their way to catch the subway to whatever this week's hot club downtown was. A punk rock couple dressed in identical dog collars and black leather jackets laughed and wrestled on the steps of the station's ornate marble staircase. Four hammered sailors staggered across the main floor cheerfully singing a censored version of the old "Flintstones" theme song. And in the middle of all the chaos, a homeless man slept on a bench with an open newspaper over his face, while a scruffy sad-eyed mongrel, probably his only friend in the world, waited for him to wake up.

As we walked further, we saw here and there in darkened corners a few couples kissing passionately. And sticking close to the brightly lit areas, some out-of-towners scurried like they were lost in the jungle and worried about being the main course for somebody's next meal. But no sign of Nikolai.

"Where is he?" I asked.

"I don't know, but you can bet he's down there in the concourse. He's probably watching us right now."

This information, while important to know, didn't exactly make me feel any better. I nervously scanned the huge underground room. A brief image of Nikolai hiding behind a potted palm in one of those dumb, fake nose and glasses disguises flashed through my mind. Even that didn't help. I was sweating. Classic.

David looked at his watch and licked his lips. "Okay,

I'm going in. You stay pretty far behind me and keep your eyes open. It may be a trap."

"Wait, don't you want the Diary?"

David exhaled. "Oh, yeah. That might come in handy."

I unzipped my pack and gave him the pages we'd photocopied. He cut them in half like a deck of cards.

"What are you doing?"

David handed me the extra pages. "They're crazy if they think they're getting exactly what they want before they let my grandmother go. Until she's free, Nikolai and Company are on the David Rosen installment plan. I should have thought of this earlier and hid it somewhere. I'm not thinking clearly." He fanned the pages. "Well, here goes nothing."

"Smart, David. Be careful!" I shot him a thumb's up.

He smiled. "Piece of cake!"

I waited until he was almost to the middle of the concourse before I quickly tucked my hair up under my hat and followed him. They'd never recognize me without my purple hair showing, which, if I survived the night, I vowed to dye and tone down to my original color so I wouldn't be such an easy mark. My plan was to hide behind pillars and stragglers anyway from a safe enough distance.

David went straight to the circular information booth at the center of the floor, the exact spot where the ransom note told us to wait. The big four-faced brass clock on top of the booth read five minutes to midnight. But there was no sign of the Russians.

Ten minutes passed. Then fifteen. While David stood by the booth, I lagged way behind, cruising the edge of the concourse. As the time passed, however, I ambled over and lingered next to the bench where the little dog was tied, about twenty feet away from the information booth. That way I would at least be able to hear what went down. The wiry-haired, yellow mongrel wagged his tail at me.

"Good doggy," I whispered.

The man under the newspapers rolled on his side and groaned. At the sound of his master's movement, the dog whimpered and put his paw on him. He was a good friend. Better than most people, it looked like.

As the minutes dragged past, David and I kept surveying the terminal. Once our eyes met and I shrugged. He shook his head. I began to think Nikolai might not be coming. When I started to walk over toward David, that's when we got some action.

Over on the opposite side of the booth from David, an elegant elderly man in an expensive camel hair overcoat folded the newspaper he was reading and tucked it under his arm. He acted like he was about to walk away, but then suddenly he turned and looked directly at David. Something about him was vaguely familiar. The snow white hair. The tailored clothing. My God! Now I remembered! It was the man from the limousine who shouted at Nikolai in German. I tried to warn David and called out to him, but a train rumbled by underground, and then another, drowning out my voice.

As the white-haired man moved towards David, the little dog tensed up and growled – the hair standing up stiff on his back. He tugged on his leash and whined, his nails clicking on the station's hard floor.

The man stopped not two feet away from David and stood with his back to him, but David still hadn't noticed him. I wanted to scream. He was alone for now but I knew Nikolai and the others had to be nearby. The dog snarled and pulled hard on his leash, yapping once . . . twice . . . three times. The man looked over his shoulder and stared at the dog, and when I saw his expression my stomach contracted.

He was without a doubt the creepiest-looking person I'd ever seen. Beneath the bizarre white hair, his lifeless grey eyes were the color of dirty mop bucket water, and his leathery skin was as creased and wrinkled as a Gila Monster's belly. And all the while the little dog whined, then tucked his tail between his legs and crawled under the bench. Definitely a very perceptive animal.

Finally, the creepy guy turned his attention back to David. *"Vere iss it?"* he hissed.

David spun around in surprise. The shock on his face quickly congealed into recognition, then to contempt. He stretched to his full height and challenged him. "First things first. Where's my grandmother, you schmuck?"

"That's not part of the deal, you little parasite," scoffed the old German, leaning closer and showing some teeth. He looked like he wanted to bite David.

When David gave him the copied pages, I noticed the man wore black leather gloves, which bothered me for some reason. "That's a copy of half the Diary," said David triumphantly. "When you let her go, you get the other half – and not a second before." Then David swore at him.

He was so repulsive that he flickered his tongue like a rattlesnake and licked at his bottom lip. The look on his face would have peeled paint. I could tell he hated David, but there was something else in that look, too. Some kind of familiarity. I know it sounds strange, but that's the only way I can put it. He hated David like he knew him. There was something so strange about that old man – distinguished and well-dressed as he was – something unbelievably sinister and prehistoric and deep in its sickness. And it all seeped out of him like a poisonous mist.

"Don't you think I already have a copy of the Diary?" he mocked, laughing as if David was too stupid for words. "Because of your meddling, I had to take your grandmother. You see, I don't want her interpreting it on her own and then selling whatever paintings she'd find to art dealers or museums. It's your fault I had to take her! Feel good about that? She's as important to me now as the Diary. And now I have both in my possession." He snickered as he watched David's face change.

David wilted, completely deflated and paralyzed by what he heard. I too was thunderstruck and almost keeled over. We never expected this!

While he stood there gaping with his mouth open, the old creep handed back the pages we had worked so much on without a glance. Like a wary animal, he scanned his eyes around the room as two transit policemen strolled by, twirling their nightsticks and shooting the breeze. He looked down and turned his face away.

That's interesting, I thought; he doesn't want to be seen. Suddenly I had an idea and reached for my backpack. I tore out my Nikon and started clicking away. It was noisy enough with the sound of distant trains pulling in and out to not hear the clicking, and it was a flashless camera. So he never knew.

When the policemen were gone, the old Nazi resumed negotiations with David. "You're playing a very dangerous game. A game you can't win . . . little Jew." The last word hung in the air, and David's face went white with anger.

"What do you want?" demanded David.

The old creep looked around him toward where the policeman last were and smiled a dangerous smile. "Ah, but you still haven't guessed. This little meeting is for insurance . . . to bring you to her as collateral." He waved his hand in the air and three new heavies appeared out of nowhere closing in on David. I didn't recognize any of them. Nikolai wasn't among them . . . nor Vlad or Sergei.

They were after David, not the Diary, I realized. It was all a ploy to get David on his own, one on one – so that David would think he was alone with this man in a public place bartering for his grandmother's life! No wonder it looked too easy. David and this lone cadaver-looking guy, old as the hills, and harmless-looking. It was a trick! How dumb could we be!

I had to think of something fast. They hadn't seen me yet.

Just then, a harried mom and dad loaded down with a stroller, portable playpen, bags and three squealing toddlers appeared out of nowhere. They were the break I needed as they came in close range to the old German, his bodyguards and David. Close enough for them all to be in the same frame with them. I pulled my baseball cap down low over my eyes and moved in for the kill with my Nikon.

"MARGE, LARRY, WHAT DARLING BABIES!" I called out with booming enthusiasm. I turned the automatic flash to "ON" and leaped out in front of David snapping a flurry of shots. My flash started blinking like a strobe light and the old German spun away from the exploding light like a vampire from the sun. Holding his arm over his face, he staggered blindly away from David while his three goons held their hands over their eyes as they came at me with everything they had.

I started screaming bloody murder. I screamed so loud and blew a whistle from around my neck that I always wear when I'm out late. I don't know which it was that stopped them in their tracks more: my drama queen screaming or my ear-splitting whistle. Everyone around me stood stock still, frozen like human icicles. Their paralysis lasted just a moment, but David and I took off like bats out of hell.

The police heard the whistle and came running out from another terminal blowing whistles of their own. We could hear other police whistles answering in the distance.

That's when the old German creep cleverly yelled out to the police: "STOP THOSE KIDS! STOP THEM! THEY STOLE MY WALLET! THEY STOLE SOMETHING EVEN MORE VALUABLE! STOP THEM! THERE THEY ARE!"

But we were long gone, almost out of hearing range of all the commotion. We split like road runners leaving a trail of burnt rubber under our soles. We ran like hell and didn't stop running till we were out of Grand Central, flying across Lexington and turning down 45th Street. Nobody their age could run as fast as David and me. No one, I thought with crazy satisfaction.

We collapsed behind a parked Range Rover in the middle of the block near Second Avenue, gasping for air.

Chapter Twenty

FBI Special Agent Angie Ortiz shook her head in disbelief. Disbelief at our stupidity. At least, that's what she called it. "You kids could have gotten into a lot of trouble! Killed . . . or worse!"

I didn't like that last part. "Worse"?

It was the next morning and we were in David's living room surrounded by FBI agents. At least that's what it felt like. There was a team of technicians hooking equipment onto two telephones and it looked like specialists from Con Edison walking in and out with a lot of electrical paraphernalia. Only they weren't from Con Ed.

She looked at me like I was a moron . . . or a little kid. "You want me to tell you the worst? Naw, I don't think you do. Let me just put it this way. When it comes to creative torture, the Russian *mafia* are regular Martha Stewarts of pain. They're spreading all over the world, too, and their ranks are full of ex-intelligence agents and military-types. These boys are sophisticated, cunning and cruel, I'm telling you. You don't know how lucky you are not to be room temperature right now."

She turned away like David and I were even too dumb to look at. "Hey, Rick! Do you have any more of that nicotine gum?" Another agent tossed her a pack of chiclet-type gum, and Agent Ortiz poured three squares into the palm of her hand. "On days like this, I wonder, I really wonder why I quit smoking." She munched on the gum and sighed.

As soon as David and I had made it home the night before, after our close call at Grand Central, we woke up his parents and told them everything. They immediately phoned the police. They got very emotional about Mrs. Rosen, and Veronica too, but also pretty angry at David for not telling them. The police came right over and after a lot of questioning informed us that they'd have to turn the case over to the FBI because kidnapping was "a federal crime." No sooner had they said that when the phone rang and it was an FBI agent acquaintance of David's father, pulling rank and ordering the police to "keep the identity of Dominique Rosen secret for as long as possible." We actually heard them say this. "According to instructions from Special Agent Ortiz, Assistant Deputy Director of the New York division of the FBI."

"I didn't know you knew anyone in the FBI!" David exclaimed, full of surprise.

"A woman who introduced herself to me after a concert I gave last year," David's father answered. "A real music lover who saw me in Corpus Christi and in San Antonio some years back. Anyway she gave me her card and told me that if I ever needed her, to keep the card always on me and give her a call. I always kept it on me for some reason. I don't know why." He heaved a sigh of the ages then and moaned, "Now I do."

Anyway, the police posted a couple of guards at David's brownstone and then personally drove me home to my building where one of the cops actually escorted me right to my door. Thank God, Mom had crashed again in front of the TV and I didn't have to explain why I was out four hours past my curfew – and why I came home with a police escort yet! We tried to wake her, but she was so out of it that the policeman just left.

They gave me a look of real knowing sympathy before they did, which made me feel good at first and then not so great when I thought about it after. Oh, my poor Mom.

By the time I was back at David's in the morning, the FBI squad was setting up shop in David's living room, turning it into a command center of cables, scanners, fax machines, cell phones, laptops and digital taping equipment – complete with technical types and nattily-dressed agents in identical Ray-Bans in attendance.

Agent Ortiz, who simply introduced herself to me as "Special Agent Ortiz in charge of the case" – not as the #2 FBI person in all of New York – grilled David and me for most of the morning.

"So this is it, huh?" Agent Ortiz held Joshua's Diary in her gloved hand, placing it in a plastic bag. I noticed she had a French manicure, which seemed sort of not to go with her machisma image and the really large stainless steel Colt .45 automatic that was strapped under her left armpit. Her thick black hair was done in a twist, and she'd updated her official-looking navy suit and white blouse with some cool buffalo nickel button covers.

"No wonder these *pendejos* are so desperate. Everyone's seen Van Gogh's *Starry Night* and Monet's *Water Lilies*. But think about it . . . a lost collection, filled with Impressionist originals that haven't seen the light of day in over half a century!"

David's father looked like he was in shock with everything going on around him – the kidnapping of his mother and her best friend, the near-kidnapping of his son after his concert, the intrusion of me and the cops last night, and the FBI wiring up the place this morning. But he suddenly lost his patience hearing that. "It's incomprehensible to me! Paintings of the masters not catalogued? I never heard of such a thing! How can it be?"

"Possibly studies of some of the masters' greatest paintings, or even a few lost ones that nobody ever knew about," Agent Ortiz answered with authority.

David's mother from across the room agreed. "It's possible. Some months ago a sketch by Michelangelo was discovered at Castle Howard in England that will fetch several millions. And in Turkey last summer they unearthed what are claimed to be several lost Picassos. I read about it in the *Times*."

Agent Ortiz shook her head and whistled. "Yeah, I know about that too, though they're not sure yet about the validity of the Picassos. Look, there's a big international underground trade in stolen paintings, believe you me. But a collection like this . . . well, let's just say it'd be the granddaddy of 'em all . . . and worth more than the national debt. They're using your mother like a bloodhound to help them track it down. And then with her friend there, too, for collateral. But, don't worry, I'm not such a bad bloodhound myself. I'll find her and her friend – alive. And the mob holding them, too. I wouldn't lay odds on their chances. Not when I catch up with 'em." She winked at us.

I liked her a lot, even though she'd been kind of tough on David and me. She was just doing her job. You know, trying to scare us so we'd stay out of trouble. I watched her inspect Joshua's Diary some more and put it in her briefcase. Then she held up one of the photographs I'd snapped at Grand Central.

"Hey, Rick – !"

But Rick was busy interrogating David's mother who he couldn't tear himself away from. I think he was falling in love with her or something. After all, she was beautiful and elegant and incredibly smart – plus she kept feeding him espresso and homemade muffins.

Agent Ortiz shook her head. "RICK!"

Still no answer.

Then she shouted: "AGENT MCMAHON!"

Agent McMahon jumped. "Yes, Ma'am?"

Ortiz showed him the photograph. "You sure you don't recognize this character?"

McMahon shook his head. "Nope. He's not in our computers either. I've already called D.C."

"Maybe we'll still be able to get some fingerprints off the Diary," she said. Then turning to David and me, she raised her voice with some sarcasm – "At least if the crucial evidence we need wasn't completely smeared off by young Sherlock and his sidekick here!"

I felt like I was two inches tall. David blushed and looked down at his feet.

Turning back to Rick, Agent Ortiz gave him the picture. "Scan it and email it to the Wiesenthal Center in Los Angeles. Fax it to them too. *Muy pronto.* They might have something. And tell them we really need their help. This guy's dangerous. Now, he's desperate. That's a bad combination."

I didn't really get what she was talking about, but I was curious. She seemed a lot more concerned about the weird white-haired German at Grand Central than about Nikolai and the rest of his gang. That was interesting. I filed it away for later.

The phone rang and David's father left the room to answer it. Agent Ortiz shushed everybody, motioned to McMahon to turn on the intricate recording equipment he set up earlier, and then clicked it on as Ortiz signaled David's father to pick up the receiver. But it was a false alarm; it wasn't the kidnappers.

"One more time," Ortiz turned her attention back to

us. "You kids stay out of this! You'll only get hurt, or – "

David and I chimed in together. "Worse!"

For the first time all morning, Ortiz almost smiled. "Right. Worse! In a way, though, I sort of admire your *cojones*. You remind me of me . . . . "

David frowned. "Our what?"

Ortiz laughed. "Well, in the barrio of Corpus Christi, Texas, where I grew up, *cajones* means your street smarts, your, you know, toughness. That's a loose translation, anyway. Now is there anything else I can help you with? I have to get to work."

"Thanks for giving me my camera and film back," I said.

Agent Ortiz finally broke down and smiled, showing a set of white teeth straight out of a toothpaste commercial. "My pleasure," she chuckled, digging around in her briefcase. "Here's my card and cell phone and pager number. You call me if you see any of these guys. It's unlikely. I repeat – unlikely. But you call me, okay?" She waited for our answer.

"Okay," I said finally.

"Yes, ma'am," David replied in earnest.

"Good answer. And I'm serious. You two shouldn't mess around with these characters. They're predators. You're good kids. Stay that way. Good and alive. You know where to find me. I'll be at the Midtown office. Sleeping is optional for me this week. I've also assigned some agents to watch the house, both your schools and your apartment building, Lauren, just in case."

I didn't like the sound of that one. "Just in case?"

She ignored that and went on, as though she were thinking aloud. "But I don't know how long I can keep that number of personnel tied up. I'd say a week, tops. But something should break by then." Then she called Agent

McMahon over to her and motioned him out the door.

I stood up and casually strode over to the hallway and heard her say to him, "Look, you and I know that once the press gets a hold of this, the Russians'll dump their human cargo fast. Either that or – "

"Right . . . smuggle them out of the country."

"And we can't keep tails on these people indefinitely. As it is these kids are pure trouble. We'd have to lock them up to stay in one place," Ortiz whistled out the side of her mouth.

"Yeah, try it," he laughed.

"Well, keep close to them and tell the others to stick to them like glue. They're our window here. I can feel it. But we don't have much time. We've got to crack this one fast or there'll be a leak to the press, in which case it's all over."

"How many tails you have in mind?" I heard him ask her.

"Ten in double shifts for one week only. Then it's all up for grabs. We'll not be able to keep it secret past then. And only you and Ed will know about Dominique Rosen. As far as the others will know, they're following orders to stay on these people's asses. No more. So keep a zip on it. And if anything else comes out, it's all about the friend kidnapped – Veronica."

"They're gonna wonder what the hell's going on, no? All this for one woman they never heard of?" asked Agent McMahon. I heard him flip a page in his pocket notebook. "Veronica MacFadden?"

"That's why we're gonna get to the bottom of this right away. No one's alive anyway – is my call – after this week. You know that as well as I," said Agent Ortiz. "Let's get back in there. There's something I forgot to tell the kids."

Hearing this in total shock, I managed to open the door as if just showing up and blurted out, "Oh, there you are,

Agent Ortiz. You said 'just in case' before. What do you mean?" I asked, feigning utter air-headedness.

"Just in case anybody special shows up." She put her hand on my shoulder. "Which I highly doubt. They've probably gone underground now that we're on the case. We've already put word out on the street in Manhattan, Queens, Brooklyn and the Bronx that if . . . er . . . the kidnapped victims . . . catch so much as a cold, there's going to be hell to pay, courtesy of Uncle Sam."

Then she went back in the room to say something to David's father and mother, while the technicians were putting away their equipment and closing up shop. She checked out all their work like an ace electrical engineer (which we found out later she really was) and whisked the technicians and all the extras out the door. Then she spoke privately to two other agents who looked like they were going to be "part of the furniture" I heard her say. And next she turned to a Bureau technician she was leaving behind with us and reviewed the plan.

When she was done with all the details, she told David's mother and father that she had to get back to her office but that there'd be protection for everyone of us, and that she'd be returning later.

David's father asked her then about Joshua's Diary. "What are you going to do with it? I heard you say you'll try to find fingerprints. We'd like to have it back as soon as possible."

"Of course, I understand. I'm also sending it over to the high-tech lab at the Bureau to have it photographed with digital cameras and scanned with ultraviolet and infrared filters to see if there's any hidden text. Those kids did one very brave thing. They managed to get this Diary and it very possibly may reveal the identity of the ring-leader behind the kidnapping of your mother and her friend. And they managed to copy it too. Amazing. We'll also contact Interpol as well as have some other international agencies check out some of the locations mentioned by Joshua, even though much of it's in code. We'll try to crack that, too. We've got to take the copy along with the original for now. They'll get the full treatment in different ways, of course. The original will go to our Lab, while we study the copy for clues."

"Yes, of course, I see," David's father said. "Well, that's encouraging." But he didn't sound very optimistic.

"Look," he added, "my mother and my uncle – Joshua – who I've never met, have been victimized twice. By sadistic henchmen first and now by art-looting sellers of souls next. My family has suffered so much. It's hard to part with this Diary right now. Will its pages be soaked in dyes and that kind of thing? How damaged will it be after your Lab specialists are finished with it?"

Agent Ortiz looked sympathetically at him. "No, that's not the process. And, look, I completely understand," she answered with genuine sympathy. "If the Tech Lab is low on volume now, I'll make sure you have this back in a week. It will be designated as an exhibit of the highest priority. I'll rush it through, I promise you, and get it past all the red bureaucratic tape. You have my word on that."

David appeared behind me at that moment, and Agent Ortiz, noticing him, said, "Come here, I want to tell both of you something, between you and me." She led us out into the hallway and fired away. "You two have to promise me you'll just do your part and keep your noses clean. Don't say anything about this to your friends. To nobody. You got that? Lives are in danger if you do. No gossipy phone calls now, right?" she seemed to single me out for that one.

"And one last thing," she added. "I see that you two have

ants in your pants. So stay out of the way. *Comprende?*"

"Comprende!" I repeated with emphasis.

"Right answer," she laughed. "That's two in a row. Keep it up. *Adios* for now." Ortiz picked up her briefcase. "McMahon?" Her partner didn't answer. Ortiz rolled her eyes. "MCMAHON! LET'S MOVE IT!"

McMahon moved it. He still had a muffin in his hand when they went out the door.

"She's pretty cool," I said after the door banged shut.

David stretched. "Formidable, you mean. I'd hate to get on her wrong side."

"So . . . are we going to stay out of trouble like she said?"

David smiled. "What do you think?"

Oh, great – now we had to worry about Nikolai . . . and getting Agent Ortiz mad and saving Mrs. Rosen and Veronica, I thought. And I wouldn't have had it any other way. Before Ortiz and McMahon's shut the doors to their car, David and I were already hard at work.

*

"Come on, let's go to my room. I've got something I want you to see," David called to me, climbing up the stairs.

Talk about an offer I couldn't refuse. He shut the door behind us and I thought, wow, he really does like me. Seeing his room for the first time, it looked like he'd just received a shipment from Computer City. I'd never seen so much cyber gear in one place outside a Connecticut mall. "Take a seat," he said, pointing to the bed.

Yessssss! I sat down, and my legs felt like warm Jell-O

pudding.

Then he leaned down and looked under the bed. He stretched out on his stomach and struggled to reach for something. "Ta dah!" he crowed finally, dusting off his shirt and holding up a sealed manila envelope.

"David! You didn't! I couldn't wait till we were alone to find out whether you gave the copy to your father or to Agent Ortiz. Wow! I kept listening for a clue, but didn't hear any hint of it out there between you and everyone and all!" I gushed excitedly. "You know, when you were copying it, I don't know how I didn't notice that you made two copies."

"Anyway, we're back in business. Let's see who cracks this first. The FBI or us!"

It was my turn to roll my eyes now. "Here we go again . . . ."

We spent the rest of the morning in David's bedroom scanning the Diary into his PC's hard drive. Then on his laptop I typed in a cryptogram program I learned in school to detect any patterns like repeated names, word combinations – codes and things like that. But we couldn't read Polish! We racked our brains trying to figure out who could translate it for us real quick and called language schools all over Manhattan except that it was Sunday and they were all closed. So we searched the Internet for Polish translators but couldn't come up with anyone we felt we could trust.

Afterwards, we transferred the whole file on disk to his Powerbook and emailed it to my own computer. Then I emailed another copy to my most trusted friend in the whole world who moved here from Mississippi in seventh grade and then had to move again when her father was transferred to Colorado earlier in the year. I was still heart-broken by Jamie's absence but we kept in pretty close touch. Won't she be surprised when she gets this download in Polish, I laughed to myself.

David and I were convinced that something in the Diary – a name, a date, a place, or even something we couldn't imagine yet – was the key to solving the riddle of the legendary lost fortune in art for which Nikolai and his mysterious boss seemed so eager to kill. Like I said, it was only a hunch, but it nagged at me like an itch. For one special reason. I believed in Joshua. That was easy. You see, he was sitting right next to me, his courage and image reflected in his great-nephew, David. My new boyfriend.

David's Mom brought us sandwiches, Greek salads and sodas on trays with linen napkins and real antique silverware. She seemed pretty calm now compared to how upset she was last night and this morning. She hadn't said anything to us after Ortiz and McMahon left, but this must have been her way to make everything seem normal by bringing us lunch. When we thanked her, she flashed a worried smile and said she was going to bring coffee out to the FBI guards posted out front.

"David! If she knew what we were doing . . . ." But he just shook his head and dived back into the Internet.

Meanwhile David's father, who I was told practiced for hours before concerts, was playing the hell out of his violin out on the terrace. It didn't sound like ordinary practice to me, but then, after all, it was his mother that was missing. There was something in his music that was so moving, so touching, that it could only have been a real cry from the heart. It went way beyond any music I'd ever heard. All afternoon, he played continuously and the notes soared up to the sky like a ladder to the angels.

When the sun set, the computer screens bathed our faces in indigo light. Or maybe I just imagined that – I was so bleary-eyed. David's Dad finally stopped playing, and the only sound in the whole place was the tap-tap-tapping of our fingers as they raced over the keyboards.

At one point, I took a break and rubbed my eyes, squinting out the window. Night blanketed the city and a silver crescent moon floated low on the horizon. Manhattan's towers sparkled like they were draped in strands of diamonds. Mrs. Rosen and Veronica were somewhere out there. I wondered what they were doing that very moment. Were they safe? Were they hungry? Were they scared? Was Mrs. Rosen re-living the other nightmare she barely survived when she was a teenager? I knew I didn't have time to rest and went right back to work.

Around 10:00 p.m., we called it a day. David yawned and stretched his arms to the ceiling. "Tomorrow I'll get this translated if it kills me. Then we'll go online. I want to get into some databases and cross-reference some of the names and places Joshua mentions. There's got to be a clue in the text someplace." He stretched and massaged the back of his neck. "I hope."

I stretched, too. "So we'll meet back here after school?

"Not here. Definitely not here."

This threw me. "Why not?"

"Because I'd be surprised if by tomorrow the FBI doesn't have this place bugged out the wazoo. Any heavy traffic through my modem and line might tip them off that we're, um, you know, not staying out of trouble. I'm sure they can read my email. I mean, the Feds are really catching up – "

"With?"

"Hackers. No, it's better if we avoid my system altogether, but I have a solution. Cyberia."

"Pardon? Like Russia?"

"Not Siberia. Cyberia. It's a coffee house in

Morningside Heights, near Columbia. You know where the Cathedral of St. John the Divine is?"

I nodded. "I know it all right – I love that place! But I haven't been there for a long time. Ever since – " I stopped, feeling the searing pain of loss I went through when I was nine years old.

"Ever since what, Lauren? It's okay. You can tell me." I must have looked really stricken or something because David grew real concerned. He was so encouraging and we'd been through so much together that it was like a dam burst inside me.

I suddenly blurted out a stream of stuff I hadn't talked about in years. "When I was little, my family used to take me to the Blessing of the Animals. My first time in church and there was a live elephant leading a procession of all kinds of animals to the altar for a special mass before thousands of people streaming out onto the sidewalk – that's how many people try to get in to see it. Lots of people bring their own dogs, cats, monkeys, parrots, and you hear whale songs and wolf howls above the singing of many choirs and the most incredible music throughout. All in honor of the earth and saving the environment. My grandparents, who said they never had much use for religion, joined because of the beloved head of the Cathedral, Dean Morton. They used to say if there's one man who's made a difference in the world today, it was Dean Morton."

Memories started to bubble up after being buried for so long, and I told David that had been the most wonderful time of my life. My parents were real happy then too. That was when my whole family became part of Cathedral life: the soup kitchen and shelter for those in need, the stone masons still constructing the place, the civil rights events, the poets in residence, the concerts, the Native-American commemorations every Thanksgiving in honor of their traditions and the loss of their land. And, from the Cathedral's environmental work, globally and locally, how I learned about the sacredness of all living beings as vital links in the web of all of creation.

But my grandparents were killed in an accident when I was nine, and my father ran away for a while . . . and my mother began to fall apart when he closed himself off and eventually shut the door on my mom and me. That's when they became drop-outs from life and were always going at it till they just gave up on each other. And I sort of just closed up and gave up on them. And everything else, I guess. And my mother, well, she brought me along to some things, but then finally said it was all too much for her and that she couldn't handle it any more.

"Anyway, that was a long time ago, and I'm a lot tougher now," I said, though David didn't look at all like he believed me. I surprised myself by how much I unloaded on him, but I trusted and respected him more than anyone else my age. Somehow with him, it didn't hurt as much to go back there . . . back to the source for me of so much love and so much light I'd felt cut off from ever since.

When my eyes started to burn, I suddenly changed the subject fast. "Now how'd I get on that track? I'm not normally like that. Wow, I sure bent your ear. I'm sorry."

"Don't apologize, Lauren. I'm really glad you did. I know you a lot better now that you told me about your family and the – "

"The Cathedral! Right, that was it. You were saying – "

"Oh, yeah, the café across the street. Well, Cyberia is right across the street from the Cathedral. It's one of these new cyber cafes, you know, a joint that lets you surf cyberspace while you sip a cappuccino. Basically, it's modeled on some kind of old 50's beatnik coffee house theme, only they've updated it by installing multimedia computer terminals and modem linkups. To be honest, it's a little too trendy for me, but it's close to school and, um, well, I sometimes hang out there."

"You don't need to apologize . . . fashion boy."

David laughed, then threw a pillow at me. Of course, I got right back at him and the mother of all pillow fights began. What a great release it was from all the tension we'd been under! I really kicked his butt. Definitely.

*

It was Thursday afternoon. Outside Cyberia's front window, rain showered down in sheets. We were marooned indoors with all our work still cut out for us. Nearly a week had passed and still no word about Mrs. Rosen and Veronica. No phone call came from Nikolai and his weird collector boss. They knew the FBI and police were staked out at the house.

It was real tense at David's house. His mother had almost stopped eating, and his Dad had canceled all his upcoming concert appearances in London, Paris, Milan, Copenhagen, Madrid, and other places I couldn't remember, for the season. His parents were home all the time waiting for a phone call from the kidnappers, so we told them we had to meet at Cyberia every day after school to get our homework done. Agent McMahon and another agent were always with us anyway; well, not far behind us anyway in the shadows.

David was right about Cyberia. It was basically a trendy West Side coffee bar, a glorified Starbucks, featuring lots of PC stations, exposed red brick walls, high ceilings, major industrial duct work and employing only the pale and multiple-pierced. Or so it seemed. Every other table was occupied by some scruffy, facial-haired dude studying and smoking French cigarettes, or an Anne Rice wannabe dudette dressed in black lace, scribbling in a notebook and sipping a tall latte – diet, of course. I liked the place a lot.

Each afternoon after we ordered cappuccinos in these really dorky big mugs, David and I staked out a PC station and hit the data trail. A couple of times Agent McMahon stepped out of the woodwork, so to speak, and came inside to make sure everything was okay. He said the Bureau had some leads in the case but that things were moving kind of slowly. He also questioned us about what we were doing, which was puzzling to him, for he had absolutely no clue about our own intensive investigation.

"HOMEWORK!" we'd groan with mock exaggeration and long faces. He even sat with us one day before we started our research, and David even offered him a cheese Danish and a large mocha coffee.

Amazingly, news of Mrs. Rosen's kidnapping hadn't reached the papers. David's father, after hearing Agent Ortiz on the subject, had been adamant about no leaks to the press because he was convinced it would place his mother's life in further danger. So somehow Agent Ortiz really had managed to keep everything under wraps for now. Reporters and TV cameras staked out in front of David's home would hinder any possible leads and negotiations with the kidnappers, according to Agent Ortiz, and force the kidnappers to take desperate measures.

Also I overheard Agent Ortiz say to McMahon that "any inkling of a treasure trove of lost paintings by the masters would cause such pandemonium in the art world that it would attract the global press with even more antsy reporters and

TV cameras swarming all over the place. Not to mention movement in underground circles here and abroad. Then they'd really be combing through overlapping networks of art thieves and underworld buyers, which would make this case nearly impossible to solve."

But how long could the secrecy of Dominique Rosen's kidnapping last, we all wondered, before people grew suspicious? Especially friends, colleagues, students. David's father and mother were warned that this could not possibly last for longer than a couple of more days before there was a leak. So each day that passed was countdown time. As it was, we learned it was the last day of the tails on all of us. David and I knew we were in a desperate race against time. Waiting for us at the finish line, there were only two options. Life . . . or death.

The biggest coup for us that week was when David found a Polish-born Rabbi at his synagogue. He told him it was for a history project, and the Rabbi was overcome with emotion when he realized what it was. Seeing a copy of an actual Diary of a Warsaw Ghetto hero made the old guy drop everything, and he began translating it aloud to David who took notes as fast as he could. Of course, David missed some school that day but he went outside and told the agent assigned to him that he was too upset for school — that was, after all, the first school day of that week right after the kidnapping — and that he was meeting with his spiritual counselor instead.

"Good thinking, David!" I slapped him on the shoulder when he told me later that day. "Cool excuse."

Finally, today David got the finished translation back from the Rabbi, and we slapped palms high in the air when he burst through the door and I saw his jubilant face. "IT'S DONE!" We quickly scanned it onto a compact disk so we could read it on a monitor. Now with the translation, we finally had something we could really sink our teeth into.

And Joshua left us a lot to chew. His entries were fascinating. Joshua's experiences were like nothing I ever imagined. As for the paintings, he never said anything straight out. But from what we could piece together, he fought the Nazis for weeks after the rest of the family fled through the sewers. Joshua never knew they'd been captured. Eventually, he made it out of what was left of the Ghetto, too, but not before he made the Nazis pay . . . dearly. His bravery, his constant planning, his network of contacts, his experiences with others in the ghetto and the conditions they lived in, were jaw-dropping. His Diary revealed the whole incredible story, describing his heroic actions in the most modest, matter-of-fact terms.

There was one line scribbled in the Diary that said:

Mila 18 is no more. We are on our own.

David explained to me that Mila 18 was the headquarters of the Jewish Fighting Organization. In the final days of the battle, nearly 200 young Jewish fighters died there, killed by gas and dynamite. Others vowed never to surrender to the Nazis and committed suicide like their ancestors did two thousand years ago at the mountain fortress called Masada.

History, David told me, says that on May 16, 1943, the Germans blew up Warsaw's main synagogue and declared the uprising over. It wasn't, according to Joshua's Diary. Not by a long shot. Scattered remnants of Warsaw's Jews, hiding in the smoking ruins, continued to fight back hard. Joshua led the survivors in a defiant series of hit and run raids. Daring ambushes and desperate hand-to-hand combat crackled to life on the smudged pages. The very pages of the Diary were soiled with smoke and dirt . . . and blood.

Then finally it was all over. *"We will go to the forests before it's too late —"* read a scrawled entry.

David explained that when things became hopeless, some of the Resistance fighters fled into the deep Polish forests to continue the fight as guerrillas behind the Nazi lines where most of them died. And that against all odds, only a few lived.

"I'm curious about this 'we' part. He keeps saying it." I scratched my head. "Who else is he talking about?"

David took a sip of cappucino and licked the foam off the top of his lip. "I know, I know. But there's . . . wait a minute!" He sat straight up in his chair.

I pulled my chair closer and sat next to him, knee to knee, shoulder to shoulder. "What?"

"Look!" he pointed to the computer monitor. Just above his fingernail were two letters – C.W. "And here they are again," he said, scrolling down.

Suddenly David got really excited. "Oh, my God! What if it's Chaim? I didn't think of that before. What if – wait . . . let's see something here." He wrote down the letters C-H-A-I-M.

"How did you say it? I took a stab and it came out sounding like *'Chayem.'*" "Chayem?" I repeated. He shook his head. Wrong. I tried again. *"Chime?* What does that mean?"

"It's a name. Well, it rhymes with 'chime,' but it's pronounced 'Hime' – with a long 'I' – you know, like 'time' or 'climb' or 'crime.' But with an 'H.' It's a man's name. Joshua's friend. Remember?"

"Oh," I said, a little confused. I thought Mrs. Rosen mentioned a name beginning with 'H' – like it was a Polish name I never heard of. Yeah, I remember now. It rhymed, well, *rhyme . . . dime . . . sublime."* I was getting carried away now and starting to show off.

"Yes, but with a 'CH' which in Hebrew is pronounced like an 'H.'" David put his hands behind his head and leaned back in his chair. "Here, let me show you the pronunciation in Hebrew," he said, as he wrote out the letters phonetically. "'C' is like 'H' – you see?"

"Oh, yeah. Now I get it."

"Joshua's younger friend who fought with him in the uprising. You know, the one who escaped from the train to Treblinka and saved my great grandmother and the children when they were left alone? She called him a young Samson when she told us what he did single-handedly to five Nazis. Remember?"

"Right, the great strong guy who saved their lives."

"Don't you see what this means, Lauren? Read this part."

"Where? Oh, yes, I see what you mean." I found the sentence and read it aloud:

Today, C.W. and I found a hiding place
for the canvases in the woods.

I frowned. "I . . . I understand that he's finally talking about the missing paintings. Right?"

"Right!" echoed David. "But, don't you see? What if Chaim survived the fight in the Ghetto? What was his last name? Let's try and remember my grandmother's story about him. C.W. Chaim . . . what? What does the "W" stand for?

"David, I can't remember. After everything she told us that night, who could remember a name? As it is, I thought she said a Polish name that began with an 'H.' There was so much she said that night," I said, wishing I could squeeze the memory out of my brain somehow.

"C.W. – C.W. – C.W.," David repeated again and again. "His last name. It's on the tip of my tongue. I'll get it. Let me think. Oh, what was it?"

He was clearly wracking his brain while mine was utterly blank. I could never remember the name. If only Mrs. Rosen were here to tell us! And now that we had our real tangible first clue, it seemed, we couldn't remember the most important name in the story she told of her time in the resistance. No one else could tell us either. Not David's father even – because she made a point of saying she'd never shared her story with him. We were frustrated out of our minds now.

"Wienstein? . . . Wientraub? . . . Werner? . . . Wolman? I've got to get a phone book and look up the W's. Maybe we'll recognize the name!" he exclaimed as he ran to the manager of Cyberia and begged him to loan him his phone book. When he returned with the big fat Manhattan directory, we combed down the list of W's . . . going right to the end without recognizing anything. Zilch. We shook our heads and then dived right back at it again from the beginning of the W's again. But this time we said aloud the first name – "Chaim" – before every single name that began with W.

We didn't have to go very far the second time. The W-A's were right at the front of the list. We started again. Wallace . . . Walkman . . . Warner . . . Wasser . . . Wasserman! "IT'S *WASSERMAN*! CHAIM WASSERMAN! THAT'S HIM!" Saying the full name aloud had jogged our memories. We both recognized it at the same time. What a break this was!

"Okay, now what? Now that we know the name, what do we do it? Could he have really escaped?" I repeated. "Your grandmother said she didn't think he made it because of all the dangerous missions he and your uncle were on."

David ignored my practicality. "It's a slim chance, an infinitesimally slim chance, but maybe he's still alive in – I don't know – Europe or Israel or maybe even right here in the United States!   If he is, he's bound to have some important information.   Something we can, you know, trade to the Russians in exchange for my grandmother and Veronica!"

"Do you really think he's alive?   Let's face it, what are the odds?

"Bad.   But what if he's still around and we don't look for him?   I'd never forgive myself.   No, I'm going to work the Web and search every database I can access . . . and then some. If this guy's breathing, I'll track him down.   Then we'll go to the FBI."

Initials . . . and now a name.   What did we have to lose?   For the first time, Joshua had given us a lead.   I glanced out the window.   "Thanks," I whispered, as if to Joshua.   And then I thought of him and Mrs. Rosen's family and Mrs. Rosen and Veronica and the old German and his thugs . . . and the FBI not coming up with anything . . . and tomorrow without our FBI protection any more.

My mood changed fast.   Each image in my mind had gotten me more and more depressed.   C. W.   The hunt for Chaim Wasserman.   IF he was alive.   A big "IF."   I knew this was such a long shot.   And I wasn't very hopeful, I have to admit.

Out front, a taxi splashed by.   The streets were slick and grey and the sidewalks bobbed with black umbrellas.   I took a sip of cold coffee.   More caffeine was imperative.   We'd just gotten our first break in the case.   Now it was up to us to do something with it.   No matter how hard it would be.

Chapter Twenty-One

We were both poised at our computers when David came out with something completely unexpected. "At this point it would help if we prayed. We need all the help we can get!"

I was surprised. "You really believe that, don't you?"

"You don't?"

"Well, it's just not cool, you know, I guess, for me and my friends. Besides, I look at my parents . . . and all the crooks in politics . . . and the world's such a mess – that I think how can there be anything else? And if there is, nobody pays attention any more or listens or believes . . . or remembers how to maybe . . . except for a few. Then again maybe it's the other way around. Nobody's listening to us or remembers us out here . . . lost . . . 'lost in the stars.'"

"I've felt that. Until I heard something right at this Cathedral here . . . ." David looked outside the window at the vast edifice of the largest gothic cathedral in the world.

"But you're Jewish!" I interrupted.

"From a Rabbi who was asked to speak there."

"Really? Oh, that's right, they hold all kinds of events like for everybody. I'd almost forgotten. I mean it's been so long since I was part of it all – since my family, you know, sort of suddenly disappeared." There was that sharp pain again that just ripped through my chest. But then I remembered something. I remembered my mother carrying on for a while for my sake. "My mother used to still bring me here for a long time after . . . after we lost everyone. She actually did that on her own when I was a kid . . . until she couldn't get out of bed any more on most weekends. She's not a complete loss," I added. At least she tried, I thought to myself.

"So what were you going to tell me?" I asked, changing the subject.

"Well, something they have every November is an Interfaith Concert of Remembrance dedicated to all the victims of the Holocaust. And my father played there once when Rabbi William H. Lebeau spoke. Well, until that night, I'd turned away from God because I couldn't believe in anything. But his words that night made me realize that the Nazis had won in a way for me."

"Really? What did he say?"

"I remember it word for word because I asked for a copy of his talk afterward and he sent it to me. He said, *"The perpetrators of the Holocaust wanted not only to usurp God's Power over life and death; they conspired, also, to silence forever God's Voice that has thundered throughout the ages: 'You shall not kill . . . . Love your neighbor as yourself . . . . Justice, justice shall you pursue.'"*

"So they wanted – "

"Right! And that meant they'd succeeded with me because they *wanted* to wipe out God. They created such a monstrous nightmare that it overwhelmed everything I'd been taught and blotted out the vision of God for so many others. Well, I wasn't going to give them one thing they wanted, not one thing! Especially that! Not after all those who died because of their faith . . . all those they killed just because of who they were!"

"Yes, I see what you mean . . . ."

"And last Sunday . . . remember when my father played like crazy all afternoon when he found out what happened, and we thought he'd cancel his solo appearance that night like he canceled his European tour for the rest of the season? Well, he did play, after all, that night – remember? And you know what he told me afterward? That he remembered something else Rabbi Lebeau talked about at that very same Interfaith Concert of Remembrance. Something about music – which made him go on that night."

"What?"

"*Music can help us reclaim, not only our common humanity, but also assure that God's call for love and harmony will be heard over the dissonance of evil.*"

"That's beautiful," I said.

"Of course my father only had to make a brief appearance at the concert that night and he rushed home right after his solo to join my mother waiting with the FBI in case there was a call. Too bad my mother and I didn't hear him because the next day critics said he never played better. My father told us he wasn't playing. He was *praying.*"

I got real quiet then, utterly lost in my thoughts. These were things I'd never considered before. Just because there are monsters doesn't mean they can take away what you believe. And love and harmony <u>can</u> be greater than all the atrocities that evil commits, just so long as we don't give up and lose sight of the bigger picture.

"And, you know, Lauren, another thing," David said. "We always think we can do everything ourselves. We're just not used to asking for help. From anyone. Least of all, God."

He was making a lot of sense. I couldn't imagine losing all one's relatives in the Holocaust. I thought about what his family had been through. And then I thought about mine.

I had lost my inner family – my wonderful grandparents when they were killed so suddenly and my parents when they fell apart at the seams. There was an emptiness I felt at the heart of things. David was real close to his mother and father . . . and his grandmother. I hadn't known what that felt like since I was a kid. They really cherished one another and didn't take each other for granted. A long time ago I knew what that was like. For me though, since losing any hint of family, I stopped believing in anything because it hurt too much to go back there to the great times in my childhood. I hadn't been prepared for the horrible blow of suddenly losing everyone and everything that meant anything to me. Well, who is . . . when something truly awful happens? And then my father and mother refused to talk about it – like nothing had happened.

It was like I was unfinished in some way. Not just because I was young and had a lot to learn. It was more than that. I had never thought about my having hit a wall when I was nine that just stopped me cold, stopped my whole emotional center, and stopped me from believing in anything or caring about anything because it hurt too much.

Finally I said, "Well, if you can believe that, after all your family suffered, then I can too."

I closed my eyes and whispered, "Please, God, I've not spoken to you in a long time. Remember me? Well, it's not for me that I pray, but for Mrs. Rosen and her friend Veronica. Please, please help us find them . . . and keep them safe till we do." I opened one eye and then added, "Oh! And please help us find Chaim Wasserman!"

*

For the next hour, David cruised the information superhighway. He attacked the web on Yahoo, AOL, Google,

Excite, and every other search engine or server he could think of, trying to get a listing, any listing, for Chaim Wasserman. First, he posted messages on the big news groups on AOL and Yahoo. Then he dragged me down to the New York Public Library on 42nd Street where we not only logged onto computers but also searched their massive phone book bank for their listings from every major and not-so-major city in North America.

And that's when he hit pay dirt! David found eighteen Chaim Wassermans spread out over the country from Montpelier, Vermont to Truckee, California. Seven of them were in the New York metropolitan area alone. We were really excited.

David then took out his calling card. "I've got a few calls to make!"

I gave him a thumb's up. "Go for it!"

With a spring in his step, he raced to find a pay phone that was free. Twenty minutes later he came back dragging his feet. "They're all the wrong age or born in America," he moaned, collapsing in the chair and holding his head in his hands.

"All of them?"

"Well, not all of them. Two of them are dead and I got one busy signal. Oh, and five didn't answer." He cleared his throat and heaved a long sigh. "This is going to take a lot longer than I expected." But already he was booting up his machine and going back to work. He looked exhausted, but he wouldn't give up. "I'll call the other five again in a little while."

I stood behind him and felt an incredible urge to touch his shoulder, as if to comfort him in some way and show support for his painstaking efforts. We'd been through so much already that it felt okay to do that, like old friends, or new friends, or partners in crime or, rather, partners in solving a crime. Achhh, I realized I was thinking too much about it so I just put my hand down impulsively and rubbed his shoulder. It seemed to seal a bond between us as he looked up at me and smiled.

David then clicked into the web sites of the Holocaust Museum in New York and Washington, D.C., the Simon Wiesenthal Center in Los Angeles, and the world-famous Yad Vashem Institute in Jerusalem, explaining what they were to me as he copied down their phone numbers. While everybody at all four places was really nice, he said, they couldn't help him. Not a trace, not a rumor, not an atom of the Chaim Wasserman from Joshua's Diary seemed to exist.

Finally I went back to my terminal, but David soon recaptured my attention. Not like that's ever a problem. "Come and look at this crap!" he said.

There was a bright red web site on his screen, but even at first glance something looked real strange. From its menu David clicked on something called "Cyber Nazis" with a full color picture of their leader-god, Adolph Hitler, and the words *Ein Reich, Ein Volk, Ein Fuhrer.* "What is that stuff?" I asked, confused.

"All lies! The Internet is a helluva useful tool, but also full of garbage like this!" David clicked again and we saw a photograph of skinheads making the Nazi salute, followed by the mailing addresses of white supremacist groups and a list of recommended books. A bunch of other sites he scanned were equally as horrible.

It was so sickening to me I felt covered in raw sewage . . . like I needed a bath. I felt like the whole world did. I couldn't believe this was out there and so up close on the screen. Hatred. Pure hatred. Jew, Jew, Jew, Jew – the word ricocheted off the screen in the ranting, raving, obsessive lingo of neo-Nazis and anti-Semites.

"Imagine if they controlled all the air waves!" David grimaced in disgust. "They did in Europe. Imagine if that was today and they controlled television, the media and all the web sites with their propaganda. I saw one once that urged blacks to thank whites for slavery! And now, what was maybe only a few hate-speech web sites a while back has mushroomed to hundreds."

"That's awful!"

"And getting more slick and sophisticated, full of graphics and animation, subtly drawing the viewer in before unveiling the real message of hate."

"But, David, wouldn't people realize right away that it's all that screwy racist stuff and just exit outta there?"

"Sure, I bet a lot would. Those in the know. But the whole point is that what's up there on the screen gives a kind of phony stamp of legitimacy to it. You know? It appears as if it's real – anything on the screen does – to others."

"Yeah, aimed at the young, impressionable and ignorant. The clueless!"

"Right, the very young and uninformed. But also aimed at angry, alienated souls they scout around for, hooking them in to join a movement so they can blame their misery on others – whether Jews, African-Americans, immigrants, whatever. Innocent, vulnerable scapegoats. So that every racist loser, every church-burning redneck wannabe, white supremacist and Nazi groupie – when they use cyberspace – can feel like they're connected to something really big and feel important."

I whistled in amazement. "I never realized the dark side of the Internet was so powerful."

"And spreading like wildfire. I think that evil wastes no time looking for any weak spot, any advantage to spread its poison. Surfing the Internet innocently or with just plain curiosity can suddenly make one a prime target for what's cleverly presented as information, but which in reality is far from the truth. Also, I read that German neo-Nazis are transferring their Internet sites to the U.S. because of the German government's crackdown outlawing those sites after all the hate murders of immigrants there. So it's onto greener pastures over here in the land of the free where anything goes."

"Unbelievable! After all that happened to your family – your grandmother and Joshua – and so many millions more. It makes you wonder if anything will ever change. If people are capable of that, then anything can . . . and . . . and . . . what's the point?" I stammered, a little shook up by what I saw on the computer screen.

"Lauren," he said tenderly. Now it was his turn to touch my shoulder. "Come with me, quick. I want to show you something. Let's leave our jackets and stuff here; we'll be right back." He then turned to a young guy doing research nearby and asked if he'd watch our things for a few minutes.

"Okay," I said, a little bewildered, following him into what I noticed was called the D. Samuel and Jeane H. Gottesman Exhibition Hall. There was a sign that said *"WHAT PRICE FREEDOM."*

"Whenever I see the crap we left behind on the screen," David said earnestly, "whenever I come in contact with the machinery of racism, I will always think about this incredible exhibit. My father and I came for the opening a few weeks ago. Do you know about it?"

"No."

"Well, feast your eyes. It honors those who dedicated and even sacrificed their lives for freedom – freedom of speech, of thought, of religious worship, of self-government. People like the student dissidents of Tiananmen Square, Nelson Mandela, Vaclav Havel, Thomas Jefferson, Lincoln, Thoreau, John Peter Zenger, Anna Akhmatova, Gandhi, and others. If only this could be shown in every city in the country and had its own web site that was well known or was part of the mainline web servers somehow. And if only every school had a course or grade requirement to study it and the whole subject of freedom and what it means."

For a few minutes we were very quiet, taking in the records and old documents and photographs and words of those whose ideas and courageous actions literally changed the world. One line about truth caught my attention: "The power of truth is such that when you try to attack it, your very assaults reinforce and validate it." It was by Galileo. I looked at the rest of the exhibit and was filled with such a sense of purpose that I found myself brimming over with inspiration and determination.

"Wow!" I gasped, unable to restrain myself. "Look at the company we're in! I never thought of it that way before. Yeah! All right!" I shouted with excitement, punching David in the arm.

David got a real kick out of my enthusiasm and started to grin in spite of himself.

"Ugh! – And just look at the company they're in," I sneered, thinking of the hate propaganda we just saw on the computer screen. "Adolph Hitler! Yuk!"

"Yeah, worlds apart, for sure. But not enough people realize the difference." Walking away from the exhibit reluctantly, David said, "Maybe we'll come back when there's more time – when everything's okay and we find Chaim Wasserman and get my grandmother and Veronica back and everything's back to normal. And we'll bring them, too." He sounded like he really believed it, too.

Back in the computer room, David said, "The important thing to remember is that there are lots of white supremacy and militant religious groups multiplying here in this country and all over the world. Today computer web sites and the mass media churn out more information than ever, while at the same time there's more intolerance than ever. More information and less critical thinking. You know? It's like people are going crazy or something. And I worry that it's somehow just the beginning all over again. Like my grandmother said last night. Well, nothing like an uninformed, indifferent public – or impoverished people kept in the dark without any access to education – to help extremists succeed. That's all it takes."

He clicked off the site. "Like tanks mowing helpless people down," he added.

When he said that, I thought of the Chinese students in Tiananmen Square – especially the famous TV image of that one boy who held back a whole tank column with his hand. What a guy! I never forgot the pictures I saw of him and the tanks. Also, I remembered a movie I saw once about Harriet Tubman, *A Woman Called Moses*, with Cicely Tyson playing the incredible woman who carried hundreds of slaves out of the South time and time again at great risk to her own life. What makes someone do that? What makes one person stand up to so many? I wondered about that aloud.

"Right, I know what you mean," David nodded. Where does that kind of strength come from? What does it take to have such courage and defiance that one person can face down a column of tanks like that boy in China in Tiananman Square, or serve an unjust prison sentence for 25 years without going insane and then come out to lead and save your country like Nelson Mandela did – "

"Or fight back in the Warsaw Ghetto against the Third Reich, despite meager weapons and numbers?"

"Or stand up to the terrorists on Flight 93 and rush them bare-handed when they were headed for Washington on September 11th and – who knows – the White House or the Capitol Building. What amazing heroes!"

I was filled with awe thinking about the contrast – the individual against the overwhelming majority . . . or the individual against the armed oppressor. And I felt it was personal to me for the first time – all of these figures – the Chinese student and Mandela and Harriet Tubman and the heroes on Flight 93 and Mrs. Rosen and Joshua.

I picked up the copy of Joshua's Diary and held it next to my heart. I believe in you, Joshua, I thought to myself, making a promise. And I'm gonna help free Mrs. Rosen and Veronica and redeem your name. If that helps put me in all your company – even way back at the end of the line – well, then I'm proud, real proud to be there.

I turned to David, but he'd already taken off. He was right back on the pay phone. One thing I've learned about him is that he's stubborn as a bulldog.

He told me later that it was like a light bulb flashed in his head and he thought of another place he could try. "Steven Spielberg's people at *The Survivors of the Shoah Foundation* where they're compiling a massive, one of a kind, multimedia archival database of Holocaust survivors' testimonies," he said. Although Chaim's name wasn't in their files, they were super helpful to him and said they'd put their team of researchers to work on his case right away. David thanked them, ran over to me to tell me about it and then doggedly attacked his terminal again.

Meanwhile, I kept returning to the Diary translation David had finally gotten today. I read it over and over again. It was trying to tell me something. But what? A lot of the entries were curious, to say the least. Was Joshua a smuggler?

Maybe. Was he cooperating with the Nazis? No way. But what was he doing? I didn't have a clue. But after staying with it a while, a pattern was slowly beginning to emerge in front of my eyes like a ghost materializing out of a fog. Slowly something began to dawn on me.

"DAVID, TAKE A LOOK AT THIS!" I shouted with excitement.

> *Today I found an abandoned root cellar in*
> *which to hide Monet and Manet. They should*
> *be safe here until the spring thaw.*

David looked at me. His eyes were red, bloodshot, exhausted. "And?"

"And that's it," I answered. "But . . . I don't know. Something is really strange here. "I mean, it's bizarre. He talks about these paintings almost like they're alive."

David quit typing and took his hands off the keyboard. Now he was listening. "Give me some more examples."

"Okay, here goes. This is from June of 1944."

> *Matisse is getting too warm in the hayloft C.W.*
> *found for her. She must be moved to more*
> *comfortable surroundings or will be jeopardized.*
> *Waffen-SS patrols are active in the village.*

"Now, does that sound like he's talking about a painting to you?"

David shrugged. "Oil canvases are delicate. You know that. Temperature, humidity, all that kind of stuff has to be controlled or they'll get damaged. Think about art museums. You've noticed those little machines in galleries that measure the atmosphere. In fact, the exhaled breath of all the people who go see the Sistine Chapel is one of the main things that threaten to ruin it. Also, Europeans often refer to things in terms of gender."

I pretended I knew that. "Yeah, that goes without saying."

Satisfied, David clicked the mouse on his terminal and resumed his hunt for the elusive C.W. Chaim Wasserman. But something about the Diary still didn't seem right to me. What it did feel like was a mystery. I kept on reading. Then sure enough, in the next minute, I had another question for David.

"Where's Canaan? Somewhere in Poland?"

"No. It's the ancient pagan name for the Promised Land. Palestine. You know . . . Israel."

A tingle went up my back. "Well, listen to this, David."

> *August 3, 1944. Wonderful news! Today I*
> *received word that Degas, Van Gogh and Pissaro*
> *are safe in Canaan. Thank God. Cassatt is already*
> *thriving there.*

"What do you make of that?"

"I don't know. Maybe he found a buyer or . . . or got the paintings out of Poland somehow. After all, he was an artist. Maybe he was just trying to keep the paintings out of the Nazis' hands. Who knows? Maybe Canaan's a code word for an art dealer or something." David shrugged.

I went off at him. "But, David, earlier you said you didn't think he was a smuggler! I'll grant that someone, a painter especially, would worry about valuable art work, but do you honestly believe he would spend this much time on . . . on collectibles, for cryin' out loud, when his people were dying?

That's not the Joshua your grandmother told us about!"

He looked up in surprise. "No, I . . . I don't believe he'd do that either."

"So what is he doing then?"

David didn't have an answer and just looked out the window. Finally, he sighed. "I'm stumped."

"This guy is a real hero, David. Whatever he's doing, he's not fencing paintings!" Flipping through the pages I said, "Look, here's another one."

> *September 1, 1944. Tonight C.W. and I will*
> *escort Renoir to the Karski Monastery where*
> *he'll be safe with Gauguin.*

"There.   Would anybody say they were going to escort a painting?   They might carry it or transport it or ship it.   But 'escort'?   I'm totally not buying it!"

David stood up. "You may have something there. Stay with it. I'll be back in a few minutes. I'm going to try that Wasserman number again in San Francisco where I got the busy signal earlier. And the five no-answers."

On his way to the phone, poor David collided with a punky-looking girl with green hair and black lipstick. Man, he was tired. He had to be punchy to miss her.

I, on the other hand, was so full of coffee I was wired. I felt like I could see the back of my eyeballs. I tried to focus all this energy on the Diary. What I couldn't get away from was how worried Joshua was about the paintings' safety. He was obsessed with it. He continually moved them from place to place to avoid detection by the Germans. It would have made more sense just to bury the paintings some place and forget the whole thing.

Joshua seemed particularly concerned for Monet

and Manet. They were usually with him or C.W. and were mentioned on nearly every single page. In fact it was in relation to them that the word "smuggle" appeared for the only time. I scrolled up the screen to reread the passage:

> *Hear, O Israel, The Lord Our God is One.*
> *Monet and Manet have been smuggled out*
> *of Sheol and are with me as I write this!!!!*

Four exclamation marks. Why? I thought about that. Nobody gets that excited about a picture. You only get that excited about a . . . a person. That's when an intriguing thought came to me. Maybe you could call it a hunch or intuition. Whatever it was, I kept it in mind while I read the last few pages of the Diary.

The final entry was particularly mysterious. It was a single sentence hastily scribbled in pencil that simply read:

> *Cezanne is missing!*

The rest of the pages were blank. That was it. . . the end of Joshua's Diary. It ended so abruptly that you just knew something terrible happened right then and there.

"LAUREN!!!!"

David scared the hell out of me so bad I practically jumped out of my seat and hung upside down from the ceiling like one of those cartoon cats. I whirled around and spotted him waving at me from the bank of pay phones at the far end of the room. I raised my hands palms up and mouthed, "WHAT?"

"IT'S HIM!" he shouted, as everyone in the room lifted their heads up and a guard tried to ssshhhhh David.

Omigod! Nikolai! I thought. I flinched and searched

frantically around me.

"Not him!" David read my body language. "HIM!"

"Who?" I squinted my eyes.

David beamed like he couldn't quite believe it himself. He practically started jumping up and down.

"HE'S ALIVE! IT'S HIM! I CAN'T BELIEVE IT! C.W. – CHAIM WASSERMAN!" he shouted, punching the air in a high five salute with the telephone receiver. "IT'S REALLY HIM! C.W.! THE ONE AND ONLY! THE MAN HIMSELF! I GOT HIM! LAUREN, WE DID IT! WE FOUND HIM!"

Chapter Twenty-Two

I ran top speed over to David. As I came screeching to a stop, almost knocking him down, he cupped his hand over the receiver and whispered to me, "He's so overjoyed he's crying. He got really excited when I told him I'm Joshua's grand-nephew."

"YES!" I cheered, throwing my right arm high in the air. I was ecstatic! This was the miracle we needed!

David went back to listening and furrowed his brow. "Oh, yes, sir, well, that's what I wanted to tell you – " But then David's mouth fell open instead. From the looks of things, he couldn't get a word in edgewise.

"Actually, I'm her grandson," David said proudly. "What?" He paused uncomfortably and cleared his throat. "Yes, she's been living here in New York, sir." Then David jumped and held the phone away from his ear. "Yes, sir, under a different last name because she married a long time ago . . . . Of course, how could you know?" Standing a yard away, even I could hear Mr. Wasserman yelling in happiness.

To me, David whispered as he covered the receiver again, "He thought she died at Auschwitz." Then after a moment of listening he answered, "How did I find you? Well, it's kind of a long story – OH, NO!" Suddenly David grabbed my arm and jerked his head towards the door. Agent McMahon was weaving through the aisles towards us, a steaming cup of coffee, with the plastic lid still on, jiggling in his hand.

"I'll handle him," said David, shoving the phone at me. "Here, Lauren, you take over. Talk to him –"

I stared at the phone in confusion. What do I do now, I thought. "H-Hello?" I asked hesitantly.

"To whom do I have the pleasure of speaking now?" I heard a courtly, elderly man's voice say on the other end of the line. His accent immediately reminded me of Mrs. Rosen's. Old fashioned, polite . . . and wonderful.

"It's Lauren . . . Lauren Robinson. Mr. Wasserman, I'm a friend of David's. Well . . . uh . . . he . . . uh . . . had to speak to someone who just arrived."

"Oh, how lucky I am today. It's a pleasure to meet you, my darling."

That clinched it. Well, I sure was ready for an adopted grandfather.

"How did you find me? No one ever has until now – and decades have passed. How did you do it?"

I wasn't sure where to start, so I jumped right in. "Mr. Wasserman, this is kind of hard to believe, but we located you after we read all about you in Joshua's Diary –"

Mr. Wasserman went very quiet. I could hear him start to breathe faster. For a second, I worried that we were going to give him a heart attack or something.

"Are you there?"

"Yes, I'm listening – go ahead. Take your time. There is nothing I would rather do in the whole world than hear what you have to say. You saw my name?"

"Well –" I took a deep breath. "No, your initials – C.W. But we figured out who you were from David's grandmother who told us about you . . . last week."

Then as best I could, I told him the whole story about how Nikolai appeared at Veronica's with Joshua's Diary and kidnapped her as a hostage to get Mrs. Rosen to play along with them. How it had gone from bad to worse when they then took Mrs. Rosen even though they said they wouldn't because her celebrity shielded her. That we were to blame because David lifted the Diary off Nikolai at the Met . . . and how they chased us afterward and kidnapped Mrs. Rosen when they couldn't catch up with us. I told him who she really was, the famous sculptor Dominique Rosen, but that the outside world didn't know yet she was missing. About our showdown with the mysterious German at Grand Central Station and the FBI coming on the scene.

I told Mr. Wasserman how desperately we had tried to find him – after only realizing today that the C.W. in the Diary was the same person Mrs. Rosen had told us about in her story – and how badly we needed his help. I told him David only got the translation today, but that if we'd been able to read Polish we'd have made the connection long before this. And how worried we were because David's family hadn't heard a thing from the kidnappers. How they had threatened David's family and me and there had been FBI tails on David, his parents and me –- but that today was to be the last day of the security detail assigned to us all. How the FBI hadn't given up, but just that they could only keep a small number of agents on us for a week, what with everything going on in New York. How they thought each day that passed without word made the outcome worse – because I overheard one of the agents on the case say that 'the kidnappers have both their ransom and their prey.' And that it didn't look good at all.

For several seconds after I finished, he didn't make a sound. His voice was hoarse at first and then became deep and low, burning with anger and intensity. In his somber, measured words, 55 years or so evaporated like they were nothing. Suddenly the Jewish warrior, the freedom fighter and defender of his people, lived once again in the fiercely courageous voice I now heard on the phone. "I would give my life for Joshua and his family!"

I truly understood what he meant after Mrs. Rosen's story. I felt a powerful current move through me from the force of his emotion. A real surge of hope.

"Listen to me, Lauren. Tomorrow morning I will be on the first flight to JFK. We must find Dominique and her friend! When and where shall I meet you?"

Wow! He was coming right away! Amazing! I felt better already. "I get out of school at 3:00 pm. Any time after that is great," I answered, giving him Cyberia's address and phone number. That sounded real stupid to me. Here he was coming all the way from San Francisco and David and I had to be in school? Ridiculous! "But we'll skip school!"

"No, that's not necessary," he said. "The first flight out of San Francisco wouldn't get me there till the afternoon because of the time difference. I'll be there even if I have to take the red-eye. But give me a phone number just in case."

"Sure," I said. David's phone was bugged anyway by the FBI. So I gave him mine instead.

"Very well, then, my child. I'll see you at 4:00 pm tomorrow afternoon at the coffee shop."

"Mr. Wasserman?"

"Yes?"

"Thanks for coming."

His voice cracked with emotion. "No, thank you, Lauren. Thank you for finding me. You and David are so resourceful and brave, you make me very proud. Perhaps an unseen hand guided you to me. You can count on my help. Until tomorrow then. God bless you."

I stood there, awe-struck and speechless. I actually just spoke to C.W.! Chaim Wasserman! He was alive, after all, and he came right out of the pages of Joshua's Diary from 1943! Unbelievable! Then I thought of what he said at the end and it hooked me. Could my prayer earlier have really helped? Amazing thought. I gently put the phone back in its cradle and turned around to see David still entertaining Agent McMahon, which apparently involved the New York cheesecake glazed with lots of cherries that David brought with us from Cyberia.

*

The next morning David appeared at my apartment just before I left for school. The doorbell rang as my mother was in the bathroom getting ready for work and I was downing some orange juice and toast. When I peered through the peephole, I was completely shocked to see him standing there. It wasn't part of our plan and I knew something awful had happened. What was he doing here? I unlocked the dead bolt and threw open the door in a nano second.

"David! What's up? What a surprise! Come in, quick. Mom's in the shower. She can't hear us." My Mom knew absolutely nothing of what was going on; I figured I had to shield her or she'd go to pieces. "I was just about to leave for school. What happened? You don't look so good."

"Nothing's happened. But – Lauren, I can't explain. Just take this please." He handed me what felt like a book wrapped in paper.

"Wha – What is it?"

"It's Joshua's – " he paused as if he couldn't say it.

"The Diary? David! You mean, the real thing? You got it back from the FBI? What's going on? Why me?"

"Yes, the real thing. Agent Ortiz returned it to my father last night – she said they were finished examining it. That they found fingerprints of a guy named Helmut Kluger, who turned out to be some Nazi mastermind the international courts and the Simon Wiesenthal Center have been trying to track down for years. They caught up with him once but he escaped, and it's been years since anyone's seen him."

"Oh," I whistled, trying to take in this information about the decrepit-looking old German whose personal bodyguards or whatever chased us all over the City after David stole the Diary from Nikolai at the Met.

"Turns out Helmut Kluger was an official in the German high command, an *SS* commandant, and an organizer of the concentration camps. And there's more. I had a dream last night. A bad dream. I just know this isn't safe in our home. Please hold it for me. And show it to Chaim later after school ... uh ... when we all meet. I want him to see the real Diary. He was there with – look, I just don't want it on me or at the house. Dad doesn't know I took it. He put it in the safe at our house, but I know the combination."

"But why don't you give it to Chaim Wasserman yourself at Cyberia after you're done with school today?"

"Lauren, there's no time to talk now! I don't want it on me. I have a bad feeling, that's all. Here, take it!"

I heaved a sigh and shook my head. "Are you sure?"

"Yes," he said, handing it over. "If anything happens to me later, tell Chaim everything. He'll know what to do. I just don't want to take any chances."

"David, don't talk like that!"

But David turned back toward the door then, clearly not himself. "I gotta go."

"David!" I called. "Wait! I'm worried about you. Are you sure – ?"

276

"Lauren, we'll talk later. I've got to go now."

"Okay, David. Later. I'll see you later," I repeated. But as I watched him rush down the hall, it struck me that I might not ever see him again.

*

All day long I carried Joshua's Diary in my backpack from class to class with my other books. I only took it off my back during classes and placed it carefully on the floor under my desk so that my foot never left it. I even wore my backpack during lunch, which a friend teased me about – "Got something goin' on that we don't know about, Lauren? Like some love letter in that backpack you're not taking any chances about?" – at which point everybody laughed. I wasn't in the mood for any of them but sort of forced a smirk. Another friend threw out a crack about not seeing me around much lately. "Real busy with stuff at home," I replied, making a face. "Oh," they said, all-knowingly, thinking I meant Mom's condition these days after the divorce.

Ordinarily, Fridays drag on bad enough, but today was like some kind of parallel universe until three o'clock when the bell rang and I shot out of school like a cannonball. Then the day finally started for me.

Running all the way from the subway to Cyberia, my hand touched the door at 3:30 p.m. No FBI tail could have kept up with me unless they ran like an Olympian athlete. But there was no tail today; it was the first day we were on our own. I was way early, but David was probably already there, I said to myself, hoping against hope. My stomach weakened as I recalled his surprise appearance at my place before school in the morning.

I ripped my Discman off my head and quickly checked my reflection in the glass door. Well, my hair was a little crazy and I was flushed from my 400 meter dash, but otherwise I didn't look too totally scary. I'd even worn a dress for the occasion, a sort of long Anna Sui-looking floral print. I'd completed the look with an old-fashioned knit sweater I found last year at a thrift shop in Soho and a pair of pole-climber boots. I think I was going for kind of a contemporary, urban-retro angle. It worked . . . mostly.

Pushing open the door of Cyberia, I couldn't wait to meet Chaim Wasserman – as much as I couldn't wait to lay eyes on David after the strange things he said when he gave me Joshua's Diary earlier. But there was no sign of David, which confirmed the sensation I had at the pit of my stomach whenever I thought about him all day.

I shrugged off my concern, reminding myself that I was thirty minutes early, and focused on finding Mr. Wasserman. I knew he was there. The place wasn't crowded at all. Just a few Columbia students sitting around drinking latte and talking or lazily tapping away at one of the terminals. The pony-tailed dude serving coffee behind the bar yawned.

Then I saw him. Over in the corner furthest from the door sat a stocky older man in a beret. I would never have guessed it was C.W. because he looked so much younger than he could possibly be, for I knew that he was in his early teens during the Warsaw Ghetto uprising. That was over 55 years ago. Yet this was the most powerfully built, healthiest-looking, fittest older man I'd ever seen. He looked like he ate nails for breakfast and washed it down with a spinach drink like Popeye. If you didn't noticed the wisps of gray hair under his cap, no one would ever dream this was a man past the half-century mark.

He was sipping espresso and his alert brown eyes peered out from under the whitest, bushiest eyebrows I'd ever seen, taking in the room and not missing a beat. Dressed in a navy turtleneck sweater, a tightly-belted Burberry's trench coat with grenade rings, gray wool slacks and black slip-on Keds tennies – he was nothing at all like I pictured him. In fact, he looked like he just stepped out of a James Bond movie. As the heavy.

I walked over to him and cleared my throat. "M-Mr. Wasserman?"

"Lauren?"

I nodded. "Yes, sir! I'm really pleased to meet you. This is a real honor." I stuck out my arm to shake his hand.

Leaping out of his chair like he was spring-loaded, he wrapped me in a tight bear-hug, like I was family, and kissed me on both sides of my face the way Mrs. Rosen does. "Lauren!" He held me at arm's length and just gazed at me as if we knew each other always and hadn't seen one another for a very long time. "How good it is to meet you!" Then he kissed me again. I was sold!

Life is funny. My new best friend was a 70+ man from San Francisco I'd never laid eyes on till now. Not like David was replaced or anything, who's in a category all by himself of course. But Chaim and I were definitely best buddies on sight. It happens . . . and, when it does, don't ask any questions. It's just magic.

"Is there any news of Dominique? Have they called yet?" he asked with grave concern.

I shook my head. "No. But something else is going on, I think. Now I'm worried about David." I told him how he appeared at my apartment before school in the morning. "He said he had a dream. He took it as a warning or something. He had a bad feeling that something might happen to him and that he might not make it today to meet you here."

Chaim's eyebrows knotted and he frowned. "Joshua used to talk like that."

"And he wanted me to show you this –" I said, pulling out the special package in my possession and handing it to Chaim. I was just about to tell him about the Nazi big shot the FBI fingered but stopped when I saw what was happening to him.

Chaim's eyes widened with disbelief as he unwrapped the paper with great care and saw Joshua's Diary. He sucked in his breath and tears fell down his cheeks. Then he lowered his head and tried to muffle a sob, sighing deeply, longingly, overcome with emotion. Shaking his head with wonder, he stared at it for a long time before opening it and turning its pages with some effort – the handwriting of his old friend Joshua speaking out to him across the long years, across all the heroic fighting and suffering and death they went through together.

He was silent for a long time. Finally, he held the old leather book to his heart and placed it back on the table in front of him, his left hand poised on top of it, as if he couldn't let it go. In a broken voice he finally whispered, "I used to chide him about it, his habit of writing things down. 'You'll kill us all!' I even challenged him once. 'No, no, you don't understand, Chaim,' he'd say. 'They'll never find it here – and even then no one would understand what it means.'" Chaim stopped and blew his nose, with tears still falling down his face.

I wanted to ask what he meant by that, but didn't want to interrupt him.

"Joshua first started writing things down in an abandoned cellar we found and hid in for a while. We didn't stay there though. We dug another cellar that no one ever found. He kept the Diary in a sawed off drain pipe there. He'd always pull the Diary out of its hiding place there and write in it. 'It helps me to keep things straight,' he'd say to me when I'd tease him about wasting his time with it. We came back to that hideout again and again because it was the best hiding place in the Warsaw Ghetto." He paused, sighing, and then added in a far-off voice, "But we had to leave the safety of that hideout. We had our work to do."

Then he looked up at me as if remembering suddenly that I was still there. "And now you are worried about David."

I nodded my head up and down, and a sob escaped from me.

"Right now you need me. I'll look through this later," he said as he gently wrapped Joshua's Diary back in the paper that David had covered it with. "There, there," he said soothingly. "Come, let's get something warm in you while we wait for him. We were both a little early. Maybe he'll still come."

I didn't feel like eating anything but somehow my appetite always gets the better of me. Over coffee and cheesecake, we talked like we'd known each other forever.

After telling him about how I knew David and Mrs. Rosen, he told me briefly about his life in San Francisco and his wife of forty-five years who died on Thanksgiving last year. His face lit up like a Broadway marquee when he mentioned her – a Holocaust survivor, too. He told me how they met in a displaced persons camp in Czechoslovakia after both their entire families died in the Holocaust and how they decided to immigrate to the United States in 1947 and moved to California. How for years and years, they worked really hard and ended up owning a chain of movie theaters in Marin County. How as a hobby he'd been a wrestling champion and coached at the local high school for many years. And that he even studied some martial arts along with his students in a program with specialists who performed exhibitions with one another's teams after exchanging methods and training.

He was a warrior all right. I beamed as I thought of Mrs. Rosen and how happy she would be to know Chaim was not only alive and in magnificent health, but also here in New York on her trail.

Then we got down to business. I described the whole scenario again in more detail, starting with Nikolai appearing at Veronica's with Joshua's Diary – and how David and I stole it back. When I told him about the kidnapping of Mrs. Rosen the day after they took Veronica, he got very quiet and listened intently, particularly as I got to the part about Nikolai's German boss. I couldn't remember the name David had mentioned in the morning. Just that they fingerprinted him as a Nazi official at Auschwitz. I also told him that Mrs. Rosen shared her story with us, how she was taken to Auschwitz and lost her mother and sisters there . . . and how she ultimately survived to reach the top of the international art world.

Before I was through, tears were streaming down his face. And when I finished, he kissed my hand and thanked me, which started me going like a sprinkler. We were quite a pair. The waitress kept coming over to make sure everything was okay. Finally, I asked him about Joshua.

"What was he like as a person, Mr. Wasserman?"

He clasped his hands and looked radiant suddenly. "My friend Joshua was a true hero. He was the bravest and most generous person I ever met. Now that I'm older, I realize something else about him, too. I really believe –" he touched his chest with his fist – "in my heart, I really believe that he was one of the *Lamed Vav*."

"Pardon me?"

He smiled. "Yes, of course, I must explain. In Jewish tradition, the *Lamed Vav* are the thirty-six righteous men for whose sake God permits the world to continue its existence. Their sole task in every generation, unknown to themselves and others, is to do good for their fellow men and women. I sincerely believe that Joshua was one of these righteous men without whom life on Earth cannot go on."

"Wow! I knew it! I knew he was really like that!"

"Yes, he was. He was a righteous man. Of this, I am certain. More certain than even the fact that I'm sitting here."

I was fascinated by what he said about Joshua. "So, he wasn't a smuggler after all, was he? He couldn't have been."

Mr. Wasserman looked me straight in the eye. "Smuggler?" he chuckled as if privately to himself. "Of course he was."

I didn't understand. "But . . . but . . . you mean, all the stuff about the paintings is true?" I was confused and felt awfully deflated.

Mr. Wasserman's eyes twinkled. He had the strangest look on his face, almost like he was teasing me. Then he laughed. "Paintings, shmaintings! *CODE NAMES*! – that's all they were. Remember, Joshua was an artist and very creative and imaginative. Didn't you suspect? They weren't paintings at all, they were – "

I clapped my hands. "I knew it! Of course they weren't paintings. No, they were – "

"Children!" shouted Mr. Wasserman as he finished my thought, beaming with pride. "Yes, they were children. We smuggled Jewish children to Palestine! Right under the Germans' noses. That's what Joshua and I were doing!"

I gasped in astonishment. This hit me like a bombshell!

What a momentous thing! The Masters, the Master paintings, were children! All this time!

"Those Nazi murderers didn't win in the end, after all. Today many of those kids are grandmothers and grandfathers themselves. And all of them have led full and rewarding lives, thank God! Doctors, lawyers, teachers, writers, dancers, artists, soldiers, scientists . . . ah, you can't believe them! Some live in Israel, others here in this country, Denmark, England and Italy. MONET AND MANET ARE TWINS! Both of them are award-winning chemists! They're wonderful. I keep up with them especially. We write each other regularly and I visit them when I'm in Jerusalem. You know why? THEY'RE HIS SISTERS!"

I came unstuck. I howled. I squealed. I drummed my boots on the floor until the table shook. "Omigod! Omigod! Sonia and Sarah! Mrs. Rosen's younger sisters are —"

"YES!" laughed Chaim. "They're alive! This is what Joshua did! SAVED CHILDREN! He dressed up like an SS officer and walked the twins out the Auschwitz main gate right in front of that bastard . . . excuse me . . . that killer Mengele — may he burn in hell!" Chaim turned his head and spat. "Can you believe it? My God, if he'd known Dominique was alive, he'd have taken her, too. We'd heard she'd been sent to . . . we heard she'd died, like her mother and baby sister."

I was reeling. Dizzy, like I needed oxygen. This was too good to be true! I kept wishing David would hurry up. He had great aunts! I couldn't wait to tell him. I wiped my eyes — they were happy tears — and daubed my cheeks with a paper napkin. "But what happened to Joshua?" I so wanted to know about the fallen hero, the author of the pages I had read and pondered and studied so hard searching for clues. "Tell me!"

Chaim's voice dropped. Suddenly, he looked tired and swallowed hard. "We did lose one child. A little girl Joshua named Cezanne. She was a toddler. An angel with beautiful black curls and big, dark eyes. One morning she wandered away from the farm where we'd been hiding her. The Polish farmer's wife who was supposed to watch her dozed off in front of the fireplace. Cezanne wandered out into the snow. Joshua went to look for her. That's when it happened."

I gritted my teeth and grimaced. "It –?"

Chaim's eyes clouded over. "Joshua was captured by an SS patrol and taken to Auschwitz. I don't know if he ever found Cezanne or not. I . . . I imagine he was tortured. If he was, he never revealed a thing. I succeeded in getting the remaining children safely out of occupied Poland. Joshua was hanged at Auschwitz a few days before it was liberated. I'm told his body was still hanging from the gallows when the Russians arrived."

My nose was all stuffy. I tried to fight back my tears. I hadn't cried this much in a long time.

Chaim was surprised by this, but smiled at me with tenderness, and then stared down into his empty coffee cup for a long time.

I glanced at my watch. Not good. It was almost 4: 15 pm. "This isn't like him, Mr. Wasserman, believe me. Especially today of all days, knowing we were to meet you! He's now 15 minutes late. Something must be wrong. He's by himself today. It's the first day the FBI isn't tailing him. Or me," I added.

Chaim patted my hand. "These boys. They'd forget their heads if they weren't screwed on. Don't worry. He's sure to be along any minute now."

"Mr. Wasserman, you don't mean that about him. You're just trying to make me feel better. David's not like other boys. He would have called if he was held up." A flutter of fear curled my stomach and I tried to ignore it.

He shook his head then and began to drop the feel-good mask he had on for my sake. "Hmmm. So we'll wait some more and then decide what to do."

The waitress came back and asked if we wanted anything else. Chaim ordered more espresso and a decaf for me. I figured I could make myself nervous without any additional help. What else could we do for the time being except wait?

"Lauren, while we're waiting, tell me this. Is there anything else you know about these kidnappers?" Chaim asked.

"Wait! I just remembered! I got a picture of one of them! With all the excitement I almost forgot! I have it right here," I beamed, reaching for my backpack. After Agent Ortiz gave me my camera and negatives back, I told him, I had the negatives developed and they came out pretty well, according to Agent McMahon. I unzipped my pack and dug around. "Oops, sorry, that's a hairbrush," I said sheepishly, laying it on the table – all tangled with purple hair and grody-looking. I definitely gotta buy a new brush, I thought, and fished around some more.

"Take your time," he chuckled. "I'm planning to be in New York as long as David and you need me."

"Whew!" I sighed with relief, just as I was beginning to think I'd lost them, and handed Mr. Wasserman the Quick-Photo package.

He took the snapshots out of the envelope and fanned them on the table. Then he picked one up and looked at it carefully. "Unbelievable!" he whispered in a stunned voice.

"What?" I asked nervously.

"It's uncanny. A miracle," he said in awe. He pointed

286

to David in the picture. "He looks just like Joshua! The spitting image."

A big smile spread across my face. I suspected David looked like Joshua! Chaim studied the photograph again and breathed in sharply. That didn't sound good to me. The nervous thing in my stomach kicked into high gear.

Then Chaim reached inside his trench coat and pulled out a monocle tied to a purple ribbon. I'd only seen that sort of thing in old movies. He fixed the lens in his right eye and squinted. "My God, it can't be!" he gasped.

"What, what?" I jumped up halfway peering closer at the photograph from upside down. The vibrations I was getting were very, very bad.

Chaim's finger trembled as he pointed to the photograph of the German. When he picked it up, the whole picture shook. "It's . . . it's him!" he choked.

I was ready to go into orbit. "Who, Mr. Wasserman? Who?"

He squeezed my wrist so hard it hurt. And then his voice got real low and constricted. "At Auschwitz, they called him the *Curator*."

The Curator – that name sounded awfully familiar. Where had I heard it before? Was it in the book I read the night Mrs. Rosen told us her story? No! It was Mrs. Rosen herself who mentioned his name when she told us how she was forced into slave labor under his command in the concentration camp!

"I'LL TAKE THAT, OLD MAN!" An arm reached across Chaim's face and snatched the photograph out of his hand as the cold steel of a gun was shoved into my temple.

Chapter Twenty-Three

I gasped and held my breath as I recognized Nikolai's sneering voice. It was like a bad dream come true. I looked up and there he was in the flesh standing over me like Genghis Khan, a scarf camouflaging his gun from onlookers in the café. He crushed the picture of his boss in his other hand and shoved it in his pocket. The rest of the photographs fluttered to the floor like dying birds.

"Don't make a sound, either of you, or your Zionist boy friend gets his throat slit! You got that?" – he hissed in my ear. Then he slid in the booth next to me, his hidden gun now in my ribs. "We've got him in the car outside. You should have seen him speeding on his bike to get here. But not fast enough. You snooping brats made a big mistake when you called the police!"

I bolted to my feet, which Nikolai wasn't expecting. As his gun clattered down to the floor, he hit me right in the solar plexus with his clenched fist. I sucked wind and fell backward like a bag full of rocks.

Chaim's powerful voice came raging forward like a torrent bursting through a dam. "LEAVE HER ALONE, YOU MISERABLE COWARD!" Before Nikolai knew what was happening, Chaim had leaped across the table, grabbed Nikolai's arm and pushed his head down so fast that I almost couldn't follow his moves. "So, Nikolai, you've been pretty tough on old ladies and youngsters. Why don't you try on someone more your size? It might improve your manners."

Nikolai's eyes goggled in disbelief. Not only was Nikolai much bigger and younger than Chaim, but he was the mobster nobody ever dared challenge. Yet Chaim had far more power and superior skill. Nikolai had no time to examine this irony because his cheek was jammed into the table as he flailed outward with his arms and futilely strained to free himself. Chaim wasn't kidding when he said he was a wrestling coach who also knew martial arts.

Through gritted teeth, Chaim smiled grimly and threatened Nikolai. "In my time, I've killed lots of men tougher than you . . . you stinking bastard!"

Two college students at the next table stopped talking, as one of the girls nearly poked herself in the eye with the plastic spoon in her coffee cup. Three others near the counter were gaping at us as they stood as if frozen on the spot. The guy who'd been behind the counter wasn't in sight, which meant he didn't see what was happening. Or else he was on the phone calling the police.

Then Chaim lifted Nikolai's head up by the scruff of his neck as he twisted his arm behind his back. Nikolai winced in pain and his face was a hideous mask of hatred and rage.

"Where is the boy?" Chaim demanded to know. "In the car you say? Well, let's go outside and see!" To me, he said calmly, "Lauren, you stay in here and wait."

Frustated and enraged, Nikolai could do nothing but grind his teeth. He kept trying to break free of Chaim, but it was useless. The muscles in his jaw writhed like snakes under his skin as he glared down at me as if he wanted to kill me. Except he couldn't do anything to me. He was in Chaim's possession. And it was a real good feeling to look at him being controlled by someone else for a change.

"I said let's go, you bastard!" Chaim had a grip on Nikolai I'd never seen. And Nikolai seemed helpless to do anything but move like a puppet wherever Chaim led him.

By this time, the guy behind the counter appeared with his mouth hanging open. "Everything all right?" he asked weakly, not wanting to get involved. He kept a pretty fair distance away.

"Oh, just fine," Chaim called back to him. "As soon as I rid you of this scum!"

"Oh, okay," he answered, trying to be cool, but mainly relieved that they were leaving so he could go back to what he was doing.

When they reached the door, I jumped up and followed them after grabbing Joshua's Diary and throwing a few dollars down on the table. Everyone was still staring speechlessly at the whole scene. Shuffling right behind Chaim and Nikolai, I turned around and called out to Cyberia's patrons, "A disagreement about computer servers, that's all." And they went back to their conversations and coffee.

Chaim had already pushed Nikolai out the door by the time I opened it. Then he shouted at me, as if seeing me from the side of his head. "Get back and wait for me inside!" I instantly did as I was told and peered out the glass door while Chaim began to grill him about David and Mrs. Rosen.

Chaim twisted Nikolai's arm all the more when he wouldn't answer. "No problem, Nikki. I have all the time in the world to break your arm as slowly and painfully as possible." Then Chaim removed Nikolai's gun and frisked him with his free hand. As he did this, a black car across the street screeched out of its parking space and sped off down Amsterdam Avenue. A different car than the one David and I had seen in the Park.

David! I couldn't help it – I ran outside and watched the car skid around the corner on two tires. It had happened so fast. Chaim was barely out the door with Nikolai 60 seconds when the car holding David captive fled the scene.

"Nice friends, you have," Chaim said to Nikolai sarcastically. "No help for you, eh? Always thinking of themselves. But then that's the only kind of people you would know, right?" He slammed Nikolai against the wall and shouted: "I want answers from you and I want them now!"

Nikolai tried to throw a punch, but Chaim dodged him so fast and flipped him over so expertly that Nikolai slumped down and hit the pavement hard instead. He was struggling to get off the ground when Chaim hit him again, connecting blows so fast that it sounded like a jackhammer.

"Now this is what we're going to do, Nikki. You're going to tell me where Dominique Rosen is – she and her friend – and where you were taking David. Where's your hideout?"

"What makes you think she's still alive?" spat Nikolai, seething with hatred.

I crumpled over hearing the unthinkable news about Mrs. Rosen when suddenly an arm grabbed me around my waist and lifted me in the air. Vlad had sneaked up behind and held me sideways with one arm.

"THAT'S ENOUGH! LET HIM GO OR THE KID GETS IT NOW!" Vlad shouted.

No sooner had Vlad picked me up when Chaim kicked the gun out of Vlad's other hand, hit him in the neck, and then in the side so that he was forced to release me. Vlad went down hard as Nikolai leaped up and pounced on Chaim with his full weight. But Chaim threw him off easily and flipped him over like this morning's pancakes. In a flash, both of these bruisers were lying on the sidewalk, gasping for air and moaning with pain, while Chaim looked fresh and relaxed, like he was just demonstrating some wrestling holds to his team. ME!

"Now, once more, guys," Chaim said impatiently. "Where is Dominque Rosen? 'Dead,' you say? I don't believe you. She can't be dead. What? No answer? Okay, game time is over. Now it's time to scream for mercy." He grabbed Vlad again and held him in a choke hold that made him splutter and gag and beg for mercy. Then he pushed him face down and Vlad fell really hard again. I hoped against hope Chaim was right about Mrs. Rosen.

Nikolai and Vlad squinted up through swollen eyes at Chaim like he was a fortress they could not scale. They were trapped and they knew it. Mostly though, they looked like they were in shock and needed physical therapy bad.

Then Chaim demanded, "While you're thinking it over, tell me what you were going to do with the girl? Why did you follow her in there if you haven't made a move on either the boy or girl all week?"

Neither answered.

Chaim banged their heads together and pressed his fingers against their temples in a move I'd never seen before. They looked like they were hurting real bad, and their eyes were starting to bulge and glaze over with panic.

"Because the tails are off them finally!" Vlad shouted hoarsely, choking it out.

Nikolai, ever the gloating lout, added in as much of an indifferent voice as he could muster: "To show Dominique Rosen we mean business –"

Chaim smacked Nikolai across the face with a stunning blow that made his head rock 90 degrees to the right. "Oh really. And what *business* would that be?"

"What do you think?" Nikolai hissed stubbornly,

refusing to give in.

But Vlad yelled out: "After we kill the boy first, then the girl, and last her old friend!" Then he crumpled over on the ground again as Chaim held him up partially again by the neck.

So Mrs. Rosen was alive! And maybe Veronica, too, then. I felt such a wave of relief and joy at the same time that I heaved a loud sigh. "Thank God!"

Then Nikolai turned on me with that same leering, disgusting expression he had that first night, almost as if he couldn't stand my happiness. "We have someone at your building ready to pay a visit to your mother, princess. If this associate of ours does not hear from us in exactly an hour, there will be a knock on your apartment door and your mother (who is home – we checked) will answer the door to this, ah, special representative of ours. We call him *the strangler*."

Chaim slammed Nikolai's head on the sidewalk. "Wipe that smirk off your face when you address her, you lout." To me Chaim spoke reassuringly, "I don't believe him, Lauren. It's just a ruse to frighten you and try to gain the upper hand." Then he turned back to Nikolai whose head he held in a vice. "Which he'll never be able to pull off any longer! Right, Nikki?" Chaim mocked, slamming his head again. "Right? Say it, Nikki. Right?"

"Ri –!" Nikolai rasped, coughing, his mouth beginning to bleed.

"Now once more, where is Dominique Rosen?"

Vlad started to say something when he was interrupted by Nikolai, who really lost it now. "No! Shut up, Vlad! Yout've said too much already!"

"Oh big brother, I am sick of this!" Vlad argued in disgust. "It's a waste of time! Stupid to take Dominque Rosen! How many times did I . . . we should have taken the boy from the beginning! Then she would have talked. Some Nazi mastermind – he's demented, I told you that from the start. So what if the boy took the Diary! The old German had a copy. But, no, *he* had to have the great Dominique Rosen in his possession."

"Shut up, Vlad! You don't know what you're talking about!" Nikolai screamed.

But Vlad was really wound up now. "*I* don't know what I'm talking about? You're just as bad as the old Nazi. You think *you* know everything? We were to start with the girl here that day we followed them downtown! Remember? And *then* the grandson! Then the boy's father! Wasn't that the plan that night we moved in on them? Well, wasn't it?"

Nikolai didn't answer.

"But, no, *you* had to change the plan and take her lady friend with no voice instead of the girl here and the boy! I told you that night, remember? I tried to stop you. A big mistake, I told you. Achhhh! A headache and a half, that woman – all that night daring us, acting like she wanted to be a martyr. And then the two of them together from the next day– feeding energy and stubbornness into each other. They're fearless together! Dominique Rosen would never give in that way. You have to hit her where it really hurts, with the young ones. And with the family! What a waste of time! Too late now."

Vlad was spilling information all over the place. I didn't know till now that they were brothers. Nor that both David and I were to have been taken first. I seem to have blocked out the part about me from that first night.

"But the FBI guard-dogs are off them!" Nikolai yelled. "Now was the time to move in on the kids."

"They weren't that first night, you fool! We had a clear path then, didn't we?"

"You're too impatient, Vlad! You've always been that way. A hothead! And you've ruined everything by talking so much!"

"*I've* ruined everything?" Vlad shouted back at Nikolai, enraged. Achhh, you mean *he's* ruined everything – this old Hercules here! Where the hell did he come from?"

Chaimed smirked at this. "You'd be surprised." Then, still holding the two of them down like a gladiator, he said calmly but with curiosity, "Tell me this. What could he possibly do with someone that well-known?"

"Hide her in a safe place, of course."

"In this country? You must be joking. This isn't India where their most famous actor was kidnapped for months." I even knew what he meant because this actually happened recently, according to one of my classmates' reports in current events class.

"Smuggling her out of the country to Europe was the plan. Killing her, another, after getting the information he wanted."

"Shut up, Vlad!"

"Hmmm," Chaim murmured, ignoring Nikolai. Then in a commanding voice, he shouted, "Once more, where is this 'old Nazi' mastermind? You will take me to him now!"

"I . . ." Vlad faltered, "we don't know where he lives. We only met him twice. Usually we deal with him by phone and through his . . . bodyguards. I know you're not going to believe this, but he'll be at a synagogue on Lexington Avenue tonight . . . in a short while."

"No. Why should I?" Chaim scowled.

"Because I heard him say that it was a favorite place of his . . . of 'antiquities' he said . . . 'to round out the picture.' But don't ask me what he meant by that. We thought it strange too. He's the type that likes to savor things. A risky combination, I told my brother here . . . who thinks only he knows everything," said Vlad, wincing, as if preparing to ward off the next blow, this time from his brother.

"What's *a short while?*" Chaim asked.

"Soon . . . at 'sundown' is what he said."

Nikolai shook his head and sneered. "You can surprise them there, but you won't see the grandson alive – and you'll never be a match for the others. You'll get yours – !"

Chaim ignored him. "How many are in your operation?"

Vlad didn't hesitate to answer. "Seven of us, including the old Nazi. Four of us and two of his own men, his personal bodyguards, one South American and the other, German."

Chaim pressed Nikolai's arm upward behind his back more tightly. "What else have you not told me? What's the plan here? Tell me or this is the last time you ever have the use of your right arm! And after that I'll break every other limb of your worthless body!"

But Vlad answered instead of Nikolai. "His plan is to present her with the broken body of her dead grandson as a memento for not revealing anything in the Diary. After we were to beat the kid to a pulp, that is. To make her realize that next he goes after her son – the kid's father – if she doesn't decode the Diary. With the father, we were to break the fingers on his right hand so that he could never play the violin again."

"Shut up!" Nikolai yelled.

"But if you ask me," Vlad continued, ignoring his brother, "I think that unless he gets the information he wants pretty soon, he'll have no use for either of them any more. I can read him better than Nikolai."

"I said shut up, you traitor! My own brother!"

Vlad started to get really furious now, his dark eyes

glowering at his brother. "All week it's been hell!" he shouted more at Nikolai than at Chaim. "Too messy. Even without the press knowing yet that Dominique Rosen has been taken. And it's just a matter of time before they're in on the whole deal. The old broad and her friend turned out to be much tougher than we figured. What a headache! He'll either smuggle them both out right away and . . . . Either way they're history."

Nikolai was spitting a tooth out as a trickle of blood ran down his chin. "Damn you, Vlad! I always knew you were too soft for this! You coward!"

"Where again?" Chaim demanded, muzzling Nikolai. He had decided to believe Vlad. "The exact name."

"Coward? Oh, is that so?" Vlad yelled back at Nikolai. "I want *out* because I'm smart enough to know when things are out of hand," he spat at his brother in disgust. Then he looked up at Chaim, and told him where. "The Beth Hayim Synagogue on Lexington Avenue," Vlad answered. "It's at — "

"I know where it is," Chaim cut him off. "So there will be only three or four of you creeps with him if one or two are holding Dominique and her friend . . . ." he said as if they didn't exist. "Vlad, you can go now," Chaim said abruptly, waving him away. "I don't need you. You've been most helpful. The police can catch up with you any time, I'm sure, now that we know you two are brothers. You're small potatoes to me. Smart but stupid, right? So get lost!"

Vlad looked dumbfounded. He managed to rise to his feet, sheepishly looking around, hoping this wasn't a joke. His face was filled with pain as he tried to stand straight and take his first step.

"Go on, go! Get out of here!" shouted Chaim, as Vlad limped and stumbled awkwardly forward, scrambling to get away. "Get out of my sight!"

But to Nikolai he growled, "Come on, Nikki, get up, you're coming with me."

He held him in his powerful hands, one of which was behind Nikolai's neck, the other gripping his arm which he held behind Nikolai's back. As Chaim pushed him to his feet, he whipped off Nikolai's belt and tied his hands behind his back. Then he double-tied him with some kind of small Chinese rope he took out of his pocket, like meditation beads or something, or like martial arts paraphernalia.

Chaim was in charge, all right. And Nikolai – Nikki – was grunting in pain as Chaim pushed him down the street.

Chapter Twenty-Four

A half hour later to the very minute, Chaim and I waited on the steps of the majestic Beth Hayim Synagogue as the sun went down. Nikolai was tied up in the back seat of Chaim's rental car across the street in a loading zone. Chaim had already gone inside the temple and searched everywhere, but found no sign of the German "Curator" or anyone else. Motioning to the illegally parked car with Nikolai inside, Chaim said, "It'll help flag the police better."

"Yeah, well, or maybe just a meter lady," I said nervously. "But still I guess we could tell her to call the police. If only she'd come soon! The police are pretty busy these days."

Losing my cell phone, just when I could make the best use of it ever, made me wince at all the wasted hours I spent talking aimlessly with friends. On the way here we had stopped the car with traffic honking at us all over the place so I could jump out and call Agent Ortiz from a corner pay phone. But the phone was broken. And we had no luck finding a police car on the way here. None that we could get to in commuter traffic anyway. And none that we could detour off our route for because we weren't sure how much time we had. It was almost sundown now.

Chaim was concerned that if he couldn't meet up with them in time, would there be another chance at all? According to what Vlad had revealed despite Nikolai's threats, we had to get there in time before the German "Curator" smuggled Mrs. Rosen out of the country. Chaim said that even though they spotted him tangling with Nikolai, they didn't know who he was.

"I could have been just a concerned bystander trying to stop them from hurting you, for all they know. And they certainly know nothing about Nikolai waiting for us like a good boy in the car over there," Chaim grimaced with a kind of chuckle. "And I don't think Vlad has returned to warn them. He's probably in the next state by now. Whoever took David clearly knows nothing about what happened to Nikolai and Vlad after driving off with him," he added.

This did not make me feel very good. Any time I thought of David, I felt sick in the pit of my stomach. Chaim saw my expression and tried to give me an encouraging smile. I looked up at him and felt a little better. He seemed so sure of himself. Or at least hopeful. That's when I really noticed the outline of the incredible edifice behind him.

The temple's delicate brownstone facade rose into twin minarets topped by onion-shaped domes made of green copper. Whenever I saw it as a kid, it always reminded me of the Arabian Nights and faraway desert caravans. Today, as the Lexington Avenue traffic honked and roared behind me, I couldn't go to that warm, happy place in my mind. I was so scared my legs were weak. I even felt a little faint, like I was about to hyperventilate. Rolling gray clouds scudded ominous and low over the towers. The air was cool and smelled like rain. And night.

A man whistled as he walked up the steps and went inside the temple. Chaim smiled at the man and told me a beautiful story to calm my nerves, for he certainly noticed that I was this close to jumping out of my skin. "Whenever I hear someone whistling as they enter a synagogue," he said, "I think of a very wise Rabbi who lived a long time ago in Europe. The Ba'al Shem Tov, you see, was one of the great holy men in Judaic history who taught that 'God desires the heart.'"

"What does that mean?" I asked.

"Well, here's a story for you that might explain it better than any definition I could ever make. It is said that once upon a time, on the solemn, holy observance of Yom Kippur, a poor young shepherd appeared in the great synagogue of the Ba'al Shem Tov to pray with the congregation. This was back in the 18th century in Europe. The young shepherd could not read or write, however, and he was ashamed that he could not pray with everyone around him in the customary way of reading the special prayers for the service. Well, he began to whistle aloud in his heartfelt way instead, as if his voice were an instrument, for this was something he knew he could do very well. So he offered his humble gift of whistling before God with great reverence.

"Suddenly all voices came to a halt. When the congregation heard the sound of whistling above their prayers, they were aghast at such arrogance and shouted out in protest that the young shepherd was committing a sacrilege in the temple of God. Some men rushed to grab him and forcibly remove him from the temple. But the Ba'al Shem Tov called out to them to set him free. Before the whole congregation he announced that until the very moment the young boy had begun to whistle, he felt that all their prayers were unable to be heard. 'Until now . . . I could feel our prayers being blocked as they tried to reach the heavenly court. This young shepherd's whistling was so pure, however, that it broke through the blockage and brought all of our prayers straight up to God.'"*

Chaim shook his head with a smile and said, "So you see, one need not recite a prayer perfectly that one has been taught, nor read perfect prayers from a book. It is lovely to pray with and among one's community, to be sure. Ah, but what matters most of all, no matter how imperfect we are, is that our prayers come from the heart. Even through our poetry, our music, our whistling from the heart. For that too is a form of prayer."

"Oh, that is a beautiful story," I said. "Thank you for telling it. It makes me feel better." Just then, a chilly wind started up, sweeping right through me, and I shivered. "I so hope God hears our prayers tonight."

Chaim stood before me as solid as a rock. Don't be nervous, Lauren. You've come this far. I think you are destined for much more in life. And a long one at that."

Then in an another attempt to keep my mind off David and the coming confrontation, he pointed to the towers. "My wife Miriam and I attended this synagogue when we lived in New York that first year. The towers, you see, represent the two columns which stood outside Solomon's Temple. Solomon was the wisest man of his time. A good complement, don't you think, to his father, the warrior King David? Those are the two hands of God – wisdom and power."

King David. That reminded me. Oh, God! David! I loved him so much my heart hurt. I had to be brave. I just had to.

Chaim looked up at the sky. "It's getting dark. Soon it will be sundown and the Sabbath will be here. It always makes me feel good. I love it so." He turned up the collar of his trench coat and tugged his beret low over his eyes. Suddenly he was the youthful hero in Mrs. Rosen's story, young and strong and brave . . . and not afraid to die. I realized I was in the best company I could possibly ever be. A warm feeling of peace came over me and my breathing slowed down. Maybe everything was going to be okay after all, I thought. I prayed that I was right.

People began to arrive and enter the synagogue in pairs and groups. As Chaim had explained, it was the start of the Sabbath. I envied them. Wrapped up in their own private lives, whatever they were, they were still in a much better place in life than we were.

Several minutes passed. No one had gone in for quite a while when suddenly the front doors of the synagogue creaked open, and from out of the shadows emerged Sergei with two other tough-looking guys I'd not seen before. And someone else behind them. The decrepit-looking, old Nazi they called the Curator.

When I saw his clamped, mask-like face, I felt like I was in the presence of something inhuman, and that I was going to die. I thought of what Chaim and Mrs. Rosen said about him. This was Hitler's *SS* commandant who relished taking the possessions – money, clothing, family heirlooms, even the hair and gold teeth – of all the men, women and children he and his men led to the gas chambers and execution pits. For a second, I thought about running. But only for a second. I stood there on the steps and forced myself not to move. It was the hardest thing I've ever had to do.

Impeccably dressed in his camelhair overcoat and elegant suit, this living embodiment of Adolph Hitler's crazed dreams slowly descended the stairs and gave us a sarcastic, regal wave. Diamond cufflinks glinted next to his black gloves when he lifted his arm. Then he stopped a few steps above me. "Lovely. You brought a guest," he said looking at Chaim. "Come with us down to the side of the temple. There is much too much going on in the front here. We'll have more privacy there. Come," he coaxed. "There is a nice courtyard set back from the street."

Chaim squared his shoulders and spread his feet for balance like a boxer poised to fight. He didn't move.

"Do you really have a choice?" he asked imperiously, staring at Chaim.

"Allow me to introduce you to my colleagues," he said, stepping down to the sidewalk and walking around the side, while Chaim and I followed his heavily accented voice. "This is Sergei, whom the young lady has already had the pleasure of meeting," he smirked, plainly enjoying his moment. "And this is my right arm, so to speak – my dear Julio – a very special young man I raised from an orphan in South America before moving back to Germany. And this is my left arm, my dear Dietrich."

He looked around, realizing he was missing two members of his gang, and asked, "Where are Nikolai and Vlad? You are unattended. Where – ?" Then he shrugged, looking at Chaim and me, sizing us both up, knowing that it was they who were supposed to bring me here. Well, I was here, all right, and with Chaim Wasserman, the great hero of the Warsaw Ghetto. And they were nowhere in sight.

"Am I to take it that you are here of your own free will?" he asked me. But before I could answer, he turned to Chaim.

"And you are?" the old Nazi inspected Chaim, lingering over his face like a man gazing at his prey. He lifted one eyebrow. "Are you a survivor – one of them? Jude?"

Chaim didn't answer but instead returned the question in kind. "Are you one of *them* – one of the Savages, Bloodsuckers, Child murderers of the Reich?" he spat back at the venomous SS commandant like an angel of judgment.

A few people passed by on the street and whirled their heads around, their eyes popping out of their heads. They were at least 30 feet away, and it was dark enough in the courtyard that they couldn't really see us. But they sure did hear Chaim. Were they on their way to the evening service, I wondered?

The Curator gasped at first, then tried to collect himself. He circled Chaim slowly, studying him in detail . . . then came to a standstill directly in front of him.

"Do I know you? . . . *Herr* . . . *Herr* . . .?"

"*C.W.* to you." Chaim stared at him, narrowing his eyes like a wolf keen for the hunt. The old Nazi gasped in recognition at one of the codes in Joshua's Diary, and was still trying to take this in when Chaim asked a question of his own. "Why here at this holy temple, if I may ask?"

"Irony, I suppose. Although, I must admit, I do admire Hebrew antiquities . . . to death. I've collected quite a few over the years."

In one quick move, Chaim closed the gap between them. Sergei, Julio and Dietrich attempted to seize Chaim, but the former *SS* commandant waved them off and stood his ground. "I'm well aware of your record," Chaim said scornfully. "You're the parasite-abomination they call the *Curator!*"

The leer on the Nazi's face quickly faded. His cheek erupted in a violent spasm, which died just as quickly as it began. "Are you quite sure we haven't met before?" he asked, strangely held by Chaim's defiance despite three guns on him. "Who are you? The girl's grandfather?"

"No, not her grandfather. I never saw her before today."

The Curator raised his eyebrows. "Yet I feel somehow that we've met."

Chaim stepped before him and got in the old Nazi's face. When he spoke, his voice was powerful, relentless, without mercy. "Through the six million you and your pack of beasts destroyed! Yes, I know who you are, you murdering fascist bastard! You were the fleshpicker part of the Nazi that systematically killed millions – then made money off their blessed remains! You are worse than a vulture, a cannibal! And if you cause so much as a finger to be laid on this child or Dominque Rosen or her grandson or her friend, so help me God, I'll kill you with my bare hands and make this holy sanctuary your tomb!"

The effect Chaim's words had on the old Nazi was so dramatic that it was like a dam burst inside him. The Curator immediately began to shake and quiver like he was caught in the coils of a vessel-popping seizure.

"So! You are one of them!" he screeched, his face blanching white with fury. "Je –" he started to say. But suddenly his voice changed to a sickening note of pleasure. "Wait . . . C.W. . . . C.W. himself! *Mein Gott*! A survivor who smuggled paintings! Where did you come from? How fortunate we are – "

The old Nazi was now just about salivating at the prospect of "C.W." before him in the flesh. "So Dominique Rosen was holding out on us. No matter, we don't need her or anyone else now that you're here. Coming to sacrifice yourself for her? I'm touched by your sentiments. I'm curious where you've been all this time, but no matter. You'll have plenty of time to tell me when you return to the continent with me as my guest."

Enjoying this new turn of events to the hilt, he languidly waved a gloved hand back towards the synagogue and chuckled. A veil of darkness was in his laughter that gave me the creeps. Then, turning to his men, he said in a low voice: "Get rid of the others immediately. Dietrich, call and tell them to dispense with them at once. We leave for Europe tonight."

I watched Dietrich click his cell phone open and put through the order of death for Mrs. Rosen, Veronica . . . and

David. He tried to call twice but it was clear he couldn't get through.

The Curator started to wave his men forward when Chaim shouted: "Dominique Rosen doesn't know I even exist! You know, you and your kind were all so demented – you're all the same. You're no different. You live in a world of such darkness you can't see the obvious!" Chaim chuckled and said in a mocking voice, "Oh, you want the hidden works of the masters, eh? HA! As if you had a right to them – "

The Curator still on another track altogether hissed back, "You'll see. We have special ways to make you talk about the paintings, which I will enjoy very much in your case – "

"As if it were your right!" Chaim shot back. "All of you master beasts who never had a right to anything, not to one life of all the millions you took! Not to one painting, not to one child – !"

The Curator had no clue what Chaim was talking about. He was enraged at being mocked and challenged. Anyone could see he wasn't used to being talked to this way. His men even seemed surprised that he let Chaim go on as long as he did. But Chaim seemed to fascinate him. Then too he was the great "C.W." of Joshua's Diary, which the Curator had taken such pains to study, to go to the lengths of kidnapping over, and still be in the dark about. He seemed in no hurry at this moment because he held all the cards. He had Dominique Rosen and the collateral of her grandson and friend. And now he had C.W. and me.

"You're nothing but a reptile, lower than anything that crawls in the earth – you and your kind!" Chaim seemed to be just getting started.

"We should have finished the job when we had the chance to rid the earth of you subhuman scum forever!" The old Nazi cackled and jerked like a maniac. Spit flecks flew from his lips as his body shook with the current of hatred that surged through his body.

What I saw jolted me. Like the sun suddenly appearing from behind a cloud, a revelation burned itself into my brain. It hit me that I was looking at nothing less than the face of evil. I would never have believed it without seeing it firsthand with my own eyes. This was far different from reading about it in a book or seeing it on a screen. This was naked evil – the soul of darkness itself.

"Subhuman, eh?" Chaim answered with great dignity. "You know the word, all right. You invented it. It is yourselves you see wherever you look; *you* are the subhumans. To be human means to be gloriously alive, to cherish life and protect it. You have neither passion for life nor compassion. You have no empathy, no capacity to suffer with others, therefore no capacity for love or joy. It is you who are not human. Yes, *you*, who hate life so and those who have no need of you, who take no notice of you, who look upon your dark and alien soul as something to turn away from in repulsion. So you destroy them. I don't presume to comprehend the pleasure you took in genocide and damnation. I know that only the inhuman can hate the human so. That is what makes you monstrous imitations who know down deep that life excludes you. Why? Because your very heartlessness and need for self-worship removes you from the human. So in your rage you kill and destroy that which offends you by its very essence: life, love, child-bearing, the continuous cycle of creation. You choose death and destruction. You are nothing. Nothing. Nothing at all. You have to kill and maim to make yourselves feel puffed up – and concoct a ridiculous mask of myth and illusion with all your disgusting swastikas and symbols to hide the reality of your hideous core of impotence and nothingness. You are pathetic!"

Chaim had really gotten to him because the deranged Nazi absolutely could not control himself. Panting and pacing like an animal, he shrieked back at Chaim: "But, you know, Jew, no one really cares what happened to you! *Mein Gott!* Today some people don't even believe it when they're told! But you and I know the Truth! You and I know what we did!" he beamed with leering pride, almost conspiratorially.

Chaim went on, roaring over the old Nazi's voice. "YOU WHO ARE DEAD INSIDE! You who have the souls of reptiles, you who nearly drove humanity back to the age of reptiles and shrouded the world in darkness! You who hate life so much that you must kill others to lift yourself up, to exalt yourselves. You have no life! You are the walking dead!"

The old Nazi was horrified at Chaim's words. "That is not true! We had a dream! A glorious purpose –" he started to say. Then his voice got lower and yet more excited at the same time. "With my very own hands and devotion to my Fuehrer and the Aryan master race beating in my heart, I exterminated you Jews and your children! We were better than you. We could never kill enough of your precious offspring to erase every one of you from the earth and end your race – forever! Achhhh, to this day, I can still hear you begging for your worthless lives!"

Suddenly striking like a cobra with lightning speed, Chaim's hand lashed out and seized the Nazi by his mottled, wrinkly throat, lifting him off the ground. I'd never seen anyone move so fast. Sergei and the other two bodyguards tried to stop him but merely looked like they were doing it in slow motion next to Chaim.

"I'm going to rip out your larynx unless I see Dominique and the boy!" he roared murderously as he held the old Nazi by the throat. To Sergei and the bodyguard, Chaim spat: "Touch your guns and he's history! Drop your weapons – now! And slide them over to me. Carefully, very carefully!" Chaim's fingers tightened in a vice grip, his nails going white with the pressure as the choking Nazi gurgled and squawked like a parrot.

As Sergei and Julio took their guns out of their pockets and slid them along to Chaim, Sergei whipped out a cell phone and motioned to Chaim that he needed it to produce David. Chaim signaled an OK and Sergei clicked open the phone, said a few words, and snapped it shut.

We heard a car door slam shut around the corner, and soon David hesitantly appeared. David was alive! My heart leaped with joy. "David!" I called and waved wildly at him.

Then I saw another man behind him. A giant of a man with a gun who called out something in Russian. He grabbed David from behind and frog-marched him down the steps, the cold barrel of the pistol mashed to his temple.

His face lit up with a holy fire, Chaim yelled at the Russian giant while still holding the old Nazi's throat in a death grip. "I'm not playing! Release the boy! Now!"

Unsure of his next move, the Russian holding David glanced at his boss for approval. But Chaim tightened his hold, squeezing harder and harder like a boa constrictor cinching down on a squealing pig, and the Nazi Curator's eyes bulged as if on stalks. His tongue shot out from his mouth and in desperation he gnawed it bloody as he struggled to scream. Finally, one arm flopped and the old Nazi frantically waved off the German. "*Nein*, Leonid," he rasped.

Leonid got the message loud and clear. He holstered his pistol and let go of David.

Free of the Russian, David leaped down to join me and I hugged him tight. Smiling with relief and rubbing his arm, he spoke softly in my ear. "Thanks for coming, Lauren. I've been thinking about something all day. And that is that I take back everything I said about you in the beginning! Oh, and another thing. You've really got guts!"

I winked and squeezed his hand. "Wouldn't miss it for the world." I bit my lip and tried not to cry. Then I went ahead and just said it. "I love you, you know."

"I know. I've known ever since we hid behind the bushes in the Park. I love you, too. And I always will."

When I heard that, I could have circled above the temple like a human Lear jet.

Meanwhile the Curator began to splutter and wheeze as Chaim eased up his grip only slightly. What happened next went so fast that I didn't see it coming. Sergei jumped me and pulled out a knife aimed at my throat, as David shouted "NO!"

"Let him go!" ordered Sergei. "Or she gets it here and now!"

Chaim released the old Nazi instantly.

The Curator, regaining his composure and recovering enough to rise to his feet, stood there blinking for a minute and massaging his throat. "Thank you, Sergei," he whispered, trying to regain his voice. "I have a nice bonus for you for your act of bravery and brains." Then he meticulously brushed off his clothes as if he'd simply tripped and stubbed his toe on a leisurely walk down the block. Clicking his heels together – he actually did that! – he made a fake little bow to me.

"Well," he grimaced and announced, "this has been most entertaining, but unfortunately I'm afraid our little tea party must come to an end." Turning to Chaim, he spat, "Foolish man. If I die, Dominique Rosen dies. I have given strict orders, you fool! Move over there –- over *there*! Away from me! I don't want you anywhere near me!" the Curator shouted, cursing at him in German. "But make no mistake about it, *C.W.*" – he spat – "you're coming with us in chains!

311

We have ways to make you talk about the paintings. You of all people would remember our methods!"

To Dietrich, Sergi, Julio and Leonid, he barked: "Keep your guns on the kids and shoot them if this intruder so much as blinks!" Then turning to me, the Curator said: "Now I want that Diary. The original. I know you have it! I want it now!"

I stood stone still and didn't move a muscle.

"Hand over the Diary!" he shouted at me. "I'm warning you. I want that book. You and that boy stole it from us. It is mine!"

"It is not yours!" Chaim roared back.

"Shut up! I found it and I claim it as mine!"

"We do not have it," Chaim said, iron-faced, trying to deflect attention from me and clearly stalling for time.

"I know you have it!"

"What makes you think we do?" Chaim baited.

"My loyal Sergei saw you with it in the coffee shop earlier today through the window. Nikolai, Vlad and Sergei were to bring the boy and girl. Sergei brought the boy. I see that Nikolai and Vlad had some trouble with the girl and –" he sneered – "you." Then he lost his patience. "Come now, we are out here long enough! I want this finished! Men, take them now!"

Chaim intervened with a clear ring of authority in his voice. "First, we have to see Dominuqe Rosen! You'll get absolutely nothing until she's free!"

"What? You are in no position to bargain with me!" he said scornfully. "Who do you think you are?" Then the old Nazi looked bored with him. "All in good time, all in good time. She's safe, probably wondering why her friends are tarrying so. But first things first," he simpered. Leonid meanwhile had reached down for the two guns that belonged

312

to Sergei and Julio. It was only then that I noticed they had silencers on them. Leonid and Julio pocketed them and pointed them at Chaim.

Once again the Curator addressed me and stuck out his hand. "The Diary, if you please, Miss."

Sergei moved his knife away from my throat a few inches, and I turned to David, who nodded and said in a terrified voice: "It's okay. Do as he says, Lauren."

Gently, slowly, I unhinged my backpack and put it down on the steps. Dietrich and Sergei glared at me like they wanted the personal pleasure of tearing me limb from limb, while the Curator licked his lips in anticipation. Julio and Leonid's guns were in their pockets and clearly pointed at David and Chaim who looked on, stone-faced, impenetrable. I knew he was planning something.

As I bent down to open it, the Curator shouted, "Wait! Sergei, you open it! And watch him, Julio – keep your gun on him!" he spat in the direction of Chaim.

If they only knew, I thought, what Chaim knows about the "paintings." Yeah, I thought, watching Sergei rummage around in my backpack – we'd probably all be dead. Nazis don't have much a sense of humor or poetic justice, for sure. I looked over at David who winked back at me. He doesn't know yet himself, I thought with excitement. Nor that his great-aunts are alive.

Finally Sergei reached to the bottom and pulled out the manila envelope with its precious contents. I felt sick as I watched him open it and pass the worn leather volume penned in Joshua's own hand to the grotesque, serpent-like old Nazi.

The Curator's eyes were fiery now and flashed with greed, and his lips started to spit even. After inspecting the envelope's contents, he sealed it back again. Satisfied, he smiled and said, "Now see how easy that was?" Then he stepped out of the courtyard and scanned the side street we were on, as if looking to see if anyone was in sight. Satisfied, he came back and turned to Dietrich and Sergei. "Kill the boy and girl and take this *C.W.* intruder with us!"

Turbo-charged by adrenaline and love, I did something without thinking. I brazenly stepped in front of Chaim and David. If this was the end, at least the bad guys were going to get a piece of my mind. "Wait a second! You should know something first!" I shouted.

Sergei drew his gun, but the Curator motioned for him to wait. The withered old Nazi swiveled his head like an iguana. "Yes, my little Jew bitch?"

"I'll take that as a compliment," I answered cheerfully, my head held high. "In fact, it's the best one I've ever received."

Puzzled, the old Nazi cocked his head like he couldn't quite believe his ears. David and Chaim were grinning at me from ear to ear.

I figured I'd already crossed the line so I went with my feelings, and they didn't disappoint me. I put my hands on my hips and rested one of my boots on the step above me. Then with my voice steady and calm – where did this come from? – I started out quietly . . . like I was talking to a complete idiot.

"There's something you ought to know, Mr. Curator, or whoever the hell you are: THERE ARE NO PAINTINGS, YOU JERK! Repeat, no paintings! They were the code names for children they were saving from your kind. And they're all still alive! That's right – alive!" I leaned so close in his face I could smell his moldy breath. "In Israel, in England, Italy, Denmark, and right here in the good ole USA!"

The old Nazi blinked, unsure of whether to believe me. "You're b-bluffing," he stuttered, aghast with outrage and horror.

"N-no, I'm n-not," I mimed in exaggerated mockery, really drawing on my worst, most insufferable behavior, according to my Mom. "It's the truth! And, for your information, I've learned something these last few days. THERE ARE SOME THINGS IN LIFE YOU CAN'T KILL! YOU CAN'T KILL TRUTH! YOU CAN'T KILL MEMORY! YOU CAN'T KILL HOPE! AND YOU CAN'T KILL LOVE! NOT EVER!"

He couldn't take his eyes off me. It was like I'd mesmerized him with my mighty powers or something.

I crooked my finger. "Come here, you." Really in my element now.

He twitched. *"Vass?"*

I grabbed the lapels of his overcoat. "There's one more thing you can't change." Then I got nose to nose with him, pausing one perfect second for effect, and shouted, "You guys got your damned asses kicked!"

The Curator's voice boomed out in a wild shriek like a madman. "Shoooot her!"

Chaim suddenly reached out for Julio and actually picked him up and hurled him at Sergei and Dietrich. Leonid whirled around to fire his gun at Chaim and shot Julio unintentionally instead who blocked his aim in mid-air. Julio crashed down on Sergei and Dietrich and they all dropped like bowling pins to the pavement.

At that very moment, like the hammer of God, a black Chevy Suburban jumped the Lexington Avenue curb at the corner and steamed up the sidewalk in an ebony tidal wave. Before it even stopped rolling, Agent Ortiz somersaulted out the door with a twelve gauge shotgun.

I called to her at the top of my lungs from the courtyard, at which point she jacked the shotgun and yelled, "FREEZE, ALL OF YOU!" Three other agents jumped out of the car with her. Then she cussed at everyone and threatened our low-life hosts with blowing off their heads if they got any second ideas.

The bodyguard blowhards didn't even put up a fight. Sergei, Dietrich and Leonid threw up their hands, while Julio was doubled over in pain, holding his bleeding stomach. The Nazi Curator, whimpering like the true coward he was, flung down the pistol he'd suddenly drawn out of his coat and tried to run. Except that David shot forward and slammed him to the ground in a textbook diving tackle.

"Holy Moly!" I called out to him. "Where'd you learn to do that?"

David yanked the Curator's arm up behind his neck in a patented all-star wrestling chicken wing hold. "I'm a big JETS fan," he answered with a grunt and let him go in disgust.

But the Curator scuttled toward the corner and up the stairs of the synagogue backwards like a crab. For once in his life, he was helpless and at the mercy of those he loathed. No longer was he the one in control. The expression on his face at that moment – betraying the same violent terror he was responsible for forcing countless innocent men, women and children to feel before he murdered them – was a picture I would always remember with some satisfaction for the rest of my life.

Led by none other than Agent McMahon himself, a posse of shouting FBI agents surged forward, their snub nosed revolvers pointed straight at his heart as Chaim scaled the steps, locked eye to eye with the panic-stricken Curator. Futilely trying to escape, the old Nazi's back collided with the synagogue's heavy door. He had nowhere else to run. It was all over.

The way I saw it – it took over a half a century, but the

truth, as it always and forever will, had caught up with him at last. And today, truth was personified in the very life and imperishable self of my new best friend Chaim Wasserman, the old Warsaw Ghetto warrior. As N.Y.P.D. sirens wailed in the background, Chaim kept coming up the stairs like the Grim Reaper, implacable and unstoppable, claiming the Nazi Curator's life as his own right to destroy.

Suddenly lost in his own private hell, the old Nazi screamed in torment like a wounded beast and clawed at his chest. Then his face swelled up like a purple, blood-engorged balloon, as if he was in the midst of a massive coronary. Choking and moaning, he pirouetted and fell backwards down the steps in slow motion, sliding to rest at Chaim's feet. In death, the German's cold lifeless eyes were locked on the stained-glass Star of David above the synagogue's entrance.

At that very instant from inside the building, the cantor's voice soared gloriously into the cool night air, lifting *Shabbat* prayers to the heavens.

David and I stood there gaping at the sound, as if the voice of the divine broke through all the madness at that very moment. Finally I said the only thing I could think of. "That was cool." Not much of a thing to say, I admit. But it sure seemed right. And it was certainly sincere.

David called out: "Where's my grandmother? What happened to her?"

Agent Ortiz snapped her fingers and waved to somebody on the street. A black FBI sedan screeched to the curb and a ray-banned agent leaped out, opening the rear door. Mrs. Rosen stepped out like a diva at a Hollywood premier and with her – Veronica at last!

I whooped and clapped my hands. She gave us a demure wave and then watched, half-smiling in satisfaction, as Nikolai was led past her in handcuffs. "Will the world ever be

317

rid of your kind? – you who hate the living so – " I heard her say to Nikolai. But he said nothing.

"MRS. ROSEN!"

"*BUBBE*!"

David and I bounded down the steps to greet her. This time . . . just this time – he beat me – nearly bowling her over with a great big bear hug. "You're alive!" he cried.

Mrs. Rosen stroked his hair. "Of course, I am, darling. What did you expect?"

Just then the paramedics rolled the Curator's stiff body by on a gurney. Mrs. Rosen blanched when she recognized him.

"I'm sorry you had to be at his mercy again after all these years," I said, throwing my arm around Mrs. Rosen's waist. It must've been an awful week."

Mrs. Rosen lifted her chin. "Well, actually, I never even saw him – just his underlings – but I'm not surprised he was behind all this." She watched the Nazi's corpse being roughly loaded into the waiting ambulance. "He once said nobody would believe what they did to our people. I know . . . and I know they failed," she whispered with feeling, putting her arm around David . . . her grandson . . . the youngest descendent of her family.

Well, that did it. My emotions got tired of waiting and I broke down and bawled for joy. I even sat down on the sidewalk for a while. Man, it was one of those sobbing, shoulder-heaving, epic ones, too. But it didn't last long, for Mrs. Rosen helped me up and smothered me with kisses and the most loving, sheltering embrace. Then she held my face in her hands and looked at David. "She's spirited, isn't she?"

David answered with a sigh, "Whew! You don't know the half of it! She sure surprised me. I'd never have believed this was the same girl the day this all started."

An expression of deep concern crossed Mrs. Rosen's face. "Oh, Lauren, does your mother know where you are? I hope you didn't take any risks on my behalf," she shook her head slowly and added, "but it seems you have."

"Mrs. Rosen, for you? You bet I – oh, but it was nothing really, nothing at all," I beamed, embarrassed and starting to blush.

David jumped in then. "Yeah, some nothing! You should have seen her!"

Always thinking ahead, Agent McMahon in the meantime had stepped back into the Suburban and brought out a thermos of coffee and a box of Dunkin' donuts. "On me," he called, offering them with great generosity to us all. "Good work!" he shouted, smiling and biting into a cinnamon twist. "You guys took out the Nazis and the Russian Mafia in one day!"

Just then Agent Ortiz, who'd been overseeing the special police units handcuffing the bodyguards as well as Nikolai strapped in the car, stuck her head in the midst of all of us and hollered: "Didn't I say you kids were trouble? Eh, McMahon? You better believe it! Big time!" Then she chuckled as she strode off back to the round-up. "Just like me when I was their age."

While we passed the donuts around, Mrs. Rosen told us how she got away. "The imbeciles didn't know I'm fluent in Russian and German. Anyway, I overheard a couple of hours ago that they were planning something here – by the way, why on earth here? – has anyone discovered why? The two uglies who were guarding me and Veronica got drunk on vodka and passed out. So with the others already gone to fetch their boss, we escaped rather easily," she said, pleased with herself as she peeled off a piece of heavy electrical tape still clinging to her wrist from the ordeal she'd been through. "Then we just strolled down to the corner gas station and called 911."

She made it sound so easy. But I know this week had to have been hell on her and Veronica as I thought of the threats and treatment they both must have gone through. And how she must have been sick with worry wondering all the time what had happened to her family.

"So they were bluffing just now when they said they'd killed you and that you and Veronica were still being held by them," I blurted out. The moment I said it though I wished I hadn't been so blunt. They'd been through so much, I could have at least spared them this late news flash from the Curator.

"Perhaps they weren't bluffing at all. Their boss and the others did not know we'd only escaped ninety minutes ago," Mrs. Rosen murmured, shaking her head.

"Why did they keep their silence all week?" I asked, changing the subject real fast. "And where in the world were they keeping you?" I was just overflowing with questions.

Mrs. Rosen sighed. "For one thing, I heard them say that their boss was called out of the country suddenly on some urgent matter and they were not to do anything till he returned. And for another, that you all had heavy security around you for the time being, which I was glad to hear. As for where they held my poor Veronica and me – in a dingy apartment above an abandoned restaurant somewhere in Brooklyn. She was so very brave," Mrs. Rosen said, smiling, and squeezing Veronica's shoulder. "God bless you, dear friend. You went through so very much on my account. I can never make it up to you enough."

Veronica's eyes flashed. "Dominique, now you know I have the devil in me! I just had to find it again! I haven't had this much excitement since I was a kid! I feel young again! Filled with inspiration! I can't wait to attack life and my work. I was getting in a rut. So was my work. Don't feel bad. I've told you a thousand times. If anything, it is I who should thank you!"

Mrs. Rosen chuckled at that. "You know I – " she started to say, but her voice broke off as she suddenly noticed Chaim. While we had all been talking and laughing with relief, he'd silently joined the group. She was startled when she looked at him, but she didn't recognize him at first. Turning to David to say something, she suddenly moved her attention back again to Chaim and studied his face like she was trying to find a key . . . a key lost in the past. Her lips silently moved. Then her eyes lit up like stars. "Oh, my God! Can it be? Can it actually be YOU?"

He smiled and bowed his head slightly, his eyes filling with tears. "Hello, Dominique. It's been a long time."

She put her hands to her mouth and tears began to flow. Then they fell into each other's arms, two long-lost friends and battle-scarred warriors who hadn't seen one another for almost 60 years and who never thought they'd lay eyes on each other again. "Of all times to find you again!" she sobbed. "Oh, Chaim . . . Joshua's Diary . . . I felt so alone all week, so hopeless and guilty about my friend and my family and Lauren. It's as if you came back to life at this hour when we needed you so much. I know you had something to do with this scene here at the temple . . . the children's safety . . . God bless you, dear Chaim." As they held each other, they both cried.

Wait till he tells her about her twin sisters, I thought as I stood there watching their emotional reunion with happiness.

David and I decided to leave them alone and started walking over to where Agent Ortiz was standing talking to some reporters who appeared out of nowhere. "Yes, you're right, that's Dominique Rosen over there," I heard her saying. "True, there was an incident here; no, I have no comment at this time."

Then we moved up the street a bit, away from a crowd of spectators that had begun to form. I couldn't get out of my mind the sight of Mrs. Rosen and Chaim reuniting after so many years when they each thought the other was dead. "Do you think we'd have been okay, you know . . . uh . . . do you think we'd have been able to do what they did during the Nazi insanity of World War II if that had happened to us?" I asked David.

"I think so." Then he thought for a moment and said with real conviction, "Absolutely . . . I know so! You and me."

"Dear Dominique," we heard Chaim's voice rise above all the commotion around us, as they moved toward us. "You have no idea the courage and resourcefulness of those two. They'd have fit right along side us in the Resistance. They were magnificent!"

"Way to go, pardner," I nudged David with my elbow.

"Yeah, way to go . . . pardner." He shot me a high five. Then David put his arms around me and we kissed. For a long time.

*

Many months later, there was a spectacular reunion celebration at Mrs. Rosen's. It took some doing – and some tracking. But everyone was there who'd been a part of Mrs. Rosen's life. Chaim, Veronica, the twins Sonia and Sarah, David and me, his parents, my parents, even Agents Ortiz and McMahon. And Degas and Van Gogh and Picasso and Renoir and Matisse and Gauguin and lots of other wonderful people, along with their sons and daughters and grandchildren too many to count.

The adults rejoiced in making one loud champagne toast after another, and were raucously in the midst of yet another when the doorbell rang. I was the only one who heard the bell – Mr. Antonelli downstairs was alerted to send up everyone who came asking for Mrs. Rosen – and put my Diet Coke down and ran to answer the door.

A stunning woman in an emerald green Chanel suit stood in the hall. Her dark hair was pulled back in a fashionable up-sweep with curls casually cascading around the front and back of her head, and she had the face of an angel.

"How do you do, dear?" she said, greeting me cordially. "I'm Dr. Stein from Tel Aviv University. I'm so sorry I'm late. My flight was delayed and I came directly from JFK Airport."

"Oh!" I exclaimed, taking her coat. "No problem. They're all here and there's plenty of food left, believe me. I'm really glad you were able to make it. Mrs. Rosen will be so happy." I shook her hand. "I'm Lauren," I said, introducing myself, "a neighbor here in the building. But I'm also a student of Mrs. Rosen's."

The beautiful woman could see I didn't know who she was. She paused in the entryway a moment, looked at the boisterous, exuberant gathering going on inside, as if fully absorbing the scene before her, and there were tears in her eyes. She turned back to me and smiled warmly.

"I'm Cezanne."

The End

AUTHOR'S NOTE

*The reference to the Warsaw Ghetto on p. 147 of this book is gratefully quoted from Rabbi Joseph Telushkin's remarkable book of history entitled Jewish Literacy, p. 369.

*The story of the great 18th century European teacher and rabbi, Ba'al Shem Tov, which appears at the beginning of the last chapter of this book on p. 301, is based on Rabbi Telushkin's recounting of the young whistler in the temple and his imagined quotation of what was said in response to those who wanted to forcibly remove him. This is also gratefully quoted from Jewish Literacy, p. 216.

Jewish Literacy by Rabbi Joseph Telushkin
Copyright © by Rabbi Joseph Telushkin
By permission of HarperCollins Publishers, Inc.

\#

The temple referred to in the final chapter is loosely modeled after the beautiful Central Synagogue in New York City. The New York Times called this 132-year old landmark an "architectural treasure" in a front page story in 1998 when it was almost destroyed by fire.

\#

On November 23rd, 1991, in New York City, Rabbi William H. Lebeau was invited to address an audience at The Cathedral of St. John the Divine's "Second Interfaith Concert of Remembrance" in honor of all Holocaust victims. His extraordinary words referred to on pages 256-257 of this book were heard by many that night and never forgotten, and he is gratefully quoted with admiration and deep appreciation. His full address appears at the end of this book.

ENDNOTE

Drawing on captured German documents newly available from Russian archives and more than a half-century of Auschwitz studies, researchers in Poland have compiled what experts call the most complete and authoritative history of the vast killing center for the Nazi extermination of the Jews.

Called simply 'Auschwitz 1940-1945' and just issued in English, it is a five-volume work of more than half a million words that has been under preparation by Auschwitz-Birkenau State Museum since 1979. Replete with names of killers and victims, it fills 1,799 pages, including construction plans for the gas chambers and crematories, prisoner lists, first-hand accounts, rare photographs, an almost day-by-day calendar and a 49-page bibliography.

By the time Soviet troops liberated Auschwitz and its subcamps 56 years ago yesterday, an estimated 1.3 million people had been shipped there and at least 1.1 million, including 960,000 Jews, had died there, the history establishes. Because fleeing guards burned millions of documents – while leaving behind others from the so-called Hygiene Institute and infirmary as exculpatory ploys – the exact toll will never be known.

'It is by far the most comprehensive in its detail and level of source material,' said Rabbi Irving Greenberg, chairman of the United States Holocaust Memorial Museum, which will be selling the work.

Using lists of victims and other camp documentation recently retrieved from Russia, the Auschwitz history offers new computations of the death toll, including the fate of 232,000 deportees under 18. It profiles many of the nearly 8,000 SS men and women who ran the camp and who, the book says, largely escaped justice after World War II. It tallies property plundered from the prisoners: gold teeth and hair by the trainload and convoys of empty baby carriages that, one former prisoner re-called, 'were pushed in rows of five, and the procession took more than an hour to pass.'

But the study also devotes nearly 400 pages alone to the often-overlooked camp resistance movement: the operations of Polish underground cells; an ill-fated mutiny on October 7, 1944, in which 451 prisoners died; and 802 escapes that helped smuggle out news of the killings to an often uninterested world.

The history includes accounts secretly recorded by anonymous doomed prisoners assigned to execution details who buried their testaments like time capsules around the Auschwitz grounds. It also cross-references Nazi memoirs and testimony from a welter of war crimes proceedings, including the trial of the camp's commandant, Rudolf Hoss, who was hanged in 1947.

For many years after the war, said Teresa Swiebocka, a curator at the museum, the Polish Communist authorities played down the singular victimization of the Jews. Since the fall of Communism, scholars say, the distortions have been redressed, as the book reflects.

— Excerpt from "Auschwitz Revisited: the Fullest Picture Yet"
by Ralph Blumenthal, The New York Times,
January 28, 2001, p. 8.

It is a privilege to be here.   I want to thank everyone whose vision and dedication made this evening possible.

Dean Morton, I want to thank you and the congregation of the Cathedral of St. John the Divine for opening the doors of this house of God, in love and friendship to all of us.   We are men and women of many different faiths and backgrounds.   Children of God – all of us in God's image – we have come together seeking solace through this shared experience of remembrance.

On this night of hope, we remember the victims of humanity's darkest night.   But God must also be remembered.   The perpetrators of the Holocaust wanted, not only to usurp God's Power over life and death; they conspired, also, to silence, forever, God's Voice that has thundered throughout the ages, "You shall not kill.   Love your neighbor as yourself.   Justice, justice shall you pursue."

Tonight it is appropriate, as Jerry Jacobs, Chairman of this commemoration suggests, that we turn to the international language of music to celebrate life, and honor the memory of all victims of the Holocaust.   Music can help us reclaim, not only our common humanity, but also assure that God's call for love and harmony will be heard over the dissonance of evil.

The Prophet Elijah teaches us how we might best hear God in tonight's music.   In the process, we will find each other.

Elijah, fleeing from Ahab, fearful for his life, hid in a cave of darkness. He longed for God's encouragement. He heard the command:

"Come out of your darkness and stand on the mountain of the Lord. And behold, the Lord passed by and a great strong wind rent the mountains and broke in pieces the rocks, but the Lord was not in the wind; and after the wind an earthquake; but the Lord was not in the earthquake; and after the earthquake a fire; but the Lord was not in the fire; and after the fire, a still, small, silent voice." When Elijah heard the silent voice of God's Presence, he was strengthened to go forward.

Tonight we will hear the wind-instruments, but the Lord will not be in the wind; and the drums and percussions will cause this sanctuary to quake, but the Lord will not be in their thunder; the mixture of voices and instruments and the motion of the conductor will generate energy like fire, but the Lord will not be in the fire.

God's Presence will be in the still, small voice of silence made audible by the contrasting sounds of music. In the silence, we will hear the sound of our own breaths. Breathing silently in cadence, we will find each other. We will find the commonality of our souls – silent souls bestowed by our common Creator – that reveal neither color, religion nor language.

In the silence, we can breach barriers that separate us and in that way honor most appropriately the memory of those who died when both the Majesty of God and the dignity of the human being were desecrated. May the music of this night encourage us to come out of our darkness and together stand on the mountain of the Lord. There we can hear the still, small voice and have the strength to go forward.